WHERE IS FORREST?

Tales of an Escape Artist

BY HANS M. BRODER, JR.

TABLE OF CONTENTS

ACKNOWLEDGMENTS

I owe special thanks to all the individuals who provided information on past events which I included in the book. I was able to interview and obtain family history from Larry Allgood, a relative of Forrest Turner, and older Henry Countians who were familiar with the Turner family. Historian Gene Morris provided valuable historical information. I received details about the old Henry County Work Camp from David Whitson, a former guard.

I visited the old site of the Jonesboro Dental Lab and Shingleroof Campground in McDonough. I used memories from my visit to Henry County Work Camp before it was closed in the late 1960s, my class trip to and walk through the inside of the Atlanta Penitentiary during college and my tour of Alcatraz Prison while in San Francisco to describe those facilities.

I read the following books which provided historical information about Henry County and Atlanta. These include, *Henry County Georgia, The Mother of Counties* by Vessie Thrasher Rainer, *True Southerners, A Pictorial History of Henry County, Georgia* by Gene Morris, Jr., County Historian, *Shadow of Death, Tommy Callahan* by Freda Turner, *I am a Fugitive from a Georgia Chain Gang!* by Robert Elliott Burns, *Living Atlanta An Oral History of the City 1914-1948*, Chapter Six, "Underside" by Clifford M.

Kuhn, Harlon E. Joye, and E. Bernard West and "The Forrest Turner Story," a 1974 campaign brochure by Forrest Turner.

I relied on various archived newspaper articles from the following newspapers: *The Atlanta Constitution, The Atlanta Journal, The Macon Telegraph, Macon News, Valdosta Daily Times, Columbus Ledger, Buffalo News, Palladium-Item, The Sentinel, Daily News, The Anniston Star, Tampa News, The Newnan Times, Herald Henry County Weekly, New York Times, Henry Herald, The Macon Evening News, Savannah Morning News, Philadelphia Inquirer, Casper Morning Star* and others. These newspaper articles were obtained through the Newspapers.com website.

I relied on Ancestry.com to learn about the individuals featured in the story using census data, marriage certificates, death certificates, birth records, draft registrations, criminal records, prison records, and burial information. I watched on YouTube reruns of the quiz show, "What's My Line?" I listened to "Oral History Interview With Forrest Turner," June 24, 1979, Digital Library of Georgia. I obtained records from the Brown House library, the home of Henry and Clayton County Genealogical Society.

I obtained ideas from reading penal reform, prison pardon and parole records, and other related information about the Georgia Penal System available on the internet. I relied on resource materials obtained from Wikipedia, Encyclopedia.com, and New Georgia Encyclopedia.

I owe thanks to my wife, Lyndy, who helped in the editing of the manuscript, my daughter, Mia Broder, who provided the research and design and my brother, Michael Broder, who provided the illustrations for the book. I also owe a debt of gratitude to Hugh Morton, friend and fellow author, for his review of the text.

PREFACE

You are about to read an inspirational story of a man who lived in the rural South during the 1900s. *Where is Forrest? Tales of an Escape Artist* recounts the life and times of Forrest T. Turner. A member of a large family who eked out a living during the Great Depression. Born and raised in Henry County, he lived his adult life in the Atlanta metro area. As a wayward young adult, he spent fifteen years as a prisoner or a fugitive. Finally, paroled, he became a responsible and respected citizen determined to atone for his earlier wrongdoings.

His introduction to crime began with the hauling of illegal moonshine from the North Georgia mountains to Atlanta. During his "Thunder Road" days he was able to elude the revenue agents who tried to catch him. But his undoing came when he was arrested for a crime he did not commit. His punishment was hard labor at a South Georgia work camp. There he was shackled in leg irons and joined other convicts performing work on county roads.

Forrest Turner was a law breaker and a "jailbreaker." Labeled as the next Harry Houdini, no chains nor prison bars could hold him. The book provides details of when, where, and how he was able to achieve such escapades. Forrest Turner became a folk hero for the wrong reasons. The newspapers described him as "Georgia's

Number One Bad Boy" and as a fugitive he was on the state's "Most Wanted List." As a debonair, witty and sought-after banditt, he received as much local newspaper coverage in Georgia as did the movie stars.

The book takes a hard look at the penal system while Forrest Turner was imprisoned, including the mistreatment at work camps and chain gangs. As a means of punishment, convicts were subjected to periods of time in sweatboxes and isolation. The use of "balls and chains" and leg irons was employed to reduce the number of escapes.

In addition to the life story of Forrest Turner, the author also introduces the reader to many of his fellow inmates, including those who joined him in his many escapes. The book provides information about their criminal backgrounds and what became of them after they left prison. The author will acquaint you with the detectives who pursued and recaptured him and the wardens and guards he outwitted. Also included are the two men who were most responsible for his parole.

Much is written about the work camps and prisons including Alcatraz in California and "Little Alcatraz" in Dallas, Georgia. They were known as "The Rock" on an island in San Francisco Bay and the other the "Rock Quarry Camp" in Paulding County. The investigation of Reidsville revealed the surprising scandals and mismanagement at the Georgia State Prison.

Two chapters tell stories of legendary characters who made their marks during the period. Bonnie and Clyde whose Midwest bank robberies, murders, and demise made national headlines. Robert Burns was sentenced to hard labor at Georgia work camps after his arrest in Atlanta for theft. His book describing the miseries he endured while on chain gangs became a "best seller" and movie. As a result, the American public became aware of the mistreatment of convicts which would create momentum for prison reform in the South.

Where is Forrest? Tales of an Escape Artist should be considered as historical literary fiction. The story follows actual events as covered by the newspapers. However, to enhance the story the author took certain liberties. To emphasize the Turner escapes and breakouts, the newspaper headlines are featured in bold print. The book also attempts to present events in chronological order. The book also refers to important historical occurrences of the period. A timetable of these events and a location map of where they occurred can be found at the end of the book. The author begins each chapter with an italicized summary of its content. The book concludes with the author's "Ode to a Legend," a poetic tribute to Forrest Turner.

PART I
THE INTRODUCTORY YEARS

1   THE FIRST ARREST

Forrest Turner's youthful days were not without mischief. His mother said that her son was a good boy, but he did get into trouble from time to time. Some of his dishonest deeds were minor and were the result of being poor. He was resourceful, nevertheless. When an opportunity arose, where he could make some easy money, he was not afraid to take the risk even if he had to break the law. Hauling moonshine was his first foray into making real money. Unfortunately, the demand for bootleggers ended with the repeal of Prohibition. Ironically, his first arrest was not the result of running moonshine, but by riding in a stolen car.

***

In August 1934 Forrest Turner was nineteen years old and was still living with his widowed mother and siblings. Burdened with his circumstance of being a young man in a large family with limited income, he had an obligation to share in the paying of the family expenses. Luckily, the neighborhood drug store owner knew the Turners and was compassionate toward their situation. The owner hired young Forrest to work behind the counter of the soda fountain and serve cups of ice cream, shakes, and floats.

Forrest Turner possessed a unique charm and had a lighthearted ease about him. His personable manner suited him well. People enjoyed his company. He was smart, not so much that he was overbearing, but just enough to talk his way out of any difficult situation. With his innate talents it was a certainty that his life's journey would be far from the ordinary.

While Forrest Turner had a job, he did not own a car. Though it was becoming more common in the 1930s for families to own automobiles, the Turners had only one. The car was used mostly by his older brothers, whose jobs provided higher pay and were further away. As an alternative he had learned early that his two feet could get him anywhere, even if that included hitching a ride.

It was Friday, August 26th. It was an uncomfortably warm, eighty-eight-degree late afternoon. He had a little cash in his pocket and more importantly he had a ride and a planned evening in Atlanta to enjoy.

Vincent Baker, better known as Bill, was a boyhood friend of Forrest Turner. Recently, Bill Baker had experienced an encounter with the law. Forrest Turner was not one to judge. He too had tempted fate plenty of times in his moonshine running days. But those days were not on his mind as Bill picked him up in a different car.

TURNER, 19, FLEES COURT AFTER HEARING SENTENCE

"Forrest Turner Sentenced for Auto Theft Flees"... "Deputies Caught Off Guard Escorting Prisoner"... "Raced Down Hall and Out of Courthouse"... Deputies in Pursuit on Atlanta Street"... "Captured and Returned to Courthouse Detention Room"

The first time Forrest Turner made the headlines was in a brief article in an Atlanta newspaper referring to an escape attempt on August 26, 1934. His flight to freedom caused momentary excitement at the Fulton County Courthouse.

Forrest thanked Bill for the ride. "Where did you get this car?" Forrest asked as he closed the passenger's side door.

Bill replied with a sly grin, "Oh I borrowed the car from a friend."

Forrest Turner didn't think much of the remark. Bill Baker always had something going on and he was more interested in getting out of Hapeville for the evening. Knowing who owned the car would not have changed the outcome. He would learn that detail soon enough.

Traveling on Boulevard they were heading northwest toward Atlanta. They were plotting as to which girls they might run into. Suddenly Bill Baker noticed in his rearview mirror two policeman in a patrol car closely following. He grimaced under his breath. Hearing the siren, Forrest Turner quickly looked out the back window and suspected his evening plans were about to fall apart.

The patrol car pulled up alongside and the officer inside motioned for Bill Baker to drive over to the shoulder. A sense of dread overcame Forrest Turner. He wasn't exactly sure what they did wrong. At that time, the State of Georgia did not give driver's test or issue driver's license. The state did however require each vehicle to be registered and display a tag. It was the tag that alerted the officers.

Speaking through the rolled down window, "We have received a report that this car had been stolen. The call came from a Mr. Glass who lives at Fort McPherson. Do you know anything about it?" asked the officer.

"No, Sir," replied Baker.

By now Forrest Turner noticed the second officer approaching the car from the rear. He saw the officer with his right hand resting on the handle of his pistol which was still in his holster. "He must be expecting trouble," Forrest surmised. "But he couldn't imagine why."

"You two young men step out of the car and put your hands on the roof while my partner frisks you," ordered the officer. "I mean right now!" After finding no concealed weapons on their person or in the car, he began asking questions. What are your names, where are you going, and what are you doing riding in Mr. Glass' car?" Unable to give reasonable answers, they were taken to po-

Forrest Turner
Convicted of Auto Theft

lice headquarters, booked for car theft, photographed, fingerprinted, and locked in the county jail pending a trial.

Bill Baker had an arrest record of an earlier theft, but Forrest Turner's slate was clean. It was Forrest Turner's first taste of jail. He didn't want any part of it, he didn't deserve to be there, and he didn't steal the car. But without money for a lawyer, Forrest Turner was dependent on the court-appointed public defender to represent him. The young attorney fresh out of law school met with the two young, accused thieves at the county jail.

Forrest's heart was still pounding when they met with the court-appointed public defender, who had only recently passed the bar. The lawyer was nervous, he did not have much experience, but he hid it well.

He started with Bill, who looked indifferent. This surprised the lawyer. As he was reading Bill's file he said "I am sorry but there is not much I can do for you, Mr. Baker. You have already been convicted of an earlier crime, found guilty, and sent to a work camp." The next bit of information surprised the new lawyer. "However, the record shows you have not completed your sentence. What happened?"

"I escaped, Sir" confessed Baker.

He moved on to the second gentlemen, "As for you Mr. Turner, you are nineteen years old, and this is your first offense. I recommend that you plead guilty to the auto theft charge. You will certainly receive a probated sentence with no time in prison." Forrest Turner honestly believed the lawyer and followed his recommendation.

Bill Baker and Forrest Turner waived their rights to a jury trial. Instead, they appeared in front of the judge in Fulton County

State Court a week later. The courthouse was on Central Avenue, seven miles from his family home in Hapeville.

"How do you plead, Mr. Baker?" Guilty Your Honor.

"How do you plead, Mr. Turner?" Guilty Your Honor.

Unfortunately, this was not the only auto theft case on the judge's docket that day. They were becoming all too frequent, and he felt he had an obligation to clean up the streets and make an example of Bill and Forrest's actions.

"Well, gentlemen the court mandates me to be tough on car thieves. We cannot have young men in Fulton County stealing cars. To discourage others I am sentencing you to serve three to five years of hard labor in one of Georgia's work camps. Let me add that I realize that you are a first-time offender, Mr. Turner. But the fact that you were riding in a stolen car with your friend knowing he was a convicted criminal, and a fugitive makes you guilty by association," proclaimed the judge. "Call the next case, bailiff!"

Bill Baker and Forrest Turner were then escorted out of the courtroom to the courthouse detention room where all the accused would await a hearing or a trial. A bus transported the prisoners to the courthouse in the morning. After all the cases were heard, those found guilty were returned to the jail.

Forrest Turner was in shock and disbelief over the judge's decision. Angry with the unjust and unexpected stiff sentence, Forrest Turner was not about to go to prison. His head was spinning as he thought to himself, "How could this be happening?

Vincent "Bill" Baker
Convicted of Auto Theft

I didn't steal a car. I am innocent." When the deputy began fumbling around trying to find the right key to open the door to the detention room, he saw his chance to flee. He pushed the deputy to the floor, dashed down the hall and escaped through the unguarded rear door.

"Stop!" yelled the deputy as he got back to his feet. "Stop that young man!" he shouted to the deputies who were at the other end of the hall. The surprised deputy managed to unlock the door and restrain his other prisoner. Bill Baker had not expected Forrest to flee and was unprepared to run. He was peacefully secured into the detention room.

The parents of a young man who was scheduled for a hearing for his reckless driving were standing in the hallway. Upon hearing the commotion, they witnessed a young man race by them, exit the courthouse, and disappear down the street. Immediately two armed deputies, Joe Harper and F.L. Rhodes, who were standing by the courthouse entrance, pursued on foot.

Once outside Forrest Turner ran away from the courthouse as fast as he could. He was breathing so hard that he did not hear the commands; "Stop or I will shoot!" yelled one of the pursuing deputies. Looking around to see who was chasing him, he accidentally fell into an open coal pit. Exhausted and dazed from the fall, Forrest Turner surrendered to the two deputies who were not far behind. They were relieved that the chase was over. He had run down Central Avenue and made it as far as Hunter Street. He was handcuffed and returned to the courthouse where he joined Bill Baker in the detention room. His exciting flight to freedom lasted only thirty minutes.

On the same evening Bill Baker and Forrest Turner along with the others who were sentenced that day were bused back to jail where they remained until the Georgia Prison Commission determined their destination. After a short stay Bill Baker was sent back to Rome to finish serving his sentence for robbery. Forrest Turner was sent to Thomas County Work Camp in Thomasville, Georgia. Accordingly, he became one of four thousand seven hundred convicts serving sentences in Georgia prisons and county work camps.

It was Forrest Turner's first escape from the grasps of the law, but it would not be his last. Thus began his legend as an escape artist.

2   THE BEGINNING

To understand why Forrest Turner resorted to criminality one must look at his roots and the surroundings in which he was raised. What influenced him and other family members to pursue breaking the law? One cannot help but notice the similarities between the Turner families' deceased relative, John Henry Holiday. The notorious gunslinger and outlaw, Doc Holiday was born in Griffin, Georgia. He became a dentist before moving west for health reasons. Forrest Turner would also become a law breaker and denturist. Many speculated that Forrest Turner had inherited some of Doc Holiday's genes.

The Turners were not unlike many rural Henry County families in the early 1900s. They lived off the land and were eking out a meager subsistence. There were eight boys and three girls in the Turner family. In addition to being a farm laborer, his father worked at a small garage. The mother was very devout and a good homemaker. She did her best to raise her boys, encouraging them to become productive citizens.

It was a tough time. Even the most well-to-do families depending on agriculture struggled to make ends meet. There were few options for a young man to get ahead. Forrest was ambitious and determined to enjoy a better standard of living than his parents had provided. People accepted their fate and made the most out of what life offered. Most of the children who were born in that era overcame economic challenges and became law-abiding, honest, hardworking adults. Forrest Turner wanted more and chose a less acceptable path to achieve life's rewards. To do so, he must first escape from the drudgery of his daily routine that was leading him nowhere. He eventually became an accomplished escape artist.

***

Forrest Turner was reminiscing about his younger days growing up in McDonough. The thought of being locked in a prison never entered his mind. He remembered when his older brother Otis set a trap to catch a raccoon that he had spotted in the woods behind the house. He placed a wooden box with a trap door where he had previously seen the animal. Attracted by the smell of food inside, the hungry raccoon entered the opening tripping the trap door. The bewildered animal had locked himself inside.

Forrest recalled, "My brother wanted to keep the raccoon as a pet. He put him in a cage in the barn and fed him once a day. Everyone enjoyed staring at his cute pet. The raccoon was very unhappy. It tried desperately to escape, but it could not. The frustrated raccoon finally quit clawing against the wall of the cage as his return to the wild appeared unlikely. It no longer had the freedom to roam the woods and be with the other animals. I looked at that depressed raccoon and saw the tears in its eyes. That night I snuck into the barn and let it loose. My brother was sore at me for a long time. I just couldn't stand seeing that caged raccoon suffering any longer."

While sitting in the Fulton Tower waiting for his transport to Thomasville, the raccoon saga entered his mind. He realized how that poor raccoon must have felt. "It's just not fair to lock an animal or person in a cage. Whenever someone is penned up without their will, they should make every effort to get free regardless of the consequences," Forrest reckoned.

He thought about his parents, Inez and Justus Turner, and his siblings. How disappointed they all were when learning of his arrest. Especially his mother, who cried when she heard that his sentence was time on the chain gang. She was a good mother.

The Turners were a long-time Henry County family. Luke, Forrest's grandfather, was born in 1844 and his grandmother, Eliza, was one year younger. His father, Justus, was born in 1878 and raised in the community of Beersheba, now known as Ola. His mother was a member of the Cleveland family born in the small rural town of Locust Grove, Georgia in 1886. If it weren't for the Southern Railway depot, the town's existence would not be known to folks outside of Henry County. They were married in 1902. Justus Turner was stern with his children when he was at home. Work occupied most of his time. Apparently, he was not strict enough with some of them, including his son, Forrest.

Forrest Turner wished he could spend more time with his brothers and sisters. Forrest Theron was the seventh of eleven children. He was born in McDonough on February 8, 1915. He couldn't remember their birthdays but could remember the years of their birth. First there were his brothers William "Willie" Edgar in 1903, Charles Adel in 1905, Henry Lucas in 1907, then his baby sister Ruby in 1910, followed by his brothers Luther Justus in 1911 and Otis Smith in 1913. Later came his brothers, Chester George in 1916 and Lee Hugh in 1918 followed by his baby sisters Lillian in 1920 and Barbara Daphine in 1925.

The Turners lived in the country. The rooster was their alarm clock, the aroma from the kitchen meant it was time to eat, the setting sun told them their day's work was done, and the sound of crickets was their signal to go to bed. They made their living as sharecroppers and farm laborers. With seven strong boys the family farmed several acres and managed to cultivate, plant and harvest the crops by themselves. During the off season, Justus Turner worked as a mechanic. By watching and helping his father in the garage, Forrest became familiar with automobiles. From that experience he developed a passion for cars, especially those with high performance engines.

He recalled his father saying how good farming was in the early 1920s. At that time sixty-nine percent of the people in Georgia were rural and made their living farming. High cotton prices and record crops ensured that small farmers throughout the state including Henry County made a decent living. But that changed as overproduction, depletion of the soil, and the arrival of man-made fabrics led to the fall of cotton prices. Then came the dreaded boll weevil. The Turner family was barely surviving. In October 1929, the New York stock market crashed followed by the Great Depression. Rich people, businesses, and banks were going broke. As if a farmer's life was not bad enough, in 1930 began Georgia's worst drought on record which lasted for two years.

Life in Henry County became a challenge, especially for large families. Most had no electricity, no running water, and no indoor toilets. Healthy meals were a luxury and limited to once a week. Diets consisted of molasses, fatback, and cornbread when their gardens gave out. There were few doctors in the area and the closest hospital was miles away.

Agriculture had no longer provided an adequate income for rural families. Without meaningful crops, the farmers could not pay their mortgages, and many began losing their land through foreclosure. Sharecroppers had to abandon their dream of owning farmland. Only the very wealthy were able to own land. As a result, most rural families began to move to the cities to find work.

After the death of Forrest Turner's grandfather, his father moved the family from McDonough to Hapeville. In the late 1920s the growing community of over forty-two hundred people offered employment opportunities no longer available in rural farm areas. Hapeville was situated in the southern part of Fulton County near the new College Park airport. Their home at 910 Central Avenue was in the heart of the town near the Sylvan Road intersection. The Atlanta West Point railroad line and the depot made the community accessible to travelers.

The transition from Henry County and the move to Fulton County showed promise, until his father, Justus, unexpectedly died in March 1930 at the age of fifty-one. He left behind his wife Inez and a house full of children. Forrest Turner was just fifteen at the time. For the Turners, hard times got tougher as Georgia felt the worsening impact of the Great Depression. During that period only about half of the people in the city of Atlanta and surrounding areas had full-time jobs. Everyone in the family old enough to work was forced to find part-time work.

The Civilian Conservation Corps, known as the CCC program, gave Forrest Turner his first job after leaving high school. It wasn't until he met a fellow who was transporting moonshine from North Georgia to Atlanta that he saw the opportunity to make some real money. Forrest Turner convinced the man to allow him to go along. After a couple of successful trips, he was hooked. Tempted by the excitement of breaking the law and the extra money, he soon found a way to become a hauler of moonshine.

So, what attracted Forrest Turner to associate with people who were committing crimes? He admired his neighbor, Bill Baker, who liked to steal cars and the bootlegger he met while working in the CCC program? To enrich themselves they had the courage to defy the law. "I need to be like them. That's the only way I can get ahead," Forrest surmised. "I am going to take some chances." Had the economic times been better and had he not moved to the city, Forrest Turner's future may have turned out differently.

3 PROHIBITION

The prohibition period during the 1920s and early 1930s for most people meant it would be more difficult to buy and drink alcohol. Even though it was unlawful and frowned upon by the churchgoers, the consumption of alcoholic beverages did not stop. The illegal manufacturing, transporting, and selling of whiskey, moonshine, and other spirits offered economic opportunities to those who were willing to ignore the consequences. Forrest Turner was one of them.

***

Following World War I there was national concern over the amount of alcohol consumed in America. Alcoholism, public drunkenness, and family violence had become a national problem. It was perceived that the only way to curtail drinking was to remove the availability of alcoholic beverages. In 1920 the Eighteenth Amendment to the Constitution made the production, distribution, and sale of such products unlawful. The law did not make it illegal to drink, but it just punished those who had a hand in providing the beverage.

Remote areas in North Georgia became sources of liquor referred to as moonshine for consumers in the cities. Moonshine was distilled from corn and syrup during the night. Manufactured using only the light of the moon prevented revenue agents from detecting the smoke from the stills, hence, the name moonshine. F.B.I. agents were constantly on the lookout to destroy liquor stills and arrest the moonshiners. To transport the illegal liquor, distillers hired drivers who were willing to take the risk to haul the moonshine to distributors who sold the spirits to thirsty customers. In the nineteenth century, those smuggling and concealing illicit liquor and valuables in their boot tops were called "bootleggers." Hence, the transporters of moonshine were labeled bootleggers.

The amendment had good intentions but not the desired results. Prohibition did not reduce alcohol consumption in the long term. Americans who wanted to imbibe, continued drinking, and used illegal methods to obtain alcohol. Syndicates emerged, political corruption, and crime increased. In some cases, people became ill or died from drinking bad alcohol. State governments lost the tax revenues from alcohol sales. Those working for distillers, restaurants, and entertainment businesses lost their jobs. President Roosevelt, who saw nothing wrong with having a glass of Falstaff beer or Burgundy red wine, supported and signed a bill to legalize their sale. While Americans were coping from the after effects of the Great Depression, public sentiment toward alcohol changed. The ratification of the Twenty-first Amendment officially ended Prohibition in 1933.

To many Americans having a drink or two after payday or at a party was a way of life. "I am not going to let the government tell me what I can eat or drink," said a fella who was buying a mason jar of moonshine from a man on an Atlanta street. For many of the farmers living in the North Georgia mountains brewing moonshine was the only way of making a decent living. Although bootlegging was illegal, those who were willing to take the risk were able to make a couple of quick and easy dollars at a time when good paying jobs were scarce.

If it hadn't been for the CCC, Forrest Turner would never have learned about the moonshine business. Those who made the spirits needed runners to bring the beverage from the North Georgia mountains to Atlanta. "I tried the stuff," he once said. "It burned my mouth, and it didn't taste good, so I spurted out the shine before it could make me sick. No one in these parts considered running moonshine to be illegal. It felt like I was doing the folks a service. It was a way for me to support my mother and family. I didn't make or sell alcohol. I just hauled it for those who did. Most of the client's customers were well-to-do, doctors, lawyers, and other middle-class professionals. I made many trips to Dawsonville."

Forrest Turner drove a V-8 Ford which was provided by the moonshiner. It looked like an ordinary car, but it had heavy-duty shocks and springs to safeguard the crates holding the hooch from breaking on the bumpy mountain roads. The seats in the back were usually removed so more jugs of alcohol could fit. The engines were souped up to outrun police officers and revenue agents. In his "hot rod" he had extra license plates and a set of hub caps that he could use to change the appearance of the car. He had cans full of nails and boards with spikes sticking out so that he could throw them out the window to discourage the pursuers. The car was equipped with a police siren and red blinking lights hidden behind the grill. When the lights were turned on, the car looked and sounded like an unmarked police car wanting to pass. "It took a lot of imagination to fool the revenue agents," he bragged. "I managed not to get arrested."

Forrest Turner continued, "I was a good driver when I started bootlegging, but to outwit the law I had to learn how to maneuver the backroads. Those curvy mountain dirt roads were a challenge especially when I had to drive with the lights off. One time when I had a full load of shine, I saw a police car quickly approaching from behind with its lights flashing. I slowed down and did a 'Bootleg U-turn.' Now I was headed in his direction. I decided to 'play chicken' with him. I gunned the engine, grabbed the steering wheel as tight as I could and was about to close my eyes expecting the worst. Luckily for both of us, he veered his car onto the shoulder in plenty of time to watch me speed by him. I saw his brake lights in my rearview mirror as I safely raced away. He didn't come after me. The agent wasn't about to risk his life over a few gallons of moonshine. That was the last time I tried that stunt."

Some of the best customers for moonshine were soldiers at Fort McPherson which was located down the street from my house. On payday there wasn't enough alcohol to satisfy all the soldiers. Since they were protecting their country, law enforcement agents seldom bothered them unless they became too unruly. In those cases, the MPs would get them out of jail and take them back to the base to spend the night in the stockade.

Moonshine was readily available up and down Peachtree Street. Most folks with money knew where the bars and night clubs, called "speakeasys," were located. The nightlife in the 1930s never slowed down in Atlanta.

Forrest Turner continued to work for the drugstore. On the days when he worked the evening shift and didn't mind losing a little sleep, he would make a haul. On weekends he made several trips north. He would deliver the alcohol to garages, warehouses, and secluded places in Atlanta. As soon as the crates filled with gallon jugs were unloaded, he got paid. When the amendment passed in December 1933 making drinking legal again, the demand for bootleggers began to slow down; however, ten months later, Forrest Turner didn't have to worry about being chased by revenue agents, he and Bill Baker were sitting in jail.

4   HENRY COUNTY WORK CAMP

When passing a crew of convicts working on a road, young Forrest Turner often wondered who those men were and what crimes had they committed to be sent to the chain gang? The Black and White convicts were divided into separate crews, but both did the same grueling work. Each crew had its own individual guard armed with a shotgun watching and supervising them. He assumed that they had to be murderers or had committed terrible crimes. That could be the only justifiable explanation as to why they were being punished and treated so severely. Because they were chained together, they had to be dangerous. Forrest Turner never imagined that one day he would be a member of a chain gang.

***

Everyone growing up in Henry County in the 1920s and 30s was familiar with the convict camp in McDonough. Traveling west on Hampton Road (Highway 81) about two miles past McDonough Square there was a narrow dirt drive exiting to the left. Following the drive down a gradual hill of five hundred yards one reached the front gate of Henry County Work Camp. The compound was composed of the main wooden building, a shop, and a storage shed. The camp consisted of pastureland for the cattle, a pond, and cultivated fields for growing corn and vegetables.

The camp could accommodate forty-eight convicts. All the convicts were dressed in typical workcamp clothes, white shirts and pants having black stripes. Trusties, not expected to escape, were not closely guarded and roamed freely in and out of the compound. Two convicts were assigned to the kitchen to prepare meals for the convicts and staff. Two convicts worked in the shop to do the maintenance chores for the compound and two more were assigned to the washhouse. The other convicts were members of the chain gang spending their days outside the camp doing road work.

Most of Henry County's roads were dirt whose maintenance included filling washed out potholes, repairing bridges, cleaning out ditches, and swing blading shoulders. The "sweat box" was found outside of the main building where convicts who broke camp rules were confined as punishment. The outhouse was situated over a small creek which carried the waste away from the camp.

The Henry County Work Camp was like all the others found in counties throughout the state. Controlled by the prison commission, convicts were assigned to the camps by the state. One of the state's most notorious prisoners, Leland Harvey, was sent to Henry County twice. The first time was in July 1924 after he was convicted of robbery in Fulton County. He was eighteen years old. He was there for a brief time before being reassigned to another camp. He constantly tried to escape. His few successful escapes ended in his immediate recapture.

After one of his successful escapes, he went home where his parents convinced him to surrender. Because of his youth and the fact, he voluntarily surrendered, Governor Hardman gave him an unconditional pardon in August 1927 on his promise that he would go straight. Two days later, however, he was arrested in Atlanta for stealing another automobile. During his brief period of freedom, he reassumed his criminal behavior. As a result, Leland Harvey was convicted of auto theft and sentenced to five years hard labor. The prison authorities assigned him to Henry County Work Camp for the second time to serve out his sentence.

TWO CONVICTS ESCAPE HENRY COUNTY WORK CAMP

"Dangerous Convicts on the Loose"... "Harvey and Smith Overpower Guard"... "Vehicle Commandeered"

The local newspaper reported the unexpected flight from the work camp.

While at the Henry County camp Leland Harvey befriended a seasoned criminal named Aubrey Smith who had a long history of petty crimes. He had bounced around several work camps before landing in McDonough. In December 1928, the pair saw an opportunity to escape. While working outside the compound they were able to overpower a lone guard who was assigned to watch them. They were able to wrestle away his gun. When the other two guards heard the commotion and came to investigate, they used the stolen guard's gun to disarm them.

"You three fellas walk back to the main building, get inside, and close the door before I have to shoot you," hollered Leland. The guards cooperated. When they were out of sight, Leland Harvey and Aubrey Smith raced five hundred yards to the paved highway. To their good fortune a car was approaching. Rather than run over the two convicts standing in the road waving their arms, the motorist stopped. Leland Harvey quickly pulled the driver out of the car and left him screaming, stranded on the side of the road. In the meantime, the guards retrieved new firearms from the office storage room and ran to the highway. The two convicts jumped into the car and headed west just as the guards were arriving. Out of firing range they helplessly watched the fugitives drive away.

"Are you hurt, mister?" asked one of the guards, who was out of breath having run from the camp to the main road.

The infuriated driver angrily responded, "I thought one of them was going to shoot me! I should have run over the two first and then stopped. I need that car to go to work."

Although escapes from Henry County had occurred in the past, they were rare. Leland Harvey's and Aubrey Smith's escape was bold and unexpected. Warden Davis told the press that had a motorist not come along and stopped, the guards would have had time to arm themselves and prevent the escape.

For two days there were no signs of the fugitives. Police had staked out his parents' home in Macon, thinking that they may go there. However, the fugitives had other ideas. After their escape they drove to Atlanta, ditched the car which they had stolen and stole another one. On the evening of the third day Leland Harvey drove to the Milledgeville State Prison Hospital. Posing as the brother of one of the patients, he asked to see his brother, Arthur Smith, a renowned car thief. The hospital was half a mile from the main prison building and housed convicts who were suffering from tuberculosis. The compassionate guard allowed the visitor into the enclosure to see his supposedly sick brother. Once inside he disarmed the guard and stripped him of his keys. He then forced the guard to escort him to the building where Arthur Smith was held.

Once inside Leland Harvey freed his so-called brother and locked the guard in his vacated room. Seeing what was taking place, an inmate in another cell begged to be released. Leland Harvey freed the bootlegger named Jack Lynch. Together they were able to climb out a window and reach their vehicle before being noticed. Having grown up in Macon, Leland Harvey and the Smith brothers were long-time friends

Warden Davis and the guards at Henry County Work Camp were eagerly waiting for news of the escapee's recapture and their eventual return. Instead, word reached them that they had entered the prison hospital and released two sick inmates…and that they were still on the loose and their whereabouts were unknown.

A few weeks later Leland Harvey and Aubrey Smith entered a nightclub around midnight and spent the early morning hours celebrating. Buying drinks for every friendly face in the place, they soon became the toast of the club. As dawn arrived the waiter presented the pair with a two hundred and twenty-five-dollar bill.

"This bill is outrageous!" Harvey, having had one too many drinks, protested. "We haven't received that much food or drink." In anger and at Aubrey Smith's insistence they paid the bill and left.

"Turn the car around Aubrey!" ordered Leland. "We are going back to get our money!"

While Aubrey Smith guarded the back door, Leland Harvey entered the front door displaying an automatic pistol. He ordered the couples to continue dancing and yelled at the orchestra to play a lively number. He ordered all the guests and employees to stand against the wall. "I bought you drinks and got the orchestra to play you a special tune. Now it's time for you to tip me. I want you to hand over your cash and jewelry. Be generous now," he politely demanded.

In the meantime, Aubrey Smith calmly walked down the line relieving them of their valuables. He gave the bag to Leland Harvey who looked inside. "This should cover the amount of the bill," he said as he rushed out of the ballroom. Two security guards who heard the commotion were waiting and quickly detained Leland Harvey. The police arrived shortly thereafter. During the confusion Aubrey Smith, who was several steps behind, had time to get lost in the crowd and slip away.

On February 18, 1929, Leland Harvey, now twenty-three-years-old, was arrested in Miami after robbing twenty guests and employees at a nightclub. He pleaded guilty to the nightclub robbery charges. He then faced a prison term in Florida.

He was a fugitive from Georgia where he was serving a five-year sentence for robbery. Since his escape, he had accumulated a lengthy list of thefts and holdups in central Georgia. Macon Police also wanted him for crimes he committed there. Leland Harvey was extradited to Georgia to answer for those crimes and complete his sentence for the auto theft charge before being returned to Florida. His arrest brought an end to another chapter of the youthful bandit's career. The jewelry and one hundred dollars in cash were returned to the victims.

Warden Davis at the Henry County Work Camp was glad to learn the prison commission was not returning Leland Harvey to McDonough. He was heard telling his guards, "I feel sorry for folks at the prison who are in charge of keeping Harvey locked up."

It would be a few years before Forrest Turner and Leland Harvey met again. One of the chain gang convicts Forrest Turner saw working on the roads in McDonough as a young man might have been Leland Harvey.

5 BONNIE AND CLYDE

The death of Bonnie Parker and Clyde Barrow made front page headlines in every newspaper in the country. Forrest Turner read with interest the backgrounds of the pair considered as "Public Enemy Number One" by the F.B.I. The couple were the most feared and dangerous outlaws in the southwestern United States. The early life of Clyde Barrow in many ways parallelled the boyhood of Forrest Turner. Born in Texas in 1909 Clyde Barrow was also raised in a rural setting. Struggling to raise seven children as a sharecropper, his father moved the family to the city seeking a better life. Instead, they moved to the crime-ridden West Dallas area known as the "Devil's Back Porch." Justus Turner on the other hand relocated his family to Hapeville, a rapidly growing but peaceful community on the Southside of Atlanta.

Times were difficult during the Great Depression. Twenty-five percent of working adults were unemployed and dependent on bread lines for meals. Without money to buy needed items, some of the impoverished resorted to stealing. For Clyde Barrow and Forrest Turner their petty offenses would mushroom into more serious crimes. Bonnie Parker was a bright child and as an adult wrote poetry. One of her poems was a premonition of her and Clyde's eventual fate.

***

Bonnie Parker, born in Texas in 1910, was the middle child of three children. After her father died when she was four, the family also moved to Dallas. Clyde Barrow met Bonnie Parker through a friend and a friendship followed. He soon took a liking to the chain-smoking gal. Their legendary saga began in 1926. Clyde Barrow was introduced to crime at the youthful age of seventeen when he began robbing stores and stealing cars. Shortly after he met Miss Parker he was arrested and convicted of auto theft. In 1930 the judge sentenced him to work on a prison farm at Eastham Work Camp near Lovelady, Texas. Bonnie Parker often visited him. On one visit he convinced her to help him escape.

"Bonnie, I appreciate you coming to visit me. You are the only friend I have. "If you help me escape, we can be together again," Clyde begged. "We make a real good team, and I really miss your company."

During the next visit she hid a gun under her dress and managed to smuggle it into the prison. Clyde Barrow used the weapon to escape. Thus began their adventurous relationship.

He was soon recaptured and returned to the prison farm. The association with hardened criminals re-enforced his determination to defy the law. Considered by the other convicts to be somewhat gay, Clyde Barrow was abused in prison. He blamed the guards for overlooking the mistreatment he was receiving. He therefore developed a hatred for the law and those who enforced it. He was paroled in February 1932. He exited prison as an angry, emotionally troubled man, no longer the mischievous youth, who had entered. He was also missing two toes, which he had purposely chopped off, to avoid doing road work.

He and Bonnie Parker immediately went on a crime spree. Their rampage included auto thefts, bank robberies, and hold ups of small businesses throughout the mid and southwest. When his brother, Buck, and his wife, Blanche, joined the pair, they became known as the "Bonnie and Clyde Gang." For the next twenty-one months details of their exploits received national attention. By publicizing their misdeeds, they became the modern "Jessie James Gang" of the South. Their numerous bank robberies often ended in shootouts with police. Their fast cars, however, allowed them to outrun the posse and highway patrolmen. The gang was surrounded in a wooded area where Buck and Blanche were shot and captured. Bonnie and Clyde managed to escape and continued their criminal crusade.

When two unsuspecting patrolmen saw a couple sitting on the side of the road near Grapevine, Texas in what they thought was a broken-down car, they stopped to help. As they got out of their patrol car, Clyde Barrow fearing arrest opened fired and killed them. The incident created quite a stir among law enforcement in Texas greatly enhancing the urgency of catching them. The director of the state highway patrol convinced Frank Hamer, former captain of the Texas Rangers, to come out of retirement, to devote full-time to the capture of the cold-blooded killers.

For four weeks he followed their trail through several states without success. Finally, Ranger Hamer got a tip that Clyde Barrow had relatives in Louisiana and decided to go there in hopes of finding them. Parked on the side of the main highway leading into Bosler Parish to observe traffic, he and a patrolmen waited. A 1934 gray Ford sedan drove by at a leisurely pace. The surprised Hamer sat up in his seat and remarked, "I believe that was them. A man and a woman are in the car! That's the same gray Ford they were driving when they eluded police in Texas."

In an unmarked car, they followed the pair at a safe distance so as not to arouse suspicion. When Frank Hamer reached a telephone, he phoned the sheriff in the next town. "These murderers have killed several policemen. Shoot them if you have to, but don't let them get away!" he told the sheriff who quickly recruited a posse of deputies and a host of volunteers with guns. Knowing the direction the bandits were likely headed, the lawmen set up an ambush several miles further down Highway 154. Frank Hamer raced to catch up with the bandits.

When Clyde Barrow saw that they were being followed, he stepped on the gas. The wild chase resulted in the two vehicles reaching high speeds on the narrow two-lane, black-tarred country road. Once Ranger Hamer was certain that the pair were headed in the direction of the expected ambush he discontinued the chase. The confident outlaws were able to outdistance the pursuing car and assumed they had once again avoided capture. However, after topping a hill in Bienville Parish, he noticed a deputy, disguised as a farmer, standing in the road beside his broken-down truck with his hand raised, motioning him to halt. He slowed as if he was going to stop and help. At that moment, the deputy dove for cover under his truck. Something didn't look right.

Then Clyde yelled, "Bonnie, it's a trap. I'm getting the hell out of here!" It would be his last words. Realizing they may be sitting ducks, he reached for his sawed-off shotgun and began to speed away. But it was too late. Suddenly from behind the bushes a swarm of lawmen armed with rifles and machine guns barraged the car with bullets. The Ford, riddled with bullets, veered off the road and careened into the ditch.

Frank Hamer arrived at the scene and witnessed the shooting. Once the firing subsided, he cautiously approached the wrecked Ford. Seeing the motionless and bleeding pair inside he raised his arms and waved to the officers to hold their fire. In fear of getting shot, he hollered as loud as he could, "Stop shooting! Stop shooting! Bonnie Parker and Clyde Barrow are dead!"

They had shot their way out of familiar traps, but not this one. Bonnie Parker slumped over motionless with a shotgun in her lap. Clyde Barrow was seated upright with his head tilted back on the headrest, never having grabbed his machine gun. The posse had fired one hundred and sixty-seven bullets which punctured the Ford. Clyde Barrow was struck twenty-five times and Bonnie Parker twenty-three. The lifeless pair were no longer a threat. Law enforcement, the bankers, and the people of the Midwest could "rest easy." The month-long chase was over.

Frank Hamer remained at the ambush site for an extended period. He did not allow anyone to disturb the car or the bodies inside. He wanted to make sure that the newspapers covered the capture in its graphic details. News photographers, reporters and hundreds from the neighborhoods flocked to the gruesome and bloody scene. There was not a single tear in the eyes of the on-lookers. These bandits had met a justifiable end. In their twenty-one months of terror, they had committed fifteen bank and countless filling station robberies. They murdered at least nine police officers and four civilians.

***

Bonnie Parker dropped out of school and got married at the age of fifteen. When her husband was jailed for robbery her attraction toward Clyde Barrow began. She was a bright child. Her talent for writing poetry was discovered when investigators uncovered her poems while searching for evidence at their hideaway. She had foreseen that their odyssey of crime would soon end and penned the following poem.

The Story of Bonnie and Clyde

By Bonnie Parker

You have read the story of Jesse James

of how he lived and died.

If you still are in of something to read,

here's the story of Bonnie and Clyde.

Now Bonnie and Clyde are the Barrow gang.

I'm sure all of you have read.

How they rob and steal.

And how those who squeal,

are usually found dying or dead.

There are lots of untruths to their write-ups.

They are not too merciless as that.

They hate all the laws:

suffer are stool pigeons, spotters and rats.

From weariness some people have died.

But take it all in all,

our troubles are small,

Till we get like Bonnie and Clyde.

Some day they will go down together.

And they will bury them side by side.

To a few it means grief.

To the law it's relief.

But it is death to Bonnie and Clyde.

After reading the newspaper article about the death of Bonnie and Clyde, Forrest Turner mentioned at the dinner table. "It's a heck of a story. I kind of feel sorry for them. They were surprisingly good at outsmarting the law."

"You see, in the end they were caught and killed. Let that be a lesson to you," Forrest Turner's mother commented. "Murdering thou neighbor isn't God's way."

The death of Bonnie Parker and Clyde Barrow on May 23, 1934, set the stage for the emergent of new legendary outlaws. Little did the public know that a young man from McDonough, Georgia would become one of them.

6 WELCOME TO THE CHAIN GANG

Forrest Turner arrived in Thomasville after a half day's ride. As he entered the gate and got his first glance of the inside of the work camp, the reality that he was about to become a convict began to sink in. He started to curse under his breath, "Why in the hell, am I sent almost to Florida when Fulton County has a handful of convict camps." He wished he could be closer to his family and friends. He had grown angrier by the mile. He was mad at Bill Baker for getting him into this mess. He was mad at his court appointed attorney for suggesting he plead guilty. And most of all, he was mad at the judge for the stiff sentence. He felt that everyone had betrayed him. If he had the money, he could have hired a better lawyer. With better representation he probably would have gotten a probated sentence. As had always been the case, money could buy you anything you need in Atlanta, even freedom.

***

Before 1908 non-violent prisoners were leased out to private businesses for compensation to the counties where they were incarcerated. The newly enacted legislation specified that going forward, convicts sentenced to work camps were to be prisoners of the state. The state dispersed the convicts to the counties to work on county roads and highways. The State of Georgia allotted a certain number of prisoners to each participating county. Georgia was the first state to implement work camps for road work. The use of chain gangs quickly spread throughout the South.

It was perceived that it was more humane to allow the prisoners to work in the fresh air and sunshine rather than to keep them locked in cells. The convict labor proved to be beneficial as the use of prisoners improved the state's road infrastructure. In political circles a popular saying arose. "The reason Georgia has so many new roads is because bad boys build good roads. We owe our improved roadway system to the road gangs."

To keep the convicts from running away and to decrease the number of men needed to guard the convicts, the chain gang system was employed. One hundred forty of the Georgia counties had approximately one hundred fifty chain gangs in 1935. State convicts were assigned to these counties. The cost to the county was the expense of their room and board. At the same time, the state was able to lower the inmate population at local jails and state prisons. The state provided little oversight, leaving the individual wardens in total control.

With little money to update and modernize the work camps, living conditions and food were horrible and medical care was non-existent. The treatment of convicts was appalling and dehumanizing. In some areas convicts were treated worse than the pre-Civil War slaves. Convicts had no rights and were subject to hard labor from sunup to sundown in harsh conditions with little concern for their health or well-being. Once one entered the work camp his or her means of exit were limited to the following: make your time, buy a pardon or parole, escape or die. Unfortunately, to many the most likely outcome was death.

Besides the treatment by the guards, which varied from work camp to work camp, the type of work the convicts were expected to do also determined the harshness of the work camp. Convicts who quarried stones for road construction saw their days pass monotonously with backbreaking labor. Road crews in the Georgia summer heat didn't fare much better. While wielding picks, swing blades, and shovels, convicts were often injured. Mosquitos, gnats, snakes and flies harassed road crews. Sunburn in the summer and frost bite in winter were commonplace. Work camps used the "sweat box" to punish runaways and the serious transgressors of the rules. It was a living hell.

***

The Thomas County camp was one of the toughest in the state for prisoners. Few convicts escaped and those who did were eventually caught and made to regret their flight. R.W. McMillan, the warden since February, had the reputation of being one of the meanest and most unforgving because he ridgidly imposed strict rules to ensure that convicts stayed put. They were in leg irons twenty-four hours a day, chained as they slept and when transported to the roadways. He had ignored pressure from the prison commission to relax the work camp's inhumane treatment of convicts.

Shackled Forrest Turner and Fellow Convict
Inspect Abandoned Railroad Tracks

The Thomas County Work Camp was a compound with rundown wooden buildings having metal roofs. It was enclosed by a sixteen-foot wooden fence resembling a fort. Beside the gate was a guard tower that overlooked the compound. Inside was a guard armed with a loaded rifle. The building occupied by the convicts had a mess hall on one end, sleeping quarters in the middle and washroom on the other end. There was a separate maintenance shop. The main building served as the headquarters. It was occupied by the guards and the warden who had a separate office.

Immediately upon arrival the new convicts were issued their work camp clothes. They were told to strip down and put on a two-piece black striped suit with no underwear. They were also issued brogans but no socks. The guards didn't care if the shoes or the clothes fit. "The horizontal blacked stripes make me look like a zebra," Forrest thought to himself. "Lastly, the guard gave me a hat that he thought would fit me."

Next Forrest Turner was escorted across the yard to the maintenance barn where Trusty Sam, a blacksmith, riveted shackles around each ankle. Sam was a convict who had only a few years to serve and was not a threat to run. Each shackle had an iron ring the size of half a dollar that was positioned to the inside of each ankle. The Trusty placed a short chain with thirteen links called the "ankle chain" between Forrest Turner's ankles into which the blacksmith attached to the ends to the ankle rings and closed the link with the pounding of his hammer. The Trusty counted the links and pointed to the seventh link whereby the blacksmith attached one end of a short three-foot chain called a "strad chain." On the other end of the "strad chain" was a four-inch ring. "If you grab ahold of this ring at the end of the 'strad chain' like this and lift the 'ankle chain,' you will be able to walk more easily and avoid tripping over the chain," the Trusty told Forrest. He continued, "You see, when you raise the 'ankle chain' it will reduce the stress on your ankles and lessen the pain."

The shackles also referred to by the convicts as leg irons made walking difficult. Shuffling back to the main building, Forrest Turner struggled to walk. He realized that running while attached to these cumbersome leg irons was almost impossible. Once inside he heard the arrival of trucks and a pickup. He watched the weary chain gang crew slowly exit the back of the truck trying not to fall as they jumped out. They walked into the dining area found in the main building. He heard the barking bloodhounds as the guards attached a leash and led the dogs to their pens.

Forrest Turner followed the other convicts into the mess hall. There the trusties were placing the convicts' dinner plates on the long wooden tables with benches attached. The convicts walked to their usual places and sat down. After all the convicts were seated, he shuffled his way to the only unclaimed plate on the table. It was to be his assigned seat while at the work camp. He sat on the bench with his back to the table, raised his two shackled legs, swung his body around to face the table, and lowered his legs. Forrest Turner was proud that he made the turn with just one try. He noticed that the Black people and Whites sat at separate tables and that only about one third of the convicts were White.

"Hey kid, what are you in here for?" asked one of the convicts.

Forrest replied, "Riding in a stolen car."

"Is that all! I thought you had committed a murder or something really bad," said the inquisitive convict with raised eyebrows. "As for me I killed two people. It was in self-defense, don't you know."

The day's ordeal had been too much for Forrest Turner. He had no appetite, and the food didn't appeal to him either. He was not his jovial self. He just sat there staring at the convicts. Their long, gloomy faces filled with despair. Most quietly finished their serving in fear of being punished if they had not. Most had washed their hands, but the dirt was deeply ingrained and visible in the crevices of their skin. All were unshaven and reeked of sweat. It was a sobering sight. He knew that soon he would look the same. He was exhausted, His tired body begged for sleep.

There were two rows of uncomfortable looking beds positioned side by side with upright milk cans that served as toilets placed at the foot of the beds. Once all the convicts were lying on their beds another chain called the "night chain" was inserted through the upper four-inch ring of each convict's "strad chain." The ends of the "night chain" were wrapped around posts found on the outside of the building and secured with a padlock. The slack in the chain and the three-foot distance of the "strad chain" allowed the convict to access the toilet can, although awkwardly.

Forrest Turner struggled to sleep. Every time someone got up to relieve himself, the movement tugged the night chain. The rattle was constantly waking him. He had just dozed off when he felt and heard the "night chain" being pulled through his "strad ring." Two hours before daylight the convicts marched to the mess hall. Breakfast consisted of black coffee, hoecake, and small pieces of fried pork or beef sides with a spoonful of sorghum syrup. He took one look at the contents of the plate and turned up his nose. A convict gave him the spoon left for him on the table. "This is your spoon. Don't lose it, or you will be eating with your hands," said the convict across the table. Forrest filled his spoon with syrup and then tasted the dark brown liquid with the tip of his tongue. "This is awful. I can't eat this!" he complained.

The convict quickly spoke up, "Forrest, you had better get used to it. This what you are going to get every day…like it or not. If you are not going to eat it, slide your plate over here? I am still hungry."

After breakfast everyone marched out into the yard and assembled in squads of twenty or so. Guards were yelling at convicts to move quicker and shoving those who weren't keeping up. Blacks and Whites were put in separate squads. Guards threaded the "day chain" through "strad rings" after each member of the work details was seated in the truck. The loaded truck with secured convicts headed to the work site.

During the truck ride Forrest Turner quickly learned the proper "chain gang language" from the other helpful convicts. Warden McMillan and the guards required each reply to be either "Yeah, Sir" or "Nah, Sir." To wipe sweat from one's brow the convict would have to announce, "Wiping it off" and wait for the guard's response, "Wipe it off." To remove one's shirt, it was "Taking it off" followed by a reply of "Take it off." The guards considered the use of the wrong language as an insult punishable by a slap in the face or punch in the gut. The perturbed Forrest Turner sarcastically commented, "You need permission to do everything in here. I wouldn't be surprised if you need permission to breathe."

"Kid, welcome to Thomas County Work Camp," the convict said with a smile.

First daylight work began. Around 11:30 a.m. Forrest Turner heard the guard holler "Lay 'em down," which meant it was time to break and eat. The rest period couldn't have come soon enough. He hadn't worked this hard since his cotton-picking days as a youth. A meal of corn pones and boiled dried red beans was dished out by a trusty. At 1:00 p.m. the resting convicts heard the command, "Let's go back." Then around 6:00 p.m. came the call, "Lay 'em down."

The convicts were loaded into the truck, chained, and returned to the work camp. As Forrest Turner exited the truck, a guard inspected his leg irons, frisked, and "sniffed" him. He would learn that if a convict didn't smell bad, he hadn't worked hard enough and was subject to punishment.

Upon hearing the announcement, "Come and get it," "Get your feed," everyone headed to the mess hall. There prepared for the convicts were corn pones and fried pig's fat with sorghum syrup. The food was not to Forrest Turner's liking, but he was starving. He hoped the "slop" as he called it would stay down.

After the meal, the convicts returned to the sleeping quarters. The weary Forrest Turner was sitting on his bed when Warden McMillan entered asking the guards if any of the convicts were causing trouble or were seen not working. Two convicts who had arrived the day before were caught sitting down instead of shoveling dirt. When threatened they stood up but were too exhausted to work. They spent most of the afternoon leaning on their shovels, using them as props. The two convicts who had not done their share of work that day were pointed out by the guards.

"Bring those men into the dining hall," Warden McMillan ordered. There the guard removed the men's shirts, and had one of them face the whipping post. The crying convict was told to wrap his arms around the whipping post where the guard tied his hands in preparation for a whipping by the warden with his leather strap. Seeing the strap in the warden's hand, the convict pleaded, "Don't hit me, I promise do better tomorrow!"

"So, you do not want to work, 'eh.' Then I will show you the consequences if you don't," voiced the warden as he began to apply his punishment. The yells and screams echoed through the building and sent chills through Forrest Turner's body. The second convict had to be forcibly dragged to the whipping post where he received the same treatment. It was their first introduction to the whip. The warden only flogged each man five times with light strokes instead of the usual ten with full force. It was considered more of an attention getter than a serious beating. Nevertheless, to the new men it was painful and left bruises. To Forrest Turner it was a lesson in obedience.

In 1923 the governor outlawed the use of leather whips, however, some wardens continued their use. "It is the only effective way to discipline these worthless human beings," Thomas County Warden McMillan said. "The governor knows nothing about running a prison work camp, so why should he tell me how to control these convicts."

Fortunately, Forrest Turner's farming background prepared him for the rigors of road work. He had lots of experience in handling shovels, pickaxes, and rakes. "Thank God it is October, the brutal South Georgia heat is still many months away," he rationalized.

As darkness set in the exhausted convicts went to their beds. Many were too exhausted to undress and slept in their soiled clothes. Saturday was a washday where the convicts could take showers and were issued clean striped uniforms. The guards threaded the night chain through each convict's "strad ring" and attached the ends to the outside anchors. The room was immediately filled with silence.

His first full day at Thomas County Work Camp was one he would never forget. Sleep came easy. The dreadful thought entered his mind, "Is each day going to follow this same routine for the next three years or so? I don't know if I can last that long."

The drudgery of working on a chain gang was bad enough with a sympathetic guard who respected human dignity, but when overseen by a "southern redneck" who treated convicts as slaves, the experience became intolerable. Forrest Turner had to decide whether to stay put and survive the cruelty for the remaining term of his three-to-five-year sentence or leave. He had served for just over a year and a half. The decision was an easy one. He would try to escape. The opportunity came on August 28, 1936. The headlines read.

SOUTH GEORGIA POLICE SEARCH FOR RUNAWAY CONVICT

"Young Convict Flees Work Camp"... "Twenty-One-Year-Old Fugitive At Large"... "All out Search Underway"

The local newspapers in Thomasville and surrounding areas reported the escape of a convict from a road gang in brief articles. The newspaper described the convict who fled Thomas County Work Camp detail as a white male, 5'11", 161 pounds, brown-haired, and blue-eyed and goes by the name, Forrest Turner. It also mentioned that the Atlanta car thief had eluded guards and bloodhounds and that few such escapes have occurred while under the stern Warden McMillan's watch.

***

Forrest Turner had confided in Robert Colton, a fellow convict, asking him for help when the time came to run. "When you see me ask for permission to go to the bushes. Please create a distraction to occupy the guards' attention," he instructed Colton.

In the meantime, an accomplice of Forrest Turner had been in the Thomasville area for days prior to the escape attempt. He was following the activity of the chain gangs from a distance. Not to draw suspicion he had stolen a local license plate and replaced the Fulton County plate with one bearing the name Thomas County. Bill Baker had passed by the road crew and was able to get the attention of Forrest Turner, who immediately recognized him.

For several months, unbeknownst to the guards, Forrest Turner had painstakingly filed down the leg irons and covered the cut marks with dirt in preparation for a future break. He could slip out of the loosened leg irons with just a little effort. Returning to the same location as the day before, the squad of convicts was finishing the cleaning of ditches on a dirt road. When Bill Baker drove by the gang of workers, it was Forrest Turner's cue that his ride would be waiting in the nearby woods. There were two guards and two vehicles to elude. One of the trucks was driven by a guard who transported the convicts. A second pickup brought the caged bloodhounds. It was a hot August day in South Georgia.

During the noon lunch break he put his plan into action. He approached the guards who were eating their lunch. "I have a bad stomach. I had the 'runs' last night. I desperately need to get to bush before I mess all over myself," he begged the guard while grimacing and holding his stomach. The guard told him, "Go to the bush but don't take too long."

As soon as Forrest Turner reached the bushes and was out of sight of the guards, Robert Colton let out a yell and fell to the ground. "Clutching his chest, I am in pain!" he moaned." At first the guards ignored him. But when one of the convicts yelled to the guards that convict Colton was in trouble, they rushed to investigate the problem. Robert Colton put on an incredible act pretending he was terribly ill. "I think he is having a heat stroke," surmised one of the guards. "Let's give him some water."

While tending to the downed convict thinking he may not make it through the day, the guards forgot about Forrest Turner who had gone to the bushes.

In the meantime, he was able to remove the leg irons and run. He was soon spotted by Bill Baker, who escorted him to the hidden vehicle. As they sped down the road, Forrest Turner was busy in the back seat changing out of his convict stripes into regular street clothes which Bill Baker had brought. He didn't know how much of a head start they had. He was simply happy being in a fast-moving vehicle heading south.

When the guards realized that Forrest Turner had not returned, one went to search for him in the bushes. All he found was a lonesome pair of leg irons lying on the ground. Forrest Turner was the last convict they expected to escape. He was well-liked by the guards and had not created any problems since his arrival at the work camp. Now he was a fugitive.

One of the guards ordered the convicts back into the truck. Two convicts carried the ailing Colton. The other guard radioed the work camp to ask for help. "Don't worry he can't go far on foot," one guard told the other. "We have eight hours of daylight left to find him." Once they were chained the other guard let loose the two dogs and followed them through the brush. Once the dogs reached an abandoned dirt road the trail went cold. Most escaped convicts were recaptured within twenty-four hours. But by the time the reinforcements arrived and let loose more dogs the fugitive Turner and driver Baker were miles away.

"The last I heard you were locked up somewhere," Forrest asked.

Bill replied with a smirk, "I just recently got released. I guess it was because of my age and good behavior. I thought I owed you a favor since I got you sent to the chain gang."

"Is this your car?" Forrest asked.

Bill replied, "No, I stole it yesterday. How do you like it? It has a big motor."

"Here we go again. If we get caught in this car, we will both be back in the chain gang for life," Forrest complained. "But nevertheless, I am thankful you came to get me."

During his stay at Thomas County Work Camp, Forrest Turner had managed not to get flogged. But he couldn't remember the number of times he was struck with a whip, poked hard in the back with the butt of a shotgun or slapped in the face. He had seen other convicts die from being unable to cope with the harsh conditions and lack of proper medical care. He was fortunate to have survived.

That night the two celebrated Forrest Turner's escape while safely many miles from the work camp. Now he hoped to put the sad memories from the chain gang days behind him. Meanwhile, at the work camp, Warden McMillan was beside himself. "There will be no more escapes," he preached to the convicts the evening following Forrest Turner's successful flight. "Your portions of food have been reduced by half for the next week," he screamed at the convicts. Robert Colton knew that it would be a while before his opportunity to follow Forrest Turner would be possible.

7 ROBERT ELLIOTT BURNS STORY

If Forrest Turner had read the book or seen the movie, "I am a Fugitive from a Georgia Chain Gang!," he would have known what was in store for him at Thomas County Work Camp. Instead, he hadn't expected to be subject to the same harsh treatment as was inflicted on Robert Burns thirteen years earlier. The most incredible documented story of time spent as a chain gang convict belonged to Robert Burns. He was sentenced to a Georgia prison work camp in 1921 where he labored on the chain gang. He escaped and led a productive life in Chicago while a fugitive until he was found. He returned to Georgia to complete his sentence only to escape again. During his period of freedom, he began to chronicle the hardships and cruelties convicts endured by those on a Georgia chain gang. These published accounts were the precursor of prison reform. He was known as the "man who broke a thousand chains." Although change in the treatment of prisoners was slow in coming, Forrest Turner would eventually benefit from the reforms.

***

Robert Burns was born in New York in 1892. He was a successful young accountant at the start of World War I. He enlisted as a combat medic in the Army. During his time in the service, his duties kept him near the front lines, tending to the wounded and dead. While he was there, the troops were engaged in some of the bloodiest conflicts in France. He survived the war physically but returned suffering from "shellshock syndrome." Unable to obtain needed medical treatment from the Army, nor hold a job, he became a drifter riding on freight trains from town to town. In 1921 the mentally ill and disheveled, Robert Burns wearing nothing but worn-out shoes, and rags arrived in Atlanta.

A fellow approached Robert Burns on Pryor Street. Figuring out that he was penniless and hungry, he offered to buy him a meal. "I know the owner of a diner who cooks a pretty good hamburger," he said. Robert Burns was beside himself. He hadn't had a hot meal in ages. While the owner was grilling the burgers, the stranger pulled out a gun and demanded money.

"What's going on? What are you doing?" the surprised Burns yelled.

The stranger then pointed the gun at him. "Go to the cash register and get all the money!" When he hesitated, the stranger yelled, "If you don't do what I say, I will shoot you both!"

He emptied the cash register. At that moment, a policeman came in and noticed the robbery taking place. A gunfight ensued and the stranger was shot and killed. The stunned Robert Burns put the money in his pocket and ran out the back door. A second policeman saw him leaving the diner and stopped him.

When he was questioned, he told the arresting officer, "I didn't do anything!"

The officer searched his pockets. "If so, what are you doing with this money?" he demanded to know while showing him the contents.

The officer escorted him back to the diner, where the owner named him as one of the holdup men. Robert Burns was arrested and taken to jail for stealing five dollars and eighty cents. During his appearance before the judge, he pleaded his case, "Your Honor, I was just an innocent bystander!" The judge had no use for a drifter, especially one from the North, and did not believe his story. "Since the stolen money was in your possession and you were running away, I find you guilty. I sentence you to a term of six to ten years on a chain gang," said the judge.

He was first sent to the chain gang at Campbell County Work Camp. When Campbell County became a part of Fulton County in 1931, the work camp was renamed Bellwood Work Camp. It had the reputation of being one of the tougher convict camps in the state. Robert Burns was five foot five inches tall, weighed one hundred and twenty-six pounds, and wore horned rimmed glasses. He spoke with a Yankee accent...a convenient target for the guards to harass. There he was shackled, endured back-breaking work at a nearby rock quarry, had constant beatings, and received meager rations. In desperation he made the decision to escape. He had a member of the chain gang bend his shackles with the precise strike of his sledgehammer. When he returned to the work camp that evening, the guards didn't notice the damaged shackle. At an opportune time the next day, he slipped out of the damaged shackles and fled.

On foot he managed to outsmart the guards, bloodhounds, and police who were in pursuit. When the bloodhounds caught up to him, he stopped, bent down and began to pet them. "Come here boys. Good boys," he said to the dogs. They became his friends and followed as he continued running. Once he reached a river he jumped in and swam downstream for twenty minutes. The dogs followed along the bank. He exited the river on the other side leaving the dogs behind. While on the run he passed a farmhouse whose farmer's laundry was hanging on a clothesline. He borrowed a shirt and a pair of overalls. In dry and clean clothes, he continued walking and running the long twenty-mile journey. When he reached the main road, a truck driver picked him up and carried him to Atlanta.

He bought a ticket and was prepared to board the arriving train when he recognized the warden and guards standing on the platform. His heart raced as he hid behind an auto parked by the station. The warden had guessed right. Fugitive Burns was heading north and would have to catch a train. The warden with his guards were there waiting for him.

Suddenly a hobo was seen in the railroad yard causing all the guards to abandon their watches and dash after him. By the time they realized they had chased and captured the wrong man, their fugitive had boarded the train and was heading north. Once the train reached Chattanooga, Robert Burns could rest easily. His freedom was assured.

He soon arrived in Chicago, where he began to recover his lost years. The ordeal at the work camp had given him time to overcome his war illness. He found a job as an accountant for a lumber company. His savings allowed him to buy rental property and eventually become a publisher of a magazine. Despite being a wanted fugitive in Georgia, he became a respected and successful businessman in Chicago. He married in 1926, but his unhappy marriage ended in divorce three years later. He had fallen in love with another woman much younger than his wife.

Unexpectedly, the vindictive estranged wife informed the authorities of his whereabout. While awaiting his fate he authored articles in his magazine of the atrocities occurring in the Georgia chain gangs. The Illinois governor originally refused to send him back to Georgia but eventually signed the extradition papers on the promise that he would be pardoned when he arrived. In 1929 Robert Burns returned to Georgia expecting a quick pardon. At the hearing, the biased judge considered him to be a habitual criminal and deserved to belong on the chain gang. To his displeasure, the state had reneged on its agreement. He was immediately sent to the Troup County Work Camp to finish his sentence. There he was assigned to do road work.

Frustrated when his parole requests were denied, he began to plan another escape. Using the money his brother had sent him he paid a local farmer who lived near the work camp to drive him out of the compound. When the car arrived, Robert Burns ran through the compound, jumped in the vehicle as the driver sped away.

Although bullets peppered around the car, they made their escape without injury. Concealed in the jump seat he made it to Atlanta undetected. There he caught a bus to Chattanooga. He successfully eluded the police who were watching the bus terminals and train stations. Through good fortune and minor miracles, he slipped out of Georgia again and made it to the home of his brother in New Jersey.

In 1931 the country was amid the Great Depression. Robert Burns was struggling financially; he used his free time to chronicle his life story. *I am a Fugitive from a Georgia Chain Gang!* The book became a best seller.

Robert Elliott Burns
"While Georgia may say I escaped from justice, I emphatically state that I escaped from injustice."

Its influence on public opinion about human suffering equaled the tragic events told by Harriet Beecher Stowe in her novel, *Uncle Tom's Cabin.* The heart-breaking story was made into an award-winning movie and released in 1932.

The book and movie were an embarrassment to the State of Georgia's prison officials. The warden at the Troup County Work Camp denied the charges of the brutality imposed on its convicts. The Georgia Prison Commission came under fire. In return, it unsuccessfully sued Warner Brothers for slandering. Secretly, Georgia officials were trying to find Robert Burns and return him to one of its chain gangs. When the governor of New Jersey refused to extradite him, there was an underground effort by the state to kidnap and return him to Georgia. Detectives were watching his family's activities, reading their mail and seeking information from neighbors of his whereabouts. This time, however, he was safely hidden and protected by friends and family.

He was still a fugitive and the fear of being returned to Georgia haunted him. Nevertheless, he would remarry and have four children. Not to embarrass them he lived an unassuming life avoiding the publicity that was normally befitting a famed author. In the meantime, he longed to rid the stigma of being a fugitive. It was many years before the last chapter of his prison odyssey was finally written.

Robert Elliott Burn's book and movie were credited for the eventual abolition of the chain gang system in the South. Until then the humanitarians and advocates of better treatment of prisoners were in the minority. But after the release of the movie the prison reform movement began to receive public approval. Pressure on legislators resulted in new laws and changes in prison policies.

It was unfortunate that Forrest Turner was already at the Thomas County Work Camp when Robert Burns' chain gang movie reached the Georgia theaters.

8   THE GREEN CAR GANG

In 1936 the City of Atlanta and the surrounding areas were terrorized by a band of thieves who became known as the "Green Car Gang." Although the gang was credited with the theft of several cars, it was the Green Ford in which they were riding when captured that gave them their dubious title. The Turner brothers and Bill Baker living in Hapeville along with Robert Colton from Mississippi made up the group of youthful and brash bandits. Lieutenant C.E. McCrary who headed up the investigative unit for Fulton County labeled the gang as the most menacing bunch in Georgia. His phone was ringing off the hook by angry folks who were victims of their unlawful activities.

Forrest Turner, Bill Baker and Robert Colton all had been convicted of crimes, served time in work camps, and escaped. They were considered fugitives in the eyes of the law. They were young and foolish. Their time spent working on chain gangs only increased their indignation of the law. The other Turner brothers, Henry and Lee, had no prior police record but eagerly took part.

Forrest Turner entered prison as a naïve first offender, but after a year and a half at the work camp he became educated in the ways of crime. He was surrounded by seasoned criminals who eagerly shared their experiences. With the new-found knowledge he hoped his criminal exploits would propel him and his gang into Georgia history books along with the other famous bandits. He was determined to avenge his cruel and unfair incarceration at the work camp.

***

Growing up in McDonough and eking out a living was a struggle. The Turner family was underprivileged. Having a pocket full of money to spend, nice clothes to wear, and fancy new automobiles to drive were luxuries neither he nor his parents could afford. The brothers, Henry, Lee, and Chester, were envious of Forrest when they met him secretly after he had escaped from the Thomas County Work Camp. He was wearing expensive polished leather shoes, a double-breasted suit, and a fedora.

Henry asked, "Forrest, I know you are stealing money and automobiles. Aren't you afraid of getting caught again and going back to the chain gang?"

"The way I look at it. I may get caught tomorrow, next year or maybe never. It doesn't matter. To me it's worth it. I enjoy this lavish lifestyle. And I am smarter than most of those fellas who are trying to catch me," Forrest explained with a laugh.

Lee continued, "I hear that being on a chain gang is awful."

"Yeah, it is. You just must find a fast way out as soon as you get there," Forrest recommended. "If you and Lee join me, I will show you how you can become rich without having to work. You will enjoy outfoxing the law at the same time." Thus, a gang was created who went on a rampage of holdups and robberies. They had managed to stay one step ahead of law enforcement who had conducted a massive manhunt for them. The gang's fortunes were about to change.

***

FORREST TURNER AND GANG ARRESTED IN ATLANTA

"Five Young Men Members of the 'Most Wanted Gang in Georgia,' Arrested"... "Three were Brothers, Cornered by Two Brave Detectives on an Atlanta Street"... "Safely Put Behind Bars Last Saturday Night"... "Arrest of

Gang to Clear up Scores of Recent Holdups in Fulton County"

Those were the headlines in the major Georgia newspapers on December 13, 1936. Fulton County police officials considered the arrests a major crime bust.

The young men, who were charged with suspicion of robbery, identified themselves as Forrest Turner, and his two brothers, Henry and Lee Turner all from Hapeville, Bill Baker also from Hapeville, and Robert Colton from Marks, Mississippi. The five were boxed in while sitting in their automobile on an Atlanta street before they could drive away and flee from detectives. The passengers surrendered without resistance.

Lieutenant McCrary assigned detectives Leo Nahlik and Melvin Coppenger to take whatever measures needed to arrest the gang who were frightening the citizens of Atlanta with their frequent holdups. To date the detectives have had little success in identifying the gang members or finding their hideout. All tips had led to dead ends. Finally, an anonymous tipster called the police station to inform the detectives that one of the bandits may be living in a rooming house at 1000 Boulevard near 10th Street. Thinking that it was another wild goose chase, they drove to the location in Leo Nahlik's personal car. Finding nothing out of the ordinary, Detective Nahlik, who was driving, considered leaving. "Another false alarm." He told Melvin, "Besides it will be totally dark soon."

"We should park across the street where we can keep an eye on the place for a while. The gang may show up later," suggested Melvin.

Leo quickly replied, "Sounds good to me. I have nothing better to do."

After a couple of hours, a vehicle pulled up to the front of the rooming house.

"That's a brand-new dark green Ford, not the type of vehicle a boarder of a rental house would own. And it's the same color as reported by some of the victims," remarked Leo.

1936 Green Ford

The detectives could see that several men were riding in the Ford sedan.

"I think it's them," the surprised Leo said with a degree of anxiety. "We need to call for backup. Go find a phone, Melvin!"

"You're right," replied Melvin not taking his eyes off the sedan as he dashed to a neighboring residence.

Five passengers got out of the vehicle and entered the building. A brief time later the passengers came out of the rooming house and got back into their car. The driver cranked the motor and began to ease forward.

Without hesitation or regard for his safety, Detective Nahlik drove his car directly to the front of the sedan thereby blocking it and forcing the driver to stop abruptly. Detective Nahlik jumped out armed with his double barrel sawed-off shotgun. He ran over to the driver's side, went to one knee, and pointed the shotgun into the face of the stunned driver of the sedan.

"If you make a move, you will get a mouth full of buckshot. You won't have to worry about shaving ever again. Just at that moment Detective Coppenger appeared out of the darkness and raced over to the passenger side flashing his loaded service revolver. "Don't reach for your weapons," he warned. "I have never missed from this distance." Caught by surprise, the occupants slowly exited the sedan with their hands up. "Don't shoot, we give up," said the front seat passenger.

The driver of the Ford sedan was the fugitive, Forrest Turner. Stepping out of the sedan with his arms raised, he told Detective Nahlik, "We had you outnumbered, but you got the drop on us. If we had seen you coming, we would have had enough guns to put you away," commented the boastful Turner.

With the captives restrained, the stress of the moment subsided. Detective Coppenger asked, "Is there anyone else in the rooming house?" He was amused by Forrest's unexpected and frustrating remarks.

"No one is in the house. You know you would never have caught us if someone hadn't tipped you off," Forrest complained.

When two backup police cars arrived a few minutes later, the policemen were astounded that the two detectives had already single-handedly taken down the notorious "Green Car Gang."

After the gang members were safely behind bars at the Fulton Tower, Lieutenant McCrary met with anxious reporters who were seeking details of the arrests. "We have seven suspects under lock and key," said the Lieutenant. "We believe the five young men and two ladies were responsible for numerous holdups and thefts that had occurred over the last three months."

"Can you tell us a little about the suspects you are holding," a reporter asked.

"The gang's leader is Forrest Turner. He is presently a fugitive from the Thomas County Work Camp. We think twenty-one-year-old Turner is the mastermind," he continued. "Second in command is Vincent 'Bill' Baker. Forrest Turner's trouble began when he and Baker were convicted of auto theft two years ago. Baker is eighteen years old, 6'1", blond-haired with a liberty tattoo on his arm. R.L. 'Robert' Colton, who served time with Forrest Turner at Thomas County Work

Fulton County Jail
Known as Fulton Tower
Located at 208 Butler Street,
Atlanta, Georgia

Camp, is the third member of the gang. The twenty-five-year-old diminutive Colton at 5'6" and a hundred thirty-four pounds has many arrests and was already a seasoned outlaw before joining the gang at Forrest Turner's invitation. He is a career criminal from Mississippi. He had committed a string of crimes and served eighteen months in the Atlanta Penitentiary. Baker and Colton were born bad and will always be in trouble with the law. I feel sorry for their poor parents who had to try to raise them."

Lieutenant McCrary added, "Forrest Turner's brothers, Henry Turner and Lee Turner, are the other members of the gang. In addition to the five men, we also arrested a Mrs. Virginia Colton, a bride of two weeks, and an Ann Lewis, nineteen, girlfriend of Forrest Turner. At this time, we are not sure what involvement they had in the robberies. We are holding all of them on suspicion of robbery for now.

"We learned that the Ford sedan was reported stolen from A.C. White Motor Company in Cartersville. It is undamaged and is being returned to its owner. We found enough guns in the vehicle to equip an army."

"What sort of guns did your men find?" asked one of the reporters.

McCrary responded, "I can tell you that Turner had a Luger automatic in his possession. Turner also claimed to own the convertible 'Tommy' gun which has a special drum which holds fifty cartridges. The gun was found in a closet at the boarding house. It shoots like a military machine gun. This fella Turner is one of the toughest fugitives in the state. What does someone need with a gun like that?

"Robert Colton had in his possession a powerful 38 caliber Winchester rifle. On the floorboard we discovered a 4 caliber Derringer. In a bedroom my men found a variety of clothes, including a closet full of overcoats varying in color and style."

"I guess they wanted to appear as wealthy gangsters," another reporter remarked.

Lieutenant McCrary replied, "I suspect all those items were stolen in Nashville, Tennessee. They are smart dressers, but I think they will look better in stripes, don't you?"

"Yesterday was a momentous day for our Atlanta Police Department," he continued. "We think the gang is responsible for some thirty unsolved cases of robbery in Atlanta and other parts of the state. The fella Turner was very boastful and wisecracking when taken to headquarters while the others were subdued and sullen. He told one of the officers that the guns aimed at him didn't scare him; that it wasn't the first time that someone had threaten to shoot him. He also bragged about the gang's successful robberies.

"Some of the people we held up were easy targets. It was like taking candy from a baby," Turner said with a wide grin.

I told him, "If you fellas are so smart why are you in jail? He had no wisecrack reply."

The Lieutenant continued, "These hoodlums were holding up innocent people and taking their hard-earned money and valuables. This Turner fella and his gang should be ashamed of what they were doing instead of bragging about it."

***

The stolen property found in the rooming house at the Boulevard address tied the gang to several robberies. There the officers found a portable radio set stolen in a holdup on Stewart Avenue. In an automobile parked nearby that was thought to have been driven by one of the other gang members, the detectives found a license plate removed from a Hudson automobile stolen from Smith Motor Company in Griffin. That blue sedan was later abandoned in the woods near Jonesboro. According to victims, it was the same Hudson that was used by the gang in other recent robberies. When Forrest Turner was searched, the keys to the stolen and abandoned Hudson were found in his pocket. "I guess I should have thrown those keys away," Forrest told the detective with a sheepish grin.

Turner and company displayed a certain arrogance by never concealing their faces when committing a crime. They never expected to get caught so it did not matter who saw them. If caught, if ever, they would simply deny any involvement in the robberies. They were confident that victims would be too afraid to testify against them.

To bring charges against the individual gang members the state needed more evidence. Since they were riding in a stolen car, all they could be charged with is auto theft or abetting the theft. Without a confession which was not always easy to get, the state would need concrete proof that the gang committed the other alleged crimes.

"Unless you catch an accused in the act, find stolen items on their person or have an eyewitness who can identify the perpetrator, juries will always side with the defense," Detective Nahlik said. "One is innocent until proven guilty, you know."

Detectives Nahlik and Coppenger began contacting the hold-up robbery victims, inviting them to take part in a line-up.

Nahlik spoke to J.R. Adams. "I understand you are the owner of a filling station on Whitehall Street. You reported a theft on December 2nd."

"Yeah, two men came into the station and demanded money. I gave him the sixty-five dollars I had in the drawer. The well-dressed man thanked me as he and the other man ran out the door," complained Mr. Adams.

Nahlik asked, "Do you think you can identify him if you saw him again?"

"Yeah, I know I can," he confidently assured.

Nahlik suggested to Mr. Adams, "Come to the stationhouse next Tuesday. We are conducting a line-up. All the gang members will be present, and a host of victims will join you to try to name their robbers. We want to clear up as many of the robberies that have occurred in the last two months as possible. We think the gang could be responsible for some if not all the robberies."

Detective Coppenger talked with C.L. Ewing who ran a filling station on Spring Street. He reported that two men robbed him of his cash and took his Derringer.

The five charged bandits marched in and lined up along a blank wall. The bright lights aimed at them made it easy for the victims to see their faces. At the same time the accused in the lineup could not see the robbery victims who were there trying to identify them. In total fifty robbery victims from the Atlanta area attended the line-up at police headquarters. There they got their first glimpse of the gang members. Seven of the victims were robbed of cash in amounts ranging from seven dollars and fifty cents to sixty-five dollars. Three individuals lost one hundred seventy-five dollars, a pistol, and an overcoat. All these victims were able to name one or more of the young men in the lineup.

Lee Turner
The Youngest Turner Brother

Later photos of the suspects were shown to the victimized merchants whose businesses were out of the area. The operators of a roadhouse between Adairsville and Rome recognized Forrest Turner and Robert Colton as the men who had stolen three hundred dollars and a Lugar automatic pistol. The same firearm was found on Forrest Turner when he was arrested. The detectives had amassed enough eyewitnesses and evidence for an air-tight case.

In Georgia and most states, the circumstances of the crime and evidence collected must be presented to a grand jury. The jury consisted of up to twenty-one men and women who would then decide if the case should either go to trial or get dismissed. On December 22, 1936, the grand jury reached its decision. Forrest Turner was identified as having committed nine robberies and Robert Colton was pointed out by witnesses as having taken part in four. Bill Baker was pointed out by only one of the hold-up victims. The trio were convicted of the crimes and faced a twelve-man traverse jury trial after the first of the year. Since they were work camp escapees, they remained in Fulton Tower.

Henry Turner, the oldest member of the gang, was not identified by the witnesses and received a probated sentence for carrying a weapon. Bill Baker, who was convicted of one robbery, was put on two years' probation. Eighteen-year-old Lee Turner was not connected with any of the robberies and was not charged.

It was not to be a merry Christmas for the young bandits. They were informed by their court appointed attorney that they had zero chance of getting acquitted. On January 13th Forrest Turner and Robert Colton pleaded guilty in court to taking part in a total of ten holdups and auto thefts. The Fulton Superior Court judge sentenced each to ten years hard labor on a chain gang. The sentence to run concurrent to the years not already served. Forrest Turner remained at the Fulton Tower. He was not happy when informed that he would be transported back to Thomas County Work Camp to resume his unfinished sentence and then begin serving his added time.

The two ladies were released the following Wednesday after their arrest. They denied being involved and there was no evidence linking them to the thefts. Chester, the fourth Turner brother, would have been a member of the gang had he not been in the Cherokee County Work Camp. He was serving time for an auto theft he committed eight months earlier.

9 SMITHVILLE ESCAPE

Forrest Turner and Robert Colton became acquaintances while serving time on the chain gang at the Thomas County Work Camp. Forrest Turner managed to escape in August 1936 while Robert Colton followed three months later in November. Both had elluded detectives before being recaptured at a rooming house off 10th Street and Boulevard in Atlanta. They were arrested on December 12, 1936, and pleaded guilty to robbery charges in Fulton Superior Court January 13th. The judge sentenced Forrest Turner to ten additional years and Robert Colton to five more. They were escorted to the Fulton Tower in Atlanta to remain until transported back to Thomas County Work Camp.

Fulton County's jail, referred to as the Fulton Tower, was located on Butler Street. Built in 1898, the facility housed four hundred prisoners who were charged with crimes committed in Fulton County. The five-story stone building was capped with an observation tower, hence its name. The one-hundred-foot landmark structure was visible from miles around. It was a reminder to passersby that eventually, if they broke the law in Fulton County, Fulton Tower would be their next home.

***

MANHUNT UNDERWAY FOR ESCAPED PRISONERS, TURNER AND COLTON

"Two Dangerous Prisoners Overpower Warden and Driver"... "Escape in Route to Convict Work Camp"... "Warden McMillan Shot"... "Warden's Abandoned Sedan Found in Dawson"... "Fugitives Forrest Turner and Robert Colton Still at Large"... "Massive Manhunt Under Way"

On Tuesday, January 26, 1937, all the state's major newspapers featured the story of a prison transfer that did not go according to plan. Prison officials were baffled over how two handcuffed prisoners sitting in the backseat managed to pull out a pistol and overpower the armed warden and driver.

Thomas County Work Camp Warden, R.W. McMillan, and the County's Ordinary, Frank Jones, drove to Atlanta to pick up two prisoners at Fulton Tower. Forrest Turner and Robert Colton had previously escaped from the work camp. They left Thomasville, Georgia in the morning and were expected back at the work camp by nightfall. "It's going to be a long day, but the transfer should be routine," Warden McMillan remarked. "I don't particularly enjoy the two hundred twenty-five-mile trip to Atlanta, but I am glad to add two convicts to our road crews."

Forrest told the jailer as he was escorted to the front door, "I am going to miss all of you guards but the accommodations here could have been a little better."

R.L. "Robert" Colton
A Career Criminal from
Mississippi

"Fulton Tower is like the Biltmore Hotel compared to where you are going," joked the guard.

Warden McMillan signed for the two prisoners and escorted them out the front door to his waiting sedan. As a precaution he handcuffed Turner's wrist to Colton's wrist. He also displayed a pistol to deter any thoughts of an escape attempt. He then instructed the two to slide into the back seat. If they had any ideas about fleeing during one of the rest stops, he would only have to shoot one of them to catch the other.

Forrest Turner was being returned to finish serving his sentence for auto theft in Atlanta while Robert Colton had three years remaining for burglary in Burke County and five years for robbery in Houston County. At that time, the exhausted search by the guards, local police, and blood hounds found no trace of the elusive fugitives. Their freedom ended, however, when they were finally recaptured in December. Unfortunately, they were both now facing lengthy stays at Thomas County Work Camp for the second time.

Forrest Turner dreaded returning to the Thomas County Work Camp where he had already spent time. He served six hundred seventy-two days before successfully managing to escape. He hated every minute of his stay. Finally, he could no longer tolerate the drudgery and misery bestowed on him by the work camp and its guards. He remembered the warden's warning on his arrival, "There will be no escapes from my work camp!" It was the warden's number one rule. He had seen the leather strap hanging on a hook in his office and heard the screams of others who were punished for their unsuccessful escapes.

As punishment for his escape the judge awarded him ten years to be added to his unfinished sentence. Since the Georgia Prison Commission often reassigned recaptured escaped convicts to different work camps, he had hoped he would not be sent back to Thomasville. That was not to be. He knew that some form of physical punishment was waiting for him when he returned.

***

The trip south was uneventful. Traveling on the Dixie Highway, they were approximately two miles south of Smithville near Leesburg when it all changed. Frank Jones was driving, and Warden McMillan was seated in the front passenger side. The prisoners had been quiet for the last several miles. The warden thought they were napping when a command came from the backseat,

"Stick 'em, up. I have a gun!" shouted Forrest Turner.

Warden McMillan shocked as he turned around, "What is this?" he yelled staring at a small caliber pistol aimed at his forehead. Several things raced through McMillan's mind. This Forrest fella must be a magician. Where did he get a gun? It looks like a pistol, but I am sure it's just a toy. His first instinct was to grab his own gun and shoot. But if it was a fake gun, he would be shooting two unarmed men. Instead, he chose not to be bluffed and reached for Turner's gun. As he tried to wrestle the gun away, it discharged. Realizing that it was not a toy gun, Warden McMillan grabbed and aimed his gun at Turner to return fire. Before he could shoot, Robert Colton instinctively grabbed the warden's gun and snatched it away. It discharged and struck the warden.

After Forrest Turner and Robert Colton managed to take possession of both guns, they noticed Warden McMillan holding his chest. From the expression on his face, he appeared to be in pain. One of the bullets had grazed his right chest before entering and lodging in the dashboard. The other bullet passed harmlessly through the roof of the sedan. From the blood stains on his shirt, Warden McMillan was bleeding, but luckily for all concerned the shot caused just a flesh wound.

Meanwhile, in the turmoil, the stunned driver Jones swerved onto the shoulder of the road. The deafening noise from the firing of the 25-caliber pistol caused Frank Jones to let go of the steering wheel and cupped his hands around his ringing ears. After a few precious seconds he gained control of himself and steered the sedan back onto the roadway. When he put on the brakes with the intent of stopping, Forrest told him to keep driving. "Roll down the windows to clear the smoke out of here!" he shouted to Jones.

It was incredible that the two prisoners managed to overpower the warden while their wrists were handcuffed together. It was a miracle that no one was seriously hurt. Now each of the prisoners had a pistol. The shoe was now on the other foot. Captives Jones and McMillan were at the mercy of the soon-to-be fugitives Turner and Colton. Was it payback time for all the mistreatment they had received while on the chain gang earlier? The frightened driver didn't expect that he and the warden would be alive much longer. He didn't realize that the prisoners were highway men and car thieves, not cold-blooded murderers.

"I told you to keep driving!" yelled Forrest.

Frank Jones replied in a panic, "Don't shoot again, I will do what you say. I see the warden is wounded. We need to get him to a doctor!"

"Don't worry about the warden. Just keep driving and no harm will come to you," responded Forrest.

Forrest continued boastfully, "I guess you are wondering where I got the gun. Well, I had it with me when I got in the car. I could have produced it anytime."

Approximately six miles from Albany, Frank Jones was ordered to turn off onto an isolated dirt road. Once they reached a wooded area, he and the warden were forced to exit the sedan. "Get these cuffs off." Colton told Jones. His hands were trembling as he unlocked the handcuffs. Instead of returning the favor by handcuffing the two hostages together, they were allowed to walk away. With their mission accomplished there was no need to harm the two men. Especially, since one was wounded.

Forrest Turner took the wheel leaving the men stranded in the woods. The county ordinary and warden were able to find their way back to the main road where a motorist picked them up. Upon reaching a residence which had a phone, the occupant called the local police, who arranged transportation for the wounded warden. He was sent to Pittman Memorial Hospital in Albany, treated and taken to his home in Ochlocknee, Georgia where he could recuperate.

"I guess we won't be going to Thomas County Work Camp any time soon," joked Forrest with a laugh.

Robert was quick to reply sarcastically, "Yeah, seriously I was looking forward to going there."

During the car ride north, Forrest and Robert were discussing the hidden gun trick. "I told you my plan would work," said Forrest.

Colton asked, "Forrest, how did you come up with idea to hide the pistol where you did?"

"From the number of times I have been in jails and prisons, I knew exactly how and where the guards were going to frisk me. Not expecting to find one they just overlooked the gun. I guess they never had someone try to smuggle a gun out of prison. Likewise, Warden McMillan saw no need to frisk us. Wow! Wasn't he surprised!" Forrest replied laughing as he shook his head.

Several hours later the police received a call about the theft of a vehicle in Dawson, Georgia. While investigating the theft, the police spotted the warden's stolen sedan nearby. It became clear that Colton and Turner had ditched the warden's car and stole a second vehicle to continue their escape.

***

Disturbed by the breakdown in security by allowing two armed and dangerous fugitives to escape, the Fulton County Grand Jury convened to investigate the occurrence.

Thomas County Ordinary Frank Jones testified, "The gun must have been placed in the sedan while we went inside to get the prisoners. I was told by one of the prison guards that the Turner brothers were seen in front of the Fulton Tower prior and after the transfer. They could have slipped the gun into the sedan when no one was looking."

A telegram sent to the jury by Detective Leo Nahlik disputed Mr. Jones' claim. "I was assigned to observe the prisoner transfer and to be ready to act in case of an escape attempt. The department was warned that an attempt might be made. I was armed and ready. Sitting in my car I was watching the activity outside Fulton Tower. I had the sedan in full view during the time Warden McMillan and Ordinary Jones were in the tower. No one came near the sedan until the warden returned with the prisoners," Nahlik wrote in the telegram.

The second question posed by the foreman of the Grand Jury. "Did anyone frisk the prisoners either before or after they were handed over to Warden McMillan. Whose responsibility was it to do a "body-search" of the prisoners coming and going? Someone should have done a better job in checking the prisoners for weapons!" No one said a word. The guards in charge just gave one another a blank stare.

The finger pointing continued. Warden McMillan, who had made the long trip from Thomasville with Frank Jones, was irritated by the assumption that he was at fault for allowing his prisoners to have a firearm when placed in the back seat. "Aren't jailers at Fulton Tower supposed to search prisoners for hidden weapons before releasing them?" the warden asked.

Jailer Holland was quick to respond, "When we turn over prisoners to sheriffs or detectives, it is up to those who are signing for them, to make sure they are clean. "I don't know whether Colton or Turner were properly searched before they left the Fulton Tower. I was standing at the front gate when they came through. At that time, I warned Warden McMillan that he should watch them closely. They are two bad actors," I said.

After listening to the testimony of all those who testified, the Grand Jury decided that both parties were at fault for not taking the proper precautions in searching for weapons on the prisoners. It was summed up by the foreman. "It looks like Turner and Colton had outsmarted the both of you. I blame both the jailer and the warden for allowing the escape."

In the meantime, Forrest Turner was filling his pockets with cash as he robbed anyone who presented themselves as easy prey. One of his victims was W.C. Tibble, a laundry truck driver, who forked over thirty-five dollars while delivering clothes to a home on Dill Avenue in Atlanta. Later a stolen automobile was found. The wrecked vehicle was heavily damaged and abandoned after striking a telephone poll. The two occupants who fled were thought to be the fugitives Forrest Turner and Robert Colton.

Thinking that Forrest's brothers or neighbors may somehow have been involved in the escape. Lieutenant McKibben ordered detectives to bring in Henry Turner, Chester Turner, friend Bill Baker, and Colton's wife, Virginia, and female companion Ann Lewis for questioning. When threatening each member of the group with arrest unless they came clean, resulted in no new leads, the detectives were forced to allow them to return home. Detectives were certain the group knew more than they admitted. The Turner brothers were outside Fulton Tower when their brother was escorted to the sedan. But there was no evidence to prove that any of them had aided in his Smithville escape.

***

The statewide manhunt had not resulted in the apprehension of either man or offered any clues as to where they might be hiding. Frustrated Warden McMillan promised a hundred dollars to anyone who could provide information leading to the capture of the wanted men. "We normally do not offer rewards for the apprehension of escaped convicts. However, these two in my opinion are the most violent criminals in the state," he revealed to the press. "They nearly killed me. I want them caught before they hurt someone else."

To avoid being recaptured, Turner and Colton knew they had to leave Atlanta. Every law enforcement officer was on the lookout for them, especially now that there was a handsome reward. The hefty sum being offered had attracted attention. Their escape had made the headlines of every newspaper in the state. Their faces boldly displayed on the front pages, made them recognizable by everyone who followed the stories in the newspaper.

As marked men they had to ditch the car. Driving by a parking lot in Atlanta there was a fast automobile begging to be stolen. As Robert Colton tried to break into the car, the operator saw what he considered suspicious activity. He left his station and ran with gun in hand to prevent the theft. "Get away from that car!" he shouted.

To avoid getting shot Robert Colton began to grapple with the man to take away his gun. During the scuffle shots were fired slightly, wounding the operator. Robert Colten was unhurt and successful in stealing the car. "That was a close call," Robert told Forrest as they headed south in their "new wheels," a 1936 Ford Roadster.

Detectives were updated daily as to the progress of the manhunt. Lieutenant McKibbon suggested to his men to be on the lookout for a roadster which had recently been stolen. On a night in late January, a motorist was speeding down Edgewood Avenue in Atlanta. At the intersection of Edgewood Avenue and Fort Street the driver crashed into another unsuspecting vehicle, hurling it into the air and causing it to land upside down. Two patrolmen who were in the area saw the accident from a distance and immediately identified the vehicle as the stolen roadster. They knew the driver had to be the fugitive, Turner. The damaged roadster managed to speed away even with a damaged front end. The detectives pursued Forrest Turner through the south side of town, where he was familiar with all the back roads and easily outmaneuvered the detectives in the darkness. The accident victim miraculously was uninjured, but his automobile was totaled.

Fearful of being spotted, Forrest Turner and Robert Colton hid the Roadster and stole another car. They headed to the Georgia coast. The fugitives resurfaced on Thursday January 29th in Savannah when a grocery store was robbed. The bandits entered a store filling up two bags of provisions. Instead of paying they held up the cashier at the store and made off with the groceries and supplies plus twenty-two dollars and change.

Fifteen minutes after fleeing the scene, an officer in a patrol car recognized the passing vehicle as stolen. He and all law enforcement officers were provided with the license plate number. He anxiously turned on his siren and began chasing the vehicle. Forrest Turner, the driver of the vehicle, hit the gas pedal and sped away. Thinking that he had outdistanced the patrol car, he drove the vehicle into the parking lot of an abandoned garage and parked in the rear. The police officer, however, saw the vehicle turn into the garage and followed. When the pursuing officer arrived moments later, he drew his firearm. Robert Colton surrendered without resisting. While the officer was cuffing him, Forrest Turner hiding in some underbrush managed to flee and avoid recapture. Robert Colton's freedom had lasted only three days. He refused to name the man that ran away, but the detectives knew who he was. The hunt for Forrest Turner continued.

10 SCARBOROUGH BREAKOUT

After his incredible escape during the transport to Thomas County Work Camp, Forrest Turner wanted to return certain favors to convicts with whom he had shared work camp time. He and James Lawrence, a fugitive from Florida, decided to free a convict from the Cherokee County Work Camp. Slim Scarborough was there serving a life sentence for his participation in the murder of a Putman County School Superintendent. Forrest Turner had read about the highly publicized murder trial and was acquainted with the murderer Scarborough, who was doing time at the work camp.

***

When a new arrival entered a prison or work camp, the first question directed to him by the inmates; what did you do to get locked up? Likewise, when Forrest Turner first met Slim Scarborough, he asked him the same question. He learned that he and his fellow convict Slim were sentenced for having committed different crimes, but both had much in common. Each was a member of a large family. They enjoyed reminiscing about the earlier days before their troubles with the law began. They soon developed a friendship which lasted for many years.

Slim was quick to give Forrest his life story. He began, "I was the oldest of ten children living in Tampa Florida, eighteen and ready to leave home. We had a barn behind the house which had sleeping quarters. My parents rented the place for nearly nothing. At that time two young drifters named Frank McClellan and Ted Coggeshall were the renters. When the two young men were ready to leave, they invited me to go with them to travel north. I didn't know them very well, but they gave me the opportunity to leave home. I didn't tell my parents because I knew they would stop me from going.

Simeon Joseph
"Slim" Scarborough
Wardens called him
"Slippery Slim"

"We left around midnight in a stolen car. We drove north to Macon. When we were nearly out of gas, we were forced to abandon the car and begin hitchhiking. Slim told me that while approaching the town of Eatonton, Georgia they were picked up by a friendly man who turned out to be Professor Wright, the superintendent of the Putnam County Schools. He said he was a former teacher and thought nothing of picking up young men. Something he had done many times without incident. I hopped into the front seat next to Professor Wright while Ted and Frank climbed into the backseat. We hadn't gone far when Frank told Professor Wright to pullover and stop. When he stopped and asked why, Frank told him that we wanted his car and that he should get out. He stopped all right but refused to surrender the vehicle. That's when Frank slugged him from behind on the back of his head. I was shocked. I couldn't believe what I was seeing. I should have done something to stop the attack, but I did nothing."

Slim kept talking as he lowered his head, and his eyes glazed over. Forrest could tell he was ashamed of what happened next.

"Frank and Ted jumped out of the car and pulled Professor Wright from the front seat and forced him to the ground. When he continued to resist, Ted struck him several more times until he was just lying there motionless. I thought they had killed him. While I stood there watching them, they dragged him into the woods. Professor Wright, however, was only unconscious and was able to crawl back to the road where he was picked up by a farmer. He was in serious condition by the time he reached the hospital. The injured Professor Wright lived three days before he passed away.

"We took the professor's car and continued driving north. State highway patrols throughout the state were on the lookout for the stolen car. We got as far as Athens, Georgia before we were spotted and arrested. Several witnesses had seen the professor offering us a ride. Others who knew the professor noticed three young passengers riding in his car. When I was arrested, I told the local sheriff that I didn't take part in the attack against the professor and that I had not been in trouble before. Since I was in the professor's car when arrested, the sheriff was certain that all three of us were equally responsible. He then pressured me into testifying against Frank and Ted. He said if I did, I wouldn't be charged. After I wrote down what had happened in exchange for immunity, the lying sheriff who accepted my confession changed his mind.

"We all went to trial. The jury debated over the verdict but in the end found us all guilty. Slim told me that he regretted being involved in the senseless and brutal murder of the popular and respected professor. My mother and father were outraged and embarrassed that one of their boys was charged with murder but were pleased that I chose to confess. The judge sentenced me to life imprisonment while the other two received the death penalty. They were later executed by electric chair at Milledgeville State Prison," Slim said.

Slim Scarborough shared his life story which resulted in his incarceration twelve years earlier. Like Forrest Turner he was sent to a work camp for a crime he didn't commit. "Slim doesn't deserve to be on a chain gang," he tells James Lawrence. "Let's break him out." Forrest Turner began planning for another daring rescue of a chain gang convict.

MACHINE GUN WEILDING OUTLAWS FREE CONVICTED MURDERER

"Scarborough, Figure in Sensational Murder Case Escaped"... "Freed from Chain Gang in Canton"... "Two Machine Gunners Threatened Warden's Son and Guard"... "Police on the Lookout for Two Fast Cars"

The news of the liberation of a convicted murderer from a chain gang stunned the citizens of Cherokee County. The guards were totally surprised when two armed men freed Slim Scarborough who had just recently entered the work camp. One of the culprits was thought to be the notorious fugitive, Forrest Turner.

Forrest Turner knew that the chain gang was working on a particular stretch of road outside the City of Canton. Not to raise suspicion, he traveled the road a couple of times during the afternoon hours after the bus had returned the convicts back to the work camp. He needed to get familiar with the road. Knowing in advance the whereabouts of the curves and intersections were necessary for a speedy getaway.

He had passed by the convict crew and spotted thirty-year-old Slim Scarborough with a shovel in his hand. "He looked depressed and didn't bother to look up. I don't know if he even noticed the black 37 Chevrolet sedan slowly passing by," he told James Lawrence. "We only have two guards stationed, one on each side of the road to overpower."

It's a chilly Monday morning, on the 8th of February 1937. Nine miles east of Canton, Slim Scarborough and eighteen other convicts had just begun working. James Lawrence, in a black 37 Ford sedan, passed by the gang and stopped. Forrest Turner following in the Chevrolet slowed to a stop as convict Scarborough asked him for a cigarette. When the guard came to tell him to get away from the car, Forrest Turner jumped out and aimed his machine gun at the surprised guard, Sonny Haney. At the same time James Lawrence exited the Ford and aimed his machine gun at the other guard. "Now don't let this little gun scare you. It can shoot twenty rounds before you can say good morning," Forrest casually ordered.

To avoid being harmed the guard quickly obeyed Forrest Turner's command to unlock Slim Scarborough's leg irons. Without hesitation, Scarborough jumped onto the running board on the front passenger side of the sedan. Both vehicles sped away in the direction of Alpharetta.

The breakout was easier than Forrest Turner had imagined. It happened quickly and efficiently. No shots were fired. Their mission was carried out in less than ten minutes. By wearing a hat pulled down over his forehead and an overcoat with the collar raised, Forrest Turner had hoped to conceal his face so that neither guard could recognize him.

"I can't thank you enough Forrest. I don't know if I could have stood another day of this chain gang work," said Slim. "Where are we going?"

Forrest Turner replied, "Not to Florida, the state patrol will be watching your family's house."

Local sheriff, Lee Spears, reported to the press that the sensational escape was well planned and executed. "It's the work of two experienced criminals," he was quoted. "The guard was able to remember the license plate number of the Chevrolet. The car was stolen from Main Street Garage in Canton. All local police and highway patrolmen were on sharp lookout for a Chevrolet heading south in hopes of seizing the fugitives before they left the state.

The warden reported that Slim Scarborough was a life-term murderer who had been transferred to Cherokee County chain gang only nine days earlier. "We want him back in our work camp where he belongs," he continued.

Detectives Nahlik and Coppenger who were on the hunt for Forrest Turner heard on the police radio of the Scarborough escape. "No doubt that is some of Turner's work. Who else could pull off such a clever breakout," Nahlik surmised. "This is the fourth successful escape involving 'Jailbreaker Turner.' However, it's not the first time he broke someone out of a work camp. What will he do next?"

The detectives wasted little time before driving to Canton to interview Sonny Haney and the other guard. Detective Coppenger handed the two men a photograph of Forrest Turner. After a long look each thought that one of the men threatening them with a machine gun could be this Turner fella. "It kind of looks like him. It was cold. His hat and coat had covered him up pretty good," said guard Haney as he pointed at the photograph. No one was able to name James Lawrence. Detective Nahlik predicted that he and his partner would catch the fugitives Scarborough and Turner within a few days. "We know where to look," he told Mr. Haney.

11 TOURIST CAMP CAPTURE

When a clever prisoner managed to escape from prison, he usually went into seclusion. He traveled as far away as his money and intuition would allow. He changed his name and identity. He avoided contact with family, friends, and other fugitives. He sought menial work to pay for his room and board. Such a strategy reduced the possible risk of being caught. Forrest Turner ignored taking precautions. During his periods of freedom, he returned to areas with which he was familiar. He stole money and automobiles. He had the audacity to break his convict cohorts out of prison. All of which brought tremendous attention to himself and his whereabouts. It appeared that he was asking to get caught and returned to prison.

Along major highways in Georgia were rest stops called tourist camps for those who were traveling through the state. Some of the facilities had cabins that were available to rent for the night or longer periods. For the frugal travelers, there were tourist camps that also had areas reserved for tents. One popular tourist camp was found eight miles south of Atlanta on the new Macon Highway.

***

Since his escape Forrest Turner had been careful to remain out of sight. He knew detectives were watching his mother's and his friend's homes. Thus, he avoided visits to Hapeville and refrained from staying too long in any one place. He reasoned that staying in a cabin at a remote tourist camp off Macon Highway would be a safe bet. It was March 7, 1937. He had been on the run since January 26th.

Detective Leo Nahlik and Melvin Coppenger, who had been in search of Forrest Turner since his sensational escape in Smithville finally got a break. A lady witnessed a man running from a store to a car parked near the front. After learning the store had been robbed, she told the policemen who were sent to investigate, what she had seen. "I thought it was unusual for someone to be in such a hurry to leave," she said. "I also noticed a lady passenger sitting in the car and that the car had a New York license plate. You don't see many of those here in Atlanta."

From the information provided, the police in the area were notified to be on the lookout for a car bearing an out-of-state license plate. According to other witnesses it was the same vehicle which had been used in several recent hold-ups. Early Sunday morning a policeman on traffic duty spotted a car fitting that description parked in the vicinity of Poplar Street in Atlanta. He immediately reported the sighting to headquarters, who notified Detectives Nahlik and Coppenger, who were at their homes. Without hesitation they responded to the call even though they were off duty. As luck would have it, just as the detectives arrived an unidentified man and woman got into the suspicious car and drove away.

"Drive around the block. Let's see if we can cut them off on Farlie Street," Leo tells Melvin who was driving.

Racing to reach the intersection ahead of the car with a New York plate, the detectives managed to block the street just as the car approached. The driver was forced to bring his car to a screeching halt. The Detectives Nahlik quickly covered the driver with his submachine gun. Unaware that they were being followed the surprised driver and passenger meekly surrendered. Sunday school goers at Tabernacle Baptist who saw the arrest, were treated to an eventful morning.

The driver of the car was not Forrest Turner but James Lawrence, a fugitive from Florida. Two weeks earlier Forrest Turner had entered Florida State Hospital in Chattahoochee and freed him. They became acquainted while both were at the Thomas County Work Camp. James Lawrence had been convicted of a felony in Fulton County. About the time Forrest Turner escaped, James Lawrence had his sentence commuted. Upon his release he returned to Florida where he was later arrested for passing worthless checks. Because his irrational behavior displayed a mental condition, he was sent to the Florida asylum for evaluation before beginning his sentence. Prison officials knew that someone had helped James Lawrence escape, but didn't know who or to where they may have fled.

"Where is Forrest Turner?" Nahlik asked in a threatening voice to the nervous driver. "And who are you and who is this young lady sitting next to you?"

The driver froze and didn't say a word. "I hate to shoot you in front of all these church goers. Resisting arrest gives me that right, you know," Detective Nahlik told the couple. "A witness saw you rob a store."

Staring at the barrel of the machine gun and afraid the detective might shoot him; he began to talk. "I am James Lawrence. While looking at the young lady, she is Ann Lewis. I am taking her to meet Forrest Turner at a cabin off the Macon Highway," he confessed.

The two were taken to police headquarters. There the detectives informed Lieutenant J.A. McKibben of Forrest Turner's whereabout. Hastily they assembled a posse to raid the tourist camp. Around 10:00 a.m. they rendezvoused at a location near the camp.

"From the information we received, Turner is in Cabin # 10," Detectives Nahlik and Coppenger told the others.

Lieutenant McKibben then spoke, "Here's our plan. I want you, two detectives, Leo and Melvin, to drive to the front of the cabin. But first, I want Officers Blair and McNaughton to circle around to the back street and set up a roadblock beyond the cabin. And Chief Dailey, I want you and Officer Cloud to block the front street entrance with your squad car. Don't let any cars enter or leave the place. In the meantime, I will follow detectives Leo and Melvin and cover the back entrance to the cabin, if necessary."

"Now there may be others with Turner at the cabin. They will be heavily armed. So, be careful!" Detective Nahlik warned.

With everyone in their assigned positions Melvin Coppenger and Leo Nahlik followed by Lieutenant McKibben drove to and parked in front of Cabin # 10. Detective Nahlik jumped out of the car with his submachine in hand, crouched behind the front end of the car with his finger on the trigger. To his surprise, there on the porch, casually sitting in a rocking chair was Forrest Turner. See-ing the weapon pointed at him, he just stared at Detective Nahlik. He had expected James Lawrence and Ann Lewis not the police.

The takedown resembled a scene from a James Cagney gang-ster movie. Except this time "Georgia's Number One Bad Man" was captured without a shoot-out. Lieutenant McKibben radioed the men at the roadblock to inform them that they had their man in cuffs. The posse of men included Fulton County Lieutenant McKibben, Detectives Nahlik, Coppenger, Blair, Chief of DeKalb County Police Department, and a DeKalb County policeman. To the surprise of Forrest Turner six armed men in four police vehi-cles had converged on the cabin. Although Forrest Turner had a 32-20 revolver in his waistband and another pistol under a nearby pillow, he knew this was not the time to resist.

"I have only been here a couple of hours. How did you find me so fast?" he asked Detective Nahlik. "I thought you fellas didn't work on Sundays."

Detective Nahlik laughing, "You know the law never sleeps."

"You fellas didn't give me much of a chance. I will tell the news-paper folks that it took six of the best policemen in Atlanta to catch me," Forrest told the group as he was being handcuffed.

Detective Nahlik just smiled, "I have been chasing you for over two months. Now we have caught you. What's that on your face? I hardly recognize you."

"Do you like my mustache? I put some wax on it so it will stand out. If you didn't notice, I also dyed my hair black," Forrest replied with a grin.

Detective Nahlik, amused by the conversation tells Forrest, "Yes, you look like one of those actors in a silent movie."

On the way to the police headquarters Detective Nahlik told Forrest Turner that James Lawrence and Ann Lewis had been arrested earlier that morning.

After turning their prisoner over to the jailer, Leo tells Melvin. "We have had a blessed Sunday. We have safely put two wanted fugitives behind bars today."

Forrest Turner's taste of freedom lasted only forty days. During the period he had amassed a trail of angry robbery victims and prison breakouts that had confounded law enforcement all over the state.

PART II
THE LEGENDARY YEARS

12 DETECTIVES NAHLIK & COPPENGER

Back in November and December of 1936 numerous holdups occurred in Atlanta and surrounding Fulton County. According to the victims and witnesses, these crimes were committed by Forrest Turner and his youthful gang of bandits. It was not known whether the thefts were a result of need or simply for their contempt of authority. Taking foolish risks by breaking the law were thrills often sought by immature and naïve youths. Forrest Turner and his gang's frequency in terrorizing unsuspecting victims had become a major concern to the citizens of Atlanta. It was not that the robberies amounted to a lot of money, but they had an adverse monetary impact on everyday working people and small business owners who could afford to be robbed the least. In any case something had to be done to catch these delinquents and stop the thievery.

As a result, Lieutenant McCrary, head of the Atlanta Police Department, assigned his most capable detectives, Leo Nahlik and Melvin M. Coppenger, to devote their full attention to their leader's capture. Forrest Turner had bragged to his brothers that he was smarter than those who were after him. That was the case until he came face to face with his new adversaries at the tourist camp.

***

Just the name "Nahlik" was an indication that Leo Benedict Nahlik was not the typical southern-bred detective. Far from it, he was a bi-lingual transplant from Watseka, Illinois. He was born in 1906 to immigrant parents, Leopold and Genevieve, who left France in 1904 to start a new life in the United States. He dropped out of school in the tenth grade as did many young men during the Great Depression to support their families. He began as a news reporter covering activities at the Atlanta Police Department. He found crime solving and police work to be interesting and applied for a job there. Leo Nahlik was hired by the department in 1932 where he showed his adept skills as a detective. At six foot and two hundred pounds he was an imposing figure to those he arrested and was seldom challenged.

His partner Melvin Coppenger was born in 1908 to Arthur and May Coppenger in Tellico Plains, Tennessee. He was a tall thin man at six feet, two inches. He was the better-educated, more intellectual and reserved of the two. On the other hand, Leo Nahlik was the "take-charge" fellow. The detectives had distinctly diverse backgrounds. Despite their differences they made a good team.

Leo Nahlik with the Machine Gun and Melvin Coppenger

Looking from above meet with Forrest Turner after his arrest

The detectives had been on Forrest Turner's trail since January 2, 1937, when he took "French Leave." The slang term used by detectives meaning the prisoner had taken an unauthorized leave of absence. The Atlanta Police Department had a list of unsolved crimes. The detectives suspected that Forrest Turner and his gang were the culprits.

The Monday following his arrest Detective Nahlik had the opportunity to question Forrest Turner about his activities while on the loose. He had hoped to trap him into confessing to some of the unsolved crimes. It was March 8, 1937, when he paid him a visit.

The guard at the Fulton Tower unlocked the cell door where Forrest Turner was sitting on his bed. Detective Nahlik entered and reintroduced himself to Mr. Turner. "We didn't have time to finish our conversation the other day."

Instead of an arrogant and "smart-aleck," the twenty-one-year-old prisoner the detective met was a good-humored Forrest Turner who politely answered every question. The conversation was filled with laughter and humor as they kidded one another.

"You and Robert Colton have become quite the celebrities after you overpowered the warden and his driver in South Georgia. The escape was an embarrassment to the Fulton County Police Department. In fact, the Grand Jury who investigated the incident was extremely critical of those involved in the transport of the prisoners. It accused the guards of failure to follow security procedures at the jail and the Thomas County warden of being careless in letting you escape. No one could figure out how you managed to get possession of a gun. Forrest, tell me about the gun you used in your escape," asked Detective Nahlik.

Forrest Turner boastfully responded to the questions. He was eager to tell him how all that went down. "First of all, I had someone slip me the gun while I was in the local jail. That was three days before I was transported to Fulton Tower. I know your next question. I carried the pistol in my belt near the middle of my back and covered it with my shirt. Later I tied the pistol on a string, strung it around my neck and let it hang down to my back."

Nahlik surprised by Forrest Turner's response, "Didn't anyone question the string and the bulge in the back of your shirt?"

"No, I had it covered up. From the number of times I have been searched, none of the guards ever patted down my back, just my hips, and the inside of my thighs and legs. A couple of times I had to lower my pants," Forrest continued with a grin.

When as a kid working in the fields at home, I wore a wet scarf around my neck to keep cool and avoid sunburn on hot July days. That day I wore a scarf to hide the string that was draped around my neck. As it turned out, I could have just as easily carried the gun in my pocket." he laughed derisively. "No one bothered to search me."

Forrest Turner continued, "The warden handcuffed my right hand to Robert Colton's left before we got into the backseat of his sedan. I was seating on the driver's side behind Frank Jones. My left hand was free. During the ride I was able to maneuver the pistol under my shirt from my backside to my stomach without creating suspicion. It came as a relief since sitting with the gun poking me in the back was so uncomfortable. When we got far enough down the road, where there was little traffic, I was able to fish out a razor blade that I had hidden in my back pocket. When I cut the string, the gun fell into my lap. Since I am right-handed, I used my right hand to grab the gun. With Robert Colton's hand handcuffed to my hand we awkwardly pointed the gun at the warden. While he was pretending to hand over his gun, he instead foolishly grabbed my gun and tried to wrestle it away. During the scuffle both guns discharged. One bullet missed everybody. The other grazed the warden's chest. Shooting the warden was an accident. I regret that he was wounded."

"Once you dropped off your two hostages, where did you go?" asked Nahlik.

Forrest Turner responded, "Well, we left Leesburg and headed to Columbus, Georgia. The sedan was equipped with a radio. On the way we listened to a radio dispatch that accused us of supposedly holding up a man at a grocery store parking lot in Atlanta then stealing a car. If the police were looking for us in Atlanta, we felt safe in Columbus. No one would be looking for us there. We subsequently abandoned the Warden McMillan's sedan and borrowed another."

"I had a conversation with Savannah's Chief Detective McCarthy trying to get a lead as to where you might be headed," said Nahlik.

Forrest replied, "Yeah, I was waiting in the car when Robert Colton went into the Savannah grocery store. I thought we had gotten away with the holdup, until the damn policeman began chasing us. I decided to hide the car behind a garage. Unfortunately, the patrolman saw us. I jumped out of the car and hid in some bushes. While he was arresting Robert, I got the hell out of there. I stayed out of sight during the day. I stole an unlocked car that evening, parked in a secluded spot and went to sleep in the backseat."

Forrest Turner was enjoying himself while he told the detective what he did a few days later. "You may not believe this, but I visited Robert at the Savannah Jail. I had hoped to spring him if I could. But mainly I wanted to check to see if he was all right," he informed Detective Nahlik as he listened with interest.

The detective shaking his head and laughing, "How in the world did you manage that."

Well, I made the deputy on duty at the jail believe that I was there to deliver a message. I was impersonating a messenger, you see. I told him that I had an important telegram to give him. He believed me. He let me hand-deliver the telegram to Robert. We couldn't say much since the deputy was standing behind me. You should have seen the expression on Robert's face. He looked unharmed. The jail was too busy for me to free him. But before I left, I had a friendly conversation with the deputy. 'You need to watch that fella,' I told him. 'He is up to no good.' as I calmly walked out the front door."

"I can't believe that!" replied Nahlik after a momentary pause and a puzzled look. "You know the judge gave Colton another twenty years."

"Sorry to hear that," Forrest said as he revealed another one of his bold adventures. "I also recently visited friends at the Fulton County Police Station. The deputy at the police station didn't recognize me. I can honestly say that while on the run, I was back in jail for a short time, but this time on the outside of the 'steel bars' instead of on the inside."

Forrest Turner had managed to stay one step ahead of the law. He told Detective Nahlik that he and his posse nearly caught him last week. A group of men were following a pack of barking bloodhounds. Each man was holding tightly to the leash so his dog couldn't run away.

"I held my breath as the dogs came within a few feet of finding me. They were sniffing the ground but scurried by the underbrush where I was hiding. I saw you and your detective friend trailing the group. When you told your companion that the dogs were useless, I clearly heard you. I almost giggled out loud when you asked why the dogs couldn't pick up my scent," he revealed to Nahlik.

Forrest Turner continued, "I want you to know that I barely got away during one of my holdups. Two pellets from a shotgun blast grazed my wrist and caught me in the stomach. He raised his shirt and showed the detective the scar on his abdomen and pointed to a scar on his wrist. I doctored myself up and I am fine today. I've been shot at before, but this was the first time I was hit."

***

Detective Nahlik revealed that he succeeded in finding him by checking the movements of his girlfriend. He described Forrest Turner as a modern-day Casanova. The fact that he had female relationships may be the reason he never left the state. Forrest Turner's alleged associate, James Lawrence, was arrested earlier in the day in downtown Atlanta while taking a woman friend to see him at the tourist camp.

"I followed your pretty girlfriend for a week, hoping that she would lead me to you," admitted Detective Nahlik.

Forrest responded, "You did huh. Well, on one occasion I had planned to visit her but spotted what I thought was a man sitting nearby in a parked car. So, I eased on by. I decided that I didn't need to disturb him from his nap. I am sure the man was disappointed when I never showed up."

Forrest jokingly complimented Detective Nahlik, "I still say you are plenty good for the kind of work you are doing. I was hoping they would demote you to a patrolman before you caught me."

"I can't understand why you didn't make a run for it at the tourist camp," Leo asked. "You saw us driving up."

Forrest laughingly replied, "Listen fella, I own one of those machine guns. I know what they can do."

Forrest Turner did admit to aiding the escape of convicted murderer Slim Scarborough. But he did not free his brother Chester Turner who was also at the Cherokee County Work Camp at the time. "I made no effort to spring him. The nineteen-year-old kid only had a few more months to go. Why would I want to make trouble for him?"

"While I was on the loose and staying at this boarding house, I was awakened by a knock. To my surprise it was a policeman standing at the door. He said he was warning neighbors of a dangerous fugitive seen in the area. Rubbing my eyes and yawning I told the officer that I hadn't seen anyone. That I had to get up early in the morning to go to work and needed to get back to bed. The officer apologized and left. Boy, will he be surprised if he ever realized how close he came to being a hero," Forrest bragged to Detective Nahlik.

That day while questioning Forrest Turner in his cell, Detective Nahlik sensed that there was a different person underneath the boastful image he tried to project. "He is a different type of criminal. I hope he gets himself straightened out," he murmured as he left the jail.

***

To resolve a number of robbery cases, Detectives Nahlik and Coppenger had Robert Colton transported from Savannah to join Forrest Turner and James Lawrence in Atlanta to take part in a lineup. On the evening of March 11th, a host of victims gathered at police headquarters to decide if any of the men standing in the lineup had robbed them. It was part of the investigation process to which Forrest Turner was all too accustomed. He had hoped his new "Hollywood look" would confuse and create doubt in the minds of the onlooking victims.

Nevertheless, five men positively recognized Forrest Turner as their holdup man. Among them were a laundry truck driver, a café operator, a filling station owner and an unsuspecting bystander who were robbed of cash, a wristwatch and a handgun. Forrest Turner and Robert Colton were pointed out as the ones who stole four dollars and an automobile from a traveling salesman leaving him stranded along the highway. However, none of the witnesses named James Lawrence as their holdup man. The detectives had enough witnesses to charge Forrest Turner and Robert Colton.

After the lineup Forrest Turner was placed in a lone cell on the third floor of the Fulton Tower. Extra precautions were taken, as rumors reached detectives that an attempt might be made to spring him. No attempts were forthcoming. Robert Colton was sent back to Savannah.

The hearing was held on April 11, 1937. Forrest Turner and Robert Colton, dubbed by the press as notorious bandits and escape artists, pleaded guilty to a total of fifteen robberies and automobile thefts committed since their escape in January. The presiding judge in Fulton County Superior Court sentenced Forrest Turner to serve a minimum of thirty additional years on top of the twelve years still to be served from the old sentences. Robert Colton received a sentence of a minimum of eighteen in addition to the thirty-eight years he was already serving. James Lawrence was sent back to the Florida State Hospital for the insane. The State Prison Commission assigned Forrest Turner to Sandy Springs Work Camp in Fulton County and Robert Colton to the work camp in DeKalb County.

Detectives Nahlik and Coppenger were proud of their accomplishment as they put away "Georgia's Number One Bad Man" for a lifetime. They had spent many hours in their effort to catch him.

"So, what is your opinion of this young Turner fella," Leo asked Melvin as they left the courthouse.

Melvin replied, "I sort of like the guy. I wish he wasn't a thief. He is not like the lowlife crooks we must deal with from day-in, to day-out."

"Yeah, he is a clever one." Leo added.

Melvin countered, "I suspect he will be back on the loose before we know it."

13 HENRY TURNER SHOT

With the leader of the gang, Forrest Turner, shackled and closely watched by guards at Sandy Springs Work Camp in Fulton County and the life-long criminal, Robert Colton, back in the DeKalb County Work Camp, the gang's number was reduced to three. Although Forrest Turner directed the old gang to many successful robberies, he avoided violence whenever possible. One can only imagine what would have occurred if he were still in charge. He did not prefer kidnapping people as a means for making money. "Multiple things could go wrong," he once said. What started out as a simple kidnapping and routine robbery ended in tragedy for the Turner family. A gun battle during a high-speed chase ended in a wreck. Driver Henry Turner was shot after he exited the car.

It is ironic that the only member who was not a fugitive was the one who was killed. He had been paroled for his earlier auto theft charge. All the others were prison escapees on the run.

***

FULTON POLICE KILL MAN INVOLVED IN KIDNAPING

"Gainesville Girl Kidnapped and Released"... "Police Spot Car"... "High Speed Chase Ensued"... "Gun Duel Raged Between Kidnapers and Fulton County Police"... "Suspect's Auto Goes Over Embankment into Nursery"

Car Wrecked"... "Henry Turner Shot and Killed, Men Escape, Posse Follow Trail. Suspects at Large"

Up till now all the publicity that Forrest Turner and his gang had received did not include violence. These June 9, 1937, headlines had more of a morbid tone. A story of a kidnapping, armed robbery and shootout with police gone bad was a perfect script for a Hollywood movie.

The saga began in Gainesville where a gang, including Bill Baker, Henry Turner, and Bob Jarrard were on the run from the authorities. Fugitive Baker, who recently escaped from Floyd County Work Camp, was the gang's leader. He was joined by a fugitive, Bob Jarrard, who recently escaped from Cherokee County Work Camp along with Chester Turner nine days earlier. Chester Turner chose to stay behind. Henry Turner was the driver of the Chevrolet. An attractive blond eighteen-year-old girl named Verline Stargel was the kidnap victim.

While they were cruising around Gainesville, they spotted Miss Stargel as she was walking near her home around 9:00 p.m. Seeing the girl, Bill Baker told Henry Turner, who was driving the Chevrolet, to pull over and stop.

"Do you need a ride? "Bill asked politely speaking through the rolled down window.

The surprised girl not recognizing those in the car replied, "No thanks, I am almost home."

At that moment Bill Baker jumped out of the car and ordered her to get into the back seat. As he pointed his pistol at her, Bob Jarrard got out, held the door open and motioned for her to get in. The startled and frightened young girl abided his command and got into the car with the three strange men.

It was a mystery as to what motivated the trio to take the girl. Perhaps, the men hoped that she would become a member of the gang. Without Forrest Turner and Robert Colton there was extra room in the sedan and travel would be more pleasant if accompanied by a female. They drove to Flowery Branch where they spent the night and then headed to Atlanta. The next morning, they held up a Safeway Service Station near Mount Zion Church on Stewart Avenue. They managed to steal nine dollars and forty-five cents from the cash drawer. Frightened by a motorist who pulled into the station to fill up his car, they sped away. A short distance down the road Henry Turner pulled into a wooded area and parked the Chevrolet to allow the passengers to take a restroom break and change their clothes.

"We want you to stay in the car. If you get out, I will shoot you!" Baker threatened Stargel.

The three disappeared into the woods with a bag filled with clothes. Instead of staying in the car, the unguarded Miss Stargel managed to exit the automobile and flee. When they returned, she was nowhere in sight. Rather than looking for the missing girl, they left and drove toward Atlanta. In desperation Miss Stargel ran to the nearest farmhouse and reported her kidnapping to the occupant, who informed the Fulton County police.

To avoid the car being identified by the police, Henry Turner had removed the license plate from the Chevrolet before staging the service station robbery. In the confusion of the girl running away and the rush to leave the area, the kidnappers forgot to reattach the plate. Shortly after noon on Thursday two officers from the Fulton County Police Department while sitting in their patrol car in East Point near Georgia Military Academy noticed a vehicle pass by with a missing plate. Trying to figure out why the owner was driving without a tag, they followed, drove alongside and motioned for them to pull over. Instead of stopping Henry Turner, stepped on the gas and sped away. What was to be a routine stop for a missing license plate violation ended in a high-speed chase.

Henry Turner was very familiar with all the roads in and around East Point and Hapeville. Since he had lived in the area, he had traveled the streets many times. Nevertheless, he was in a panic. First, he pulled out of Church Street, then he turned onto Dunlap.

"Turn on Vista!" shouted Bill. Unnerved by the irritating instructions coming from the backseat, he barely made the turn. The car tires were squealing as he doubled back to Main Street.

"Speed up!" hollered Bill into Henry's right ear as he leaned forward to get a better view. Henry Turner pushed down the gas pedal to the floor reaching speeds up to ninety miles per hour on the straightaways.

"Shut up Bill! I know where I am going," yelled Henry as he gripped the steering wheel as tightly as he could. He feared he might lose control at any minute. Looking in the rearview mirror, he saw the patrol car keeping pace.

At that moment Bob Jarrard sitting on the driver's side tells Henry," I know how to slow those fellas down." He, rolled down the window, turned, and began shooting at the pursuing patrol car. Bill Baker sitting in the back seat immediately slid over to the driver's side to avoid being shot.

Hearing the gunshot the driver of the patrol car, Wilson Gilbert, crouched down to where he could barely see over the steering wheel, while his partner, Ed West, returned fire. He could see bullets striking the fleeing Chevrolet several times. With Henry Turner weaving all over the road it was hard for Bob Jarrard to shoot accurately. "I am sure I hit the front end of the patrol car," he shouted. Bullets fired by Officer West from the patrol car struck the trunk of the Chevrolet and the rear window. Glass from the window sprayed on Bill Baker who was now lying down on the seat covering his head with both hands.

"Speed up, I am getting shot at!" screamed Bill. "When is this guy going to run out of ammo?"

Racing down Main Street Henry Turner was unable to shake the pursuing patrol car. In a desperate effort to escape he nearly flipped his vehicle again as he turned onto Mercer. "Don't turn onto this side street. It leads to a dead end!" yelled Bill who was now sitting up. It was too late. At the intersection of West Mercer and Pierce Streets, Henry should have taken Pierce.

When Henry Turner reached the end of West Mercer, he realized they were trapped. As he looked back, he saw the patrol car quickly approaching at a distance. "Oh my God! I can't turn around," he thought to himself. Without thinking his instincts told him to speed ahead. He hadn't counted on vaulting over and down a twelve-foot embankment. The vehicle came to an abrupt halt resting in the flower beds at Mount's Nursery on Rugby Street in College Park. Upon impact Henry Turner's head struck the steering wheel. He was momentarily in a state of confusion. Fortunately, the car landed on its four wheels allowing Bill Baker and Bob Jarrard to leap out and dash away.

In the meantime, Officer Gilbert brought the patrol car to a stop just short of the edge of the embankment. He jumped from his vehicle and ran toward the wrecked Chevrolet. He began yelling, "Stop or I will shoot!" He had only one target, the dazed Henry Turner who was barely able to exit the wrecked car. As he tried to run, he became an easy target. The officer did not miss.

Several shots did indeed strike the patrol car's radiator and windshield. In the gun battle the two officers were hit. Officer Gilbert had a flesh wound to his arm but was able to drive. Ed West had taken a shot to the shoulder and remained in the police car nursing his wound. He was unable to chase after the two fleeing fugitives who sought cover in the nearby woods. Fortunately, the officers were not seriously hurt.

When Officer West reached Henry Turner, he was lying motionless in the grass with his eyes closed. The officer slowly rolled him over. He had a bullet wound to the back and died at the scene.

Word of the dramatic shooting and high-speed chase through the streets in College Park reached headquarters. All available men were ordered to proceed to the site of the wreck and search for the kidnappers still on the loose. Scores of bloodhounds were used in the search as police and deputized citizens scoured the surrounding area. Around midnight the search was called off.

In the wrecked vehicle investigators found a sawed-off shotgun, gas bombs, and pouches of tobacco taken from earlier robberies. The gunfire by Officer West resulted in two bullets entering the trunk of the Chevrolet. The two holes in the rear windshield were made by the reckless Bob Jarrard when he was shooting from inside the fleeing Chevrolet.

***

Warden Clarke asked one of the work camp guards to bring Forrest Turner to his office after he returned from his quarry duties.

"Have a seat Forrest, I have some sad news to tell you, "The warden began in a serious tone of voice.

Forrest made a humorous guess, "Oh, am I going to be sent back to the Thomas County chain gang?"

"No, it's worse than that. I am sorry to tell you, that your brother Henry has been shot and killed while trying to avoid capture," explained the warden. "He took part in a kidnapping and a robbery. He chose to run rather than give up. A convict named Bob Jarrard, who escaped from Cherokee with your brother Chester and Bill Baker were with him but got away."

"What about my brother Chester?" Forrest asked.

The warden responded, "He was not with them."

Forrest angrily replied, "I should have known Baker would get my brother in trouble. Just like he did me when I hitched a ride with him and was arrested because he stole the car."

Forrest stunned and in tears, asked the warden if he could attend the funeral. "Yes, Forrest, I will arrange the travel, when the date is set," promised the warden.

Meanwhile the police had no luck in finding the whereabouts of the others. On June 12th, Landrum Skinner, a night watchman reported that he saw two men answering the general description sneak aboard a slowly moving freight train in Fairburn heading north. "The men appeared out of the darkness and boarded the train about three hundred yards from our construction site," said the watchman to the investigator. "The fact that the train was moving, caught my attention. They didn't appear to be hobos, so I assumed they were on the run."

That same day, under constant watch by two armed patrolmen, Forrest Turner, attended the funeral services for his deceased brother, Henry, who was shot and killed by a Fulton County policeman. Escorted from the Fulton County chain gang, he wept as the rites were administered in the chapel of Howard L. Carmichael Funeral Home. And again, later at the gravesite at Hill Crest Cemetery.

As Forrest Turner was transported back from the gravesite to the Sandy Springs Work Camp, his mind wandered. For a moment he wondered whether a life of crime was worth the publicity and notoriety he was receiving. Yes, he had money, fine clothes, and girls. But he was constantly on the run when he wasn't incarcerated. The problem now was that he had accumulated so many years to serve, he was certain he would never be free again...a hopeless situation. Now his older brother Henry, who was twenty-nine years old, had been killed. Somehow, he must reassess his predicament.

The unexpected death of Henry devastated the Turner family. Chester Turner, from the pleas of his mother, agreed to give himself up. On Thursday, June 17th, Detectives Leo Nahlik and Melvin Coppenger came to Mrs. Turner's home where Chester Turner surrendered peacefully. Mrs. Turner told the detectives, "I do not want to lose another son to a confrontation with the police. The family was disappointed that he and seven others had overpowered the guards to escape from the Cherokee Work Camp."

Chester had only a short time left of his remaining sentence. If he had stayed, he would be paroled and could have rejoined his family. Like his brother Forrest the temptation must have been too great for him not to take advantage of the opportunity.

Detective Nahlik nodding his head replied, "I understand Mrs. Turner."

Chester made a special request to the detectives, "I am ready to complete my sentence. I hope no more time gets added to my sentences. As a favor to me and my mother I ask if I could be transferred from Cherokee County Work Camp from where I escaped to a Fulton County camp so I can be closer to my mother."

Detective Nahlik looked at Mrs. Turner and promised, "I will do my best to look after your boy, Chester."

"Thanks," said Chester. "I want you to know I was not involved in the kidnapping of the Gainesville girl, nor did I commit the slew of robberies of which I am accused."

"We know Chester," said Leo as he escorted him to his car.

F.B.I. fingerprints proved that the third member of the gang was Bob Jarrard. Convicted of murder in Hall County in 1935, he was sentenced to life imprisonment. He escaped from Cherokee County Work Camp along with Chester Turner and six others last month. He was the one with the gun who began firing at the patrol car causing the running gun battle. He was also identified as the culprit in several local robberies. Based on his aggressive nature when he recklessly fired at the pursuing police car, Bob Jarrard should take some of the blame for the fatal shooting of Henry Turner.

On June 19th Bill Baker entered a South Rome drugstore where a Floyd County convict guard, Joe Lawrence, recognized him. An old girlfriend and former acquaintance of Forrest Turner was a passenger in Bill Baker's car. When he did not immediately return and a police car arrived, she tried unsuccessfully to drive away. The two were taken to the Rome Police Station and questioned. Having no evidence connecting his passenger to the robberies, the police eventually released her. Unlike Forrest Turner, she avoided a trip to a work camp.

It was not determined if he was there to rob the place or buy medicine. In either case he was in the wrong place at the wrong time. He had escaped twelve days earlier from the Floyd County chain gang. Last week he was spotted in College Park where he presumably was hiding out since his escape. Shortly thereafter, a warrant for his arrest had been issued for the holdup of a hardware store in Holland, Georgia. There the bandit stole one hundred and forty-seven dollars and other store items including a knife. The same knife was found in the wrecked vehicle which came to rest in Mounts' flower garden following the shootout with police and the death of Henry Turner. The discovery of the stolen knife left behind as Bill Baker fled tied him to the theft in Holland, Georgia.

As of July 1, 1937, the surviving members of the "Green Car Gang" were in jail or in leg irons at different work camps. Forrest Turner was sent to Sandy Springs, Robert Colton to DeKalb County, Chester Turner to Fulton Tower and Bill Baker to Troup County. The separation of the group brought an end to the notorious "Green Car Gang." As fugitives the bandits were charged with at least twenty robberies and auto thefts. The Fulton County Police Department and the many victims took comfort in knowing that Georgia's most notorious young outlaws including Bob Jarrad faced long prison sentences.

14 GEORGIA STATE PRISON AT REIDSVILLE

The Georgia State Prison known to locals simply as Reidsville opened for business in 1936. Located in rural southeast Georgia approximately two hundred miles from Atlanta and sixty-six miles from Savannah. Reidsville became the new home for convict Forrest Turner. To his surprise he was immediately approached by an inmate who asked for his help in fleeing. His first of several escape attempts from Reidsville soon followed.

***

Forrest Turner was transferred from Bellwood Work Camp to Reidsville in June 1938 where he joined Georgia's most notorious criminals; not because he was a violent offender, but because of his frequent escapes. He had become a thorn in the sides of wardens throughout the state. No one had been able to keep him in their work camp very long. The state had spent money and countless man hours tracking him down.

Asked why he continued to escape, "Because I didn't like it there, I just left," Forrest replied. Since Reidsville was considered "escape proof," leaving was not an option whether he liked it there or not.

Forrest Turner was apprehensive about his transfer to a maxi-

Georgia State Prison at Reidsville, Tattnall County

mum-security prison. Since his recapture on March 7, 1937, he had spent time at Atlanta's Fulton Tower and various work camps in Fulton and Troup Counties. In his opinion, the officials at the prison commission were shuffling convicts from one work camp to another without a good reason. His transfer was intentional as the wardens and the commission chose to move him before he could carry out his next escape. Nevertheless, he was looking forward to not being shackled and chained. But on the other hand, he dreaded being penned up behind Reidsville's bars all day.

Travelling down the roads of South Georgia, the ride approaching Reidsville became bumpy and rough. The scenery was miles and miles of pine forests, wire grass pastures filled with grazing cattle, cotton fields, and an occasional farm. Traffic was limited to a few pickups and slow-moving rickety old logging trucks hauling logs to the sawmills. "One could easily get lost in all those trees," escape-minded Forrest thought to himself. To pass the time he chatted with the two prison officials who were escorting him to Reidsville.

In the distance he finally got his first glimpse of the prison. Forrest Turner leaned forward looking through the wire grid partition separating him from the officials in the front seat. Though it looked small on the horizon, he easily recognized how Reidsville had earned its reputation as a state-of-the-art prison. He was taking it all in as the buildings grew taller and more imposing the closer, they got. "This place is out in nowhere," he told the prison officials who were driving. "Living in this new building will be a vast improvement over the rundown shacks I stayed in while at work camps."

The first feature that came into view was the guard observation station in the tower above the top floor. Mounted on top of the tower was a flagpole with two flags fluttering in the breeze. His eyes quickly moved down to the tall, concrete building capped with a cupola. As he got closer, he saw there was a lantern etched on the frontside. "The prison building is impressive," Forrest commented.

The official who was driving added, "Yes, there are eight cell blocks that can hold up to two thousand inmates. Up on the fifth floor, the prisoners call "Death Row," is the electric chair. It's already burned several butts since it was moved here from Milledgeville. There are more than nine hundred acres surrounding the prison, which includes several farms. The complex also includes a women's prison. In case you are getting any ideas, the women are separated from the men in a separate building. They don't do outside work and are confined mostly to their dorms."

As they passed the gate and drove into the yard, he got his first up-close glimpse of the front side of the five-story building. Its massive size overwhelmed him. His head turned from side to side as his eyes tried to inspect every inch of the prison. The building had rows of windows secured by steel bars. "Behind one of those windows is a cell that will be my new home," he assumed.

"Turner, you see those fancy sculptures just above the building's entrance. It shows convicts performing various trades. It's a reminder to the inmates that this is a learning and working prison," the other official remarked.

Forrest commented, "I see why they say that Reidsville is an escape-proof prison; the building and the outside walls are made from steel and concrete, the razor wire on top of the wall makes it dangerous to climb over and the guards in the tower are ready to shoot anyone who tries."

The official was quick to say as he looked at Forrest, "Those guards are marksmen. On occasion you can hear them practicing their shooting in nearby woods."

***

Shortly after Forrest Turner arrived at Reidsville, a prisoner named Terrell Loughridge cornered him. "I understand that you have made several successful jail breaks. Me and my friends need your help in getting out. Of course you are welcome to join us," said Terrell who was serving time for the murder of his father.

Pleased that his past escapes had gained him notoriety in the prison, Forrest didn't hesitate to answer, "Yeah, I began looking for a way out the minute the cell door was shut behind me. I will let you know when I come up with a plan." The opportunity came when Forrest Turner and a group of men were working in the yard. It would be his fourth escape. When Reidsville's prison was designed and built, it was considered escape-proof. That reputation was soon discredited as Forrest Turner and others managed unauthorized leaves of absence.

REIDSVILLE BREAK IS LED BY TURNER

"Five Notorious Convicts Are on The Run"... "Forrest Turner and Four Other Convicts Escape from Reidsville's Prison"... "Last Seen in Stolen Vehicle Heading South"... "Guard and Young Boy Taken Hostage and Feared Dead"

The newspaper headlines on July 11, 1938, reported Forrest Turner's latest prison escape. A feel-good follow up story the next day mentioned the fate of the hostages. Mrs. McCullough publicly thanked the kidnappers for releasing her husband and water boy, unharmed. "We were praying for them," the tearful Mrs. McCullough told the reporter who interviewed her by telephone.

***

Guard T.W. McCullough was overpowered in the yard as he was

picking up his lunch basket which was left for him by a member of the kitchen crew. He was struck from behind by one of the prisoners. Dazed, he fell to the ground. When the guard came to, he was staring at his pistol pointing at him. The prisoners led by Forrest Turner and Terrell Loughridge also included Tom Burroughs, Luther Kilgo, Wilbur Futral, and Chris Anglin. They ordered the guard and a waterboy, who saw the assault, to go with them to the home of Captain Larrimore. As head of the guards, his house was within the compound.

Guard McCullough with a pistol poking into his back knocked on the door. "Miss Larrimore these fellas want the keys to your father's car and any guns you have in the house," he said nervously as beads of sweat were noticeable on his forehead.

The young girl recognized the possible consequences if she did not obey. She feared for her and Mr. McCullough's life and handed over the keys and the two pistols hidden in a kitchen drawer. Taking the guard and the boy with them, the prisoners stole the car. The seven packed into the sedan built to seat six people and sped out of the prison compound. Terrell Loughridge and Tom Burroughs sat in the back with the two hostages in the middle. Luther Kilgo and Chris Anglin had squeezed into the front seat next to Forrest Turner who was driving.

Terrell yelled from the back seat, "Can't you go any faster? I am sure Assistant Warden Sims has everybody within fifty miles looking for us."

Forrest Turner didn't say a word. He just eased down on the gas pedal. Driving at high speeds on unfamiliar roads in an overloaded car was a challenge even for a good driver. After topping a hill, the road made a sharp turn to the left. Forrest Turner let off the gas and turned the wheel. The front seat passengers slid into him, not allowing him to finish turning the steering wheel. As a result, he lost control of the car as it ran off the road, struck the bank, and came to an abrupt halt. With steam rising from the radiator the car wouldn't restart. The uninjured and confused fugitives crawled out of the wrecked car which had come to rest in the ditch.

The wreck occurred near the city of Glennville. From a distance a curious and concerned motorist saw a group of men standing on the side of the road. Herbert Brannan, the passing motorist, stopped his car to investigate. "Can I give you fellas a hand?" he asked Forrest who was standing in the road waving his arms.

As Mr. Brannan approached the men, Terrell Loughridge accosted him and demanded his keys. The fugitives commandeered his car. In the confusion Guard McCullough and the waterboy ran into the woods and disappeared. Rather than chasing after the two hostages the fugitives instead chose to take Mr. Brannan as their captive. Forcing Mr. Brannan into the back seat they sped away and continued their flight in the direction of Ludowici.

In the meantime, the guard and waterboy ran to a farmhouse from where they called the assistant warden. With the location of the fugitives and description of the vehicle they had hijacked, the prison officials had information needed to issue a statewide alert.

Learning that the escapees were traveling in his direction, Liberty County Sheriff Sikes and Deputy Strickland drove to the highway, parked out of sight, and waited. When the stolen car containing the fugitives flew by, the Sheriff switched on the siren and gave chase. As the police car gained on the fleeing vehicle, the deputy began firing. The inmates who had the two stolen pistols in their possession returned the fire. During the exchange, some fifty shots were fired. One of the bullets fired by the deputy struck the trunk of the fleeing car. The running-battle continued until the fugitive's car left the road and careened into a ditch near Riceboro.

Forrest Turner was hoping to avoid getting struck by a bullet. He had overestimated the intelligence of his fella inmate passengers. Wanted notorious criminals who chose to shoot it out with lawmen seldom won. As was the case with John Dillinger, Pretty Boy Floyd, Baby Face Nelson, and the forementioned Bonnie and Clyde. When lawmen were instructed to take down criminals, "Dead or Alive," it presumably meant "Dead", if they resisted! At that moment he thought of his brother Henry Turner who had been in a similar situation.

Fortunately, the dazed fugitives, who were out of ammunition struggled to exit the wrecked car and were in no condition to challenge the sherrif and deputy. Tom Burroughs had a minor bullet wound to the leg and needed assistance.

Forrest Turner told the sheriff, "You need to tend to the hurt man who is lying in the backseat." Sheriff Sikes walked over to the wrecked car and discovered a seriously wounded passenger. He immediately had him rushed to a Savannah hospital. The bullet that struck Mr. Brannan was fired by the deputy, who was not aware that he was a passenger in the fleeing car.

Forrest Turner and the other men were taken to Long County Jail. The wild ride through three counties covered seventy-two miles. His escape lasted only one day. Once again, the man who the Atlanta police consider as the city's "Number One Public Enemy" along with four other escapees were recaptured. It's the first time that Forrest Turner had two accidents in two different vehicles on the same day.

***

The Long County Grand Jury met in the Ludowici Courthouse to hear the evidence against Forrest Turner and the other four escapees. They recommended that the accused stand trial for their escape from Reidsville, car thefts, resisting arrest, and causing the wounding of an innocent citizen. The foreman of the grand jury recommended to the presiding judge that Forrest Turner receive the death penalty recently permissible under Georgia state law, should the twelve traverse jurors find him guilty.

Forrest Turner pleaded guilty and did not have to face a traverse jury. Thus, avoiding the potential of receiving the death penalty. Instead, the judge added twenty years to his already lengthy sentence. He now had up to sixty years to serve. After his hearing he was transported back to Reidsville.

Embarrassed and frustrated, the warden ordered Forrest Turner to be placed in one of the solitary cells. "Let's see if you can get out of here," he told him as the guard closed and locked the cell door.

Isolation and the inability to converse with other inmates was the most severe punishment Forrest Turner was to endure. At least while on the chain gang he could enjoy the sunshine. "Confined to this hole is pure misery," he would tell the warden later.

15 WHERE IS FORREST?

When construction of the new Georgia State Prison in Reidsville was completed, the state's most hardened prisoners were sent there. They were systematically moved out of the old state prison in Milledgeville and from the various county work camps. Escape artist Forrest Turner was one of the arrivals. He was told by the deputy who had transported him to Reidsville that he would find the new maximum-security prison a difficult place from which to flee. Forrest Turner soon proved him wrong. As a result, recapturing him became the utmost priority for the prison authorities, but first law enforcement had to find him.

***

FORREST TURNER BREAKS REIDSVILLE

"Twenty-Three-Year-Old Forrest Turner Escaped"... "Sixth Time in Four Years"... "Under Sentence Totaling Excess of Forty Years"... "Concealed Inside Truck Leaving Prison"... "State Highway Patrolmen and Posse in Search"... "Highway Traffic Throughout Central and South Georgia Closely Watched"... "Turner's Disappearance Angered Prison Officials"

Hence, the headlines of November 29, 1938, newspapers read. In what direction did the elusive fugitive go? Prison officials and detectives were confounded and clueless as to Forrest Turner's whereabouts.

After his months of confinement in solitary ended, he was reassigned to work in the prison yard. When a work truck was left unmanned, Forrest Turner could not resist the opportunity to jump into the back, crawl under some trash and wait. He went unnoticed when the truck in which he was hiding drove out of the prison. Forrest Turner was on the loose again. This time he had better luck escaping. Being alone he didn't have to contend with a car full of annoying inmates.

"Here, There, Everywhere, Where Is Fugitive Forrest Turner?" was a headline of a later newspaper article written December 15, 1938. The article paraphrased the famous lines from the classic novel, *The Scarlet Pimpernel* written by Baroness Orczy in 1905.

> *"We seek him here, we seek him there,*
>
> *Those police seek him everywhere.*
>
> *He's probably in heaven or in hell, one supposes,*
>
> *The elusive Turner disappeared right under their noses!"*

Forrest Turner, who recently made his second escape from Reidsville Prison, was seen by everyone except by the police. Reports had reached various police departments of sightings of the elusive escape artist. Everyone who spotted a person who remotely resembled him called the police department. The police detectives acted on these tips regardless of how far-fetched they appeared to be. Hopes were always high as police rushed to the area of a possible sighting. The results were always the same. The person they tried to arrest was not Forrest Turner. When the police were certain they had him, he had managed to flee and vanish into thin air before they arrived.

Local barbers always had several newspapers available for those who had to wait their turn for a haircut. The shop also had older gentlemen who showed up on a regular basis to get the latest gossip or to read the free newspapers. The barbers welcomed visitors so they could have someone to talk with when they were not cutting someone's hair. The escapades of Forrest Turner were always a hot topic.

"I read here that this fella Turner has escaped again," remarked one of the gentlemen.

Another asks, "How many does that make?"

"I think this is his fifth. No, maybe it's his sixth," answered another. "He has escaped so many times I can't remember how many."

At some barber shops the regular customers placed bets trying to guess how many days it would be before he was caught. There was one certainty about the jail breaker, Forrest Turner; he was always going to escape, and he was always going to get caught. You could bet on it. And they did. Oh, the bets were usually limited to a cup of coffee or a coca cola.

When the headlines reported that Forrest Turner had been recaptured, one of the fellas would read the newspaper article aloud so everyone could hear the details. The barber would stop cutting hair so he could listen even though he had already read the article before opening his shop. He was always amused at how intently they listened to every word.

Someone would ask, "How many more years is the judge going to add to his sentence? "Probably ten more years," someone guessed. "I think that will give him about seventy years." Shaking their heads, one commented, "My goodness, that sure is a long time." The barber interjected with a chuckle, "The next time the judge won't be sentencing him in the number of years but in the number of decades."

***

The pattern was always the same for Forrest Turner. The minute he entered a prison he looked for an escape route. "How do I get out of here?" he thought as he surveyed every inch of the facility. When the opportunity presented itself and the escape was successful, he had to prepare himself to survive as a fugitive. First, he must get rid of the prison uniform and obtain civilian clothes. Only the best suits and accessories would do. Second, transportation was necessary. It would have to be a newer model known for speed. And finally, and most importantly, it was the money. To obtain these critical items they would have to be stolen. Detective Nahlik knew that after every prison break, there would be a rash of burglaries and thefts. For each occurrence Forrest Turner had to be the culprit. Law enforcement knew where he had been but had no clue where he was headed.

Forrest Turner's success in eluding the police was because he never stayed in any one place very long. While most citizens spent their days working, Mr. Turner was vacationing. He had a lot of free time on his hands. He and his gang spent much of their time cruising around. When they saw a person or a business that posed no threat, a holdup soon followed. It was a certainty that when he needed money to support his lavish lifestyle, he simply stole it. Seldom did he allow too many days to pass before he would strike again somewhere in the state. Many times, it was convenient for the police to blame him for robberies he did not commit.

"Forrest Turner was not a loner," Detective Nahlik said. "He was always joined by one or more accomplices during his robbery forays. He's the one who held the gun and gave the ultimatums. Then another cleaned out the cash register or confiscated the valuables from the victims. One was on the lookout for the police. While another remained in the getaway car with the motor running. The theft and the getaway took only a few minutes.

Following his escape from Reidsville an all-out search for Forrest Turner began again. It took the concentrated statewide effort by law enforcement and detectives Nahlik and Coppenger to track down all the leads which were being reported.

A Mississippi newspaper article stated that Forrest Turner was apprehended in Jackson. He had sawed his way out of a local jail where he was being held on a burglary charge. Shortly thereafter he was recaptured. When Detective Nahlik learned that Jackson police held a Forrest Turner, they were prepared to ask for his extradition to Georgia. After further inquiries they discovered their captive was a young Black man using an alias, not their Forrest Turner.

Police needed fingerprints to prove that Louie Propes, a twenty-three-year-old painter from Atlanta, was not their fugitive. Police arrested Propes because he had an amazing facial resemblance to Forrest Turner. He was released and given an apology.

Lieutenant J.A. McKibben, who oversaw the bureau sent a message to all detectives and policemen under his authority. The message included the instructions, if necessary "Shoot-to-Kill." He was frustrated with all the useless tips that led to the arrest of the wrong people.

Shortly thereafter speeding Edward Long, a twenty-one-year-old radio repairman, caught the attention of two policemen sitting in a parked squad car. The policemen began to follow the car to issue a speeding ticket. When they turned on their flashing red lights, Edward Long refused to stop. Aware of a recent bulletin sent by Lieutenant McKibben, the policemen assumed the driver in the car was the fugitive, Turner. Giving chase one of the policemen began to fire at the fleeing vehicle striking three of the tires. As a result, Mr. Long wrecked his automobile and was then shot in the leg as he tried to run away. Mr. Long talked with police from his Grady Hospital bed.

"I don't know why the police started shooting at me. I was just trying to get out of paying a ticket," he said as he raised his voice in anger. "And I wrecked my car!"

"I am sorry" said the officer who fired the shot while being questioned by his supervisor. "When Mr. Long jumped out of the car, I swore he looked just like Forrest Turner. When he didn't stop running, I fired at him. He shouldn't have run away."

Annoyed by the incident, Lieutenant McKibbin sent out another order to all detectives and those involved in the manhunt, "Be sure you know who you are shooting at!" it read.

The shooting of a civilian only added to the frenzy of police activity from Macon to Atlanta in the search for the elusive fugitive. Special squads of shotgun-armed detectives were stopping every suspicious-looking high-performance vehicle on the main highways. Two detectives reported that they had collided with each other in their rush to aid another officer who reported spotting fugitive Turner. Neither driver was hurt but both vehicles required extensive repair.

The Rockdale County Sheriff reported to Atlanta Police that he saw a lifelong acquaintance of his, a traveling salesman, show his brand-new car to a stranger in a Conyers parking lot. He thought nothing of it, until his friend reported that his automobile was missing later that day. Thinking back, the sheriff recollected that the stranger he had seen resembled Forrest Turner. As a result, police learned of the probable vehicle Forrest Turner was driving.

Then there was a filling station operator in Griffin who was forced to hand over fifty dollars from the cash drawer. He was certain that one of the two bandits who held a pistol was the ubiquitous Forrest Turner. From his photograph he was positively identified by victims who were robbed in Spalding, Pike, Troup, Merriwether, Clayton, and Fulton Counties. It was hard to imagine he was in so many places at the same time.

News from Villa Rica and Dallas reported that Forrest Turner, the leader of the gang, held up two hardware stores and made off with weapons, ammunition, and cash. This time he was seen driving a stolen 1939 Ford with Florida plates.

Knowing that witnesses could identify the getaway car, he always kept stolen license plates handy. An East Point dry cleaner witnessed Forrest Turner changing license plates on an automobile on Sylvan Road. The owner recognized him from his photos in the newspaper. He alerted the Atlanta Police Department. When the officers arrived, the automobile with the stolen plates was nowhere in sight.

It was one of the few times fugitive Forrest Turner was able to enjoy the Christmas season as a free man. He had escaped six times and helped others break out. To date no Georgia prison had been able to hold him long.

"So, where's that damned, elusive Forrest Turner?" Baroness

Orczy would have poetically written if she was still alive.

> *"Determined to put fugitive Forrest Turner back in jail,*
> *Detectives searched and searched but to no avail.*
> *He vanished into thin air, his whereabouts unknown.*
> *So, to where on God's earth might he have flown?"*

16 CUMMING WORK CAMP BREAK

During Forrest Turner's "French Leave" from Georgia State Prison in Reidsville, he again outwitted police and prison officials. His next feat defied belief and baffled prison authorities. Who would have the audacity to enter a county work camp to release convicts just thirty-five days after he himself escaped from prison? Every law enforcement official in the state was on the lookout for the fugitive. His photograph was displayed in all the newspapers. Only Forrest Turner would have the courage to pull off such an incredible feat. The guards at the work camp at Cumming in Forsyth County were his unsuspecting victims.

***

NOTORIOUS TURNER POSES AS ATTORNEY LIBERATES CONVICTS

"A Daring Forrest Turner Executes a Well-Planned Break"... "Poses as Attorney and Fools Guard"... "Single-Handedly Frees Five Dangerous Convicts"... "Burglars, Safecracker and Bank Robber on the Loose"... "Two Sedans Used, One has Alabama License Plate"

On January 3, 1939, Forrest Turner captured front page headlines in all Georgia newspapers. His claim to fame had been limited to his frequency of escapes from prisons and chain gangs. Yesterday he showed another one of his clever abilities; that is how to enter a work camp and release convicts.

Forrest Turner had made an agreement with Jack Gamble to break out two of his cohorts from the work camp. He would receive a cash payment if successful. Jack Gamble, a thirty-eight-year-old, convicted murderer and burglar, was on the run. He had escaped from Colquitt County Work Camp earlier in December and wanted to free his former work camp buddies. The opportunity to free someone from a work camp piqued Forrest Turner's interest and he eagerly accepted the challenge. The two men to be freed were Jack Devine, a thirty-four-year-old with a long criminal history and twenty-year-old Charles Bryant recently convicted of armed robbery.

Forrest Turner parked his Ford in the visitor parking area by the front gate. Jack Gamble and his wife were in a second car hidden from view, but in a position to watch the activity at the work camp. Forrest Turner with nerves of steel, calmly walked in the Forsyth County Work Camp in Cumming at 2:00 p.m. He entered dressed in a sharp-looking suit and overcoat while holding a legal file folder in his hand. Posing as an attorney he walked into the office expecting to find Warden Gordon. The warden, however, was out taking a sick convict to the doctor's office at the city square and left the senior guard in charge.

"I am a defense attorney. I am here to see my clients Jack Devine and Charles Bryant," he confidently and assertively told the guard, Deuce Garrett, in the work camp office. Forrest Turner remembered the two long-term convicts from the time they all served together at Reidsville. They were just recently transferred to Cumming. Assuming that he was speaking to an attorney, the guard without hesitation escorted him across the grounds, through the gate and into the kitchen. In the kitchen were the unsuspecting work camp's cook, Carl McCormack and two visitors, John Fowler, and his young son, Charlie.

"This is the kitchen!" Forrest asked the guard again. "Where can I find my clients, Mr. Devine and Mr. Bryant?"

When the guard hesitated, Forrest Turner pulled two pistols from his overcoat and threatened the surprised group with harm unless they cooperated. He then pointed the pistol at the three-year-old Charlie.

"Don't harm the boy," the guard pleaded as he stepped in between Forrest Turner and the frightened boy.

Forrest told the guard, "I got a deal for you. I will take the boy here and let you keep your convicts, or I will take my clients Devine and Bryant and leave you the boy. It's your choice."

With keys in hand and directions to the barracks, he found and released the two men plus three of their convict friends. Jack Devine and Charles Bryant ran and hopped into the sedan driven by Jack Gamble which had just arrived at the gate. Bryan Schwab, a burglar and safecracker, Jack Green, a bank robber, and A.S. Ross, a burglar from Forsyth calmly followed Forrest Turner out the front gate. Once out of the compound they leisurely walked across the parking area and jumped into Forrest Turner's Ford sedan.

"Are you really a lawyer?" asked Bryan Schwab as Forrest floored the gas pedal, spinning his tires as he raced away from the work camp.

Attorney Turner replied laughing, "Yeah, Emory Law School class of 1937. My secretary will send you a bill for my fee."

Later when Warden Gordon was informed of the escape, he was shocked that five of his convicts were participants in the breakout. Since he was always vigilant about staying at the work camp during the day, he suspected the sick convict, who he had taken to the doctor, had faked his illness to draw him away from the camp. Without the warden on duty a breakout from the camp was less difficult.

A witness reported to the warden that he had seen a man in a suit and a woman wearing a fur coat sitting in a car near the camp minutes before the breakout. The sedan had Alabama plates. From the description given by the witness the man in the car resembled Charles Bryant's former work camp friend, Jack Gamble.

Forrest would later say while grabbing and rubbing his tie, "I didn't know if I could pull it off. It went smooth as silk."

The work camp was once a cotton oil and fertilizer plant that had been recently converted to a work camp. Since it opened six weeks earlier, there had been three other escapes. "I could have broken out of that work camp the first week I was there," he bragged.

The daring feat not only added to his notoriety but put him on top of "Georgia's Most Wanted List."

A couple of days after outlaw Turner masterminded the unbelievable escape of five convicts from the work camp, he was seen in his former hometown of McDonough. Chief Hightower of McDonough reported that four men had stopped at a filling station to have their vehicle's brakes examined. Forrest Turner was thought to be in the area to visit family members who lived in the county. The station attendant said that the mechanic repaired the Ford. Shortly before lunch the group headed east toward Covington.

***

Forrest Turner and the elusive fugitives chose to go in separate directions. Jack Devine and Charles Bryant left the state while Bryan Schwab stayed with Forrest Turner. Forty-one-year-old Jack Green, originally from Texas, went west to start a new life. A.S. Ross also left for parts unknown. As the massive manhunt continued, few reliable leads surfaced as to their whereabouts. However, in Villa Rica during the night of January 21st two robberies occurred. The thieves entered the town's two hardware stores by prying the locks off the front doors. Inside they broke into the cash register, helped themselves to the cash, and hauled off shotguns, pistols, and ammunition. A man fitting Forrest Turner's description was observed near the scene.

Forrest Turner was able to enjoy the Christmas Season as a free man. During his hiatus from prison, he was doing his Christmas shopping at "gun point" and not paying for the gifts. He was Santa Claus to five convicts at the Cumming Work Camp who he freed. But on January 31, 1939, his Christmas vacation came to an end.

During the month-long manhunt Forrest Turner had been seen by witnesses in Atlanta, Griffin, Manchester, Zebulon, Villa Rica, LaGrange, Conyers, and McDonough. When the police went to investigate, he was nowhere to be found. Finally, information from a reliable source proved correct.

Acting on a tip the police chief, deputies and state patrol raided a cabin nine miles from Augusta. The men surrounded the cabin around four o'clock in the morning. They tossed tear gas through the windows and waited for the occupants to react. It didn't take long for Forrest Turner and Bryan Schwab to stagger out of the front door in their night clothes, gasping for air and rubbing their eyes. "I wish you hadn't come so early," Forrest Turner told the officer as he was being handcuffed. "I was having a restful sleep one minute and the next I was overcome by gas. I couldn't breathe. My wonderful dream became a nightmare!"

Once the air in the cabin was breathable, the officers entered and found an arsenal of weapons, dynamite, nitroglycerin, and burglary tools. All of which were stolen. "We found enough food to feed an army," said the chief to a reporter. "They had intended to stay for a long time."

The police doing the raid were surprised and relieved that the two didn't make any effort to resist. Taken to Augusta Police Headquarters in his bathrobe, Forrest Turner was questioned about twenty unsolved robberies that occurred since his escape in November. He denied committing all the robberies except one. The district attorney chose not to pursue charges against Forrest Turner for other crimes he may have committed. One conviction was all he needed to put him away. He stayed in the Augusta jail awaiting trial.

At an earlier legislative session, the lawmakers passed a law whereby "robbery by force" was a capital crime, punishable by death in the electric chair. The possibility of execution loomed as Forrest Turner pondered his fate. Could he be the first convicted thief to be put to death under the new law?

The upcoming trial on February 14th was receiving a great deal of publicity. Forrest Turner knew the district attorney had him dead-to-right. He also knew the local traverse jurors would show no mercy, so he agreed to waive his rights to a trial by jury. Forrest Turner would take his chances with the Richmond County Superior Judge, A.L. Franklin.

"How do you plead to a charge of robbing Murphy's News Stand in December of twelve hundred dollars, two diamond rings, and two overcoats?" asked the judge.

"Guilty Your Honor," Forrest replied.

The judge asked, "What say you, before I pass sentence?"

"I'm not really as bad as I am painted to be," he said to the judge. "I am just a poor country boy, who has lost his way. Have pity on me, Your Honor."

Judge Franklin, not convinced by his remarks, sentenced Forrest Turner to an additional ten to fifteen years of hard labor.

"Son, let me tell you this. You just haven't the courage to go straight," he said with a stern look. "I have looked at your miserable arrest record, how disappointing."

"Yeah, I have Your Honor," Forrest answered. "I have a bit of respect for the new warden at Reidsville and his treatment of inmates. I will become a model prisoner. One day you will read in the papers about me and how I turned my life around. You will be proud of me."

The judge listened and nodded, "I hope you will son. But I doubt it. I want to warn you that while I am not sending you to the electric chair now, if you come before me again, you may not be so lucky."

After the hearing, a deputy returned Forrest Turner to Reidsville Prison. He now has seventy-nine years to serve. He was thankful not to be sent upstairs to the death row cell block to await a date with the infamous electric chair. Instead, he was moved to a high security cell on the fourth floor.

While sitting in solitary confinement Forrest Turner wondered who tipped off the police. He suspected that his girlfriend may have been the one. Later he learned that it was Jack Gamble. The authorities traced him and his wife to Covington where they were seen catching an east bound bus. When the bus arrived at the Augusta Bus Station, the police were there waiting for them. After his arrest Jack Gamble negotiated a deal with Chief Wilson. He would give the location of Forrest Turner's hideout in exchange for a pardon. Three days after Forrest Turner's arrest, Governor Rivers consented and granted a conditional pardon. In making the decision the governor considered that the capture of the state's most wanted fugitive, Forrest Turner, was more important than the release of a convicted murderer, Jack Gamble.

17 SO MANY JAIL BREAKS!

Before Reidsville Forrest Turner was setting records for the most escapes from Georgia work camps and prisons, he was not alone. Numerous jail breaks were occurring throughout the state. With at least one work camp in each county, thousands of convicts were supervised and watched by a limited number of guards. Convicts working in chain gangs on remote roads, in quarries and on large farms were constantly slipping away. Most were recaptured within twenty-four hours. The escapes, which had advance planning and with an accomplice on the outside with a car had more success.

***

Most of the convicts in the work camps were uneducated men who had lived in poverty. The majority were Black. The post Great Depression period was a challenging time for those poor souls. Many resorted to theft for survival. The punishment was most likely a trip to a work camp to be a member of a chain gang. Aside from the forced labor, the living conditions while at the work camp were equal, if not better than what they were experiencing at home. They had a place to live, three meals a day, and clothes to wear. Those convicts had no desire to escape. On the other hand, there were those who came from more comfortable environments who dreaded their time at the work camps. They were constantly looking for ways to escape.

The conditions and security at the forced work camps came under scrutiny. The prison commission recommended more humane treatment of convicts. In so doing, it forbade the use of twenty-four-hour restraints at the camps. During that period, the prison commission also began sending newly sentenced felons to individual work camps instead of to the overcrowded state prison. To reduce further the number of existing inmates in the state prison, the commission also transferred prisoners out to the work camps. The consequences resulting from the transferring of hardened criminals to county work camps increased the number of escapes. The situation soon developed into an unmanageable problem for the Georgia penal system.

The county work camps were run by the local county governments, but were required to follow state guidelines. Local commissioners hired the warden, who hired and fired the guards. The convicts were leased to work camps by the prison commission in exchange for the cost of their room and board. Convicts could be transferred from one work camp to another with the approvals from the commission and the wardens at the respective work camps. Some wardens preferred only Black convicts while other wardens preferred only Whites. Forrest Turner didn't mind working with the Black convicts. He knew when a guard was itching to pick on a convict, he would choose a Black first. That meant that the guard would probably leave him alone. Nevertheless, he hated to see any convict get roughed up needlessly by a guard.

The number of convicts in each of the county work camps varied. When convicts completed their sentence, died or escaped, their replacements became necessary for the work camp to have enough manual laborers to perform the road work. Since the jails were full of prisoners, there were plenty of convicts to go around.

Because of the unusually high number of escapes, the governor called a special meeting at the State Capitol. The one hundred and fifty wardens and assistants, who attended the assembly, had the opportunity to voice their concerns and discuss practical solutions. The panel at the head table included the governor, chairman of the prison commission, head of public safety, and a host of other officials.

Governor Rivers was the first to speak. His office had been flooded with complaints about the number of prisoner flights. "Something must be done about these escapes in order to restore confidence back to the Georgia penal system," he said. "Citizens in the small communities who live near work camps are afraid that one of the fugitives might do them harm."

The panel was then shown a list of names of the recent escapes and the fugitives still at large. Forrest Turner and his friends were first on the list; Robert Colton, Slim Scarborough, Leland Harvey, ...as well as his brother Chester Turner.

Governor Rivers continued, "We are all concerned about the number of attempted and successful escapes. The commission chairman investigates each escape by sending a representative to the work camp. A report is filed and action taken to prevent future escapes. Before I announce my office's recommendations, I first want to hear from you."

One warden sitting on the front row stood up and offered his opinion, "One of the reasons for escapes is that the work camps do not have enough guards to watch over the large number of convicts. The low salaries and monotonous work create constant turnover of personnel. The temptation for an underpaid guard to take a few dollars from a convict in exchange for a favor is often too great to resist."

A representative from Franklin County commented on the eight recent escapes from his work camp in Carnesville. "The practice of turning hardened criminals from Milledgeville over to the counties was a mistake. Also, this new policy of requiring guards to be discharged when convicts escape under their watch, forces us to keep hiring untrained men. Whose idea was it, anyway? Our new and untrained guards are no match for these unscrupulous convicts, who spend every minute of the day plotting how to escape."

The opinionated Warden McMillan from Thomas County Work Camp, who was not one of Forrest Turner's favorite wardens, was next to speak, "We had a fella, a friend of Forrest Turner, who was sent to us, took it upon himself just to walk away. While working on a road construction job he was told to fetch drinking water from the creek for the men. The man never returned. I admit it is humane to unshackle convicts while they work. They could do more in less time if they weren't restrained. But the problem with that policy is that they can also run faster when they take a flight. We need to keep those shackles on them all the time, day and night... just like we used to," commented the warden.

Supervisor Glover from a South Georgia work camp at Hortense mentioned a recent escape from his work camp. He began, "A few months back we had this life-timer named Colton who was sent to our work camp. He had been there just a few days. While working on a highway, one of 'em heavy thunderstorms we get down there on occasion hit upon us all of a sudden. Because of the lightning, the two guards jumped into the cab of the truck for safety. The convicts took cover under a makeshift tarpaulin. During the downpour Colton and another man slipped out. Because of the rain the blood hounds that were brought along for such an event were unable to follow their scent. The men got clean away."

The complaints kept coming. "There has got to be better communication between the commission and the work camps. This fearless Forrest Turner has no respect for the law. Whoever heard of a fugitive breaking into a work camp letting loose a bunch of convicts? I am talking about the mess at the Forsyth County Work Camp in Cumming. This Turner fella walked in, pulled a gun, and overpowered the unsuspecting guard. No one ever breaks into a work camp. It's the convicts who do-the-breaking-out. If there were pictures of all the fugitives posted on the walls at each work camp, Turner would never have gotten past the gate. In fact, he would have been arrested right then and there," mentioned a North Georgia warden.

Governor Rivers stood up and thanked all those who made comments. "I'm sure that many of you would like to share your stories with the group, but we need to move forward with the meeting. Let me summarize some of the actions that are being taken.

"The introduction of the Georgia State Patrol a couple of years ago should begin to provide professional help to your local guards in catching your runaways. It is our plan to increase the number of cars and patrolmen covering Georgia highways. And another thing, if I were you, I wouldn't be speeding anymore. The state patrolmen love to ticket speeders. Allow me to introduce Major Philip Brewster. He is head of the new Georgia State Patrol. He has asked if he could make a few remarks," the governor continued.

"The State Patrol is committed to helping you catch runaways. We will let you and the bloodhounds chase them through the woods. We will catch them if they make it to the highways," promised Major Brewster.

"With the opening of the maximum prison in Reidsville, escapes will be much more difficult, if not impossible. We plan to send all the recaptured escapees there. Your work camps will not have to contend with these troublemaking and unscrupulous convicts anymore.

"The prison commission informed me that it had already begun the establishment of a filing system which will include the fingerprints of all existing convicts with new arrivals added as they enter the work camps and prisons. Each file will have a photograph of the convict. The system will allow local law enforcement to confirm whether their detainee is a fugitive or not.

"I and the commission have proposed to the pardon and parole board to decrease the number of pardons and paroles it grants, especially to those who are repeat offenders.

"We are going to reverse the recent policy where guards cannot shoot fleeing convicts unless done in self-defense. You wardens are right. If the convict knows that he will not be fired upon, why not run away. Wouldn't you?

"And finally, a word of caution to all of you wardens. The convicts will soon learn that changes are forthcoming thus bringing an end to the ease of escaping from a chain gang. Convicts will be motivated more than ever to take the risk of escaping rather than waiting. So, beware."

Addressing Govennor Rivers, Warden McMillan from Thomas County said, "I can tell you that you can't control convicts, if we don't use straps or lock 'em in sweatboxes after they are caught escaping."

"In this day and time there is no place for the whips or sweatboxes in our penal system," responded the governor.

"Another thing. It is my intention to do away with chain gangs. Don't look so shocked. I want to see the establishment of honor work camps. These convicts will still do road and rock work but will not require constant watch. The commission will make sure only the best-behaved prisoners will be sent to these work camps. They will be allowed to work outside the work camp without shackles or stripes. On their honor they will return to the camp after their day's work is done. What do you think of our plans?" asked the governor.

"I am sorry to say, it will never work, Governor Rivers," said the Thomas County's Warden McMillan as he shook his head. "You must be hard on these convicts, never giving them a chance to escape. If not, you might find yourself getting shot by Robert Colton, just like I was!"

The governor left the meeting and asked the chairman of the prison commission to continue answering questions and explaining the forthcoming policy changes. Most wardens were pleased with the state's commitment to toughen the supervision of convicts. One warden from one of the Atlanta work camps commented, "I believe there will be fewer successful breakouts going forward from my work camp at Dallas."

The change in the treatment of convicts began at the top. Those at the State Capitol and the prison commission realized the time had come to end the use of leather straps, twenty-four-hour restraints, and sweatboxes. Hard labor at the work camp was punishment enough without the added guard-imposed cruelty. Many of the escape attempts could have been prevented had the guards been paying attention. It would be a few more years before meaningful reform would take place.

18 "LITTLE ALCATRAZ"

When Forrest Turner became a habitual escape threat, he was moved to the maximum-security wing at the Reidsville prison. There he stayed in the cell except for brief exercise periods. Unaccustomed to the isolation, he felt that the walls of his cell were closing in on him. "If I can't get out of here, I will lose my mind," he vowed. He knew that Warden Sims had no interest in his well-being, so he got his attorney involved. As a result, the director of prisons and Governor Rivers granted his wish and transferred him.

***

While in solitary confinement Forrest Turner was not allowed to send or receive mail. In desperation he had a letter smuggled out of Reidsville addressed to his attorney Max Rubenstein. The letter asked the attorney to make an appeal to Governor Rivers on his behalf to remove him from solitary confinement. Since Forrest Turner was a constant threat to escape, the warden was taking no chances. "As long as he is separated from the other inmates and monitored by a guard twenty-four hours a day, he cannot escape," said the warden. Forrest Turner was unhappy unless people surrounded him. He loved to converse and never let the opportunity go by without a witty retort. He was a member of a large family and always had friends around. Isolation was difficult. He was in a constant state of loneliness and misery.

His letter eventually reached the Governor's desk in June 1939. The letter, having a return address of 300 1st Avenue South, Reidsville, Georgia, caught the attention of his secretary. "Mr. Rivers you might want to read this letter," she said with a smile. "It's from a prisoner named Forrest Turner."

"What does he want? Is it a pardon?" the governor asked jokingly. The letter asked that he be released from solitary confinement so he could enjoy at least a few hours of sunlight each day. He also says as a result, his health was deteriorating, but Warden Sims had refused to allow him to see a doctor.

After reading the letter, he asked his secretary to get Warden Sims on the phone. Warden Sims replied to the governor's questions. "It's not like he is locked in a dark closet over here. He has freedom to move around in his cell. I can't let him work in the yard anymore with the other prisoners. We don't know when he is liable to jump into a truck or hijack an employee's car and vanish like he has done before. As to his health, he has gained weight since his last escape. The prison doctor would have told me if something was wrong with him. Governor, he will do or say anything to get out of solitary confinement. I have learned that you just can't believe a word he says."

Following the discussion of the Turner letter with the warden, the governor and the penal director, Phil Anderson, decided to move Forrest Turner to the work camp in Dallas, Georgia. There the convicts bust rocks all day under the supervision of extra security guards. Because of the harsh conditions at the work camp, it was referred to as Georgia's "Little Alcatraz." When the director announced the transfer, he also commented, "At the request of Mr. Turner…in a short time we expect to provide him with plenty of fresh air, sunshine, and hard work at the 'Rock Quarry Camp' in Dallas, Paulding County."

On July 19, 1939, Forrest Turner arrived at the Dallas work camp.

*Paulding County Work Camp in Dallas, Georgia
known as "Little Alcatraz"*

He joined two hundred of the state's most notorious convicts. Many of them were destined to remain in prison for the rest of their lives. Slim Scarborough was assigned there, after his recapture in Florida. Unlike the other camps, Paulding County Work Camp's armed guards were instructed to pay special attention to convicts who had previous escapes. Convicts were shackled and watched twenty-four hours a day. Donned in a long-sleeved, white work uniform with the traditional black horizontal stripes, Forrest Turner made daily trips to a nearby rock pile. His squad of fifteen convicts loaded surface-rock for delivery to a crushing machine. The gravel material was used on roads.

"Little Alcatraz" was not unlike other county work camps. There was a graveled yard with a twenty-five-foot watch tower surrounded by wooden buildings. The entire complex was fenced. It was named after the notorious federal penitentiary in San Francisco, California.

Alcatraz referred to as the "The Rock" was situated on an island surrounded by the San Francisco Bay's frigid waters. The prison housed the nation's worst prisoners, bank robbers, escape artists, and murderers. Those who were successful in digging or sawing their way out of the prison had to manage the mile and quarter swim to land in sub-sixty-degree water. Few had tried, only one was known to have successfully escaped from the fortress. He had an accomplice waiting for him offshore with a boat. Clarence

Hughes sentenced for desertion was imprisoned on Alcatraz Island while it was an Army detention work camp and escaped in 1928.

Forrest Turner soon learned that labor at the quarry was far more strenuous than the road work at Thomasville. There were always periods when the shovel, rake or switchblade was laid aside, but in Dallas the busting and shoveling of rock never ended. The monotony of the work was unbearable. He had developed calluses on top of calluses on both hands. He was losing weight. The summer heat was excruciating. "Working on the farms growing up was a breeze compared to the labor at this rock pile. This place will put a man in his grave," he told the guard on the first day. The witty guard replied, "I guess starting tomorrow you need to chisel out a headstone for yourself just in case."

Forrest Turner never made it to the work camp's graveyard in Dallas. He had no need for the headstone. His future resting place would be elsewhere.

***

TURNER ESCAPES "LITTLE ALCATRAZ" IN DALLAS

"Forrest Turner and Slim Scarborough at Large"... Seven Convicts on the Run"... "Two on Foot and Five in Work Camp Truck"... "Guards and Police in Hot Pursuit"... "Warden Worthington Expects Recapture Within Twenty-Four Hours"

News that Forrest Turner and Slim Scarborough were once again fugitives on the run did not surprise the reading public. Convicts considered the hard labor at the Paulding County Work Camp in Dallas as one of the state's most dreaded camps. It also had the fewest successful escape attempts.

On the morning of August 14, 1941, Burrell Crews, serving a life sentence for murder and Hubert Dickerson, doing twenty to forty for robbery, had fled on foot. When the men were reported missing, their escape was broadcasted over the Georgia State Patrol radio. All roads leading from the work camp were filled with police cars on the lookout for the two men. Bloodhounds were summoned to search the nearby woods. Local police drove to the work camp to lend a hand. An airplane was dispatched to do an aerial search. The camp was in a complete state of confusion. It was 5:00 p.m. before someone noticed that the work camp pickup truck was no longer in the parking yard. After conducting a body count of the convicts, a prison official realized they were facing a major work camp break.

Missing was Forrest Turner, who reportedly had accumulated eighty-nine years of prison time for his crimes and escapes and life-termer Slim Scarborough, who was convicted of the 1925 Putnam County school superintendent murder. Three others included S.M. Myles, who was convicted of a 1936 murder in Whitfield County, robbers Mack Green and Frank Long, who were each serving ten years for robbery. Shortly after convicts Crews and Dickerson fled, Forrest Turner and others seized their opportunity to leave Dallas and "Little Alcatraz." The work camp was short of guards that day. The temporary responsibility of overseeing the convicts was left to Trusty Frank Long.

It was not difficult to convince Trusty Long to fetch the key to the truck from the office, especially when threatened by two convicts who had been charged with murder. With the key in hand, Forrest Turner took the wheel. Slim Scarborough forced Trusty Long to unlock the front gate.

"You sit in the middle," Slim told Frank as they climbed into the pickup. Slim joined him and closed the door. The others jumped into the back of the truck. "You fellas need to lay down until we get out of sight," Forrest instructed.

With no one stopping them at the gate, they successfully made their escape. Forrest Turner drove the few miles to Carnesville. Although they had not seen any unusual police presence, it was time to abandon the work camp truck. Convicts Turner, Scarborough, and Myles stayed together. They stole an automobile and left the others behind with the truck. They headed south.

Frank Long and Mack Green continued their escape to the north until they ran out of gas. Mack Green quickly commandeered an automobile from a motorist while Frank Long chose to remain with the stranded pickup truck. It was late evening before Trusty Frank Long reached the filling station on foot. There he phoned the work camp to report his whereabout. After obtaining gas he drove the pickup back to the work camp to surrender voluntarily.

In the meantime, Forrest Turner and Slim Scarborough reached Alabama. They had been on the run for more than four hours. Low on gas, hungry, and in need of money, they robbed a filling station in Opelika, Alabama.

When Trusty Long returned to the work camp, Warden Worthington was there waiting for him. He sternly asked Trusty Long what happened. "Well, they forced me to let them out of the front gate and they made me go with them. There was no one there to stop us. Turner and Scarborough, who led the break were talking about going to Atlanta after they stole the car. Green having no use for me left me with the pickup truck," answered the Trusty. "I hope you won't punish me. After all, I did come back on my own."

The warden thanked Frank Long and told him that he would vouch for his good behavior. Worthington continued, "Since I was called away for a meeting, I was not here. But I am going to find out where the other guards were who should have been on watch. Leaving control of a work camp to a trusty turned out to be a bad idea," he lamented.

19 THE BANK ROBBERY

Forrest Turner and Slim Scarborough had successfully eluded detectives and police since their escape from "Little Alcatraz" in Dallas. During their liberty they decided to embark on a daring robbery of a bank. Unlike their many holdups which were spontaneous and took only minutes to pull off, a bank robbery required planning. The idea arose as the pair passed a bank while traveling in north Georgia. A serious discussion followed about the large amounts of cash available in an unsuspecting bank.

***

Slim told Forrest, "So far all you have done is rob people of a few dollars or holdup a filling stations when you were out of gas. Then sometimes you rob a general store when you were out of groceries. And occasionally you would borrow a car without asking. I think it's time to steal from a place where there is lots of money."

"What do you have in mind?" the perplexed Forrest asked.

Slim countered, "Lets rob a bank. I know how it can be done. First, we must find a bank that is easy to rob and then figure out a way to get into its vault. That's where the big money is kept. The bank should not have a guard on duty and the town must not have much of a police force." They found such a small bank off U.S. 17 in Royston.

Established in 1935, the Commercial Exchange Bank on Church Street was the small town's only bank. Situated in northeast Georgia, the rural community of Royston had approximately fifteen hundred residents. Royston sat in portions of Franklin, Hart and Madison counties. If it weren't for the famous baseball player Ty Cobb, who lived there, most people in the state would not have heard of the town. Royston was only thirty miles from Athens and twelve miles from the South Carolina line.

Small community banks have always been targets for desperate people in need of cash and thieves seeking fast money. Because of the risk of holdups, banks took certain security measures to discourage robberies. The creation of the Federal Deposit Insurance Corporation in 1933 not only protected customer deposits, but it made the robbery of an insured bank a federal crime. Bank robbers could expect a fraught of trouble when pursued by the local police and agents from the G.B.I. and the F.B.I. Only the most experienced and professional thieves had success in robbing banks. Even most of them were eventually caught.

On Monday August 18, 1941, they put their plan into action. They left well before sunrise and headed to the banker's house. Once there they would force the banker to take them to the bank and unlock the vault. It was 6:00 a.m. when they arrived at the home of Branson James, who was the president of Commercial Exchange Bank in Royston. No one was up and the screen door was locked. They cut a hole in the screen door to reach in and unlock the front door. They entered the house attempting to surprise the banker. Hearing the commotion Mrs. James got up to investigate. When she turned on the lights, she met the intruders stumbling around the living room looking for a light switch.

"Where is your husband?" The surprised Slim asked as he raised his hand to shield his squinted eyes from the sudden brightness of the overhead light.

The startled Mrs. James answered, "He's asleep in the bedroom. What do you want with him?"

"We need to make a withdrawal from the bank," Forrest replied in his usual lighthearted manner.

Confused by the strange request and not knowing what to do she responded, "Well okay, it's this way pointing down the hall. Follow me."

"Mr. Banker, get dressed and take us to your bank!" demanded Forrest. "When we get there, you are to open the vault before the bank opens and before the other employees arrive."

Branson James sat up. Rubbing his eyes and half asleep, he put on his banker clothes, a white short-sleeved shirt, tie, and khaki pants. His mind was racing. Finally, he mustered up the courage to respond to the demands. "But that would be impossible! The vault has a time delayed lock. The bolts securing the door will not retract allowing the vault door to open until just minutes before the bank opens," he revealed.

"Well, what time does the bank open?" asked Forrest, a bit annoyed.

Banker James replied, "It opens at 9:00 a.m. sharp."

Slim Scarborough had not accounted on a time-delayed lock even though they had been installed at most banks since the turn of the century.

Up to this point Forrest Turner had depended on his partner to manage the robbery. With what little money he had, he seldom had the need to frequent a bank. He was beginning to wonder if Slim knew as much about robbing a bank as he led on.

"Well, then let's all go to the kitchen. Mrs. James can make us some coffee, while we figure out what to do," Forrest told the couple. "Mr. James, I am keeping a close eye on you. Don't try anything stupid," ordered Forrest.

Slim suggested to Forrest, "We'll just wait until around 9:00 then go to the bank."

Forrest didn't answer but, in his mind, it sounded like a risky change in plans. But, since they had already gone this far, they might as well see it through.

They instructed Mrs. James to stay at the house. They threatened to harm her husband if she phoned the police. "I won't call the police. Please don't hurt my husband!" she pleaded.

Then they followed Mr. James to his 1941 Oldsmobile sedan and told him to drive. To kill the time, they rode around. While traveling through Commerce they realized the Oldsmobile was running low on gas and stopped at a filling station.

"It's your car so I want you to pay for the gas," Forrest told James. "Gimme $2.00."

Forrest Turner felt uncomfortable leaving Mrs. James at her home by herself. Having second thoughts and looking at his watch he tells Slim, "We should have taken her along. Before going to the bank, we should stop at the house to check to see if Mrs. James had kept her word."

When they arrived at the house there were no police cars present. Mrs. James was in a panic. She ran to the door to see if her husband was still alive. She was relieved to see him sitting in the car and waving to her indicating that he was all right.

In tears Mrs. James pleaded, "I didn't call the police. You have got to believe me! Why did you come back?"

"We came back to make sure you hadn't. You remember what I told you Mrs. James?" Slim asserted. "Don't go anywhere and don't talk to anyone!"

Since she had been true to her word, they decided to let her stay at the house. It was a few minutes before 9:00 when they arrived at the bank. Branson James unlocked the door and entered the bank accompanied by Slim Scarborough. Forrest Turner remained in the car as a lookout. Upon entering the bank they were greeted by the bookkeeper, who was sitting at her desk.

"Good morning Mrs. Wynn. Me and this gentleman have some

business to do in the vault," he told her.

She was unaware of what was about to take place. In the vault Slim pulled out the pistol he had concealed in his pocket. "Now I want you to do exactly as I say as he handed Mr. James a paper bag which he had hidden inside his shirt," he quietly instructed him so as not to be overheard by the other employees. "Open the vault Mr. Banker and put all the cash in a bag."

He was surprised by the small amount of cash in the vault. Disappointed, he had figured that even a little bank would have more money. "Is this all the money you have?" asked Slim sternly.

The frightened Branson James, not knowing what to say, replied. "We always cash a lot of checks on Friday, so our cash is low on Monday mornings. A cash shipment will be arriving this afternoon."

"Ok, you and I are going to walk casually back to the car," Slim instructed. "You hold the bag."

As they walked by Mrs. Wynn's desk, "This gentleman has something he wants to show me. I will be back shortly," Mr. James told her. It was after 9:00. The front door was unlocked but there were no customers in the bank.

With the banker driving, Slim Scarborough was in the front passenger seat looking to see if there were any police in sight. There were none. No one at the bank nor Mrs. James had alerted the police. The robbers had just pulled off a successful bank job. "I guess Slim did know what he was talking about," Forrest said to himself. He counted the money and told Slim that there was five thousand dollars in the bag.

"You did real good Mr. Banker," Forrest said as he gave him a broad smile.

After traveling for an hour, the bank robbers assumed that it was safe to rid themselves of Mr. James. They had driven fifty miles and were near the town of Winder. "Slow down and turn left on that logging road up ahead," Slim told Mr. James.

Up to now he had felt that the kidnappers would eventually let him go. But now he wasn't so sure. As he turned onto dirt road and looking at Slim, "You are not going to shoot me and dump my body out here, are you?" he asked hysterically.

"Just drive over to those trees and stop," Slim ordered. At first the banker refused to get out of the car. Forrest opened his door and told him. "Now Mr. James, we are not going to shoot you. Believe me! But I am going to tie you up, so we will have time to get away. Go over there and sit with your back against the tree," Forrest told the frightened banker, who was unsure of his fate. "Remove that nice looking tie you are wearing and put your arms behind you."

The tree was an eight-inch pine. Small enough to where Mr. James could extend his arms behind his back with his hands reaching beyond the tree. Forrest Turner used his tie to bound his hands. Leaving Mr. James tied to the tree they drove off in his Oldsmobile.

"Did you tie him up tight?" asked the inquisitive Slim.

Forrest laughing, "Tight enough. But he should get free in about twenty minutes."

Just as Forrest Turner had promised. No harm came to the banker. He was able to free himself and flag down a traveling salesman who took him to the nearest telephone where he called his worried wife. Relieved to learn that her husband was safe, she immediately called the police.

Forrest Turner figured they had pulled off the perfect job. It's the most money he had ever stolen.

As soon as Branson James returned to the bank, local police, and detectives were there. "I admit the bank robbers treated me well. They didn't have much to say, except occasionally, one of the men told me politely, if I behaved myself, I wouldn't get hurt. One was about five foot nine, weighed about one hundred forty-five pounds, had a scar under his left ear, brown eyes, and was wearing a cheap brown suit. The other fellow was a bit shorter and was dressed in a smart blue suit," the banker told detectives. "I got a little nervous when they stopped near Winder and told me to get out. When one of them started to tie me to a tree, I figured they were going to shoot me. But thank God they didn't. The way the one fella tied me up, he knew I could get loose and wouldn't die in the woods," the banker disclosed.

When Georgia State Patrol Headquarters in Atlanta broadcasted an alert to its patrol cars and surrounding police departments instructing them to be on the lookout for two Royston bank robbers, Detectives Nahlik and Coppenger didn't pay the alert any attention. The heist of the Commercial Exchange Bank in northeast Georgia occurred a hundred miles from Atlanta. It was not their concern. "Turner is not known for robbing banks," Detective Coppenger told his partner, Nahlik.

The following week the detectives were informed that Birmingham police had arrested two robbery suspects who had a car full of weapons, hacksaw, and blades. The suspects were not willing to divulge their names, however, the police considered the two had to be fugitives from a Georgia work camp or the Royston bank robbers. Detectives Nahlik and Coppenger had second thoughts about who committed the robbery and drove to Birmingham. When the detectives arrived, they discovered their prisoners were not Forrest Turner or Slim Scarborough but instead, were Wylie Smith and Robert Laminack who were also escapees from "Little Alcatraz." Consequently, their trip to Alabama was not in vain.

After Branson James identified the bank robbers from photographs as indeed being Forrest Turner and Slim Scarborough, the G.B.I. called Detective Leo Nahlik to help with the investigation. "I know this Turner fella like the back of my hand," he told the agent. "Don't you worry. I will get the bank its money back before they can spend it all, and I will return them back to "Little Alcatraz" in no time." The next day they got their first lead when Branson James' Oldsmobile was found undamaged behind a supermarket off Lawrenceville Highway in Decatur. It was good news for Mr. James, but consequently it resulted in unwelcome news for a Decatur resident whose car was taken.

The search for Forrest Turner and Slim Scarborough was the number one priority for Georgia law enforcement. Switchboard operators at the police stations were told to report any calls of a sighting to their superiors.

An unusual call came the next morning at 2:00 a.m. Three police cars rushed to Ponce de Leon Place and set up roadblocks. Three more patrol cars came to a shrieking halt in front of an apartment. An unmarked detective's car with siren blasting followed. All the lawmen exited and stood behind their vehicles with their guns drawn. The residents, awakened by the commotion, assumed that the police must have cornered dangerous suspects. It had to be the Royston bank robbers. When all the commotion settled down it was not the robbers, but an altercation between a taxi driver and his passenger. The taxi driver had picked up the night janitor after work and brought him to his apartment. A heated and loud argument ensued when the taxi driver was unable to collect his forty-cent taxi fare.

On August 31, 1941, detectives raided a small motel in Clayton County and arrested Forrest Turner. Once at the station house, they learned the accused was not the notorious Forrest Turner, but a nineteen-year-old youth from Lovejoy with the same name.

On September 8th, Slim Scarborough robbed an airport liquor store in Hapeville while Forrest Turner waited in the car. He had intended to buy a bottle of Old Forrester Bourbon, but since no customers were in the store, he decided to have the cashier turn over all the folding money in the register. After the theft was reported, Fulton County police quickly spotted the car and gave chase. They were able to get close enough to fire several shots before the fleeing car sped away.

Three days later an abandoned bullet-riddled car was discovered in Parrot near Albany, Georgia. The 1941 Ford had been stolen from a Bainbridge man, who from photos positively identified Forrest Turner as one of the culprits. Detective Nahlik suspected it was the same car used in the holdup of the airport liquor store and was certain that fugitives Turner and Scarborough were responsible for the theft.

In the meantime, reports of their sighting were occurring throughout the South. In the afternoon of September 17th two men answering the descriptions of Forrest Turner and Slim Scarborough supposedly held up a business in Chattanooga, Tennessee and escaped with one hundred sixty-eight dollars.

Another sighting of the pair was reported the same day in Ashburn. The witness was sure it was the fugitives who were on foot heading toward Cordelle. Georgia State Patrol later arrested two men standing on the side of the highway. They were not the fugitives, but two vagrants who were later released.

Acting on what was thought to be a reliable tip, ten armed policemen on the 23rd raced to a specific street address in Atlanta. When they arrived on the street hoping to corner Forrest Turner, they soon discovered that there was no such street number. One of the policemen was heard saying, "I bet it was Turner who called in the tip. The fugitive sure has a sense of humor."

The other annoyed police responded, "But it isn't funny to me. I sure would like to get my hands on this Turner fella!"

The robbery of the Commercial Exchange Bank, a small private bank, was ill-timed for the investors as they did not recover the money stolen. Detective Nahlik learned that shortly after the robbery its board renamed their bank the Tri County Bank of Royston and obtained coverage for its depositors through the Federal Deposit Insurance Corporation.

On October 4th word came from the G.B.I. that Forrest Turner was spotted in Southwest Georgia. At the same time a major convict breakout and a kidnapping occurred. All law enforcement officers in Georgia, Florida, and Alabama were put on full alert. Detective Nahlik began making plans to leave Atlanta and travel to Columbus. "It sounds like something Forrest Turner would do. If it was him, he may have bitten off, more than he can chew this time," he said to himself. He hoped to be nearby when Forrest Turner was apprehended. He had a couple of unsolved cases in Fulton County that needed to be closed.

20 FREE THE CONVICTS

The sight of convicts doing road work brought back sad memories for Forrest Turner who was traveling through middle Georgia with Slim Scarborough and two other passengers. The temptation not to stop and help them was too great to ignore. It was an impulsive decision unlike some of Forrest Turner's past break out of convicts. The freeing of an entire road gang was a bold act of legendary proportions. For law enforcement and prison officials recapturing one or two escapees was difficult enough but trying to round up a gang of fleeing convicts was an enormous task. The fear that these felons could do harm to unsuspecting residents caused a general alarm in the area. It was a chaotic afternoon as authorities tried to ease the fears of the panic stricken public.

***

TURNER AND SCARBOROUGH BRAZENLY RELEASE 41 CONVICTS

"Two Prison Officials Kidnapped"... "Hostage Fate Unknown"... "Shots Fired"... "South Georgia in a State of Panic"... "Forty-One Convicts from the Harris County Work Camp Road Gang Liberated"... "Turner and Scarborough Suspected"... "Search Intensified for the Convicts in Columbus, Georgia"

The news came as no surprise to those who followed the escapades of Forrest Turner. On October 4, 1941 headlines reported his latest impersonation of "Robin Hood," the outlaw with a big heart.

Slim Scarborough and Forrest Turner, accompanied by Forrest's girlfriend, Betty Ann Jones, and another escaped convict, Fred Stewart, were traveling through Manchester, in Merriwether County. Forrest Turner was driving a new Mercury and slowed as he passed a group of convicts working on the road. Looking in the rearview mirror he waited until the chain gang was out of sight then pulled over to the side of the road and stopped. He looked at Slim Scarborough and said, "Do you know what I'm thinking?" Slim nodded in agreement.

Betty Ann Lewis noticing the exchange quickly interrupted, "Oh no you don't. We can't stop to help those convicts. Forrest, you don't even know any of them!"

"Well, Slim and I feel sorry for them," said Forrest while turning the car around. "We wouldn't feel right if we don't go back."

One of the most bizarre chain of events in Georgia penal history was about to unfold. The daring effort to free the convicts without a plan was foolhardy. The notion that something could go wrong never entered their minds. "We will surprise the guards. They will not know what to do with so many convicts running in all directions. They will be too busy rounding them up to chase us," Forrest laughed as he explained his thinking to his lady friend. "I suspect many will make it to freedom. It's worth the risk."

It was around lunch time. The convicts and all the guards except two were sitting on the grassy shoulder eating their lunches. Claude Almon was busy reviewing construction plans and wasn't paying attention until Forrest Turner pointed his gun at him. "Walk quietly toward the two guards who are watching the convicts," he instructed. No one has to get hurt."

Claude Almon was walking in front of them with his hands in the air. Forrest Turner branded a machine gun while Slim Scarborough had a shotgun. The other passengers remained in the sedan anxiously watching the action. Seeing the weapons pointed at them, the guards quickly surrendered their guns.

"We want you guards to free these convicts. When the restraints were removed, Forrest yelled loudly. "You cons are free, compliments of Forrest Turner and Slim Scarborough. Get the hell out of here! This may be the only chance you will ever have to escape the chain gang." Several at once jumped into the back of the work camp truck as one of the convicts began to drive away. Many of the others began to run through the woods. Some of the bewildered and confused convicts remained seated. They didn't want to have anything to do with the escape.

"Now we want you, pointing at Guard Hutchinson and Engineer Almon, to come with us. You fellas will be our insurance policy in case the police think about shooting at us," Forrest continued. "We want to be sure that no guards start following us. Since we can't fit any more people into the car, I want you, pointing the gun at the third guard, to start running toward those woods over there and don't stop." Guard Thornton began running. To emphasize the seriousness of his command Forrest Turner fired a couple of shots into the air. Immediately, the frightened guard picked up the pace and began to sprint, stumbling along the way.

The shots being fired alerted a fourth guard, who was in the bushes relieving himself. Forrest Turner jumped into the driver's side of the Mercury and forced the guards to sit next to him in the front seat. Guard Hutchinson sat by the passenger door. Slim Scarborough, Fred Stewart and the lady were in the back seat. As Forrest Turner began to drive off, the fourth guard who had come to investigate was within range and fired. He floored the gas pedal. The Mercury occupied with the kidnappers and the two hostages sped off in the direction of Columbus.

"Ouch!" yelled Hutchinson as he grabbed his right leg. One of the pellets pierced the passenger door and struck Hutchinson. Seeing the grimace expression on his face Forrest remarked, "That stupid guard doesn't care who he shoots." At that moment he reached under the seat and handed Scarborough three sticks of dynamite with short fuses. "If someone starts chasing us, light the fuse on one of them and throw the dynamite out the window. The explosion should scare the hell out of 'em! Those fellas will think twice about chasing us." Forrest said in a serious tone while looking in the direction of the hostages.

Learning of the release of forty-one chain gang convicts in Harris County prompted the warden to send out a general alarm. The head of Georgia State Patrol, John Goodwin, instructed the dispatcher to radio all patrol cars in Columbus, Macon, Atlanta, Athens, and areas in between. "Patrolmen should be on the lookout for a maroon Mercury. Do not attempt to stop the vehicle. The occupants may include two kidnapped work camp personnel. The patrol does not want any harm to come to them. If you see or learn of the whereabouts of the vehicle fitting the description, report the sighting to headquarters. Until we catch these desperadoes, all patrolmen will remain on duty until further notice."

The Georgia Bureau of Investigation hurried to the scene with all the department's available men. The Harris County Sheriff had all his deputies notify homeowners of the pending danger of armed kidnapers and runaway convicts who might force themselves into a home to use as a hiding place. All dog handlers were asked to bring their blood hounds to the scene to help the massive manhunt. "Rounding up forty-one convicts will not be an easy task," remarked one of the participating dog owners.

Once Forrest Turner reached the city of West Point about forty miles from Columbus, he parked the vehicle on a side road. There he turned on the short-wave radio. They began listening to the communication between the state policemen who were in their patrol cars and the dispatcher at headquarters. They immediately knew what roads to avoid.

Late that afternoon Forrest Turner told the hostages, Claude Almon, state highway engineer, and Neal Hutchinson, guard, to exit the car. "We are going to let you go. We want you to wait here one hour before you leave," Forrest yelled out the window to the two relieved men who were standing next to the car expecting the worst.

Of course, the hostages didn't hang around. They were able to hitch a ride to the Columbus Police Headquarters. After receiving medical treatment, Guard Hutchinson would later tell the warden, "Yeah, I was afraid at first. I figured they would shoot us and dump our bodies in the woods somewhere. When we stopped at Mulberry Bridge, I thought I was a goner. I admit that captors Turner and Scarborough treated us good. After I told them that we had families at home, they said no harm would come to us if we behaved ourselves. So, we did exactly what they asked us to do."

Meanwhile the Harris County Work Camp was abuzz. By early nightfall thirty of the convicts were back in custody. Most hadn't wandered very far, and others were sitting under some nearby trees waiting for a ride back to the work camp. Eleven were still at large. Some were running from tired bloodhounds which were in hot pursuit. The work camp truck with convicts inside disappeared in the darkness, its whereabouts unknown.

State highway patrolmen and Colquitt County police officers were on high alert when word came that the kidnappers were in the area. Acting on a tip from a witness who had seen the Mercury pass her house, two cars of ten armed officers and federal officials surprised the fugitives in Norman Park, a small town in Colquitt County. A chase pursued on crooked dirt roads reaching speeds up to seventy-five miles an hour. Forrest Turner, with the driving skills of a racecar driver, was not able to outmaneuver the pursuers. When they reached a roadblock near the town of Ellenton and tried to double back, they were trapped. Even though they had a carload of weapons and dynamite they meekly surrendered.

They were taken to jail in Moultrie. There the police officials questioned each captive individually. Betty Ann Jones, twenty-two-year-old lady friend

Forrest Turner Sits in
the Moultrie Jail

of Forrest Turner offered the following, "I told Forrest not to free the convicts. But he did it anyway. He just wanted the publicity." Forrest Turner and Slim Scarborough got the biggest kick out of listening to the police reports on the short-wave radio, especially when patrolmen had no clue as to where to look. The local radio station interrupted the country music sung by Gene Audry and Earnest Tubbs to report the convict release. Such an event had never occurred in South Georgia.

The investigator interviewed the mystery woman, Betty Ann Jones. She admitted that she and her husband Forrest were married three years ago but had to forgo their honeymoon. She said, "The only reason Forrest escaped from the Dallas Work Camp back in August was to be with me." She was being held in Harris County Jail charged as an accomplice in the forcible escape of forty-one convicts. When asked whether Betty Jones' real name was Betty Turner, Forrest Turner wouldn't admit or deny the fact. He just said that she had offered to be his wife.

At the request of Governor Rivers, the fugitives were taken to Reidsville after questioning. Officers discovered that the Mercury had been stolen ten days earlier in Fort Valley, Georgia. Forrest Turner's freedom began on August 14th when he escaped from "Little Alcatraz" and ended with his capture in Ellenton on October 4th. His feats during the fifty-one days of liberty propelled Forrest Turner to legendary status. Forrest Turner had managed to avoid harm to himself and his passengers except for one hostage. The credit for slightly wounding Guard Hutchinson went to a "gun happy" guard left behind.

At twenty-six years of age, Forrest Turner was quick to threaten those who he had robbed or held as hostage, but to date he never intentionally hurt any of them. In those days most of the publicized captures of notorious criminals ended in a shootout. Sworn not to be taken alive…they were not. When it was all over, Forrest Turner had lived another day.

PART III
THE REFORM YEARS

21 CLOUDS OF WAR GATHERING

While Forrest Turner and his fellow convicts were terrorizing local citizens in Georgia a greater threat was looming in Europe and Asia. "When will the United States enter the war?" That question had become the main topic of discussion. Like every patriotic young man, Forrest Turner had a keen interest in the war. Had circumstances been different he would have volunteered for military service. While on the run and behind bars, he read newspapers and listened to the radio for any news about the conflicts overseas. In December 1941 the unwelcomed news that every American dreaded to hear was announced. The United States and the Axis Power governments had declared war.

***

It was the 1940s. Forrest Turner was twenty-six years old when Franklin Roosevelt won reelection for a third term as president. Ed Rivers was in his last year as governor. Everyone was listening to New York Yankee baseball games on their radios after they had won four straight World Series. Babe Ruth had already retired after hitting seven hundred fourteen home runs as did Lou Gehrig after playing in two thousand one hundred thirty straight games. Ted Williams enlisted in the Army after recording a four hundred and six batting average. Former ace pilot with twenty-five kills and President of Eastern Airlines, Captain Eddie Rickenbacker, survived a plane crash near Jonesboro, Georgia in 1941.

All attention was focused on Germany's aggression in Europe. The message from a man, small in stature with a narrow mustache, was being heard throughout Europe. Adolf Hitler with the Third Reich movement wanted to reunite the German speaking people under one nation. The clouds of war were gathering in Europe. Popular opinion in America was for the United States to stay neutral. When Germany began invading its neighbors, American sentiment began to change. Poland was overrun in a matter of weeks. France, Belgium, and the Netherlands were next. France quickly surrendered and the Battle of Britain began. Germany, Italy, and Japan signed a joint military and economic agreement thus expanding the war to Asia. America's involvement became a certainty.

***

Forrest Turner and Slim Scarborough made their escape from "Little Alcatraz," but were recaptured on October 4, 1941. The fifty-one days while they were on the loose, they were accused of car thefts, robberies, and every imaginable crime that was committed in Georgia. Unfortunately for Forrest Turner, their odyssey ended, and the two men were returned to Reidsville with more years added to their sentences. The local and national newspapers had a field day printing story after story about the two. Their devious activities made headlines and fascinated the public. Their escapades, however, paled in comparison to the distrubing event that occurred two months later.

Just before 8:00 a.m. Sunday morning the Imperial Japanese Navy bombed U.S. naval base at Pearl Harbor in Honolulu, Hawaii. The unprovoked sneak attack shocked and angered all American citizens including those at Georgia State Prison in Reidsville. In the attack eight U.S. battleships, three cruisers, and three destroyers were damaged or sunk. A total of more than two thousand three hundred Americans were killed and more than eleven hundred were wounded.

Because of the gravity of the event and the uncertainties facing the country, the warden provided radios and assembled the inmates in the dining hall to listen to President Roosevelt's scheduled speech to Congress. The sketchy report of the attack by the press was filled with rumors and left many unanswered questions. It was hoped, the president would give the official details and explain what would happen next.

He began, "Yesterday, December 7, 1941 – a date which will live in infamy – the United States of America was suddenly and deliberately attacked by naval and air forces of the Empire of Japan. As Commander in Chief of the Army and Navy, I have directed that all measures be taken for our defense. But always will our whole nation remember the character of the onslaught against us.

"No matter how long it may take us to overcome this premeditated invasion, the American people in their righteous might will win through to absolute victory. Hostilities exist. There is no blinking at the fact that our people, our territory, and our interests are in grave danger. With confidence in our armed forces—with the unbounding determination of our people—we will gain the inevitable triumph—so help us God.

"I believe that I interpret the will of the Congress and of the people when I assert that we will not only defend ourselves to the utmost but will make it very certain that this form of treachery will never again endanger us.

"I ask that the Congress declare a state of war between the United States and the Japanese Empire."

No one in the hall uttered a sound as President Roosevelt continued his speech. When he completed his remarks, the entire congressional body stood and clapped loudly. At the same time the inmates rose and joined in clapping and yelling. "Giv 'em hell" one of the inmates yelled. "Give those Japanese bastards, hell!" Shortly thereafter congress by an overwhelming vote declared war against Japan. America formally entered World War II.

From that moment Forrest regretted more than ever that he was a prisoner and not a free man. He had brothers, high school class-mates and neighbors who enlisted in the military. There was a patriotic fervor by every healthy male to protect the American way of life which was being threatened by Germany and Japan.

This feeling intensified when Congress introduced the draft. Men born between 1897 and 1921 were required to register for military service. Forrest Turner received his registration card. It showed his place of address as Reidsville, Tattnall County. His employer was listed as the Georgia State Prison. He would have been thrilled if he could enlist in the Army.

October 1942, Forrest Turner was determined to be allowed to serve in the armed forces. He felt helpless sitting in prison while other Americans were fighting the Germans. It was a world war. The German U-boats were sinking U.S. ships in the Atlantic and the Japanese planes had bombed Pearl Harbor in the Pacific.

He came up with the idea of negotiating an exchange. He would swap his prison sentence for active duty in the Army as a soldier. If he survived the war and performed honorably, he would have expected a full pardon. It made sense to him. "I am sure the army could use an expert with firearms like me," he thought. "I know I can drive a tank better than any man in the army. I can help America win the war."

First, he would need someone to speak on his behalf. He knew that speaking with the warden was a waste of time. The warden had little respect for inmates and no respect for Forrest Turner. He was aware that long-term inmates would promise anything to get out of prison. They say there was no honor among felons. If there was, they wouldn't be locked up here in Reidsville.

While Forrest Turner was growing up in Henry County, one of his neighbors was John E. Goodwin. He was older than Forrest, but he was confident that Mr. Goodwin would remember him and listen to his wish.

Mr. Goodwin and Forrest Turner both eventually left Henry County and moved to Fulton County. As adults they took differ-

John Goodwin
Head of Georgia Highway Patrol

ent career paths ending up on different sides of the law; one in law enforcement and the other in breaking the law. Mr. Goodwin helped Eugene Talmadge get elected governor. In return the governor appointed him as the commissioner of public safety. One of the department's responsibilities was overseeing the Georgia State Patrol.

Forrest Turner was certain that he would take his request seriously and proceeded to send him a letter. He knew Mr. Goodwin could get into Governor Talmadge's ear. John Goodwin would never have imagined that a member of the Turner family from Henry County would become the most renowned criminal in the State of Georgia. His patrolmen had spent many hours looking for him after his escapes.

He was surprised to receive the letter and sent a message to him telling him that he would do his best to help him. John Goodwin showed the letter to the governor, who agreed to intercede. "I have got to meet this Turner fellow," the governor told John Goodwin. "He gets more publicity than I do."

Governor Talmadge would later meet Forrest Turner at the Reidsville prison. "I really and honestly want to go straight and live the life of a normal man," he tells Governor Talmadge. "I want a conditional pardon to volunteer and join the army. I will make you a promise. If I am still living after the war, I will report back to you or to whoever I am supposed to. If my military record and conduct are not to your satisfaction, I will voluntarily return to prison. If they are, I hope you will grant me a full pardon."

Governor Talmadge replied, "Well, Forrest, I will look into the matter and will see what I can do."

A few days later the governor contacted him. "I am sorry Forrest. The army has strict rules regarding prisoners serving in the army. A prisoner must be paroled and then be crime free for three months before being eligible to be drafted into the army. Since you have had so many years added to your sentence it's unlikely you will be paroled any time soon."

When the press learned of the interview, they asked the governor of his impression of the "Georgia's Number One Bad Boy," Forrest Turner, the notorious criminal.

"I have met and talked with Forrest. He's a surprisingly good boy. I sort of felt sorry for him. They have him tied to a ball and chain. Since he is twenty-seven years old, high-spirited, they are certain he will try to escape as he has done several times already if not restrained. From my review of his record, I determined that he is not a murderer but just a clever armed robber. The warden says he is one of the best workers at Reidsville when he puts his mind into it," Governor Talmadge told the reporter.

Mr. Talmadge did make one promise, "Forrest, while I am governor, I will encourage the arm forces to lessen their restrictions against young men of military age who are in the penal institutions in this country. Under the present regulations there is too much danger of a young criminal who has spent all his youthful years in prison returning to his old ways before he can enlist. By not finishing out their ninety-day probation period with a clean record, he becomes ineligible for military service. These young men would be better off to go straight from prison to boot camp. In those ninety days the army could instill some serious discipline in the youth."

The governor told the press that he would like to see Mr. Turner and other young convicts like him in the military. If they can stay out of trouble and the war continues, me or the next governor will grant him a pardon. He then could enlist.

Not everyone favored pardons to hardened criminals for any reason even enlisting in the military. When the press reported that the governor was considering pardoning Forrest Turner as one of

REGISTRATION CARD—(Men born on or after February 17, 1897 and on or before December 31, 1921)

SERIAL NUMBER	1. NAME (Print)			ORDER NUMBER
T. 3685	Forrest	Turner		T.
	(First)	(Middle)	(Last)	

2. PLACE OF RESIDENCE (Print)

910 Central Ave., Hapeville, Fulton, Ga.

(Number and street)　(Town, township, village, or city)　(County)　(State)

[THE PLACE OF RESIDENCE GIVEN ON THE LINE ABOVE WILL DETERMINE LOCAL BOARD JURISDICTION; LINE 2 OF REGISTRATION CERTIFICATE WILL BE IDENTICAL]

3. MAILING ADDRESS

same as above

[Mailing address if other than place indicated on line 2. If same insert word same]

4. TELEPHONE

5. AGE IN YEARS　30 yrs

DATE OF BIRTH　Feb. 8th, 1915

(Mo.)　(Day)　(Yr.)

6. PLACE OF BIRTH　McDonough, Ga.

(Town or county)

Henry County

(State or country)

(Exchange)　(Number)

7. NAME AND ADDRESS OF PERSON WHO WILL ALWAYS KNOW YOUR ADDRESS

Mother... Mrs. J. M. Turner, same address as above

8. EMPLOYER'S NAME AND ADDRESS

Inmate　Ga. State Priosn

9. PLACE OF EMPLOYMENT OR BUSINESS

Reidsville, Tattnall, Ga.

(Number and street or R. F. D. number)　(Town)　(County)　(State)

I AFFIRM THAT I HAVE VERIFIED ABOVE ANSWERS AND THAT THEY ARE TRUE.

D. S. S. Form 1　(Revised 1-1-42)　(over)　☆　GPO　16—21630-1　_Forrest Turner_

(Registrant's signature)

WWII Draft Registration Card

his last official acts, several readers voiced their concerns.

"Before the governor releases Mr. Turner, he might ask the hundreds of people who he robbed, terrorized, and abused. There was a bank in Royston that lost a lot of money. What about the peace officers who risked their lives trying to recapture him? In the past prisoners had been pardoned who the governor thought would go straight. They didn't. The first thing Mr. Turner will do when he gets to boot camp is to use his rifle to escape. Mark my words, he has no intentions of being a soldier," a letter to governor read.

When the last day of Talmadge's term of office ended, he did not include Forrest Turner on his list of the prisoners to whom he granted pardons. Forrest Turner's fame as an escape artist made it difficult for Governor Talmadge to release him. Nevertheless, what to do with Mr. Turner and others like him became the challenge for the next governor, Ellis Arnall.

The radios that the warden brought into the prison to hear President Roosevelt remained. The convicts had the choice of listening to baseball games, music, variety shows, and news broadcasts. Popular bands at the time were Glenn Miller and Jimmy Dorsey. The singers were Frank Sinatra, Ella Fitzgerald, and Louie Armstrong. Everyone laughed at "Amos 'n' Andy" and "Abbot and Costello." Prisoners who were not in solitary were allowed to listen in the evenings. The few hours of entertainment took their minds off the misery of prison life.

22 CHESTER TURNER'S FLIGHT

Chester, brother of Forrest Turner, was convicted and sent to the Cherokee Work Camp to serve his sentence for an auto theft in April 1935. He escaped two years later in April 1937, recaptured and escaped again in May 1937. After the death of his brother, Henry, during a police chase and gun battle, he agreed to turn himself in and serve out his sentence.

Mrs. Turner was pleased that her son, Chester, had surrendered June 17, 1937, to Detectives Nahlik and Coppenger. In a bit of remorse, he promised his mother that he would resume serving his remaining prison sentence. He said he wanted to leave prison as a reformed man. Several years had passed since then and Chester Turner was still in prison. He did not keep his promise to his mother or to himself. He escaped from the maximum-security prison in Reidsville, the former home of his brother, Forrest. Known for his many escape attempts, Forrest Turner now had a younger brother who was about to follow in his footsteps.

***

FUGITIVES IN HOSPITAL

"Turner Brother Flees Reidsville"... "Chester Turner and Sam Wheat Wreck Stolen Car"... "Turner Breaks Foot"... "Wheat Breaks Back"

Newspapers reported that while Forrest busted rocks at "Little Alcatraz," Chester pulled off a daring escape from Reidsville.

In January 1941 Chester Turner and another prisoner, Sam Wheat, escaped from the Georgia State Prison in Reidsville. Twenty-two-year-old Chester Turner was serving a four-year-term for assault and a three-year term for auto theft. Sam Wheat, also twenty-two, was serving a life sentence for the murder of an Austell grocery store operator in 1938.

Chester Turner
Forrest's Younger Brother

As part of the new rehabilitation programs which offered prisoners the opportunity to gain experience in a skill, Chester Turner was assigned to the electrical shop and Sam Wheat to the carpentry shed. Because of good behavior they were not considered a flight risk and were allowed freely to roam the yard. When J.H. Widener, a prison pipe plant worker, brought his Plymouth to the prison garage for repairs, Chester Turner was able to have a duplicate key made by a fellow inmate in the machine shop.

Before daylight early Saturday morning the 11th of January, the two managed to unlock their cell door and exit the cell block. They used one of the ladders the maintenance man left behind to climb up on the prison roof which was above the fourth floor on the main building. On each side of the prison were two annex cell blocks. They used the ladder to climb down upon the roof of one of the annex buildings, then onto the roof of the adjacent one-story office building, and finally they were able to climb down to the ground. Undetected by the guards they ran through the yard to where the employees parked their cars. Approaching the employee's Plymouth in the parking lot, Sam Wheat looked at Chester and said, "I hope this key works." A sign of relief overcame them as the key fit and the car cranked.

Although it was dark, the guards in the tower recognized the leaving vehicle as one belonging to an employee. Thus, they made no effort to halt the Plymouth as it eased through the yard and out the gate. The inmates were now fugitives heading in a northerly direction. In less than an hour they had traveled eighteen miles reaching the small community of Cobbtown in north Tattnall County.

Knowing that it would only be a matter of time before the guards realized that they were missing, Sam Wheat pushed the Plymouth as hard as he could. He had successfully maneuvered down the winding road until he reached an unexpected sharp curve. Like his brother Forrest and other escapees who were driving cars and traveling on roads which were unfamiliar to them, Sam Wheat had an accident. Speeding to distance themselves from the law, Sam Wheat lost control and smashed into an embankment. The getaway vehicle was totaled. In the collision, Chester Turner broke his foot and cracked several ribs. Sam Wheat was thrown forward smashing his chest against the steering wheel. His injuries to his rib cage and back were more severe.

A farmer who was repairing a fence heard the noise from the collision and came to investigate. When he arrived, fugitive Wheat was sitting motionless in the car. Leaning forward he had both arms wrapped around the steering wheel and his forehead resting against the back of his hands. Fugitive Turner was moaning and rubbing his foot. "Looking through the window, I believe you fellas need to go to the hospital," suggested the concerned farmer. "Yeah, I am in pain," replied Chester with a grimaced expression. "I can't open the door."

The farmer helped the two out of the wrecked car and drove them eleven miles to Metter Hospital. When the farmer reached the hospital, the two accident victims were taken to the emergency room. When the admitting clerk asked for identification, Chester Turner informed the nurse that they had escaped from Reidsville Prison. "I figured as much, based on your attire, lack of identification and no money," the nurse replied to the fugitive patient.

While the emergency doctor placed a cast on his broken foot and tended to Sam Wheat's bruises, the nurse called the local police and the warden's office at the prison. The police took the fugitives into custody and placed them under guard until a prison official could come and transport them back to Reidsville.

The furious Warden Henderson personally made the trip to Metter to pick up the prisoners. When Warden Henderson arrived, he delivered a stern message. Looking directly at Chester, "You are just like your older brother, Forrest. You just can't stay put in any one place. I have a cell on the fourth floor that we named after your brother because he was in it most of the time while he was here at Reidsville," scolded the irate warden.

The next morning Chester Turner with his broken foot in a cast was sitting in solitary confinement. On a sheet of stationary attached to the cell door was written by one of the guards as a tease, "This cell is dedicated to "Forrest Turner" our most frequent guest." Down the hall laid Sam Wheat in a back brace. In the meantime, unfortunate prison employee Widener was without transportation.

23   MILITARY DUTY

In 1942 the war in Europe raged on. Adolf Hitler was not satisfied with taking over Europe. He also wanted to include Russia in his German empire. Joseph Stalin who gained power after the death of Vladimir Lenin wanted no part of the takeover and ordered his generals to prepare an all-out defense of his country. Hitler's troops advanced to Stalingrad and expected Joseph Stalin to surrender before winter. Instead, his "Red Army" engaged in a grueling counterattack.

In the U.S., the surprise attack on Pearl Harbor had created a fear among the American people. "How can a small island nation thousands of miles away manage to bomb our country? Where was our military?" many had complained. Their spirits were heightened when Jimmy Doolittle led a successful air raid on Japan. Allied forces were also making advances in the Pacific after being victorious at Midway. The Japanese were determined to defeat the Americans at Guadalcanal and keep control of the Pacific. Japanese troops were ordered to fight till victory or death. Kamikaze pilots flew their planes headlong into American war ships with no regard for their own lives. To defeat the Germans and Japanese "Uncle Sam" needed more brave fighting men.

***

Of all the policemen, state patrolmen, and detectives who were responsible in the apprehension of Forrest Turner, none was more uncharacteristic than was Leo Nahlik. He was as unique as a detective as Forrest Turner was an escape artist. As a result, mutual admiration of one another developed.

In 1942 Leo Nahlik had the occasion to be at Reidsville. While there he asked to speak with his old nemesis Forrest Turner. Spending most of his time in his cell, Forrest was glad to have company.

"Forrest, I dropped by to say hello and goodbye," he said with a broad smile. "I am being sworn into the Marines in a couple of days, so I won't be chasing you anymore. I will be going to Parris Island as a 'buck private.' The country needs me."

"That's great. I'm happy to see you. I have been trying to get the governor to pardon me, so I could enlist," Forrest replied.

Leo responded, "Yeah, I read about your meeting with the governor and all the other misbehaving you had been doing. Everyone who is worth their salt is enlisting. My partner Melvin Coppenger decided to join the Navy last month. I hear that the Germans are beating up on my ancestors in France. I wouldn't feel right if I didn't do my part. 'Vive la France' as they say."

They began reminiscing about the past adventures they shared, especially the cat and mouse games they played. "I broke out several times, but you always caught me" Forrest admitted.

Leo responded, "We knew where to look."

"I would have fared better if you hadn't been chasing me," Forrest said with a raised eyebrow. "I never lost my love for my home, family, and Georgia. It was one of my weaknesses. While on the run I did leave Georgia for brief periods, but I always returned home."

Forrest continued, "Why did you choose to go into police work in the first place?"

"It was the excitement. Before becoming a detective, I was a motorcycle racer, a prize fighter, a newspaper photographer, and a newspaper reporter. There was excitement in all those jobs. But tracking down criminals was the most exciting game of all, and I was doing something to better my community. Yes, chasing after you, Forrest, was one of my highlights," replied Leo with a chuckle.

The conversation was very upbeat, until Leo mentioned Slim Scarborough. "If you have not heard Governor Talmadge pardoned Slim yesterday for the purpose of entering the armed services," he revealed.

With that comment Forrest's heart sank. He felt betrayed. Why wasn't he pardoned? "Slim must have used some of the money he saved from the bank robbery to buy his pardon. 'I have four brothers and three nephews who are in the military," he told Leo. "I am really disappointed."

The leave of absence of Detectives Nahlik and Coppenger left the Fulton County Police Department without its best two investigators. The tandem of Nahlik and Coppenger brought before Georgia courts some of the state's most notorious criminals. Chicago had Elliot Ness who was a thorn in the side of gangsters and mobs who were doing business there. Atlanta had Leo Nahlik known as the "gang buster" who did the same in Atlanta. The names of the two detectives for years have been the most feared words to these unscrupulous characters. Nahlik and Coppenger of the 1930s were comparable to the 1950s "Dragnet's" fictional detectives, Joe Friday and Bill Gannon. The pair solved some of Atlanta's most puzzling murders.

***

In May 1943 President Roosevelt confirmed the rumors that German and Italian prisoners of war were being transferred to the United States. President Roosevelt reported to the press, "The White House has approved the acceptance of one hundred seventy-five thousand soldiers captured in Tunisia, North Africa to be held on U.S. military bases until the end of the war. The move was necessitated because the Allied Forces did not have the facilities to house that many prisoners. The P.O.W.s will be closely guarded with many used to do farm work."

The military base at Fort Stewart in Hinesville was approximately forty miles from Georgia State Prison in Reidsville. With the war raging in Europe, troops normally stationed at Fort Stewart were deployed overseas leaving the base nearly empty. Since Fort Stewart had the available space, large numbers of the captured soldiers were sent there. Because many young farmers and agricultural hands enlisted in the military, there weren't enough workers to do the farm labor, P.O.W.s were assigned to tend to the crops and cattle in northern Tattnall County. When it proved to be too time-consuming to transport the prisoners back and forth to Fort Stewart each day, a satellite work camp was established in Reidsville. The facility was found on the outskirts of town only a few miles from the state prison.

It was unknown if Forrest Turner knew that the enemy soldiers who he desperately wanted to fight were right next door. But like Forrest Turner the enemy soldiers were in the same predicament as he... confined to a prison in a small southeast Georgia town.

24 REIDSVILLE ESCAPES

Unable to obtain a pardon to enter military service, Forrest Turner's probability of an early release from Reidsville appeared hopeless. He once again was looking for an opportunity to escape. Over the next twelve months he tried three escapes from Reidsville. The first time he teamed up with two other inmates and fled while working with a road crew. The second attempt Forrest Turner managed to commandeer a guard's car and race to freedom. In both attempts he was recaptured in less than two days. The warden concerned about Forrest Turner's propensity to flee moved him again into solitary confinement on the fourth floor.

Escaping from the fourth floor was believed impossible. Forrest Turner knew it would take a masterful plan to succeed a third time. He also needed outside as well as inside help. He confided in Leland Harvey and Allen Billingsly by sharing his plan and getting their support. The eventual escape attempt went flawlessly. The manner of how it was conducted and the number who escaped was mindboggling. The great escape would go down in Reidsville prison's storied history as the most incredible escape and crowned Forrest Turner as one of Georgia's most famous jailbreakers.

***

Outside the prison walls came encouraging news. April 18, 1942, the nation learned of the infamous Doolittle's raid on Japan. It occurred five months after Japan's sneak attack at Pearl Harbor. It was a crucial time for the American military forces. Some form of retaliation against Japan was necessary to boost morale. It was accomplished by a surprise high-risk, tactical bombing raid. Lieutenant Cornell James led sixteen B-25 bombers from an aircraft carrier and flew seven hundred and fifty miles to bomb strategic military and industrial targets on the Japanese mainland. Because it was too difficult for the large bombers to land on a moving aircraft carrier, the pilots were forced to fly to neutral China and find a place to land before running out of fuel. There were a few unfortunate casualties, but most planes landed with their crews surviving the raid.

***

TURNER WOUNDED IN ESCAPE FROM PRISON

"Turner, Guy Ezell, and Third Convict Flee"... "Trio Working on Collins-Metter Highway"... "Men Leap into a Truck and Speed Away"... "Forrest Shot in Shoulder During Escape"... "Guards Unable to Prevent Getaway"... "Fugitives Last Seen Headed Toward Collins"

Since the front pages of local newspapers were dedicated to the coverage of World War II, Forrest Turner's latest adventure on April 19th received little attention.

Forrest Turner, Guy Ezell, and Harry Smith were working on a road crew April 19, 1942. Guy Ezell was the son of a preacher residing in Rome, Georgia. In 1939 he was convicted of murdering his former manager at a shoe department store in Bibb County. The manager, upset with his performance, fired him. Guy Ezell later went to the manager to ask for his job back. When the manager refused, an argument ensued. In a fit of anger, he pulled out a pistol and shot him four times. The sensational murder shocked the members of the church and the community.

Harry Smith on the other hand was convicted of a lesser crime. His stay at Reidsville was the result of a theft charge committed in Rockdale County.

When a guard returned from delivering a load of dirt, Forrest Turner noticed that he had inadvertently left the key in the ignition. He knew it would be easy to jump into the cab and drive off. He told Guy Ezell, "When the guards are not paying attention, I am heading to the truck. You and Harry are welcome to come with me. If you decide to come, you had better run fast, or I will leave you."

When everyone had stopped working to eat their lunch, the opportunity presented itself. Forrest Turner briskly walked to the truck followed by the other two. One of the guards was quick to notice the attempted getaway and began to shoot. As Forrest Turner opened the driver's side door, buckshot pellets hit him in the shoulder. He froze temporarily but managed to climb inside and slam the door. "Are you alright?" asked Guy.

Forrest grabbing his shoulder, "I will be okay. I can still drive but it just burns a little." The truck sped away as pellets from the second shot whistled harmlessly by.

Once the escapees were a safe distance away, they spotted a 1939 Chevrolet in the front yard of a Collins resident. They hurriedly abandoned the truck and stole the vehicle. The owner witnessed the theft from her kitchen window. Figuring that the men were probably runaway convicts, she was afraid to go outside. Instead, she called the police.

They were only able to travel five miles before the alerted highway patrolman recognized the stolen Chevrolet as it zoomed by. To avoid being captured Forrest Turner steered the car off the main highway onto an abandoned road. When he tried to drive through a creek that ran across the road, the engine flooded, and the car stalled. Given no other choice they waded through the creek, ran into the underbrush, and disappeared into the swamp.

Reidsville's Warden Lawrence put out a statewide alert. John E. Goodwin, director of the state patrol, had his men begin an intensive search on the highways in the area. "I don't know what to think of Forrest," he murmured under his breath. "I had encouraged the governor to pardon him, so he could join the army. Since the governor didn't, I guess Forrest has found another way to get out of prison."

It was learned that Betty Ann Jones, female friend of Forrest Turner was reported to be in Savannah. With that information the state patrol assumed that he would try to meet up with her. By one o'clock a posse, including guards with bloodhounds and local police had entered the swamp in pursuit. Unable to see in the darkness, the search was cancelled at 10:00 p.m.

The fugitives ran until they no longer heard the barking dogs. Forrest Turner was totally exhausted. His shoulder had stopped bleeding, but what began as a burning sensation now became a painful throb. Forrest Turner sat down with his back against a large pine in anticipation of spending a cool April night in the swamp.

The next morning the trio stole another automobile and immediately robbed a local store in Collins taking clothes, bandages, and supplies. When the police were notified of a robbery at a local store, they concentrated their search along the road to Metter. Knowing that they were sitting ducks if they were seen on the main road, Forrest began looking for a hideout. He soon spotted an abandoned house in the distance. "I need to rest and tend to my shoulder before it gets infected," he told the others as he steered off the main road.

Tired and hungry he persuaded Guy Ezell to take the car and go to the nearest grocery store for food and more provisions. The City of Collins was not a large town. It was easy for officers to stake out all the retail locations where the trio might stop. When Guy Ezell arrived at the store, the officers who were watching from a distance rushed in and seized him. Guy Ezell, with a basket filled with groceries in hand but no weapon, quickly surrendered. Handcuffed and sitting in the back seat of the guard's car, he directed them to the abandoned house. Within a few minutes the other two surprised fugitives joined Guy Ezell in the back seat. The stolen merchandise was returned to the store, and the fugitives were taken to Reidsville.

Forrest Turner reconciled that his haphazard escape was a pitiful effort. Not only was he caught but he was wounded as well. Lucky for Forrest Turner, the guard was a good distance away when he fired his shotgun at the fleeing prisoners. Had the guard used a rifle the shot could have been deadly. Forrest Turner's sixth escape lasted less than two days. Trudging through the muddy swamp left him exhausted and in pain. During his liberty he spent the night in a South Georgia swamp with an aching shoulder.

It was a relief to be sent back to Reidsville and have the prison doctor tend to his wound. It was the second time he had been wounded. The other time he took pellets to the abdomen and wrist.

***

It would be approximately ten months before Forrest Turner would try another escape. He was confined to an individual cell and no longer had the freedom to roam about the yard or rejoin the road crew. Thinking that he had learned his lesson, the warden eventually moved him from isolation. He was placed in the cell block where prisoners were allowed to work in the yard during the day. However, because of his reputation he would remain under constant watch.

Forrest Turner hoped that the next attempt would be his last. If successful he would go to Canada where he would change his name and start a new life. "The police and detectives will never think of looking for me up there," he convinced himself. For the fear of getting recognized and recaptured, he would never come back to Georgia. He would get an honest job and do his best to avoid being sent to prison again. He would miss the occasional visit from his mother and siblings. But it was the only way to gain his much sought after freedom.

TURNER OUT AGAIN

"Sly Forrest Turner Fools Guard"... "Wielded Fake Gun to Gain Freedom"... "Stole Guard's Vehicle and Fled"... "Recaptured Same Afternoon"... "No Other Details Available"

On February 3, 1943, Forrest Turner had another trick up his sleeve. He used a wooden gun made from a peach crate and covered it with black shoe polish. The makeshift gun fooled the guard who surrendered his weapon and keys to his car. Within minutes the fugitive Turner drove out of the compound leaving the guard watching helplessly. A call alerted the highway patrol who spotted the stolen car, gave chase and quickly apprehended the fugitive. Thus, ending Forrest Turner's futile escape effort two hours later. The fake gun was found in the vehicle.

***

More importantly, the front-page news was Germany's first defeat at the hands of the Russians at Stalingrad. The tide of the war was turning in favor of the Allied forces. Unbeknownst to the Germans, Army code breakers were intercepting and decoding messages. As a result, the U.S. Air Force was able to find and sink the menacing U-boats.

Back at Reidsville a major prison break was about to occur that would stun prison officials and law enforcement.

TURNER AND HARVEY BLACK OUT PRISON AND LEAD MASSIVE ESCAPE

"Two Dozen Convicts Flee Reidsville, Led by Turner and Harvey"... "Power Plant Wrecked, No Electricity, Telephone Wires Cut"... "Three Vehicles Filled with Convicts Leave in Total Darkness, No Shots Fired"... "Warden Duvall on the Hot Seat"

The newspaper coverage of the mass exodus extended beyond Georgia. A New York newspaper article reported that the escape occurred in the early hours of April 16, 1943. "Twenty-four criminals including thirty-year-old Forrest Turner and thirty-four-year-old Leland Harvey broke out of the escape-proof Tattnall Prison in Reidsville. It was the largest prison break in the institution's brief history. Forrest Turner's fourth escape from Reidsville prison defied imagination. It was the crowning achievement of all his escapes. Never has anyone managed to free two dozen convicts from a state maximum-security prison without a single shot being fired. It would be the final straw for Warden Duvall who was under heavy criticism because his prisoners seemed to have their way at the prison.

The missing inmates were housed on the fourth floor, which was home for the state's most incorrigible prisoners. Thursday night April 15th, Forrest Turner and Leland Harvey orchestrated the escape. Forrest Turner was facing long-term sentences for larceny, robbery and kidnapping. Leland Harvey, who was recently transferred from Alcatraz in California, was serving three to five and eight to ten-year terms for larceny and robbery. Forrest Turner had spent months cutting through the bars of his cell. By using black shoe polish, he was able to camouflage the cut marks. The pair had duplicate keys made for the front gate and bribed a guard to smuggle in a pistol. For their own safety, the guards stationed in that section of the prison were not armed. So, when the night guard stepped off the elevator to do his midnight inspection, he was easily overpowered, stripped of his keys to the individual cells and locked in an empty cell.

***

Forrest Turner and Leland Harvey had been planning the escape for several months. To get out of their cell block and out of the front gate, they would have to take over the prison. To carry out such an impossible task, they needed the help of the other convicts on the cell block. Their best chance for escape would be after midnight when the fewest number of guards were on duty.

Forrest Turner kicked loose the cut-weakened bars and slipped through the hole. He immediately went to the elevator to wait for the night Guard Morrison to arrive. He knew the guard arrived at 12:00 p.m. to conduct the night inspection. As the guard stepped

Leland Harvey
Criminal from Macon, Georgia

off the elevator and the door closed, Forrest Turner pointed a pistol at the unsuspected and astonished guard.

"Good evening, Mr. Morrison. The convicts and I are going to take over the prison, and you are going to help us!" Forrest ordered as he pointed the pistol at him.

Morrison froze and was speechless. "How did Turner get out of his cell and where did he get a gun?" he wondered.

"We want your keys," Forrest added.

With the keys Forrest Turner freed Leland Harvey who proceeded to release the other prisoners on the cell block. He locked the puzzled Morrison in one of the cells and tied him to the bolted down leg of the cell bunk. Many of the prisoners had no prior knowledge of an escape attempt. So understandably there was pandemonium and jubilation on the fourth floor as each cell door was unlocked and the inmate released.

With all the prisoners standing in the hallway, Forrest and Leland told the prisoners of their plan. "First, three men are going down to the first floor and take over the switchboard located in the radio room. When they get in there, they will call the other guards and have them individually come up here by giving them a false pretense. When the guard gets off the elevator, I want you to disarm them, take them to an empty cell, tie them to the bunk, and lock the gate," instructed Forrest.

He added, "We don't want any violence. You hear!"

Forrest Turner remained with the prisoners and kept them under control while Leland Harvey, Allen Billingsley, and another inmate, went to the radio room and took over the switchboard. Disguising his voice, Leland Harvey phoned Guards Overstreet and Spivey with instructions to come up to the fourth floor. When each arrived, he was greeted by inmates who quickly locked them in an empty cell. Before leaving the radio room, Leland Harvey cut the main telephone line to prevent any outgoing or incoming calls.

With all the guards within the prison walls out of commission,

Forrest Turner disclosed the remaining details of their plan. Hearing that they would soon be free, the prisoners began cheering and acting like a bunch of out-of-control school children. One of the prisoners shouted, "Warden Duvall told us that the prisoners weren't going to run his prison while he was in charge, but guess who is running the joint now!"

"Settle down now," Forrest yelled. "You're right. We are now in control of the prison. In an hour we are all to meet downstairs. As soon as the power goes out, we will gather in the yard. The guards in the towers will be unable to see us but they can still hear us. So, you've got to be quiet. We will all leave from there at the same time," he told the anxious prisoners. "Until it's time to leave, you are on your own. Stay out of trouble!"

The prisoners scattered. He hoped that they would lay low and not cause a disturbance that would alert the guards in the watch tower. Some went to the guard's barracks and helped themselves to the guns and ammunition, and whatever else that was available. Some went to the supply room to gather tools and clothes which would be useful after their escape. They took all the packs of Lucky Strike, Camel, and Chesterfield cigarettes they could get their hands on. Several went to the kitchen where trusties were cooking meals for the night guards. There they enjoyed the guard's steak dinner.

Forrest Turner went up to the fifth floor referred to as "Death Row." At the end of the hall in a separate chamber was the "electric chair" which was recently moved from Milledgeville. Prisoners who were scheduled for execution were locked in individual cells and separated from the other prisoners. Once sentenced to death a prisoner could expect the execution to occur quickly. The final hope rested with the governor who had the power to commute the sentence to life. There were never more than five people on "Death Row." On this day only one prisoner was waiting for his turn.

As Forrest unlocked the door to cell number 3 and told him, "You are free to come with us."

The prisoner sitting on his bunk replied in a faint voice, "Boss, I am ready to meet my Maker. I don't want to go."

"The surprised Forrest Turner said. "Are you sure?" I figured of all the prisoners who are here at Reidsville, you would be the first to want to leave!"

The prisoner just lowered his head and remained silent. Somewhat puzzled by his answer, Forrest Turner closed the cell door and left.

The most important prisoner on this day was the one who had worked as an electrician before being arrested for burglary. He went to the power plant which was out of view from the watch tower. There he was able to disable the unit. All the lights and electricity for the entire prison went out. It was pitch black. The guards in the tower assumed it was some type of power outage. They tried to call the radio room to figure out what had happened, but the phone lines were dead.

In the darkness the group of twenty-four prisoners slowly walked into the yard and stole two prison trucks. Forrest Turner, Leland Harvey, and Allen Billingsley took Guard Morrison's sedan. From the observation station in the tower the guards had a panoramic view of the grounds and buildings. At night only two armed guards with loaded rifles were on duty. Without lighting they were unable to see the men escaping. With the key in hand Leland Harvey unlocked the front gate, and the caravan drove to freedom. The fugitives included three who were convicted of murder while others were serving time for either burglary, robbery, forgery, assault, and larceny or a combination. All the crimes occurred in Georgia with several committed in counties surrounding the Atlanta area.

Not a shot was fired, and no guards were harmed. The ease of the escape was unbelievable, especially since Reidsville was built to be escape-proof. With no communication or electrical power, it took a while before officials outside the prison became aware of the break. It was not until one of the prisoners, who had second thoughts, turned himself in at the Reidsville Police Station that the massive manhunt began. In the meantime, the fugitives had a lengthy head start.

Two of the prisoners were captured within a few hours near Lyons and Vidalia when their stolen truck overturned in a ditch. The other passengers in trucks went scurrying in all directions and managed to elude the bloodhounds. Forrest Turner abandoned Morrison's stolen sedan fourteen miles northeast of Cobbtown. He and the two other fugitives with him stole another vehicle and headed to Savannah. Several days later a fisherman found the body of one of the escapees. He had tried to cross the Ohoopee River south of Reidsville, unable to swim he drowned.

Leland Harvey's reputation as a "prison escape Houdini" equaled that of Forrest Turners. His most sensational break came on May 4, 1933 when he and another inmate forced their way out of a cell on "Death Row" at the Milledgeville State Prison. A career criminal, he was first sentenced for robbery in 1924. In 1933 the compassionate Governor Eugene Talmadge pardoned him after serving only a few years of the more than the several decades he had yet to serve. Now he was on the loose again.

Governor Arnall was outraged when the escape news reached the Capitol. He immediately called the prison. "Warden Duvall why didn't the guards in the tower shoot them?" asked the governor.

The warden replied, "The guards said it was too dark to see. They said they heard the trucks crank up, but figured it was guards leaving the prison to check on the power outage. They tried to call the switchboard to get an explanation, but the phone was dead. They had no clue that prisoners were escaping until they were long gone." "Those prisoners must have had inside help," said the governor as he slammed down the phone.

Concerned about the large number of dangerous criminals on the loose in southeast Georgia, the governor considered calling the National Guard to help in the search. He was told that most of the regiment had already been called to duty in Europe. It would be up to the highway patrol and the local police to find and apprehend the escapees, a very formidable task.

In haste he issued an executive order requiring the Georgia Prison Commission to investigate the recent escape from the Reidsville Prison. Included in the order was a requirement that the commission have their written findings on his desk within five days. The governor also said the state would pay a one-hundred-dollar reward for the return of each escapee, whether dead or alive.

***

A week later, on the night of April 24th, Savannah police captured Forrest Turner. The young escape specialist, who they learned was the mastermind of the breakout from Reidsville's prison, was unable to elude a lone policeman. A motorcycle patrolman who recognized the stolen vehicle as it was heading toward the Savannah River began chasing the three men seen in the car. He was soon joined by a patrol car from where an officer fired shots at the fleeing car. After shooting and deflating the back tires, the vehicle came to a stop. The two patrolmen rushed to the driver's side with their weapons drawn. Forrest Turner surrendered without a struggle. The passengers Leland Harvey and Allen Billingsley exited out to the other side, ran into the marsh disappearing in the darkness. Inside the car the police found a pump action shotgun and a pistol stolen from the prison.

Forrest Turner was taken to police headquarters. The next day he was allowed to give an interview to a local newspaper reporter. "Had you not been captured last night, where were you headed?" the reporter asked while standing outside of Forrest's cell.

Forrest replied, "Had the police not been so lucky in catching me, I would have made my way to Canada and joined the Canadian Army. I feel like the country could use me."

Forrest Turner was secretive about disclosing his activities while on the loose. He did admit to stealing the car he was driving in Macon and the clothes he was wearing in Anniston, Alabama. "Forrest, the police found ten nice suits and other articles of clothing in your possession; why all those business suits?" asked the reporter with a grin.

"I always want to make a good impression when I rob someone," Forrest remarked. "What do you think of this blue one I am wearing?"

The reporter studied the quality of the suit and answered with a grin, "I am afraid you won't be needing those fancy clothes at Reidsville. The warden doesn't like his prisoners to be dressed better than him. You will be wearing your old prison clothes again." Forrest Turner was amused by the comment replied, "Yeah, it doesn't take much to out dress the warden."

When the last of the escaped convicts were recaptured in Chicago, the governor paid two thousand three hundred dollars in individual rewards for the return of prisoners. It concluded the last chapter of Forrest Turner's sensational Reidsville's escape.

Forrest Turner was credited with eleven successful escape attempts. Many were short-lived. After each escape he returned to his roots, the State of Georgia. And each time he was recaptured. For his "French Leaves" he was punished with lengthy stays in solitary confinement. He recovered from the gunshots from the earlier escapes. All that remained were scars. The once boastful and the best self-proclaimed escape artist was now a beaten-down man. He had reached the low point of his imprisonment.

The worst times he experienced while in prison thus far was not the hard labor while on the chain gang but the periods of isolation in solitary confinement. Previously his stays were limited to a week or two. Now it appeared he would be in seclusion for an extended time. Forrest Turner was eventually allowed to leave confinement and work in the yard shackled and under constant watch.

Prison officials knew that there were certain times when a prisoner would do anything to get out; when he was constantly bullied by the guards, the death of a family member or Christmas. Guessing that Forrest Turner would try another escape during Christmas, the warden placed him back in solitary during the entire month of December. He was determined to put Forrest Turner where he could keep a special eye on him. As added punishment for his many escapes he was allowed only bread and water while there.

Lying on his bed he reminisced about his childhood in Henry County. Most Christmases were simple. Santa brought only a few gifts. But dinner with the family was the happiest time of the year for him. Being locked up with no one to share the special holiday prolonged the misery.

Christmas day, in depths of depression, Forrest Turner was visited by a Trusty, who was an elderly Black prisoner, Colquitt "Pap" Dwight. "Hey Forrest, I have a little package for you," he said with a smile. It was wrapped in an old newspaper and small enough to slide through the bars. "I had a little extra, so I wanted you to have it," he said. Before he continued down the hall, he paused for a few minutes to watch Forrest's reaction.

The visit was so unexpected, Forrest Turner didn't say a word. He just got up from his bed, took the package and nodded with approval. Inside the package were raisins, a stick of candy, and a cigar. When he unwrapped the package and saw what was inside, he became glassy-eyed. He couldn't remember the last time anyone had done anything nice for him, especially an inmate. He began to cry. He never forgot the gesture. "Those were the best raisins and candy he had ever eaten," he recounted.

Convict Dwight was at Reidsville only a few days when Forrest Turner saw a guard slap him and knock him to the ground. Helping him to his feet, he said. "The next time you meet a guard take off your hat, bow your head and say 'Yeah, Sir.' The guard will most likely leave you alone from then on."

While all eyes were focused on Forrest Turner and Leland Harvey, others were escaping from the farm, road gangs, and the yard. As a result, the warden, totally fed up with the number of escapes, instituted the draconian use of ball and chain to keep the prisoners at home. "With all the fourth-floor cells full, there is no room for any more recaptured fugitives," declared the warden. "Furthermore, escaping from here has become an epidemic."

Of the twenty-three convicts who escaped with Forrest Turner, all but two had at least one successful escape either from Reidsville or one of the county work camps. Forrest Turner was the first to get shackled and became a charter member of the gang.

25 PRISON SYSTEM

It has been several years since Forrest Turner entered the Georgia prison system. Much had changed from his initial stay at Fulton Tower, transfer to Thomas County Work Camp and eventual transfer to the new Georgia State Prison in Reidsville. To his disappointment, what was originally to be a short prison term had expanded to multiple years. He had experienced some of the worst conditions as a convict at Georgia work camps and prisons. His situation improved as a movement was afoot by Georgia's governor to institute prison reform.

***

In 1934, when Forrest Turner was arrested and convicted of auto theft, the Georgia prison system was emerging from a difficult financial period. The Great Depression had caused significant cutbacks in all government programs. Legislators considered prison budgets as a low priority when so many government programs needed funding. Convicts at the work camps felt the impact of the budget cuts the most. Convicts like Forrest Turner were already enduring substandard housing conditions, meager meals, and inadequate medical treatment. Inmates were forced to work longer hours on roads, farms, and in stone quarries.

During this period the number of misdemeanor crimes increased resulting in more arrests and convictions. As unemployment rose so did the prison population. The outraged public demanded stiffer and longer sentences as a means of controlling their frequency. "Repeat offenders should remain in jail indefinitely, until they learn not to rob or steal," said a recent angry victim. At the time when more prison space was needed, prison budgets were decreased. Prison facilities became outdated and overcrowded.

The Georgia prison system was in dire need of additional beds. Those convicted of murder, robbery, bootlegging, or burglary were sent to Georgia facilities. The accused were tried in the county superior courts where local juries and judges determined their punishment. Based on the severity of the crime, the guilty were either sent to work camps or to a state prison. Forrest Turner and his band of thieves populated the various work camps and prisons. The maximum-security prison in Milledgeville was so overcrowded the prisoners who were scheduled to enter had to be held in the county jails until vacancies became available.

The segregation of Georgia prisoners was paramount. Minor non-violent offenders should be moved to minimum-security prisons while serious offenders such as murderers would be housed in the new maximum-security prison. The mentally ill and drug addicted should be sent to a medically staffed institution. Juveniles and women should have their own separate facilities.

Franklin Roosevelt's administration was keenly aware of the national problem of overcrowded and inadequate prisons. Through his New Deal Public Works Program, funds were distributed to states to help pay for prison construction. Georgia used its allocation to construct a modern correction facility in Tattnall County, referred to as Reidsville. The old, antiquated Georgia State Prison in Milledgeville built in 1899 was phased out as the state's maximum-security prison. The new Reidsville's prison would take its place.

The early 1930s saw little progress in prison reform as the state was beset with economic hardships. Despite these challenges efforts slowly began to emerge that would improve the criminal justice system in Georgia. It began with the opening of the new prison at Reidsville in 1936. Followed by the election of Ellis Arnall as governor who promised to prioritize the problem of the inhumane treatment of inmates. Taking the advice from consultants, his administration initiated an aggressive agenda of change for the prison system. By having a modern facility, the state would be able to introduce several rehabilitation programs.

"All these changes and improvements to our prison systems are going to cost money," Governor Arnall predicted. "By electing me I have the full support of the majority voters in Georgia to spend the money."

Even though the infrastructure was in place, it would still be a few years before the inmates would see the benefits. How quickly these ambitious programs got established depended on Wiley Moore, the new director of the Georgia Board of Corrections. The changes couldn't come soon enough for Forrest Turner and the other prisoners.

From years of neglect, the nation's prison system was also in a mess. To accommodate the increasing number of those convicted of federal crimes, a new facility was constructed on McDonough Boulevard in Atlanta. The U.S. Penitentiary accommodated the nation's worst criminals. Those found guilty by juries in Federal Courts of racketeering, bank robbery, fraud, drugs or tax evasion were sent there...as were gangster Al Capone and swindler Carlos Ponzi. The opening of the Atlanta Penitentiary and expansion of Reidsville Prison allowed the State of Georgia to house six thousand state and federal convicted felons.

26 "EIGHT BALL SQUAD"

The mass prisoner exodus from the fourth floor was the catalyst for major changes at Reidsville. First the warden punished the violators by putting them in balls and chains and then the governor called for an investigation of the prison. During the investigation Forrest Turner was able to voice in detail his treatment while at the various work camps and Reidsville to those who came to listen. From the findings by the prison commission the governor appointed a director of corrections to initiate changes. Wiley Moore made a special trip to Reidsville to introduce his penal reform program to the prisoners. His message and promise would positively affect Forrest Turner's future.

***

The usual sentence imposed by a judge for a guilty offender was hard labor. The prisoners remained in the local jails until the prison commission assigned them to a county work camp. The State of Georgia had the distinction of being the first state to employ convict labor to maintain its roads. In the individual counties convicts were expected to do labor as members of chain gangs. At that time, the largest maximum-security prison in Georgia was Georgia State Prison located in Milledgeville. It was replaced by a modern facility in Reidsville in 1937. Reidsville had an elaborate agriculture program where inmates raised enough beef, dairy, poultry, and grew vegetables to help feed the prison population. It had a cannery, garage, and metal shop where the state's auto tags were made. The facility had workshops where the inmates performed various crafts and trades.

In southern politics, state government department heads were appointed by the governor. Many of the appointees were selected as repayment for contributions to their campaigns, some were family related, and others were loyal party members. In the past, the newly appointed department heads in state government were not always the most qualified candidates. Each new governor generally appointed those to whom he owed a political favor. The governor handpicked the director of the prison system, the members of the prison commission, and the members of the pardon and parole board. In addition, the governor had the authority to commute sentences and pardon prisoners.

Governor Eugene Talmadge appointed his cousin, Rolly Lawrence, who was a policeman in Milledgeville, as the new warden at Reidsville. Under this arrangement it was said that it was politics that managed the largest Georgia prison. The question many asked, "Shouldn't an experienced penologist be in charge of Reidsville?" As expected, it did not matter who the governor chose, the decisions and policies by the new department heads often faced criticism from political opponents. None received more public scrutiny than the director of prisons.

Forrest Turner entered the Georgia prison system in 1934. He was transferred to Thomas County Work Camp where he wore leg irons twenty-four hours a day. Over the next nine years more humane treatment for convicts was imposed. The prisoners at Reidsville who obeyed the rules and were not a flight risk were allowed to work in the prison workshops and farms without strict supervision. Those who had a history of escape attempts found themselves sent to solitary confinement. When escapes occurred from the maximum-security floor, Warden Duvall resorted to more desperate measures. Under fire the infuriated warden reinstituted the ball and chain system. Forrest Turner and a host of so-called "runners" who had been transferred from work camps to Reidsville were forced to wear a heavy ball and chain.

Surprisingly, the use of ball and chain was not considered as "cruel and unusual punishment" as prohibited by the Eighth Amendment. Thus, several prisons and work camps continued to allow their use. The prisoners at Reidsville referred to the inmates shackled with the ball and chain as members of the "Eight Ball Squad." To those not familiar with the term, the iron ball used to restrain the convicts resembled the black-numbered eight ball used in the game of pool. The combination weight of the ball and chain was approximately forty pounds and severely limited the inmate's mobility. "It was like having a boat anchor tied around your ankles," as Forrest described the heavy ball.

The governor also took exception to Forrest Turner and the three vehicles full of prisoners who drove out the front gate of Reidsville in April 1943. The incident brought the security of the prison into question. The governor suggested to the press that the escapees had inside help. "I am going to get to the bottom of this incredible escape," he vowed. He issued an executive order instructing the prison commission to make a full investigation into the management of the prison.

The members of the commission made a tour of the Reidsville Prison. They had particular interest in the fourth floor where the April escape originated. While there the commission interviewed several prisoners individually. Members of the commission were eager to speak with Forrest Turner.

"Sit down Forrest. The three of us from the Georgia Prison Commission are investigating conditions here at Reidsville. We know you have been an inmate here for several years. We would like to ask you a few questions. Nothing that you tell us will get you into trouble. So, speak your mind," the chairman, Clem Rainey said.

The chairman continued, "Reidsville is supposed to be a maximum-security prison, but it appears to have become a vacation resort for the prisoners. We were surprised to learn that the counterfeiting of coins was taking place at the machine shop inside the prison. Hidden at the farm were liquor stills operated by prisoners who distributed the moonshine to the inmates. We heard that women prisoners were allowed to have sexual activity with guards and male inmates for money. And that pass keys that fit locks including the front gate were readily available in the prison. Is it true that inmates in the metal shop were reproducing copies from a stolen key?"

To that question Forrest just smiled and nodded his head. The chairman continued, "One of the other prisoners told us he estimated there were as many as seventy-five keys held by inmates. A few prisoners were known to leave their cell at night, walk out of the prison building, roam around the yard, and go into the shops before returning to their cells by midnight. There was no telling what they were making in the shops. Would you comment on these accusations."

Forrest raised his eyebrows and smiled. "If you had money, you could buy cigarettes, whiskey, keys or even women. I was never lucky enough to share a bed with a woman while I have been here. Since I don't drink or smoke, I had no interest in the whiskey or cigarettes."

"That's too bad. Tell us more about this 'love nest' over here," one asked inquisitively.

Very amused Forrest answered, "Well, if a prisoner had the money and the desire, he could make an arrangement with one of the night guards to be with a woman in private for one hour."

Forrest changed the subject, "Speaking about money I want to make a comment about the clemency system in Georgia for us prisoners. In the past I could have gotten a pardon if I had enough money. It would have taken at least five thousand dollars. I didn't have that much," he said. "But others, who committed worse crimes than me, had the money and the right connections with influential friends, got pardons. That's wrong!"

None of the commission members made any comments. They just looked at each other. All were newly appointed by Governor Arnall, and had no knowledge that pardons were being bought.

"What are the conditions here at Reidsville?" asked one of the commission members, Vivian Stanley. "How are you being treated?"

"I would like it here much better if I wasn't tied to the ball and chain. The guard took them off before I came into the room and he will put them back on when I leave. Things seem to be looking up, however, with our new governor. One of the smartest things he has done was to take pardon business out of politics. Going forward, a prisoner must earn his parole. The appointment of Wiley Moore, who was recently appointed director of Georgia's Board of Corrections, and new Warden Duvall will bring changes to Reidsville, good changes. I might begin to like staying here," remarked Forrest with a chuckle.

"What do you know about these fake coins?" another member of the commission, Royal Mann, asked.

Forrest answered, "Yeah, I had some. They used a plaster of Paris mold. They would melt down a piece of tin and pour it into the mold. When it hardened, you had a fifty-cent piece. It looked pretty real, I admit." Forrest added, "No one in prison took a half dollar without first sticking it in their mouth and biting down on it to see if the coin bent."

"So where did you get the tin?" continued the curious Mr. Rainey.

Forrest replied, "After the numbers and letters were pressed onto a sheet of tin in the metal shop by the convicts who made license plates, they trimmed the borders around the new license plate. They then collected and saved the tin scraps to be used to make coins when guards weren't around.

"That's interesting. Where did you use the fake coins?"

"They were used in the commissary until the cashier there got wise and wouldn't take the bad money. Then the fellas stopped making the coins."

"How is it that so many of you have escaped from here? Do you care to tell us or is it a secret?" was the next question.

"Because of the limited number of guards, movement within the prison was relatively easy at night. We knew what time guards made their rounds and where they were always stationed," replied Forrest.

"So where did you get the tools and items that you used in your breakout?"

"As I said, if you had money, you could get anything, food, liquor, knives, files, and even a pistol. These poor guards are not paid a lot. They appreciated what few dollars they could pick up doing an inmate a favor," he volunteered.

Mr. Rainey asked, "Warden Duvall told us that he discovered a fifty-gallon still in the cannery and a twenty-gallon cauldron in a tunnel under the prison. How did you convicts boil the spirits without being seen?"

"The fella making the whiskey tapped into the steam pipes used to heat the prison to boil the mixture," Forrest divulged. "I was told the way some of the inmates were carrying on at night with their loud talk and singing, that they must have drunk moonshine."

Forrest Turner continued talking as he often did when he had something important on his mind. "What's wrong with the old prison system is that most prisoners have nothing to do. They have too much idle time on their hands. Once a prisoner is released, he has no skills, and no job. He soon is doing what he did before. That is to steal and possibly harm his victim. I have met ex-convicts who made their time but before too long they were back in prison. I would like to have an opportunity to gain experience in a skill. One day I am going to be paroled. If I had a job, I wouldn't be tempted to steal. When I get out, I want to be prepared to cope with civilian life with no chance of returning to prison."

***

Forrest Turner was now on the "Eight Ball Squad." The reward for having had numerous successful escapes earned him the right to

Wiley Moore
Director of Georgia Board
of Corrections

be included in that select group. Forrest Turner and Leland Harvey were the first to be fitted with the cumbersome restraints.

Governor Arnall knew that Reidsville was in a mess. He did not have to hear that from the inmates. Rumors had circulated for some time about the lax oversight at the prison. To make the change he appointed Wiley Moore to lead the Georgia Department of Corrections. Mr. Moore was a wealthy and successful businessman. He had taken the position without pay. His only goal was to reform the prison system by stressing better treatment of prisoners. Mr. Moore made a special trip to Reidsville in October 1943 to meet with the prisoners. First, he met with prisoners with lengthy or life sentences. The sixty-three inmates known as the "Eight Ball Squad" consisted of Reidsville's most notorious inmates. Many considered Forrest Turner to be the worst of the lot.

Once all the prisoners were seated, he looked around the room. "Where is Forrest Turner?" he asked. When he saw a raised hand, he motioned for Forrest to come up.

Forrest Turner slowly shuffled his way to where speaker Moore was standing while lugging his forty-pound ball. Mr. Moore grabbed a hold of the chain and picked up the ball that was attached. "Mighty heavy isn't it," he said as he looked Forrest in the eye. Forrest smiled, nodded in agreement, and painstakingly shuffled his way back to his seat.

"I'll be as good to you as you'll let me be. If you go down the line with me, to help to build up a name for this institution, I'll be in there pitching for you. Beginning today, all of you are on the honor roll of this prison. What happens to you from now on will depend on your own conduct. Beginning today all of you will be fed from the same spoon; all will get the same consideration. I don't know or care what your mistakes were in the past. Today the past is wiped out," Wiley Moore promised.

Hearing his remarks everyone's ears perked up as they listened intensely. Mr. Moore paused a moment to let the murmur among the convicts die down. "Yes, I said. You will be given a clean slate. 'Do Right, Get Out!' That should be your goal." he emphasized.

He addressed the guards who were standing in the back of the room, as the convicts listened, "Going forward I don't want prisoners cursed! I want you guards to be as courteous and decent to the prisoners as you would have them be to you." A few chants of "yeah," "you bet," and "damn right" echoed in the room.

Mr. Moore continued, "We want to work toward making the prison self-sustaining as soon as possible. A dietitian will be employed to assure every inmate gets a balanced, well-prepared meal. We have plans to add a bakery. We will install industries within the prison so that each of you can learn a vocation that will assure you gainful employment after you leave here. A placement office will be set up. When you are discharged, they will arrange interviews with businesses looking for your skill level. I am also happy to report that as soon as the cloth for new uniforms can be obtained the old 'stripes' will be discarded. With those remarks all the eight-ballers cheered. I promised the governor that I would bring this prison from the 'dark ages' to the present."

After two hours of speaking to the eight ballers, Mr. Moore addressed the other prisoners. He promised vocational training by installing classes taught by qualified teachers. He expected the Reidsville prison to be self-sufficient. He mentioned that the state would invest money to upgrade the farms to increase yields. From the skills learned by the inmates, this prison will manufacture goods needed by other institutions not just license plates. He told the women that a nursing school will offer accredited courses. "I want all of you to be informed. There is a war going on, you know. We will install radios on every floor so you can keep up with the events out in the world," he said. "For those of you who can't, or have trouble reading and writing, we can teach you how. You have an abundance of free time on your hands to learn if you want. For recreation, a baseball diamond will be built here at Reidsville. How many of you in here would like to play ball?" he asked as he searched the room looking for raised hands. "And finally, I have arranged for a full-time chaplain to come here to counsel you and offer spiritual advice. Lord knows you need it."

Everybody laughed.

Leland Harvey who was sitting next to Forrest whispered in his ear, "If they will do all that, which I doubt, I may decide to stay put. How about you?"

"It's the best news I have heard in a long time," Forrest replied. "His mind was racing. It's exactly what I told the commission board when they interviewed me. They had listened. If this is true, my prayers have been answered."

Mr. Moore continued to field questions. One of the topics that received attention was the subject of work camps. "What are you going to do about the terrible conditions at the county work camps?" a fella in the back yelled out.

Mr. Moore was quick to answer, "I would like to see the state abolish these and eliminate the use of chain gangs to work on the roads. In my brief time as commissioner, I have received many complaints and heard of an untold number of horror stories from former convicts."

The governor and I discussed the expansion plans for this prison. We are going to increase the size from thirteen hundred to three thousand inmates. We will fill the added space with convicts who will be moved from closed work camps.

Wiley Moore received a standing ovation from all the groups of enthusiastic inmates who listened to his reform plans.

The next day Forrest Turner and the "Eight Ball Squad" assembled in the yard. One by one the shackles were removed from each inmate. To the delight of the inmates and at the persistence of Mr. Moore, the balls and chains were thrown into a pile to be trucked out of the compound to a scrap yard. All that remained were the scars around ankles that would serve as a reminder of the torture they inflicted. For the first time since becoming a prisoner, a ray of hope overwhelmed Forrest Turner. The possibility that he had a chance to be paroled uplifted his spirit. "For now, I will forgo any more escapes and give Mr. Moore time to keep his promises," he tells Leland.

Mr. Moore did not expect a hundred percent participation by the "Eight Ball Squad" members to abide to his "Do Right, Get Out" policy. It took only four months before Leland Harvey made a successful escape attempt. Mr. Moore was disappointed, but proud that he was returned two hours later. Leland Harvey had asked Forrest Turner to join him, but he had refused to go.

***

A team of state penologists, considered to be experts in prison management and operations, visited the men's and women's prison in Reidsville at the behest of the governor. Their final audit gave the men's prison low marks in many categories and recommended several changes. The team suggested that a specialist be hired to inspect the women's prison. As a result, a consultant for the federal prison system, Lewis Lawes, arrived at Reidsville. He was accompanied by the director of the War Production Board and Wiley Moore to make inspections. Mr. Lawes, former warden of Sing-Sing Prison by the Hudson River in New York, considered the Reidsville women's prison as one of the worst he had ever seen. "For starters, the kitchen is filthy, and the entire dining area is filled with cockroaches, just to name two. I can go on. Both the men's and women's prisons are poorly managed," he said. "This place needs everything."

"Furthermore, the manpower in the prison is being wasted. In the midst of this war, everyone should be engaged in productive work. The Reidsville men's and women's prisons are just sitting on the sidelines," he suggested. "This place could use a truck repair shop to train mechanics and repair state highway equipment, a better shoe repair shop, prison sawmill, sewing rooms, and textile mills. With these enhancements Reidsville would be in line for government contracts to provide vital war materials. There should be an adequate kitchen where inmates can learn how to cook and bake as well as to prepare food for the other inmates. The meals would be better, especially if served with fresh bread."

Shortly thereafter, A.C. Aderhold was appointed new warden at Reidsville in February 1944. As part of the reform program the trusty system was expanded. The number of trusties at Reidsville increased to two hundred. These men were considered the most trustworthy of the one thousand three hundred and fifty prisoners who were hardened criminals. By 1948 half of the convicts at the work camps became trusties. These prisoners were allowed to roam freely in and around the compound or operate road equipment outside without leg irons or the constant watch by armed guards. Many work camps had begun to do away with stripes. The use of whips to punish and cages to haul prisoners to work sites were a foregone memory of the inhumane treatment they imposed.

"Yes, the number of runaways has increased. Most are caught and sent to Reidsville, where they will be placed in solitary confinement," said the Director Moore. "There they could be closely watched and controlled."

27 NORMANDY INVASION

It's been seven months since Wiley Moore gave Forrest Turner a new lease on life. "Do Right, Get Out" promise gave him the opportunity for an eventual parole. Freedom, which at one time seemed impossible, was now within his grasp. Thus far he had conducted himself as a model prisoner and forgone any further escapes. Although difficult at times he was determined to stay the course.

As Forrest Turner's future became more optimistic, so did the direction of the war. A major offensive by the Allies was in progress. World War II had been raging in Europe since Germany invaded Poland. America's involvement had exceeded forty-two months with no end in sight. Daily thousands of American soldiers were risking their lives. When a major counter offensive was reported on the radio that would change the tide of the war in favor of the Allies, everyone was interested in hearing the details. Forrest Turner took pride in reading newspaper articles to the illiterate inmates.

***

Now that radios and newspapers were allowed at Reidsville, Forrest Turner took a keen interest in the war. Still disappointed that he was unable to take part. He never imagined that the war would last so long. "If I were over there, the war would be over by now," he thought. It was June 1944. General Eisenhower and the Allied generals knew it would take a massive effort to defeat the well-entrenched enemy forces in Europe.

It took several days before the details of the Normandy invasion were revealed to the American public. Sitting in the dining hall, the inmates were gathered around Forrest Turner as he read the headlines from several of the Savannah newspapers. A curious guard joined them. Less than half of the inmates at Reidsville could read or write. Adolf Hitler, Benito Mussolini, or Ervin Rommel were names who were strange to them. Some had heard of Generals Eisenhower and Patton. Nevertheless, his audience of inmates were interested in the war. They appreciated Forrest Turner taking time to read the newspaper articles to them.

"It says here that on June 6th, known as D-Day, Allied troops commanded by General Eisenhower landed on five beaches in Normandy, France. It was the largest amphibious landing in history," Forrest read. "That means the attack came from the sea."

One of prisoners asked, "What do they mean by Allied Forces?"

"Well, Canada and England joined the Americans in the attack. Somewhere around one hundred fifty thousand U.S., British, and Canadian troops on five thousand ships and ten thousand planes attacked the Germans. First the Air Force and the Navy bombarded the Germans troops from the air and sea," Forrest answered. "Adolf Hitler and his generals fortified the beaches with barricades, landmines, and barbed wire to prevent the troops from advancing. Many lives were lost as the soldiers struggled to scale the cliffs under heavy machine gun fire. At the same time, thirteen paratrooper units landed behind German lines to support the advancing Allied troops."

"Did we win, Forrest?" asked the convict who was in prison for hauling moonshine.

"After a fierce battle they succeeded in overrunning the German defenses," Forrest continued. "In the latest paper it says the Americans were headed to liberate Paris, France. It's about one hundred forty miles away from Normandy. The Führer, they call Hitler, had hoped to drive the Americans back into the English Channel, but that didn't happen."

"This is good news," someone said. "Yeah, indeed, this is good news."

Forrest made one final comment, "You know that life on the chain gang was miserable and cruel. Reidsville Prison isn't much better, but neither can compare to the perilous conditions the troops face in battle. In many ways we inmates are fortunate to be alive in our cell rather than dead on a beach in Normandy."

***

The war effort affected every American. Most young able-bodied men enlisted in the military. The women worked in factories making supplies for troops and building war planes. Prisoners were contributing in other ways. The Red Cross received permission to conduct blood drives at the state's prison institutions. Reidsville had blood drives. Hundreds of pints of blood were accumulated and sent overseas.

Forrest Turner gladly donated blood. He was surprised that some prisoners refused to give, even though they were promised a dessert at the evening meal. "They had no fear of the law so why were they afraid of a little old needle?" Forrest thought to himself.

Several prisons made contributions to the war effort by producing shoes, tents, parachute packs, machine-gun belts, and other war equipment in their textile mills. Prison officials, guards as well as the public bought war bonds.

On April 12, 1945, Franklin Roosevelt died at Warm Springs, Georgia of a heart attack. The spring water there was therapeutic for his chronic polio affliction. The CCC program as part of his "New Deal" had brought relief to many financially distressed families as were the Turners. His body was transported from Warm Springs through McDonough to Atlanta and then north to Hyde

Park in upstate New York where he was buried. Citizens along the way lined the railroad tracks and filled the station depots. Onlookers removed their hats or bowed their heads in respect as his private railcar, Magellan, slowly passed. It was only fitting that the beloved President Roosevelt be honored in such a way for all the frustrations he endured trying to bring an end to the war. Shortly after his death Germany surrendered on May 7th and the Japanese Navy was in retreat.

Eleven months following the Normandy Invasion the war ended in Europe in May 1945. But in the Pacific the Japanese soldiers were determined to defend their homeland at all costs. The number of casualties was mounting. U.S. President Harry Thruman, who was just sworn into office, and the generals decided that it was time to use the country's newest secret weapon. The Pentagon reported in early August that the U.S. had dropped nuclear bombs on two Japanese cities. The death toll in Hiroshima and Nagasaki, Japan was in the hundreds of thousands. Most were civilians. A week later the Japanese Emperor, Hirohito surrendered to General McArthur. The war was over.

Members of the Turner family who served in the military began to return home. Forrest Turner wondered if Leo Nahlik and Melvin Coppenger had survived the war.

28 BACK TO SCHOOL

In addition to convincing Wiley Moore to institute reforms within the state's prison system in 1943, Governor Arnall was determined to resolve the issues at Reidsville prison. The reports he received from investigations by the prison commission and penal consultants cited numerous problems. To do so, he instructed the new warden to rectify the mess created by earlier wardens. The governor's instruction was to "clean house." The prison was the laughingstock of the nation. Thanks to Forrest Turner and others, escapes occurred on a regular basis and illegal activities inside the prison were widespread.

Warden DuVall made his intentions very clear from the onset when he announced to the press, "I am going to hire plenty of alert, high-type guards. Not the old pot-bellied, tobacco-chewing, 'shotgun toting' men hired in the past. The bribery of guards and the smuggling of contraband into the prison are going to stop! With the guidance of Mr. Moore, we are going to change the culture. We believe the way to keep prisoners here is to give them ambition. Make them feel worthy. To do that we will give them an education and teach them a trade. As a result, all the prisoners now have the possibility of learning a skill."

***

Forrest Turner was eager to take advantage of the prison's educational programs. As a farm boy he was knowledgeable about many things, but he lacked a skill that would allow him to earn a living once paroled. Understandably, Forrest Turner was excited when he met with the assistant warden to discuss the available options for vocational training. He told the assistant warden about the work he had done before going to prison. Raised in a rural environment where everyone farmed, Forrest Turner felt he already knew all there was to learn about agriculture. He had his sights set for a higher calling…perhaps in the medical field.

He continued telling his work background, "After attending Russell High, "I joined the Civilian Conservation Corps (CCC) for six months. The CCC was started by President Franklin D. Roosevelt to give unemployed boys like me a chance to work in the woods. I was expected to work forty hours a week and was paid once a month. The program provided me with work clothes, food, and medical care if it was needed.

"I remember the day of the induction in CCC. All the recruits were lined up and given a medical checkup. If a recruit passed his examination, he received shots. Each was given green dungarees and a floppy hat to wear. This city kid in front of me fainted from his smallpox shot and was lying motionless on the floor. Everyone around him stopped to look but did nothing to help. They just stared at him in amazement. I went to him and put my hand underneath his head and raised it off the floor. He was out cold but was still breathing.

I yelled! "Somebody, please bring me a cup of water!" A medical doctor heard the commotion and saw me tending to the boy. He regained consciousness just as the doctor arrived.

"The group was scheduled to work in a wooded area cleaning out the underbrush and removing the smaller pine saplings. The county had plans to create a park complete with walking trails and a recreation area. Our CCC group was called in to prepare the site for the shelters, bathrooms, and wooden picnic tables that were to be added later.

"The doctor said he was impressed by my quick reaction. He told me that fainting spells could lead to complications, but it was certainly better than getting smallpox. He continued by saying that he wished we had a vaccine to prevent polio. Examining the young lad, the doctor had no doubt he would recover.

"Instead of working in the woods he suggested I come with him to Fort McPherson Hospital. He needed a helper there. I took his advice and began doing odd jobs for him at the hospital and ran errands. From there I was able to land a job at Dr. Anderson's drugstore in College Park. I was just a delivery boy and occasionally served customers ice cream at the soda fountain. It all ended when I was arrested. Although my role there was not important, I was inspired by watching the doctors and druggists help people in need. I was not there long enough to learn any important skills, but I enjoyed the odd jobs I was asked to do at the two places."

Forrest paused a moment before making his request. "If I had my preference, I would like to work in the prison infirmary," Forrest said.

The assistant warden shaking his head replied, "I have another suggestion. The female nurses have already filled those slots, so I can't put you there. With the war going on, however, all prisons are short of medical people. The most critical need here at Reidsville is the dental assistance position. Someone who could make dental plates and dentures. Most of these convicts here have decayed and missing teeth. What do you think, Forrest?"

"I will give it a try," Forrest eagerly responded. "I can probably use a few fillings myself."

The assistant warden contacted the prison dentist to tell him that Forrest Turner would be his trainee. "He is a smart fellow. I believe he can learn how to make your dentures," he predicted.

Forrest Turner closely observed the dentist as he showed him how to make dental impressions, mix and pour dental compounds into a mold, and then shape the hard cast into a denture. He bent over to get a good look of the dentist inserting the denture into the inmate's mouth. Forrest Turner soon perfected the craft of making dentures. The dentist was amazed that he had to return very few of Forrest Turner's dentures to the lab for adjustment.

Dental hygiene at work camps and state prisons such as Reidsville was not existent. Toothpaste and toothbrushes were not available to the inmates. One could tell the approximate age of an inmate by the number of missing teeth. For the first time Forrest Turner felt that he was serving a useful purpose while in prison. He was providing the suffering convicts with the ability to eat without pain or discomfort. The positive impact he was having with the inmates in the dental lab gave him a sense of pride. He felt needed, which lifted his spirits. He no longer depended on the thrill of outsmarting the law and embellishing the publicity that followed. Wiley Moore had given him a new slate. He was no longer destined to be a prisoner for the rest of his life.

***

His fellow inmates were baffled by Forrest Turner's transformation from being "Georgia's Number One Bad Boy" to a model prisoner. One of the disappointed inmates asked, "You don't smoke nor drink and are not trying to get out. What in the hell is wrong with you?" He took the ridicule he was getting from the inmates in stride. Even the prison guards joined in the fun.

"Just for you, Forrest I am going to leave the front gate unlocked tonight," one of the guards told him in jest.

"Thanks, but I will not be going out," Forrest replied. He knew that it was high time for him to grow up, wise up, just as he was told umpteen times by his father and mother. He was determined to prove that this time his promises of change were sincere.

In October 1946 Forrest along with three other inmates were moved to Fulton Tower. One inmate in bad health was moved for the convenience of his family. Living in Atlanta, the aging siblings could make frequent visits during the terminally ill inmate's last remaining months. Dr. Freeman, sentenced to life imprisonment for murder, was transferred to perform medical services. Forrest

Turner was included in the transfer to accompany Dr. Freeman as a dental technician. The transfer was also a reward for his exemplary record and his newfound knowledge of dentistry. After a brief stay, he was promoted to a Trusty and transferred to Bellwood Work Camp in north Fulton County. It would be his home for the rest of his prison term. Forrest Turner had completed the most important phase of his journey to freedom. He was beginning to gain the respect and confidence of the prison officials. "I am older now, and know better," Forrest told the warden. "I've come a long way since that day in 1934."

Most of Forrest Turner's work at the work camp was addressing dental problems for the two hundred and thirty-eight convicts there with rotten teeth. With the urgent need for doctors and dentists to serve in the military during the war, prisons were left lacking medical personnel. Prison officials were fortunate to have two inmates who could fill the roles. One was a convicted murderer, the other a thief.

Forrest Turner recalled the first time an aching inmate came to the dentist's office at Reidsville. It was a weekend, and no one was there but him.

"My tooth is killing me," said the desperate inmate to Forrest.

After examining the man's tooth, Forrest informed him that it was decayed and maybe abscessed, and it needed to be pulled. "The dentist will be back on Monday," Forrest explained. "You will have to come back then."

In tears the man said, "I can't wait till Monday. Can't you pull the tooth, Mr. Forrest?"

"No, I just make dentures and help the dentist. I don't pull teeth," Forrest admitted.

Listening to his pleas he just couldn't stand to see the man suffer. "I can't hurt him any more than he is already hurting," he surmised. He instructed the man to sit in the dental chair. "Grab ahold of the armrests. This is going to hurt, he said. He took the dental pliers, clamped down on the tooth, twisted, and yanked hard. The decayed tooth came out. He showed the extracted tooth to his relieved patient and discharged it into the trash bucket. He handed the man a cotton pad. "Now bite down on this to stop the bleeding and take this cloth and wipe the blood off your cheek.

"How do you feel now," asked Forrest.

The patient mumbled, "Much better doc. Thanks."

"Do me a favor," asked Forrest. "Don't tell the other inmates that it was me who pulled your tooth. I might get in trouble with the dentist."

Right then Forrest Turner knew that he had missed his calling. He should have been a dentist instead of a thief. At Reidsville word soon spread to the other inmates and later to the convicts at the camps that Forrest Turner was pulling teeth. He would provide that same service many times. At Bellwood it was not unusual for him to extract teeth and then later fill the gaps with a partial or denture when the wound healed.

29   GUARDIAN ANGELS

There is a common belief in the existence of guardian angels. These heavenly spirits serve an important role in the daily lives of human beings. Those of religious faith claim it is an inherent gift from God above. They are sent to watch over us and provide guidance and comfort in times of trouble during our life's journey. Forrest Turner had ignored the advice of his spiritual guardian angel but he was fortunate to be rescued by two men. Wiley Moore and Reverand Allison helped him find his conscience.

***

When Forrest Turner was born, he was assigned a guardian angel. It was not a physical being, but a spirit buried in the depths of the subconscious part of the mind. The guardian angel telepathically attempted to influence his thoughts and actions. The presence of an angel provided him with a conscience. During times of temptation and indecision, the guardian angel mentally offered encouragement and advice. Forrest Turner ignored his guardian angel's warnings when he chose to take the wrong path, one of crime and lawlessness. Like with most criminals it appeared that he did not have a conscience as he felt no remorse for his wrongdoings. The initial thrill and euphoria from challenging authority soon resulted in unwanted consequences. The loss of freedom was a big price to pay for his indiscretions. He had "sowed his wild oats" and now he was in a hopeless situation.

Whether through fate or an act of God, two guardian angels in a physical form came to his rescue. This time a desperate Forrest Turner had no choice but to listen. First it was Wiley Moore who offered Forrest Turner a way out of confinement though his prison reform program. Then followed by Chaplain Bill Allison who guided him down the path of righteousness. "You must abide by the Lord's Ten Commandments and follow the 'Golden Rule', if you are to find inner peace," the Chaplain told Forrest. "Going forward you should no longer steal but do unto others as you would have them do unto you." As encouragement the Chaplain assured him that he had a conscience. "Let it be your guide," he advised.

***

WILEY MOORE

Seldom does a wealthy oil man take an interest in incorrigible and downtrodden convicts. However, Wiley Moore was a humanitarian and civic leader. He wasn't always rich and powerful. He worked hard to achieve his success. In repayment for his good fortune, he became a philanthropist with his time and money.

Wiley L. Moore was born in Wrightsville, Georgia in 1888. In 1920 he began working for a company that sold barrels of oil and gasoline to sawmills in central Georgia. As wealthy individuals began buying horseless carriages, he provided them with their needed barrels of fuel. He attended Lanier High School in LaGrange and later acquired his business acumen by reading business textbooks at night. During the Great Depression he expected to get laid off as were many of his friends and neighbors. But instead, his hard work paid off as he was promoted to a better paying sales manager position.

With a wife and family, he left his job to start his own oil business. With a minimal amount of cash, he was determined not to fail. His one-man operation was successful. Later he bought out his old company, merged it with an independent oil dealer, and formed an alliance with a refinery. His company, Wofford Oil Company, was headquartered on Ponce de Leon Avenue in Atlanta.

When Governor Talmadge refused to approve a pipeline for his company, he began to support his political opponent, Ellis Arnall. In 1942, Mr. Arnall won the governor's seat. One of Governor Arnall's major challenges was to clean up the Georgia Penal System. He knew just the man who could do the job. It would be Wiley Moore's responsibility to carry out prison reform in the State of Georgia. Being a wealthy businessman, he accepted the position as Commissioner of Correction and refused the twelve-thousand-dollar annual salary.

Mr. Moore heard of the harsh and cruel treatment of convicts in the chain gangs. He had seen firsthand the scars on the ankles and backs of released prisoners, now employees for his company. He had read about the countless escape attempts from the work camps. Those who were not killed during their escape faced unmerciful punishment when recaptured and returned to the camp. Governor Arnall informed him of the chaos at the state's maximum-security prison at Reidsville. His first mission was to restore law and order within the prison. After assessing the situation and interviewing prisoners, which included Forrest Turner, he prepared a reform plan. With the governor's approval, he outlined his plan to the staff and inmates at Reidsville.

***

CHAPLAIN BILL ALLISON

Since Forrest Turner was no longer considered a flight risk and his dental skills were needed in the Fulton County work camps, he was transferred to Bellwood Work Camp in Atlanta. He was familiar with the work camp, having served there before. This time he was not there to crush rocks but to make dentures. The move to Bellwood was a welcome change from the maximum-security prison at Reidsville. Forrest Turner didn't think his convict friends would miss him because he no longer had the same crim-

Reverend Bill Allison
Chaplain for the Fulton County
Prison System

inal mindset. Since his arrival he was in the company of a new bunch of convicted felons. He was alone amongst dubious strangers, knowing no one other than the two inmates who were transferred with him.

It was only a brief time before a soft-spoken gentleman small in stature came to his cell for a friendly visit. As he handed Forrest a card, he introduced himself, "I am Bill Allison, the work camp's chaplain. As the card says, I am here to render advice whether to be personal or spiritual. I must say that your reputation has preceded your arrival. I have heard many good things about you, Forrest. I am sure you and I will become good friends."

After the pastor left, Forrest Turner read the card. "My Friend: If at any time while you are in the Fulton County prisons, I can be of any service to you I will be privileged to advise you. I will be pleased to render any reasonable service in keeping with my position." He learned that the Chaplain greeted every new inmate and presented them with his calling card. At the time Forrest Turner did not realize just how true his prediction would be. The friendship that followed would keep him on the straight and narrow path toward obtaining parole.

Reverend Willard Pierce Allson was born in 1906 and raised in Gainesville. He attended Locust Grove Institute in Henry County, Columbia Theological Seminary in Decatur, and graduated from Atlanta's Oglethorpe College in 1933. He was hired by Fulton County in 1938 to be spiritual leader and counselor for convicts in the county's five work camps. He enlisted in the service and served as army chaplain at Camp Robinson in Arkansas. He returned to Atlanta in 1944 where he was appointed Chief Chaplain for the Fulton County work camps. At all times there were between eight hundred fifty and one thousand convicts in the camps.

He spent his weekdays talking to inmates and their families. He counseled them about financial, personal and domestic problems. After the convicts' release, he would buy them clothes, loan them money, and help them find jobs. Reverend Allison's mission was to rehabilitate convicts. "These are men who have made mistakes because they lacked the advantages of education," he once said.

Forrest Turner began regularly attending the weekly church services at Bellwood. "I remember his first sermon," Forrest recalled. The Reverend looking directly at me and said, "No man is beyond redemption. The phrase has remained close to my heart ever since." He soon gained Reverend Allison's respect. "Forrest, I need someone to be my assistant. I have too many convicts to look after. Do you mind helping me?" he asked.

Forrest Turner agreed to become the assistant chaplain.

Everyone in the work camp was fond of the Reverend. He asked the convicts to call him Pastor Bill. He was always seen at every work camp activity with a broad warm smile. Since it was difficult to find an unbiased umpire among the guards and convicts, he became the official umpire for inter-work camp and prison baseball games. During such a game an angry batter could not bring himself to curse the Reverend. All he would say was, "Lord please give the chaplain some glasses. He can't see nothin.'"

Both men became dear friends and allies during the five-year period while he was awaiting parole. They met separately and together with judges, lawyers, and members of the pardon and parole board to lobby for his release. Their efforts did not go unnoticed as the press, which had earlier championed him as a rebellious folk hero, now began promoting his parole. Newspaper editorials titled, "Forrest Turner has done his part" and "Would it not be in the Spirit of Christmas if the State of Georgia gave Forrest Turner a chance?" were published. The articles began to sway public opinion.

Forrest Turner now realized that Wiley Moore and Pastor Allison were his guardian angels. He had wished that they had arrived earlier. If they had, he probably wouldn't be in his present predicament. "I can never repay you for your faith in me and your dedication in promoting my bid for freedom," Forrest told each of them many times. His road to freedom had been filled with many bumps, but his difficult journey was about to end.

30 PAROLE

Forrest Turner had been promised parole by Governor Eugene Talmadge in October 1942 as his last official act before leaving office. For whatever reason, whether politics or Forrest Turner's reputation for reneging on past promises of going straight, the governor did not grant his pardon. Facing a century of prison time, an early parole was at best years away, a pardon was impossible. Based on the number of years left of his sentence he was destined to die in prison. He saw no alternative to gaining freedom except to escape. That seemed unlikely as he was confined to his cell and watched constantly. After the sensational breakout where he helped the escape of twenty-three other inmates, Forrest Turner was shackled with a ball and chain. His situation appeared hopeless.

The visionary Georgia's Director of Corrections, Wiley Moore, gave Forrest Turner a bit of optimism. If he conformed to the rules of the prison, learned a trade, and quit pretending to be 'Houdini,' he would recommend his parole. But first he would have to prove it. That was 1943. He was motivated by the opportunity to walk out the front gate instead of sneaking out the back door with a pack of blood hounds or Detective Nahlik on his trail. Under the new reform program other convicts who showed remorse and were contrite for their crimes were paroled.

***

Robert Elliott Burns had heard of Governor Arnall's effort to bring about prison reform in Georgia. It had been twelve years since his escape from the Troup County Work Camp in LaGrange. He reasoned that now would be a good time to ask for his long-awaited pardon. He contacted Governor Arnall in 1943 and invited him to come to New York. After a meeting with him the governor suggested to the Georgia Board of Pardons and Paroles to grant Robert Burns full clemency. "He is completely rehabilitated and has earned the right to be free based on his exemplary life he has led for the past thirteen years," the governor told the board. Once the governor's remarks to the board were mentioned in the newspaper a swell of favorable publicity followed. With Governor Arnall's solemn promise that a pardon would be forthcoming, Robert Burns voluntarily returned to Georgia in November 1945. The governor stood by his side during the hearing. At the conclusion the chairman announced the board's ruling; "It is the decision of the board to commute Mr. Burns' sentence for the time he has already served." Created by the robbery of a five-dollar bill and change, his twenty-four-year nightmare had finally ended. Many thought that he should have been given a medal for his service to his country, not the unfair punishment he received in Georgia.

The news that Robert Burns sentence was commuted by the Georgia Board of Pardons and Paroles would reach Forrest Turner while he was a Trusty at Bellwood. The same convict camp, where Robert Burns was imprisoned years earlier. Forrest Turner hoped that receiving his pardon would not take as long.

***

For the last eleven years Forrest Turner had been either a prisoner or a fugitive. His closest associates were either murderers, thieves or both. He was exposed to the devious minds and the unlawful ways of professional criminals. These men were his mentors. In such an environment it is difficult to foresee how Forrest Turner or any of the members from the "Eight Ball Squad" could reform. Imprisoning young boys together with hardened criminals proved to be a mistake by the justice system. The naïve young men sent to prison for unruly behavior and later released were destined to be repeat offenders of more serious crimes. It seemed to be a near miracle for Forrest Turner to succeed in his transformation back to being an honest and law-bidding person. Whether sheer determination or desperation he wanted out of the miserable hole he had dug for himself.

Wiley Moore's reform program thus far, was succeeding. Of the less notorious inmates who were paroled, few had returned to prison. However, his fellow eight ball inmates continued to escape and commit crimes while on the loose. Attempts to rehabilitate them had proven to be unsuccessful. Since Forrest Turner was considered the leader of the squad, a quick parole for him appeared unobtainable. Nevertheless, something inside was driving Forrest Turner to succeed.

***

In February 1946 Forrest Turner's primary focus was molding false teeth in the prison dental lab. He was proud of his work and his new mindset. He recounts his final years at Reidsville.

A.C. Aderhold had just become the new warden. He was aware of Forrest Turner's record while at Reidsville and wasn't ready to brag about his rehabilitation. "In view of his many escapes we can hardly send him to the post office to mail his letters unaccompanied in fear of non-delivery. I need to see more progress, before I am willing to trust him one hundred percent. But I give him credit. He is headed in the right direction."

Forrest replied in his attempt to convince the doubters, "I have worked hard, kept a perfect record, and have earned the respect and commendation of the officials here. That wasn't the case a few years ago."

On November 18, 1946, nine prisoners from Reidsville escaped by digging a seventy-five-foot tunnel from the cell block to the other side of the outer wall. One of the escapees was Charles Bryant, who Forrest Turner had liberated from the Cumming Work Camp earlier. All were recaptured within two weeks. An escapee who was the first one recaptured confessed to Warden Aderhold that the group spent nine months digging the tunnel. After the last convict was recaptured, the warden asked a guard to bring Forrest Turner to his office.

"Forrest, I was pleased that you weren't involved with the fellas who escaped through the tunnel," he said with a straight face. "I was also surprised that you never used a tunnel as your means of escape."

"You know warden, it's hard to dig your way out through the solid concrete from the fourth floor," Forrest remarked with a bit of wit.

Warden Aderhold after first laughing he got straight to the point. "The real reason I asked you to come to my office is to discuss my dental problem," he devulged. "I think I need a dental plate. I lost my second molar. The gap makes it hard for me to chew meat Forrest. I want you to look at my teeth."

The next day the warden went to the dental room at the prison. "Have a seat in the dental chair and open wide," Forrest instructed.

Forrest Turner leaned over and looked into the warden's mouth. The same mouth through which the warden had proclaimed earlier that he did not trust his sincerity. Now because of his dental discomforts he was willing to risk his dental care to an untrustworthy convict. Forrest Turner measured the bite and began to prepare a partial denture. The entire time he was thinking of what the warden had said. Instead of a mild retaliation by making a mediocre partial, he put extra effort into trying to please the warden. Two days later Forrest Turner inserted the partial. It fit perfectly. The warden thanked him.

"No charge," Forrest replied in a joking manner.

Two weeks later the warden met Forrest Turner in the hallway. "I want to tell you that you did an excellent job with my partial. I am now able to gnaw on a rough steak like I used to when I had all my teeth. I will be recommending you for parole when the board reviews your appeal."

After learning about the outcome of the warden's dental procedure, other prison officials and guards approached him to make them dentures.

Fulfilling Wiley Moore's requirements had earned Forrest Turner the transfer from the Reidsville maximum-security prison. The move to Bellwood Work Camp a few weeks later came because of his new attitude. He followed the prison rules and dedicated his energy to making perfect-fitting dentures. A good word from Warden Aderhold didn't hurt either.

At Bellwood he fulfilled the roles of both assistant to the dentist and to the chaplain. Under the watchful eyes of the new warden, he was able to show that his good intentions were genuine. The experience he was getting in the dental office would prove invaluable once he was released and had to earn a living.

***

One year after reporting to Bellwood, Forrest Turner had his first official appeal for parole. Through the urging by Wiley Moore the pardon and parole board agreed to a hearing date. He was certain that the board would rule in Forrest Turner's favor.

Reverend Allison was present to put in a good word on his behalf. "I have known Mr. Turner since he arrived at Bellwood. You as members of the Georgia Board of Pardons and Paroles are familiar with his exemplary record while there. He is an abiding Christian. He is not a man of violence, even though he was surrounded by violent men in prison. During his escapes and recaptures he never intentionally harmed anyone. I hope the record shows that during the infamous Reidsville escape, no prison property was destroyed, or a single guard was hurt.

"Let me tell a story that I was told to me by one of the inmates involved in the Reidsville's breakout. You know the one where two dozen prisoners escaped. While they were escorting one of the guards to a cell to lock up, one of the meaner convicts began cursing the guard. Apparently, the guard had been abusive toward this convict who was anxious to retaliate. When he drew back to slug the guard, Forrest grabbed his arm. "We are not here to hurt anyone. Our mission is just to leave. There will be no bloodshed. Do you hear me?" he yelled at the unruly convict.

"This is a man who has the potential to be an asset to society. When released, it is Mr. Turner's intention to attend Emory University Dental School while he works at a dental laboratory in Atlanta," Reverend Allison argued. "A prominent dentist is looking forward to having him as an assistant."

At the clemency hearing in December 1947 the board faced a difficult decision. Prison officials agreed Forrest Turner was a model prisoner and had been for four years. He had turned to dentistry with the same vigor with which he once took to illegal activities. He filled in as a dentist at Reidsville Prison during the war and continued his dental work as a Trusty at Bellwood. Because of Forrest Turner's past notoriety, a decision would be a tough one for the pardon and parole board. Whatever decision was made by the board it would have a bearing on the future of penology in the state. An early release of Forrest Turner would be an endorsement of Wiley Moore's reform program, "Do Right, Get Out!" At past hearings, the board had not always followed Mr. Moore's recommendations when it denied paroles to prisoners who were demonstrating good behavior and deserving of a release.

The conflict between the Georgia Boards of Corrections and Pardons and Paroles over who should be paroled frustrated Wiley Moore. He had given the inmates at Reidsville his word that if they behaved, they would get paroled. While some appeals were granted, Forrest Turner's was not. Mr. Moore told the press that the once notorious Mr. Turner had lived up to his promises. Now it was time for the state to live up to its agreement. Wiley Moore was hoping for an early Christmas present for Forrest. However, the board denied the appeal. The specific reasons for the denial were not immediately given. Because of his disagreements with the pardon and parole board, especially the failure to parole

Forrest Turner, Wiley Moore resigned as director of the Georgia Board of Corrections.

Forrest Turner was disappointed and frustrated by the news of the denial. "The way I look at it, I am a Trusty inside now. If they would just give me a chance as a Trusty on the outside, I believe I could become a useful citizen," Forrest vowed.

Reverend Allison, surprised by the rejection, said, "I have one hundred percent faith in my assistant Forrest's sincerity. "If he had wanted to escape from Bellwood, he could have done so a hundred times over. But he didn't. That should be an indicator of his honesty."

In October 1948 Forrest Turner filed another written appeal to the pardon and parole board. The petition included one hundred fifty names of College Park businessmen and residents. When members of the family asked for signatures not a single person refused to sign. "We would love to have Forrest back in our community. I think he has learned his lesson," one of the residents said as she signed the petition. The chief of police, law enforcement officials and civic leaders gladly signed.

The purpose of signed petitions was to show the community's support for his release. "Who else knows Forrest better than the people of Hapeville and College Park," one of his supporters said. News reporters who had over embellished his exploits with their newsprint by characterizing him as an incorrigible bad man in the past were now extolling his virtues. Letters sent to the newspapers demanded that the pardon and parole board release him at once.

Disappointing news reached Forrest Turner in December 1948 when the parole board again failed to rule favorably on his appeal for parole. Chairman of the board announced that there were still outstanding indictments on the books against him. "It is the policy of the board not to pass on a case where there is a pending indictment. Any action will be held in abeyance until the case is disposed of," disclosed the chairman. His appeal was put on hold until he could stand trial for armed robberies in Rome in 1936 and in Griffin in 1939.

***

It is now 1949. The country was recovering from the misery of World War II. Harry Truman, who inherited the presidency after the death of Franklin Roosevelt was voted back into office after an upset victory over New York Governor Thomas Dewey. In Georgia Herman Talmadge was named governor after his father Eugene Talmadge had won the election but died before taking office. The Cleveland Indians had beaten the Boston Braves for the World Series title that year. The U.S. economy slipped into recession. All this didn't matter to Forrest Turner since he was still imprisoned.

In January 1949 Forrest Turner was escorted from Bellwood in Atlanta to the Floyd County Superior Courthouse in Rome. There the thirteen-year-old robbery charge against him went to trial. The formal accusation claimed that Turner and two other men robbed a filling station operator in Rome, Georgia of two hundred twenty-five dollars on the night of October 16, 1938. It was a long time ago when he was twenty-one years of age. At a time when he was on the run and needed money. Forrest Turner knew he had robbed several people, but he couldn't remember specifically whether he did or didn't rob the filling station.

He was joined in court by Chaplain Allison, the Fulton County District Attorney, and a Fulton County Commissioner who came to Rome as friends of the defendant. The case was tried before a judge. No jury was involved. The victim's wife, who saw the robbery, was in court to testify for the state. Her husband, who was the robbery victim, was deceased. The formal accusation had been buried in the courthouse files. All but forgotten, the charge remained on record.

After the bailiff read the charges, Judge Nichols, who had reviewed the formal accusation documents, addressed those in the courtroom. "Ladies and Gentlemen, I have carefully reviewed the documents. I have found a blatant technical error in the preparation of the charges. Therefore, I am dismissing the formal accusation against Mr. Turner," proclaimed the judge as he struck the plate with his gavel. "The case is dismissed."

Everyone in the courtroom was overjoyed by the verdict, except for the victim's wife and the Floyd County District Attorney. Backed by public support to parole Forrest Turner, the judge's decision was an easy one. The relieved Forrest Turner was escorted back to Bellwood having removed one major obstacle to his parole.

To resolve the two pending Griffin charges, Reverend Allison and Forrest Turner met privately with the judge who was to hear the cases in January. The judge, however, was unable to dismiss the charges. "I have a sympathetic ear, but by law there must be a trial. The pardon and parole board is within its right to defer its review of a parole petition until the cases are settled," the judge said.

In February Forrest Turner went to trial in Spalding Superior Court on the separate five dollar and the sixty-six-dollar robbery charges which had been pending against him. Both were tried simultaneously. He had previously denied committing the two crimes. Forrest asked his attorney, "Since these robberies happened so long ago, can I repay the money plus interest and have the charges dropped?"

His lawyer shaking his head informed Forrest. "It's too late for that." said his lawyer. "It's going to be up to the judge if the charges are to be dismissed."

The case was also a "bench trial" tried before a judge with no jury present. Back on December 5, 1938, the filling station manager and the attendant both identified Forrest Turner from a picture, as one of the two men who robbed them in Griffin. The district attorney presented only two witnesses; a man who was robbed of his five dollars and another person who was present during the Griffin filling station robbery of sixty-six dollars.

The district attorney pointed to Forrest Turner sitting next to his attorney. "Is this the man that robbed your business on December the 5th?"

The uncomfortable victim fidgeting while sitting in the witness chair paused for moment then meekly responded, "I am not sure if he was the man."

The prosecutor questioned the second victim in the same manner. He was more assertive with his answer. "It wasn't him," he said. "I am certain."

After eleven years neither witness could positively name Forrest Turner as the culprit. After the closing arguments were presented by the state and the defense attorneys, the judge gave his verdict.

The judge proclaimed, "Since no evidence implicating the defendant was presented by the state, I hereby issue a direct verdict of acquittal. Case dismissed."

After the trial, a reporter asked the wife of the robbery victim, "How do you feel about the verdict today?" "Well, my late husband could never put that robbery behind him. The anger from being robbed and the threat of being killed, tormented him the rest of his life," she said.

Of course, Forrest Turner was elated with the judge's decision. However, after reflecting on the victims' testimonies during the trial, he felt a sense of compassion for them. He vowed that someday he would find a way to repay them for their loss and anguish.

Since Forrest Turner was cleared of the last charges which had been holding up his petition for parole, there was no reason for the board to delay its decision any longer. The board was duty bound to review the parole petition at its next meeting. It was hard to believe that Forrest Turner's freedom was delayed three months over thefts totaling seventy-one dollars. Finally, the parole board chairman, Edward Everett, notified Forrest Turner's attorney of the board's decision.

***

It's Saturday March 5, 1949; a day Forrest Turner thought would never come. With the encouragement from Governor Herman Talmadge, he would be released from prison. It's been six years since he made his commitment to Wiley Moore that he would go straight. Now thirty-four years old, he had spent half of his life in jails. The parole came with conditions, none of which however were a concern to Forrest Turner. His conditional parole would last for an unrealistic fifty-five years. During that period, he must report periodically to his parole officer, not to fraternize with known criminals, not to possess a firearm, and most importantly not to partake in any illegal activities.

It was still dark when he got up as the anticipated excitement of the release aroused him to the point that he could not sleep. He paced the floor as he waited for a guard to inform him that the paperwork had reached the assistant chief clerk at the work camp. To Forrest Turner the seconds seemed like minutes and the minutes like hours. Finally, the word came. Chaplain Allison had the honor of unlocking the cell gate. After signing out with the assistant chief clerk, he walked out the front door. Somehow the air smelled fresher than it had in a very long time. Greeted by reporters, he posed for the newspaper photographer while shaking hands with Chaplain Allison. The chaplain, more than anyone else, was responsible for his parole. Pastor Allison had met with individual members of the parole board many times to make the case that it was time to give Forrest Turner his freedom.

A reporter asked Forrest, "How does it feel to be a free man?"

"I have looked forward to this day more than a kid looks forward to Christmas. Once I heard from Pastor Bill that my parole had been approved, I began to count my blessings," Forrest said with a huge smile.

The reporter posed another question, "Didn't you get depressed as your parole requests stalled?"

"I never became disheartened. I received hundreds of letters from people all over the state encouraging me to be patient. They told me that I deserved to be free and that a lot of people were praying for my parole. I did not want to let them down," Forrest replied.

The reporter continued, "Now that you are free, what will you be doing?"

"Well first, in a few days, I report to work at Dr. Harold Holt-zendorf's dental laboratory as a dental assistant. Secondly, after what I have been through, I am going to devote most of my time to discourage juvenile delinquency. I want to tell young boys that crime destroys lives. I have already been invited to speak at a high school. I also promised my dear friend Pastor Bill Allison that I would visit his church. I don't know when yet, but I will call him. There is much more that needs to be done to improve our prison system. I hope you newspaper people will listen to me. I have a lot to tell you," he replied.

Forrest Turner thanked those who came to witness his release. With a suitcase in one hand and the parole papers in the other he briskly walked to his awaiting brother's car. Twenty minutes later he was hugging his mother at her Hapeville home. She had prayed that he would have the opportunity to start again as the decent, honest, and hardworking person he once was as a boy. She was confident her prayers would be answered.

PART IV
THE FREEDOM YEARS

31 THE COUNSELOR

Forrest Turner had not expected to become a guidance counselor or a social worker for troubled convicts after his release from prison. But he was good-hearted and sympathetic toward their needs. His fellow convicts had looked up to him and listened to him when he spoke. His new roll began when Dr. Holtzendorf sought his help with his wayward son and continued as Pastor Bill referred parolees to him.

***

Dr. Harold Holtzendorf was looking for a dental assistant. He had planned to open a second office. His son, Buddy, who he hoped would one day take over the practice had no interest in dentistry. When he got word that a skilled denturist was about to get paroled from prison, he agreed to meet with Forrest Turner. Dr. Holtzendorf met him at Bellwood Work Camp for an interview. Forrest Turner was able to convince the dentist that he had the knowledge and experience to fulfill the position. As a plus, the dentist found convict Turner to be very personable and a likeable sort. The interview went well, but Dr. Holtzendorf had reservations about hiring an ex-con. "Anyone who has been in prison for as long as Forrest Turner had, must have a few loose screws," he assumed. Nevertheless, he considered the hiring of

Forrest Turner as a manageable risk and agreed to take him under his wing when released.

All went according to plan. Forrest Turner enjoyed working at his Peachtree Road clinic and Dr. Holtzendorf was pleased with his work. By having an able assistant, Dr. Holtzendorf opened a second clinic in Calhoun. He and Dr. Holtzendorf traveled to the Gordon County clinic twice a week to see patients. He knew that he could trust Forrest and began to take him into his confidence.

One day he confronted Forrest. "My wife and I are worried about our son, Buddy. We believe he engages in some type of illegal activity. He does not work, keeps irregular hours, and always has lots of money. From your background I know you can find out what he is up to," the concerned Dr. Holtzendorf asked hopefully.

Forrest Turner agreed to speak to Buddy. At first, he denied the accusations. "After I revealed some of the petty crimes and car thefts I had committed, Buddy began to talk more openly to me," he reported to Dr. Holtzendorf.

"Yeah, I have been driving stolen cars from Florida to Atlanta for a fee. I don't steal them. I just bring the cars to a garage and a man gives me an envelope with cash inside," Buddy confessed.

Forrest listened and thanked him for his candor. "Buddy, I am speaking from experience. The punishments for the crimes you are committing far exceed whatever money you are getting. I recommend you stop now before it's too late. Prison time for a young man is far worse than you can imagine."

"Okay, Mr. Turner, I will think about what you said and try to find another line of work," he promised.

Forrest continued, "You have wonderful parents. They would be extremely disappointed if you get arrested."

He met with Buddy several more times. At each meeting he assured him that he was going straight. But a brief time later twenty-three-year-old Harold, 'Buddy' Holtzendorf, Jr. was arrested for armed robbery and transporting a stolen car. Later the F.B.I. also charged him and several of his gang members with passing counterfeit money. On the way to Fulton County police headquarters to pay his son's bond, Dr. Holtzendorf was a passenger in an automobile which was involved in a serious accident. The lawyer who was driving died. Although he survived, his injuries affected his ability to practice dentistry. It was truly a sad time for the Holtzendorf family.

Forrest Turner's first experience of being a counselor didn't go well. Buddy had ignored his advice. "It broke my heart when I learned that he was arrested. I'm afraid the same thing is going to happen to him as happened to me…a lengthy time in prison," Forrest told his father. "Buddy was already too deeply involved in crime. Nothing I could have said would have changed the outcome." From this experience Forrest Turner was determined more than ever to reach young adults before they became hardened criminals.

***

Fulton County Chaplain Bill Allison was an effective counselor for convicts seeking help. Many of those with whom he consulted were the trusties, "short termers" who soon would be paroled. With a thousand convicts under his care, it was difficult for him at times to reach all those who needed guidance. After Forrest Turner was paroled, Chaplain Allison asked him if he would counsel convicts once they were paroled. "I can help the convicts on the inside, but I need help for those on the outside. Would you try helping them if I refer them to you?" he asked.

Forrest replied without hesitation, "You know I will Pastor Bill. I will remain your assistant chaplain for as long as you would like."

After seeing a constant parade of guidance-seeking convicts visiting the pastor's office one morning, Forrest was compelled to ask, "Reverend, why do you devote so much time to the prison ministry. You could be the head pastor of the largest church in Atlanta if you wanted?"

Pastor Bill replied, "It's like this Forrest. I believe there is a latent goodness in every man, even a convict. It's my desire to bring this lost virtue to the forefront and discourage his future evil temptations."

With that mindset Forrest Turner, after his parole, became a counselor to parolees for many years. Those who walked out of prison and had families found support at home. Those without families were alone in a changed world and struggled to cope with their new independence. They had to fend for themselves. They could no longer depend on a strict prison schedule or have the guards dictate to them their every move. Someone had to be there to help with the transition. That person was Forrest Turner.

He gained a reputation for being able to communicate with troubled parolees. Unlike Buddy Holtzendorf, who had ignored his guidance, they listened and followed his advice. Georgia's conditions of parole required that every discharged prisoner be assigned a parole officer. Each officer had a lengthy list of parolees under his watch. The parole officer's primary role was to make sure the parolees stayed in line: they went to work, stayed crime free, and did not associate with criminals. When a parolee needed special attention with a specific problem, his parole officer was often too busy to help. The parolee would reach out to Chaplain Allison, who in turn referred him to Forrest Turner. The wellbeing of an ex-con was not always the overburdened parole officer's concern, only that the parole requirements were met. Forrest Turner on the other hand took a personal interest. He was good at comforting them and providing the help needed. Of the parolees he counseled, very few violated their parole and returned to prison.

Forrest Turner had many irons in the fire. His primary focus, however, was still to prevent juvenile delinquency. When two young prisoners, Joseph Mauldin and Earl Taylor, escaped near Macon while being transported to Reidsville, he wrote an open letter pleading for them to surrender to police. "I am not being coerced by the police," Forrest included in his written appeal to the young men.

"I know what it is like to be a fugitive, with a price on your head, to be taken dead or alive. My appeal to you is for your long-term benefit. You are young and still have an opportunity to become useful citizens. Not so long ago, I faced nearly a century in prison and at the time there was no hope for me. There is nothing on the face of the earth to compare with honest freedom. This is your only real chance. It will be only a matter of hours, days or weeks before you will find yourself confronted by law enforcement officers. Why endanger your lives, the lives of some innocent person and the policemen in a futile effort?

"No human being is so bad as to be beyond redemption. There is a chance for everyone willing to prove himself worthy to find a place in society. I have an earnest prayer in my heart that you will heed this advice, coming as it is from one who has experienced the same things you are now facing."

They were recaptured at a restaurant on North Highland Drive where Mauldin's mother worked. Forrest Turner was motivated to write the letter because the pair had committed three burglaries in DeKalb County near his home.

Sometime later Pastor Bill called Forrest about a recent parolee living in Jonesboro who needed help. His name was James, a middle-aged, uneducated Black man. He had gotten into an argument with another man over a woman. When the other man attacked him, James managed to wrestle away the knife. But in so doing he stabbed the man who later died. The jury found him guilty of murder and the judge sentenced him to life imprisonment. James was sent to the Dallas Work Camp and later transferred to Reidsville. There he was assigned to the kitchen where he learned how to cook. He later became a Trusty and had recently been paroled.

"Would you talk with him?" Pastor Bill asked.

Forrest Turner was working at the Jonesboro Dental Lab and asked James to come to his office. He did not recognize the name, but when he met him, he remembered James from his stay in Reidsville prison. In fact, he was one of the cooks during the time of his famous 1943 Reidsville's escape. The man mentioned to

Forrest Turner that he had little money and needed a job. Forrest Turner agreed to help.

While eating lunch at Butch's Chicken House, a local Jonesboro restaurant specializing in fried chicken, he spoke to the owner and mentioned James.

"You are in luck," Butch Hand said. "I have been looking for a helper in the kitchen. Forrest, if you recommend him, I will give him a tryout. Have James come to the restaurant at 7:00 a.m. on Monday. If he checks out okay, I will put him to work."

Forrest Turner loaned James a few dollars and Butch hired him. James was one of many ex-convicts who he helped. Later Forrest would tease Butch, "The fried chicken tastes better now that James is doing the cooking."

32 HERMAN TALMADGE

After his parole, Forrest Turner always included prison reform in his talks to the various groups. Upon hearing of his experiences as a member of a chain gang and as an inmate at Reidsville, the audiences were in sympathy with what he endured and whole-heartedly supported his pleas for change. But if he was to effect such a change, he would have to reach a higher authority. Some-one who had influence with the prison commission and the legis-lators. He needed to have a heart-to-heart talk with the governor.

***

Herman Talmadge followed Ellis Arnall as Georgia's governor. Originally from Telfair County, Mr. Talmadge moved to Love-joy, which is just a rock's throw from Hampton in Henry County, Forrest Turner's former home. His father, Eugene Talmadge, had earlier met with Forrest Turner and had intimated that he would grant him a pardon. Which he didn't. But all was forgiven now that the pardon and parole board finally approved his parole. For-rest Turner called the State Capitol to arrange a conversation with Governor Talmadge.

"Thank you for speaking with me," Forrest said. "I want to thank you for your help in getting me paroled."

Governor Talmadge replied, "My father told me all about you. You were quite a celebrity in Georgia in those days. As it turned out, I made the right decision. You have been a productive citizen since your release. What can I do for you?"

"You know that I promised Governor Arnall that I would promote his and Wiley Moore's prison reform program, which I have. Many of the policy changes which improved the treatment of prisoners were enacted," Forrest revealed. "But there is more that can be done," Forrest revealed.

"How is that, Forrest?"

Forrest continued, "First of all, it's the chain gangs. I can tell you from my personal experience my treatment while working on the chain gangs was cruel. Thank God, chain gangs were outlawed in 1943, thus improving the treatment of convicts. As you know there are still many county work camps operating in the state. At some of these work camps the environment is like that found on the old southern plantations during the slavery days. These work camps should be done away with."

"So, Forrest are you against work camps? Should the state build more jails and put every prisoner behind bars?"

"No governor," Forrest corrected himself. "Convicts should be allowed to work if they wish. They should have decent housing, food, and medical care. They should also receive some sort of an allowance for their work. We just need to bring these camps up to today's standards...and one more thing."

"Go ahead Forrest. I am listening," Governor Talmadge said.

"You know juvenile rehabilitation is very important to me," Forrest began. "Too many young juveniles are sent to prison and are corrupted by adult prisoners. These young men should be separated and sent to reform schools or youth camps. There they can be taught to control their irrational behavior and learn something other than stealing. They can finish their high school education and acquire skills. I don't know where I would be if I hadn't learned how to make dentures at Reidsville."

"I agree with what you are saying," responded the governor. "I have been thinking about setting up an informal committee to advise me on prison matters. Would you like to be on that committee?"

Forrest Turner was encouraged by the governor's willingness to listen. He was honored that the governor would call on him if he needed advice regarding the Georgia prisons. "I know I can help him, since I have been in most of them," Forrest surmised.

He had wanted to apprise the governor of the need to upgrade the mental hospital at Milledgeville, where he had worked as a dental assistant, but decided that he had taken up enough of the governor's precious time. "There will be other occasions to discuss those needs," he thought. He learned later that the governor was instrumental in the construction of three new buildings at the Milledgeville State Hospital. The new facilities included three thousand new beds and a state-of-the-art dental clinic. Just what Forrest Turner had hoped for.

Some other positive initiatives occurred during Herman Talmadge's administration. Several work camp facilities that the counties did not or would not upgrade were closed. A new work camp for youths was created in 1951 when the old convict work camp in Stephens County was converted exclusively for juvenile rehabilitation. It was the state's first juvenile honor work camp in Toccoa where teachers replaced guards. Useful skills such as carpentry, woodwork, bricklaying, electrical, automotive were taught. Of the two hundred and fifty transferred there, one hundred and ten young men came from Reidsville. Closer to home, Fulton County officials approved the construction of a new juvenile court building.

33 LIFE AFTER PAROLE

Forrest Turner's many escapes allowed him to stay abreast of the changing world. He entered prison at the end of the Great Depression and Prohibition and left shortly before the Korean War. Most of the major changes that occurred during his absence were influenced by the war. Modern technology introduced helicopters, radar systems, jeeps, and jets. The development and use of the atomic bomb ended the war. People began enjoying television and driving automobiles with automatic transmissions. Much had happened while he was in prison. He had a lot of catching up to do. But first he must face the challenge of coping with life outside of prison.

***

Upon release most paroled convicts were ill equipped to blend back into society. There were no halfway houses at that time to help them bridge between prison and independent life. That was especially true for those who had been incarcerated for an extended period. Time had changed their former surroundings from what they had left behind when entering prison. Their former friends and families had moved away or died. They were alone. They were experiencing a certain so-called "Rip Van Winkle" effect. Exiting prison seemed like waking from a long sleep and finding oneself in a strange new world.

The major problem facing an ex-convict was inactivity. For many it meant going home, if there was a home, and finding work if fortunate to find a job. Those without jobs or someone to motivate them to stay straight were soon back in prison. Pastor Allison had warned Forrest, "Idle hands are the Devil's workshop. You must stay busy." Forrest Turner did not have these problems. Forrest Turner had family to support him, he had a job as a denturist, and a "to do list" a mile long. He swore to himself that he was not going to put himself in a position to be imprisoned again.

All he owned was in that briefcase which he took with him during Saturday's walk to freedom. He had no money, no clothes, no worldly possessions, just his pride. He had to start over. For now, he could borrow what he needed. An important privilege of being free was the ability to go to wherever and whenever one pleased. He wanted to get a firsthand look at the changes that had occurred while he was away. To do that he needed a car, and a Georgia driver's license. It didn't matter when he was a fugitive, he was never stopped for driving without a license. Now, as a law-abiding citizen, his first mission was to obtain a license and drive legally.

On the day of his release, he had promised the Reverend that he would attend his church. It would be an awkward experience for Forrest Turner, not knowing how well a former convict would be received by those in attendance. When he did not immediately hear back from him, Pastor Bill became concerned. Two Sundays had passed, and to his elation, Forrest finally called. He had settled into his new surroundings. With an advance from Dr. Holtzendorf, and a small amount borrowed from family, he bought a used car. It was less fancy than the stolen cars he had driven while a fugitive, but it served its purpose. He had transportation and now was ready to attend Western Heights Baptist Church.

He was welcomed by Reverend Allison, who gave him a glowing introduction. Forrest Turner received a standing ovation and a rousing round of applause from the congregation. The notorious escape artist was as humble and gracious as any man could be.

He told Pastor Allison later, "It was a strange feeling to be praised rather than scorned, deservedly so, as many had done to me in the past." The memorable moment caused him to blush. He struggled to hold back his tears.

There were not enough hours in the day for Forrest Turner to try to make up for the years he had lost. He was just thirty-five years old, still a young man. Assessing his priorities he had to follow the requirements mandated by the pardon and parole board. In thirty days, he would have his first meeting with his parole officer. In the meantime, he kept a log of his daily activities and whereabouts. He had looked forward to reporting to Dr. Holtzendorf's dental clinic on Peachtree Street.

While in prison he promised himself that his penance for his bad behavior would be to counsel youth. He vividly remembered the young juveniles who were serving time at Reidsville Prison. Thank goodness for the prison reformer, Wiley Moore, who had the younger prisoners transferred to an all-youth prison. While at Reidsville he befriended an eleven-year-old lad who was in the same cell block. He was large for his age and mean as a rattle snake. He didn't belong in a cage surrounded by the worst criminals in the State of Georgia. If someone could have reached his inner soul and mind in time, his life could have had a different outcome. Forrest Turner lost track of the young man when he left Reidsville, but he suspected nothing good became of him.

Forrest Turner was a bachelor. Most men his age were married with children. While in prison he longed for a partner with whom he could share the rest of his life. He missed having a family of his own...certainly not the number of children as his mother and father had, but two or three. His wife to be would have to accept him for who he was...a reformed ex-convict struggling to resume a normal life.

While at Bellwood he met a lovely, pretty, and petite girl named June Young. She was active in the Baptist Training Union, who periodically visited prisons to conduct their mission work. Forrest Turner, who was the assistant chaplain, looked forward to her visits. Prison was a lonely place. The companionship of a lady, even for just an hour, was the highlight of his day. She was younger than him, but they shared a common bond. They loved their God.

June Young felt a certain admiration toward him because he had overcome his checkered past. The fact that he was rehabilitated and chose God over crime enhanced their affection. It didn't hurt the relationship that Forrest Turner was a handsome blue-eyed debonair looking gentleman. Forrest Turner had found God and June Young found him.

After his release, the first order of business was to confess his relationship with Betty Ann Jones, whom the newspapers had reported to be his alleged wife. He knew she deserved to hear the truth about their relationship. He finally got the courage and proceeded to tell her, "She was a lost soul who couldn't stay out of trouble. She idolized me because I was a notorious escape artist and always had pockets full of money. During my lonely days as a fugitive, she met me at my hideouts. There were occasions when she waited in the car while I was committing a robbery. In her twisted mind she considered me to be Clyde Barrow, and she imagined herself to be Bonnie Parker. It was more of a partnership in crime than a love affair. I had no real affection for her. In fact, she was already legally married to someone else named West when I met her. The last I heard she was serving time for theft in a Virginia prison."

The affair with Mrs. Betty Ann Jones West weighed heavily on his mind. He was afraid that when he revealed his relationship with her, Miss Young would no longer wish to see him. But he owed it to her to clear the air before he surprised her with a proposal of marriage.

"Whatever you did before you met me is in the past. It's the future that I am interested in," she fondly told Forrest.

Elated Forrest was overcome with happiness. "Well then, I know of no reason why we can't get married, June," Forrest divulged sheepishly.

Gushing with excitement June asked, "Is that a proposal?"

Forrest smiled and nodded his head up and down.

"Yeah, I will marry you as she hugged and affectionately kissed him. I was praying that you would ask me. Let's get married right away," she replied in a very hopeful manner.

In a matter of weeks Pastor Allison married them. It was a simple ceremony at a small Baptist Church. She was almost twenty and he was thirty-four. "A match made in heaven," the Reverend said just before he pronounced them husband and wife.

***

When Dr. Holtzendorf closed his Calhoun Clinic due to health and travel reasons, Forrest Turner went to work for his friend, Wiley Moore, constructing apartments on Roswell Road. When he wasn't working, he spent the first year making speeches, seventy in all. His "From Crime to Christ" theme attracted large crowds at each event. He gave testimonials at churches: Revival Baptist Tabernacle, Colonial Hills, First Baptist Church of Carrollton, Milner Bethel Baptist, Lawrenceville Rehoboth Baptist to name a few. Sometimes making as many as three separate talks on a given Sunday. His entire Sundays were spent attending and speaking at churches. After work on weekdays, he could be found speaking at civic clubs such as Optimist Clubs, Blackhall Civic Club, and others. He made himself available to any group within the state that would listen to his story no matter how far the drive. For his presentations he did not require a fee, but occasionally he received a small gift or token in appreciation.

When Wiley Moore's construction project was completed, Forrest Turner began looking for another job. The church goers in the pews and youth groups at the schools were overwhelmed by his message. Employers, however, could not look past his prison record and lack of a college education. He was very upfront about his past when interviewing for a job. The interviews for a well-paying job in the dental field for which he was trained weren't fruitful. They said they appreciated his honesty but then found some reason to offer the job to another candidate. His chief goal was to land a job as a dental technician. If not available, a job where he could work outside was his second choice. He preferred not to be confined behind four walls, if possible.

He was married and had responsibilities. He had no savings and was too embarrassed to ask for financial help. He had a wife with a child on the way. He finally took a temporary job at a grocery store to make ends meet.

Pastor Allison knew that Forrest Turner was trying to find himself. He had been unable to stick with one job for any length of time for one reason or another. The pastor suggested that he consider becoming a full-time minister. "Since leaving prison you have dedicated your life to Christ. You are good behind the pulpit. You enjoy counseling people, especially the youth. You should become a preacher like me," he told Forrest.

Forrest Turner thought he was getting the call to join the ministry, but he was not sure. Pastor Bill told Forrest, "A lot of people are going to encourage you to be a minister as I am doing. Don't let the urging come from the outside. Your decision must come from within. Let your own heart and soul guide you. You can give your life to God without being a minister."

During his period of soul-searching Forrest Turner agreed to make an appearance at Fulton Tower prison to speak to the inmates. It was an eerie feeling, returning to the place where he had spent many months as a prisoner. Now as a guest he shared with them his prison story, "I was once an inmate here just like you. I was a mixed-up man then with no future. Through a divine miracle I saw the light from above and changed my ways. Today I am a rehabilitated free man. This could happen to you. You must take the first step and shun the devil's temptations." He didn't know how many took his message in earnest. When he was there as a prisoner, a similar message presented to him went right over his head. He had hoped that the outcome of the meeting would influence his decision to become a minister.

To be an effective preacher he realized he must go to a Baptist seminary to study. He knew about Adam and Eve, Moses parting the Red Sea and the Crucifixion, but he was not proficient in the teachings of the Bible. Work camps didn't offer convicts the opportunity to read the Bible. Even if they did, he was not in the frame of mind to learn scripture. He had forgotten most of the Bible teachings he had heard as a youth. He also realized leaving the workplace for the classroom would be a burden to his family. He couldn't be a good student, loving husband, and devoted father all at the same time. Then there were the financial consequences. "Where would the money come from," he worried. Since he had his family to think about, the ministry would have to wait.

One of the happiest days of his life was the birth of his daughter, Sherry, born at Crawford Long Hospital on May 1, 1950. His life was trending in the right direction. His good fortune continued when Milledgeville State Hospital hired him as a dental assistant. He was performing a service that he had learned and perfected while in prison. He had been out of prison for less than two years. God had answered his prayers. He had a family, employment, and a sense of peace in his life.

In 1954 the Georgia Board of Pardons and Paroles returned forty-year-old Forrest Turner his eligibility to vote. Having fulfilled a perfect parole record for five years, his civil and political rights were restored. His conditional parole was revoked, and full pardon was granted. When Forrest Turner cast his ballot for Marvin Griffin in the November gubernatorial election, it was his first time voting since his arrest.

Forrest Turner left Milledgeville State Hospital, when he was offered a job with a major manufacturing concern. In 1959 his second daughter Maria was born.

***

The demand for making public appearances and giving testimonials continued. He always began by sharing a little history of his prison time. "Back in the 1940s I was in a hopeless state. I had accumulated prison sentences which totaled nearly a century. My faith in God rescued me from the brink of destruction," he told his astounded audience. "In 1945 I converted to Christianity."

When speaking to civic organizations and youth groups, he always allotted time for questions and answers. The inquisitive minds never failed to amaze him. He gave a group of boys at a reform school an earful of frank answers.

"Why did you escape so many times?" asked a young fella on the front row.

"That's always the first question. Each time the guards mistreated me, I considered escaping. It was my intention to serve out my time at Thomas County Work Camp. That meant being a good convict in hopes of getting an early parole. I was angry because I didn't deserve to be there. Once paroled I knew that this miserable part of my life would be over. I soon realized that an early release was not forthcoming. My patience finally ran out when I was beaten for making a smart remark to a guard. I decided that I would rather be shot and killed than spend another day in that God forsaken place," Forrest said in a remorseful tone as he fielded the next question.

"What was the worst part about being on a chain gang?" someone yelled out.

"To me it was the leg irons. It took several months for my chafed ankles to heal as the skin got rubbed raw while trying to keep pace with the other convicts doing road work." Forrest said as he bent over to untie his right shoe, pulled off his sock, and raised his foot. "Take a good look at the ugly scar. See what I mean. The other ankle looks just as bad.

"Prison was a lonely place. We were isolated from the world. At the beginning I was not allowed to receive mail or newspapers. There were no radios to listen to. The treatment was so bad that I saw convicts take razor blades and cut their heel strings to avoid the brutal road work."

Forrest Turner could tell by the look in their eyes that he had their undivided attention. Several had their hands up wanting to ask a question. He pointed to a boy who was frantically waving his raised arm. "What happened to you when you were caught?"

"At most of the work camps, convicts, who tried to escape and were caught, were either whipped with a leather strap or locked into a 'sweat box' for fourteen days. If it was his second attempt he was let out for a day and then locked up again for another two weeks. It was a steel box too small to stand up in, that had just a small window for the guard to look in to see if you were still alive. If the convict managed to survive the four weeks from what little food he was given, there wasn't much left of him when he was let out. In one of the work camps, I was put in a concrete box in a hole dug underneath the building. It was dark, damp, and cold. Not even a rat could stand to go in there. At the Reidsville prison where I escaped four times. I was put in an isolation cell after each recapture. As punishment during the Christmas Holidays, I received only stale bread and water. I must have lost twenty pounds while I was there, and I am not a big fella. You can imagine how I looked," Forrest replied.

"Were you ever whipped?" another student asked.

"I never received ten lashes. If I had, I wouldn't be here today. But I was struck with the whip many times while working outdoors on roads for breaking one of the guard's silly rules. It was painful and hurt for hours," Forrest said with a frowning look.

Then Forrest asked, "Do you boys get whippings here when you misbehave?"

The school's headmaster responded, "Yes, but we use paddles not the leather whips. While I have the floor I would like to ask a question. Can you tell us about the electric chair?"

"Yeah, I can," Forrest answered with a stern expression. "Well, for some of my time at Reidsville I was in the cell block below the floor where 'Old Smokey,' the electric chair, was situated. During my years in and out of prison there were seven executions of convicts whom I had met or knew about. I had already been transferred to Bellwood Work Camp when the only female, Lena Baker, was electrocuted in March of 1945. She was a maid who murdered her abusive boss.

"Most of those who met their death by 'Old Smokey' were either disadvantaged or Black. It's a horrible way to die and not a pretty sight to watch. People say the lights flickered when the executioner pulls the switch, and two thousand volts pass through the condemned person's body. It's not true. I hope it doesn't happen to you. But death by electrocution can be the result if you don't heed my words, Crime has no rewards just punishments!"

"Let me give you some final advice. Some think it takes guts for you to disarm a deputy or a warden and escape in his car. It takes immeasurably more guts to walk like a man and face your debt to society. The inmates at Reidsville poked fun at me when I decided to go straight," he told them. "Some of those fellas are the very ones who are in their graves or still in prison today."

Forrest Turner did not know why these boys were sent to this private school. He suspected the boys were making trouble at their homes or were suspended from their public schools. They were destined to defy the law and end up in prison. Some had parents, who became so frustrated with their sons, that they chose to pass the responsibility of raising them to someone else. Some came from households of dysfunctional families where there was a lack of discipline. Fortunately, the families had the money and the good sense to send them to a private school where they could get the discipline and education needed.

34 SHINGLEROOF CAMPGROUND

Forrest Turner had numerous speaking engagements. The two most notable were his first testimonial he gave in Bainbridge, followed a few years later by the one in Henry County where he was raised. Reverend Allison and his wife accompanied him to the Bainbridge Calvary Baptist Church engagement. On the way he offered Forrest Turner advice and encouragement. His visit to Shingleroof Campground in McDonough brought back fond memories.

***

Reverend Bill Allison, Chaplain of the Fulton County Prison System was instrumental in convincing Forrest Turner to forego his life of crime and dedicate his existence to God. When first asked, he agreed without hesitation to speak to the groups, but now he wondered whether he had the courage to do so. He had never been short of words and was comfortable talking to individuals or to a group of friends. But, standing behind the pulpit facing a church full of devout Southern Baptists was another matter. He didn't know whether he would be hit with a case of stage fright or accidentally make an off-color remark. He had gotten so accustomed to "prison speak" that an "unchurch like" word or remark was sure to pop out. It would be a challenge to use the proper language to describe his life in prison without offending the ladies. He didn't want the listeners throwing their Bibles at him, nor embarrass himself or the Chaplain.

Of all the prisoners Pastor Bill took under his wing while in prison, none were more determined to succeed than Forrest Turner. Knowing that out-of-town talks to total strangers would be stressful, the chaplain and his wife drove him to his early engagements. Forrest Turner appreciated the company and moral support provided by them. He clearly remembered one of those engagements, a long trip to a church in Bainbridge, Georgia. It was the closest he had been to Thomasville and its work camp since his escape in 1938. He had no desire to get any nearer.

Chaplain Allison stressed, "Now Forrest, here is my advice to you. Just relax and speak from your heart. You are not expected to give an eloquent sermon. The preacher at the church will do that. Let your message be about the evils of crime. 'Crime does not Pay.' I suggest you use that old phrase in your speech."

I can tell them about my time at the work camps. How I was forced to do hard labor while in leg irons. Eating awful food and sleeping in crowded conditions that weren't fit for a dog," Forrest said as he felt more at ease.

With an encouraging look, the chaplain responded, "It was a huge price to pay for your past transgressions. I know you will do well."

Just as the chaplain had predicted, his talk to the Calvary Baptist Church was a success. Although Forrest Turner was extremely nervous at first, he settled down after a few minutes. "Once I could sense that everyone in the pews had an interest in what I was saying, I relaxed," he told the chaplain afterwards.

Several members of the congregation came up to congratulate him on his inspirational message. The pastor even wrote a letter to an Atlanta newspaper saying that in all his time as a minister he had never met anyone with whom he was more impressed with than Mr. Turner. "The people in attendance were behind him wholeheartedly. We only wish it could have been possible for every person in the State of Georgia to hear this man who has turned from sin to the Savior," extolled the pastor.

***

Many more such engagements followed. The one that had special meaning to Forrest Turner was his appearance at Shingleroof Campground. Henry County was his birthplace and first home. Members of his family and former school friends were there. By now he was able to recite his presentation from memory. There was no need to have written notes tucked in his coat pocket to use if he should lose his train of thought.

The Turner family was well acquainted with Shingleroof Campground as were most people in Henry County. In summer or early fall each year families traveled to McDonough, Georgia to attend spiritual revival services. The unique event referred to as a "camp meeting" saw a pilgrimage of Christians gather for one week to renew their religious beliefs. While at the campground they could enjoy fellowship and partake in recreational activities. Visiting preachers motivated the crowds while softball and other games kept the young lads out of trouble. Those too young for softball could spend their days picking Cicada skins off the bark of pine trees and filling their mason jars at night with Fireflies. The campfire storytelling and singing entertained young and old until way after dark.

The tradition of camp meetings at Shingleroof dated back to the 1830s. Settlers came to Henry County by means of government-land lotteries. Tracts of land were available to farmers who would clear and cultivate the land, build homes, grow crops, and raise animals. In the ensuing years construction of roads, shops, churches and schools followed. Survival on a farm in those days required working from sunup to sundown with little time to socialize with neighbors. Between the planting and the harvest there was a slack period when farm families had the opportunity to meet one another and worship. Farmsteads were scattered throughout the area and travel was limited to horses and buggies. A central location in the county was needed to gather. The place required an adequate supply of fresh water and was conducive to the building of cabins. A site having one hundred acres located off Decatur Road, which came to be known as Highway 155, was chosen.

Shingleroof Campground:
Faith of Our Fathers, Faith of Our Own,
Praising Our Savior, Passing it On

The camp meetings usually lasted a week. In the early days those who came to worship slept in wagons or tents and cooked on open fires. Spearheaded by the Methodist Church, Shingleroof was now open to all Protestant faiths. The entire community was welcome. Many of the attendees stayed in the same cabins occupied by their family for generations. Over time the local citizens referred to "Shingleroof Campground" as a place to find solitude and inner peace. Surrounded by old rustic cottages, walking trails, woods, and a sheltered open-air pavilion, the campers encountered few distractions. The mornings and evenings were filled with worship services. In between participants enjoyed their leisure time, recreation and fellowship.

***

Forrest recalls that memorable day, "It was August 16, 1959, a typical summer day, hot and humid. My wife, June, and I arrived early so we could do a walking tour of the place. Our guide was preacher William Powell from the Flippen Methodist Church. I was the main speaker at the Sunday service. All the old cabins looked just as I had remembered them as a boy. Some of the cabins still had dirt floors and clapboard siding. I felt like I was traveling back in time. The buildings, religious traditions and camp atmosphere had been preserved. Preacher Powell told me that it was the one-hundred-twenty-eighth session for Shingleroof. Over the years there had been hundreds of preachers who had preceded me to the pulpit. I made a friendly wager with June. I bet her that it was the first time Shingleroof had a speaker, who was an ex-convict." She just smiled.

The Methodist District Superintendent invited Forrest Turner to the pulpit. "The gentleman standing beside me, is Forrest Turner. Since he is from McDonough, some of you are related to or may have grown up with him. The rest of you have heard or read about him. Today he has an interesting and inspiring message for you. He is the best example of a man who had a zero chance of turning away from his life of crime. But through his belief in God, he is a testament that it can be done. I give you Forrest Turner."

Forrest Turner was smartly dressed in his favorite blue suit with a matching vest. He spoke with humility, meekness, and told a simple story. His sincerity and desire to convince those to avoid life's temptations were very persuading. He said that he could not have done it without the encouragement of Chaplain Allison.

Forrest thanked the superintendent and began his message, "From 1934 to 1942 I had accumulated so many years of prison time that I would have been one hundred fourteen years old when released. I was on the brink of despair. I had gone to my knees in prayer asking that I might go free someday. The defining moment came when I realized I could escape from everywhere and everything except from God. I learned what faith in God can do for a man. I am here today as an example of the power of prayer.

"I am terribly sorry for all the stupid things I have done. I have learned my lesson. Going forward I want my life to exalt Jesus Christ and follow his example," he said in a contrite manner. While looking at a scruffy young man on the second row, Forrest said, "Don't make the same mistakes I did. Some think crime is glamorous, but all the glamor fades when you are behind bars."

He paused for a minute to take a sip from his water glass. He continued, "The only thing that I am proud of is that I never intentionally hurt anyone during my sinful days. Yeah, I threatened to shoot them if they didn't hand over their money or give me the keys to their automobiles. I am sure it scared most of them 'half to death.' But I would never have shot them."

He spoke for twenty minutes and answered questions for another forty. After he thanked those who came to hear his message, the entire congregation rose and gave him a loud round of applause.

The grounds around the pavilion were packed with campers and curious onlookers. Notification of his appearance in the local newspapers had attracted others who came just to hear him speak and hopefully meet him in person. Knowing it would be crowded, they brought blankets and sat on the lawn. Family members who once were ashamed of him, now were beaming with pride.

Forrest Turner used his trip to McDonough to visit family members who still lived in Flippen. He was pleased that cousins Charles Turner and Geraldine Allgood, accompanied by her son, Larry, were in attendance. His mother, now seventy-two, did not attend, however, several friends from Henry County were present to hear his testimonial. It was indeed a memorable day.

35 DENTAL LAB

If he had to do it over again and if he had the means and opportunity, Forrest Turner would have attended dental school. His life would have been different. He would have been a successful dentist with a waiting room full of patients. However, there was no looking back. He had to make do with what he had and what he knew. Very little was gained from his time in prison except for his knowledge of making dentures, partials and plates. His workmanship was comparable to any denturist practicing in Georgia. What Forrest Turner lacked was a license from the Board of Dental Examiners to practice dentistry. To obtain such a license he must attend and complete the course work at a dental school. At fifty-three years of age, he had no desire to attend dental school just to obtain a certificate to frame and hang on a wall in his office. Twenty years of on-the-job experience should be enough training to qualify him to practice with or without a license.

***

While working as a dental assistant at the state hospital in Milledgeville, Forrest Turner decided to open his own dental laboratory. The ninety-mile drive from Decatur to Milledgeville was time-consuming and stressful. He opened a small office on Mc-

Donough Street in Jonesboro to be closer to his home. Located a couple of miles from the Clayton County Courthouse, the office was convenient for Henry and Clayton County residents needing dentures. Dentists whose practices were to be impacted by the more affordably priced dentures offered by Forrest Turner, opposed the opening of his new office.

Georgia law prohibited the sale of false teeth directly to the public. The denture maker could only manufacture dentures for a dentist's patient based on a prescription. According to the law, the dentist must make the impression, order the denture from a denturist, and then plant the denture in the patient's mouth. At Forrest Turner's urging, a bill to repeal the law was introduced during the 1959 Legislative session. Unfortunately, the bill never made it out of committee.

Later he opened a second office thus owning and managing two clinics: the dental laboratory in Jonesboro and one in Lilburn. There he provided dentures for the indigent and elderly at reduced prices. If financial circumstances were dire enough, he would make and insert the dentures for free. He was a godsend to many needy patients. Unfortunately, the dental society was not happy with his infringement into their lucrative denture business. They were determined to put him out of business.

In August 1967, an injunction petition was filed by the Georgia Board of Dental Examiners in DeKalb County charging Forrest Turner with making and selling dentures not ordered by or returned to a licensed dentist. Accompanying Forrest Turner at the hearing was his friend and ally, Pastor Bill Allison, who was there to vouch for his honesty and integrity since parole.

Before the attorney for the dental board could make his argument, Forrest Turner's attorney asked if he could approach the bench. "Judge Morgan, I have filed an appeal on the legal points of the injunction to a higher court," he said as he handed the judge a copy of the appeal document. After verifying the authenticity of the pending appeal, the judge postponed his decision until the higher court made its ruling on the appeal. In the meantime, Forrest Turner continued his denture practice as before. He knew the dental board would continue to pursue the matter.

When the higher court denied the appeal, Forrest Turner and his attorney were back in the lower court in December 1968. After hearing the arguments from the attorneys, he delayed his decision until he could deliberate over the facts. A short time later, with both parties present, Judge Morgan ruled in favor of the Georgia Board of Dental Examiners. Based on Georgia Dental Practice laws he issued an injunction against Forrest Turner enjoining him from practicing dentistry without a proper license. The action pleased the Georgia Board of Dental Examiners, who considered Forrest Turner's dental laboratories as a threat to the dental industry.

From the very beginning his attorney had told Forrest that Judge Morgan would likely rule in favor of the Georgia Board of Dental Examiners. Expecting the worst, he was prepared to give the judge a piece of his mind. "I was authorized to do dental work as a Trusty by two governors. During that time, I 'fixed teeth' for state troopers, judges, prison officials, and hospital patients," Forrest said. "The Georgia Board of Dental Examiners are using retaliatory tactics, because I have been campaigning against dentist's unfair pricing. Dentists have placed the price of dentures beyond the means of seventy percent of the people in Georgia. I am fighting for the poor people."

The president of the board argued, "The board will oppose any legislation allowing denturists to fit teeth, unless the denturist is trained in anatomy and biophysics. It is known in our profession that there are undesirable medical consequences to the patient if the denture is ill-fitted. Also, we have had dentists who told us about patients who came to their practice complaining of uncomfortable dentures. These were former patients of Forrest Turner. Consequently, the dentist had to replace the denture."

Forrest found that statement hard to believe. "If a patient was unhappy with his denture, he was told upfront that it would be replaced free of charge. I wanted the patient to be satisfied. Why would a patient who paid little or nothing for a denture from me, and then go to a dentist and have it replaced paying a retail price? It doesn't make sense," Forrest replied.

Forrest Turner promised to comply with the injunction. However, he would work harder than ever to see that legislation was introduced to set up a special board of examiners. The board could license qualified denturists based on experience not on a dental degree, allowing them to sell false teeth directly to patients without the intervention of a dentist. To promote such legislation, he agreed to lobby its merits on behalf of the Independent Dental Laboratories Association of America. His speeches tried to expose what he claimed was a racket behind dental plates.

Forrest Turner's dental lab continued to operate under the injunction. Albeit dentists had stopped sending him business in retaliation. The underserved, poor, and elderly needing one type of dental apparatus, or another continued to seek him for his affordable service. In sympathy for these people, Forrest Turner agreed to see and help them. Word got back to the board that he was sneaking patients into his laboratory fitting them with dentures. They complained to the G.B.I. An agent assigned to investigate began watching the lab and saw non-employees enter and leave the lab. To confirm his suspicions and bring formal charges the G.B.I. needed more proof. Forrest Turner had to be caught in the act.

***

Forrest Turner's lobbying efforts had gotten him interested in politics. He was a staunch democrat. He actively supported Jimmy Carter in his campaign for governor. One afternoon a man who he had worked with during the campaign called Forrest Turner to seek his dental help for a friend of his. Eager to help, he recommended to the caller to have his friend get in touch with him. After a brief time, Forrest Turner received the call.

He introduced himself and began to describe his predicament. "I got drunk at a Jimmy Carter victory party and lost my false teeth. I woke up in the morning and the teeth were not in my glass where I usually put them before I go to bed. I looked everywhere but I couldn't find them. Could you make me a set of dentures, really quick?" he asked.

Forrest Turner told him that he was headed to Cherokee County to put out some gospel singing posters. But he gave him the address of a colleague near Canton. "Go meet the man and he will make a dental impression. I will pick up the impression on my way home and prepare the dentures in my lab later this evening," Forrest promised the caller.

He made a set of dentures and asked the stranger to meet him at a church in Canton. When the man arrived, Forrest had him try out the dentures. "How do they fit?" Forrest asked looking into the man's mouth, "They look good to me. See for yourself, look in the mirror over there."

The man appeared overjoyed and gladly paid the charge which was fifteen dollars above Forrest's cost. "Mr. Turner, I will never forget you as long as I live," the man said as he left the church.

Forrest Turner was pleased that he was able to help the man. The same feeling of self-pride he had each time a patient left his lab with a new smile. A brief time later two agents from the Georgia Bureau of Investigation appeared at the laboratory. "We are here to arrest you Mr. Turner on the charge of practicing dentistry without a license," one of the agents said while the other handcuffed him. "You had prepared a set of dentures yesterday for a man who was a G.B.I. informer." Hearing the agent's accusations, Forrest was utterly dumbfounded and left speechless. While searching the lab for evidence, the agents uncovered a small bottle labeled Novocain.

Shocked and bewildered, Forrest Turner was more hurt than disappointed. "I felt like someone had stabbed me in the heart after hearing what the agent told me. I had tried to be a "Good Samaritan" to a stranger, but he betrayed me just as Judas had done to Jesus," Forrest said later. "It was the same resentment for the law, which I had after my first arrest. I am older and wiser now. I will seek my revenge the legal way through the courts."

He was taken to G.B.I. headquarters where he was charged. He posted bond and was released the same day. He would have a future court date to plead his defense. It would take a long time before Forrest Turner was able to forgive the stranger who said that he would never forget him for replacing his dentures and the fella who asked for the favor.

In January 1971 he stood before Judge Marion Pope to defend his conviction in Cherokee County Superior Court. He was accused of practicing dentistry there without a license and the possession of an illegal drug. Forrest had pleaded "nolo contendere" to both charges. In the packed courtroom in Canton, defendant Forrest Turner gave an eloquent argument as to why he should not be punished. "The narcotic charge relates to Novocain, the agent found in my lab. It is a common anesthetic used in the deadening of the gums of patients. It was not for personal use," Forrest argued. "The Novocain was found in an old dentist's bag that was given to me some time ago. I even forgot I had it.

"I am not a drug addict or a pusher! When I was a prisoner at Reidsville, the state spent a lot of money teaching me dental medicine. During the war, when the prison dentist left to join the armed services, I inherited complete charge of the dental program at Reidsville. For a while, I was the only one there to do the dental work needed at the prison. I had two thousand men and eight hundred women prisoners, plus the guards and their families under my care. They were thankful for what I could do for them. Today I am providing teeth for needy people. For that and I am treated like a criminal. It doesn't sound fair to me.

"Your Honor, if I were in the state of South Carolina making the impressions, building the dentures and inserting them into the mouths of the patients, I would not be breaking the law. In Georgia, a dentist orders the patient's dentures from a denturist who charges fourteen to thirty dollars for each. The dentist then marks up the price for the patient to two hundred fifty to three hundred dollars if the dentures fit properly. Wouldn't you call that a racket, Your Honor?" Forrest insisted.

"I am aware that your actions appear to be in the best interest of the patient, Mr. Turner. But since you are not a dentist, it is illegal for you to possess Novocain," Judge Pope said, "You broke the law. Therefore, for the charge of possession of the illegal drug Novocain, I am sentencing you to two years' probation. One year probation for practicing dentistry without a license. I am also fining you five hundred dollars. My advice to you, Mr. Turner, if you feel the present law is unfair, then lobby your legislators to change the law."

Judge Marion Pope explained to those in the courtroom. "I probated the sentence against Turner because it wouldn't serve in the best interest of anyone. Turner's actions were not self-serving but rather an attempt to help those in need. And besides, if I send him back to prison he would just probably escape." After a moment, several people in the courtroom began to laugh.

The ill-timed humor and the verdict did not please Forrest Turner. Knowing so, the judge added an unexpected compliment. "Mr. Turner, I commend you for the dental service you provided while in prison. I am sure you relieved many a suffering inmate from tooth pain," he said with sincerity looking directly at Forrest."

The battle with the Board of Dental Examiners, which began in 1967, had made full circle. In the end he lost. The ordeal only intensified his motivation to have the law changed. "If I had a seat at the state house in Atlanta, I could convince my colleagues to amend the law," Forrest proclaimed. "I need to run for office."

36 WHAT'S MY LINE?

The appearance on the extremely popular Emmy award-winning quiz show in 1968 was the pinnacle of his fame. His unusual background and accomplishments earned him the invitation to be among celebrities. Could he stump the panel on "What's My Line?" The producers of the show were constantly looking for individuals with unique occupations. Forrest Turner's name was well known in Georgia. His talents caught the attention of the casting director in New York.

***

One day in July 1968 a lady from Columbia Broadcasting called Forrest Turner at the dental lab.

"Is this Forrest Turner who owns the dental lab in Jonesboro, Georgia?" the caller asked.

Forrest replied, "Yeah, Ma'am. This is Forrest. What can I do for you?"

She continued, "My name is Helen Moore. I am the casting director for Columbia Broadcasting Company. I handle the booking of guests for the 'What's My Line?' show here on CBS. Have you watched our show on television?"

"I reckon I have. I have seen it many times," he answered with a chuckle. "You wouldn't be related to Wiley Moore, who lived in Atlanta, but died a few years ago, would you?" Forrest asked.

Mrs. Moore politely answered, "No, I have no relatives in Atlanta. But here is why I am calling. From what I have heard, Mr. Turner, you would be an interesting guest. We have never had a former prisoner on the show, nor have we had anyone who made dentures. I learned of your wonderful reputation for counseling parolees and misguided youths. We will pay your expenses to come to New York and to spend the night at a hotel near the studio. What do you say, Mr. Turner?"

Amazed and flattered by the request he could not think of any reason not to go. "It should be fun. Will I be paid for appearing on the show?" Forrest asked.

Mrs. Moore responded, "Everyone asks that question. You will have a chance to win up to fifty dollars if the panel is unable to guess your occupation. I will get back to you when I have more details."

***

Forrest Turner had made many speeches and had many interviews, but the thought of being on television made him nervous. Shortly thereafter Forrest Turner made the trip to New York. The sheer size of the tall buildings, the hustle and bustle of the crowds, and the traffic were beyond his comprehension. None of the large towns in the South compared to the City of New York.

A taxi drove him to the Ed Sullivan Theater. The soon-to-be TV celebrity met with Lloyd Gross, the show's director, who briefed him on what to expect. He also received instructions on what and what not to do. Don't say anything unless Mr. Bruner or one of the panelists asks a question. Reframe from using bad language. When you speak, look at the camera, the one with the small flashing red light on top.

Wally Bruner came backstage and introduced himself to Forrest Turner. "Don't be nervous. Just be yourself," he said to Forrest as he patted him on the back. "We go on the air in about twenty minutes. You are scheduled to be the second contestant."

"Tell me, Mr. Bruner do you know when the show will be seen on television?" asks Forrest.

Wally Bruner replied, "It is being videotaped and should be on Atlanta TV in about three to four weeks."

*"Let's All Play
What's My Line!"*

In a soundproof waiting room reserved for the contestants was a television set. Forrest Turner was able to watch the show while waiting for his turn. After the show's music jingle ended, the announcer, Johnny Olson's, loud voice could be heard as he kicked off the show. "Let's all play! 'What's My Line!' Let's meet our panel."

Johnny Olson first introduced Nipsey Russell who he called a poet laureate and popular comedian. The witty Nipsy Russell, known for humorous poems, entered from behind the curtain. Wearing a light brown suit with a matching tie he walked to his seat behind the panel's desk. Standing behind the desk and his chair, he introduced the next panelist. "There are many rewards for being on 'What's My Line,' none better than sitting next to the lovely Joanna Barnes.

Joanna Barnes entered wearing a black dress with a two-inch collar. Underneath the collar below the chin was a pendent shaped like a star. With flattering remarks, she then introduced Bert Convy, who entered wearing a black suit, red shirt, and red tie. The flashy-dressed Mr. Convy introduced the lovely Arlene Francis. Mrs. Francis, always attired in the latest fashion, introduced Wally Bruner who entered and sat behind the moderator's desk. As the panel took their seats, the next segment of the show began.

Wally Bruner looked into the first camera and made his usual remarks to the viewing audience. "In the next few minutes, you will meet some interesting people who will try to stump our panel. "Is the panel ready?" he asked, as the second camera focused on the elongated desk where the panelists took their seats.

"Yes, we are," replied the panelists in unison.

***

During a brief commercial break and just before it was Forrest Turner's turn, the assistant director came to the waiting room to escort the anxious Forrest Turner to a spot marked by an 'X' on the floor behind the curtain. When the moderator Bruner announced," Would the next challenger sign in please!" The assistant director pulled back the curtain and whispered to Forrest, "Okay you are on. Good luck."

As he walked out and shook Mr. Bruner's hand, the surreal surroundings overwhelmed him. "Is this for real?" thought Forrest. His eyes were instantly drawn to the cameramen humped over behind their cameras. The lighting was very bright and the temperature on stage was as hot as a South Georgia July day. Under his blue suit coat and vest, he was sweating badly. "At that moment, the thought of possibly making a fool of myself raced through my mind. I don't know how many thousands of people will see me mess up," he wondered.

'What's My Line?' was an immensely popular quiz show. It had been on the air since 1950. The show had just recently been upgraded from black and white to color. The theme of the game show was for the panel of four celebrities to guess the contestant's line of work. The panelists would ask questions that required a 'yes' or 'no' answer. If the answer was 'yes,' the panelist was allowed to ask another question, this continued until the panelist received a 'no' answer. The next panelist followed the same procedure. For every wrong answer Forrest Turner won five dollars. If after ten wrong answers with no one guessing the contestant's line of work, the contestant would be deemed as having stumped the panel and won fifty dollars. It was the show's tradition to find individuals with unique if not bizarre occupations.

The first contestant was an attractive young lady. She was a college student with an interesting part-time job. She was able to outwit all the panelists except Arlene Francis who guessed her line of work after three correct questions.

The show continued as Mr. Bruner introduced the next guest. As had earlier challengers done numerous times before, Forrest Turner calmly walked over to a chalkboard and signed in. In case the panelist couldn't read the handwriting, Mr. Bruner always read aloud the signature on the board, "Forrest Turner!" He took a seat next to Mr. Bruner's right, behind the moderator's desk.

Mr. Bruner asked Forrest Turner where he was from. "I am from Atlanta, Georgia," Forrest proudly replied while looking at the four celebrities. He could not help but notice the big grin on Nipsy Russell's face. Mr. Russell was from Atlanta and aware of Forrest Turner's local fame. At that moment Forrest Turner's occupation appeared on the studio monitor and on the home audience's television screens, "Makes Dentures." The audience on cue let out loud cheers followed by thunderous applause.

Mr. Bruner informed the panel that Mr. Turner provided a product. He called on Bert to begin the questioning.

Bert Convy, "Is this a product that I might need?"

Forrest, "No, let's hope not." The audience burst out in laughter.

Wally Bruner, "One down and nine to go, flipping the first card on his rolodex that shows five dollars. Arlene it's your turn."

Arlene Francis, "While providing this product do you wear something other than what you are wearing now? You look so handsome in your blue suit."

Forrest, "Thank you ma'am, yeah."

Arlene Francis, "Is the product that you provide for people rather than animals?"

Forrest, "Yeah."

Arlene Francis, "Since you are man, would men use it more than women?"

Forrest, "No, ma'am it's not."

Wally Bruner, "That's two wrong answers and eight to go, as he flips the rolodex showing ten dollars, Nipsey."

Nipsey Russell, "I am afraid that I must disqualify myself." Looking at Forrest Turner with a broad smile, "I know Mr. Turner."

Joanna leaning over to Nipsy with her cupped hand around her right ear, "If you know what he makes, why don't you whisper the product name to me."

Nipsey Russell laughed, "No, seriously, you know I have Atlanta ties."

Wally Bruner, "I Understand. I will count that as a wrong answer and flips the card. Joanna it's your turn."

Joanna Barnes, "So, you are from the South. With your southern drawl, I figured as much. Is this a product used primarily in the Atlanta area or the South?"

Forrest, "No, it's not."

Wally Bruner flips the card. "That's four down, Bert."

Bert Convy, "Mr. Turner, if I needed your product, would I go to your place of business rather than you come to my house?"

Forrest, "I believe you will."

Bert Convy, "Mr. Turner, would your place of business be a store?"

Forrest, "No, it's not."

Wally Bruner flips the card. "That's five down, Arlene."

Arlene Francis, "Does it have anything to do with children?"

Forrest, "No."

Wally Bruner, "Flips the card. That's six down."

Joanna Barnes, "So, what you make is it more for adults?"

Forrest, "Yeah, it is."

Joanna Barnes, "Is it bigger than a bread box?"

Forrest, "No Ma'am."

Wally Bruner, "Flips the card. That's seven down."

Bert Convy, "Can I hold the product in my hand?"

Forrest, "Yeah, you can."

Mr. Bruner interrupts and whispers into Forrest Turner's ear and says to him. "You can hold it in your hand, but only when you take the denture out of your mouth. The 'yes' answer is a little misleading." Forrest nodded in agreement.

Bruner speaking to the panel, "If you are referring to a product Mr. Turner's makes as something that will fit into your hand, the answer is 'yes.' But it is not something that you would physically handle on a regular basis. I will give you a 'yes.' You may ask another question."

Bert Convy, "Will this product improve my looks?"

Forrest smiling, "Yeah, it might"

Bruner interrupts. "Indirectly it can."

Bert Convy, "Well then, is the product you make something that has a unique or pleasing scent such as perfume?"

Forrest, "No, it does not."

Wally Bruner, "That's eight down and two to go, Arlene."

Arlene Frances, "In using your product, does it come in contact to any part of the body?"

Forrest, "Yeah, it does."

Arlene Francis, "This product you make, would it be used above the neck?"

Forrest, "Yeah."

Arlene Francis, "Is it done to the face?"

Wally Bruner, "I am going to count that as a 'no.' As he flips the card. Panel, you have thirty seconds to uncover what product Mr. Turner makes. Joanna, it's your turn."

Joanna Barnes, "Does your product have anything to do with medical care?"

Forrest, "Yeah, I would say so."

Joanna Barnes, "It must involve a medical device that goes somewhere above the neck. Is it a hearing aid?"

Forrest grinning, "No it's not."

As Wally Bruner turns over the last card, he tells the panel. "Mr. Turner has stumped you and wins fifty dollars. Mr. Turner makes dentures!" The panelists and the studio audience applause.

Arlene Francis, "Goodness, that was going to be my next guess!"

Wally Bruner, "What is unique about Mr. Turner is that he learned to make dentures while he was in prison. Mr. Turner is a former convict who spent fifteen years in Georgia prisons. In addition to making dentures, he speaks to youth groups, civic organizations and churches about the evils of crime. Mr. Turner counsels and advises parolees and youth offenders as part of their probation requirements. He hopes that by telling his life story it will discourage others from making the same mistakes. He is the most sought-after speaker in Georgia.

The "Mystery Guest" followed Forrest Turner on the show and was the final contestant. Since the contestant was a well-known celebrity, the panel was blindfolded. This time each panelist could only ask one question per turn and then had two to three minutes to name the guest. Even while the "Mystery Guest" tried to disguise her voice, Mrs. Francis was able to identify her. The thirty-minute show ended having entertained the audience with contestants who had challenging professions or made unique products and featured the appearance of a movie star.

The challengers and panelists remained on stage and conversed. Of course, Forrest Turner got all the attention. He was able to meet all the celebrities. He and Nipsey Russell talked about the time when they met after he spoke to Nipsey's church. "Back in the 1930s and 1940s, you were in the news all the time. I read that you had escaped from prison many times. That's an amazing story," he told Forrest.

"Forrest, while I was carhopping hotdogs and hamburgers to customers in the Atlanta Varsity parking lot, you were stealing cars," Mr. Russell commented. "Just kidding of course. Those were the good old days before I went to Hollywood."

Forrest Turner didn't know much about Bert Convy, the singer and game show participant, nor Joanna Barnes, the actress and writer. But the 'Mystery Guest' Maureen Stapleton was one of his favorite movie stars. He had seen her in the movie "Lonely Hearts." He was familiar with Arlene Francis, the radio performer and stage actress. She had been a panelist on the show since it first aired in the 1950s. He had seen her on the show multiple times.

"She is an attractive and charming lady," Forrest told his family when he returned home. "It was quite an experience. I loved every minute of it. Winning fifty dollars plus the small appearance fee was just the icing on the cake. Forrest was a little 'full of himself' when he asked jokingly. "Do any of you want my autograph?"

37 HOUSE OF REPRESENTATIVES

Disappointed by the legal maneuvering by the dental board to shut down his dental labs, Forrest Turner was determined to change the law. While the formal accusation against him was pending in court, he was encouraged by his friends and family to take the case to the State Capitol. On June 6, 1968, he filed the necessary documents with the secretary of state to run for office. Living in DeKalb County he became a candidate for the District 75 House of Representative seat.

Forrest Turner's name on the ballot in November added an unusual twist to the representative race. Described by a reporter, "Candidate Turner is a reformed jail break artist, whose daredevil prison escapes prior to World War II put him in the international spotlight. He is a denturist, who had become a model citizen following his release from prison some twenty years ago. He was credited with helping the implementation of extensive penal reform and juvenile delinquency measures in Georgia." The flattering comments about his background in the newspapers kicked off his campaign in a positive light.

***

Forrest Turner ran as a Democrat and was unopposed in the pri-

Forrest Turner
"From the State Pen to State Capitol"
VOTE

mary. His main opponent was incumbent Republican attorney, Jim Westlake.

One item on his campaign platform was summed up in the catchy phrase, "Take the chains off denture sales in Georgia." "If elected I want to make it possible for the majority of low-income persons and those drawing welfare and old age pensions to obtain dentures at a lower cost," Forrest promised.

Prison reform, however, had been his chief mission since being paroled. Every speech he had made emphasized the need to continue the improvement of the Georgia penal system through legislation. Better rehabilitation programs and prevention of juvenile delinquency were his priority. "We have come a long way since my time on the chain gang, but we still have a long way to go," he said. "No one in the state is more qualified to speak on prison reform than me. I have always said that to analyze dirt, you have to taste it. And I've had a bellyful."

From the year he spent working in the dental lab at the Milledgeville hospital, later renamed Central State Hospital, he saw the overcrowding. The state needed to invest money in building more facilities to treat the mentally ill. "I can tell you from firsthand knowledge that the prisons and work camps are full of untreated mentally ill convicts. Some can become violent if not medicated," Forrest Turner said as he remembered his former pals, Robert Colton and Bill Baker. They had at times suffered from mental illness. "When prisoners finish their sentences and are released, the sick and disturbed ex-convicts are a risk to harm themselves and others.

"I spent a great deal of time and money trying to convince legislators and others to do something about the problems in the prisons and mental hospitals," Forrest said. "But nobody listened. The public just doesn't want to spend their tax money on prisoners and crazy people. During my campaign, I hope I can change their minds."

When asked by a reporter if his opponents would use his past criminal record to defeat him, Forrest answered with a chuckle, "One thing about this campaign is certain. Nobody can drag my past through the mud because my life is an open book. I paid dearly for my past sins. I hope to repay society for my past actions by being a good public servant. I suspect that there are plenty of corrupt people in public office now who deserve a little prison time. If chosen, I will not be one of them. It's time for these dishonest politicians to pay their dues." Another popular Forrest Turner's campaign slogan was "From the State Pen to the State Capitol."

Although his family and friends thought that Forrest Turner had a better than fifty percent chance of winning, a formidable opponent stood in his way. To win the election he would have to unseat Representative Jim Westlake, a powerful GOP leader in South DeKalb. As an insurance underwriter he was vice chairman of the House Insurance Committee. He had a lengthy list of popular items on his political agenda which he promised to deliver if re-elected.

The race for the House District 75 Post 3 seat received a great deal of attention from the press. Never has a reformed convict been a serious contender for state office. The state and nation were watching the returns to see if Forrest Turner could succeed. When the final returns were counted, Republican and Democratic candidates in DeKalb County split the number of seats. But by a count of 11,258 to 8,310, Jim Westlake defeated Forrest Turner to keep his seat. It was a good showing against a strong incumbent.

Georgia voters in the 1960s did not follow the national trends. Democrat, Lester Maddox, a segregationist was elected governor in 1966. In the general 1968 national election for U.S. President, the American Party candidate George Wallace, an independent, received forty-three percent, Republican candidate Richard Nixon received thirty percent and Democrat Hubert Humphrey received twenty-seven percent of the Georgia votes. All twelve of Georgia's electoral votes went for George Wallace; however, Richard Nixon won the presidential election. If DeKalb County jail inmates were allowed to vote, Forrest Turner would have come closer to winning.

On October 22, 1969, Forrest Turner attended the funeral of his closest friend and ally, Pastor Bill Allison. Services were held at First Baptist Church in East Point. Members of the Atlanta Fire Department and Optimist Club of Atlanta served as honorary pallbearers. As an appreciation of sympathy for the beloved Reverend, the family asked that gifts be made to the Prisoner Rehabilitation Fund. "There has never been a more compassionate man than Pastor Bill," Forrest Turner said to Helen, his widow, after the burial service. "Pastor Bill devoted his entire life to help God's rejects, like me. I am sure there was a crowd at the 'Pearly Gates' to welcome him home."

The weeping Helen Allison replied, "My husband thought the world of you, Forrest."

In September 1970 Forrest Turner ran for the DeKalb County House District 75 Post 2 House seat. This time around he ran against incumbent State Representative Leon Floyd. Representative Floyd had narrowly won the seat two years earlier and appeared to be vulnerable.

While speaking on the campaign trail he once commented in jest, "The last time I ran against Jim Westlake. I introduced myself to a woman voter. She asked against whom I was running. When I told her it was Mr. Westlake, she responded by saying, 'I like him because he is so cute.' For the lack of an intelligent response, I told her that I didn't think I looked all that bad and that she might need glasses. I suspect I didn't get her vote."

Apparently, looks did not matter. Forrest Turner lost again by a vote count of 12,660 to 11,125. The election was close as Forrest Turner managed to get forty-seven percent of the votes. He would say, "Some twenty years ago I didn't have a friend in the world. People thought I was untrustworthy and dishonest. When the votes were counted nearly half the voters in my district had enough respect for me to put me in office. To me that's a victory!"

Forrest Turner had mixed feelings about running for public office again. On the one hand, he had only lost to Representative Floyd by five hundred thirty-five votes. It made sense that the second time around he should have won. On the other hand, the negative publicity he received in January relating to the dental lab lessened his chances. Nevertheless, he was determined to try again. Whether he won or lost, he would promote his causes when speaking on the campaign trail. October 7, 1971, Forrest Turner paid the four-hundred-dollar qualifying fee to run in a special election for the Georgia House. The vacancy was created when Jim Westlake accepted the post as deputy regional director of the U.S. Environmental Protection Agency.

"If I win, I promise to donate my salary to the Chaplain Bill Allison Memorial Fund. The proceeds will provide new teeth for poor people," Forrest declared. His campaign slogan read, 'Obligated to no one but the people.' "As the saying goes, the third time around is a charm. I like my chances, this time," he predicted. He liked his chances, but not the results. He lost again. In this election three Democrats vied for the position. Of the 16,713 votes cast Forrest Turner received only 2,970 and placed a distant fourth.

When House member Representative George Ray died suddenly, Forrest Turner considered running for the unexpired seat. When Forrest Turner mentioned to June that he wanted to run for office again, she offered advice. "People tell me that the voters think that you are a one-dimensional candidate. Everyone is aware of your background, and they support your prison reform and juvenile rehabilitation causes. But they say you must align your views with the DeKalb County voter base, if you want to get elected," she recommended.

Forrest thought for a minute and replied, "That's a clever idea June. I will publish my views on crime and punishment."

"Here's are some of my beliefs I want the public to know," he continued.

"Law enforcement should have full authority to enforce the laws and officers should have the right to protect themselves. We need to get tough with criminals. Prisons should be a place for both punishment and correction. I support the death penalty to discourage senseless and brutal acts of crime. I am also opposed to gun control. Citizens should be allowed to protect themselves."

Forrest Turner's conservative stances now were quite different from when he was a misbehaving rebellious youth. He was smarter than he was then.

Minutes before the qualifying deadline he paid his fee. He was the eleventh candidate to qualify in the special election. "Many people want me to run," said Forrest. "I still have a list of items that I would like to see passed." Only ten percent of voters turned out. A disappointed Forrest Turner tied for fourth.

Democratic candidate, Forrest Turner, did not realize he had four major hurdles to overcome to win the elections. First, South DeKalb was a Republican stronghold. Democrats had a tough time winning there. Second, most of the time after a candidate had lost two elections, the uncommitted voters began to wonder why. "There must be something wrong with this Turner candidate. People must have good reasons for not voting for him. Maybe I shouldn't vote for him either," they surmised. And they didn't. Third, the untimely negative publicity stemming from the G.B.I. arrest for practicing dentistry without a license and the illegal possession of Novocain. Fourth, he didn't have the money to spend on a campaign like the other candidates did. For these reasons Forrest Turner was a longshot to win in the primaries and the general elections.

Forrest Turner had given all that he had, but he had lost. Frustrated and disappointed, he quit trying to gain a house seat. "Apparently, politics is not for me. I have spent a lot of time and money to no avail," he lamented. Instead of using the podium to get elected, he used the stage to promote the causes that were dear to him. He was sixty years old and was thankful to have the support of his family, the Lord to guide him, and his good health as he approached his retirement years.

38 THE FIVE UNFORGETTABLE CONVICTS

Forrest Turner had reached retirement. He was no longer in the public eye. He was content to lead a normal life as a senior citizen and grandfather. He often looked in the rearview mirror and reminisced about the past. The years of his youth and early adulthood were not his best. From October 1934 to March 1949 Forrest Turner spent approximately fifteen years as an inmate or a fugitive. He was in and out of work camps, local jails, including Fulton Tower and Georgia State Prison at Reidsville. He was never in an institution for long. He escaped, was recaptured and often sent to a different facility. During that period, he developed associations with many other convicts. What was it about these convicted murderers and thieves that drew Forrest Turner toward them? He wasn't interested in why they were sent to prison, and he had overlooked their faults. Forrest Turner was not a big man and no match against the bullies in prison. He defended himself with his wit and cheerful demeaner. The fellow nonviolent convicts he befriended shared a common philosophy which implied that there was nothing wrong with stealing. "Why work your fingers to the bone when you can get it for free?" The price paid for such irrational thinking resulted in lengthy prison terms for all of them.

***

Most of Forest Turner's associations while at the work camps were short-lived as convicts were constantly being moved from one work camp to another. His prison stay at Reidsville was the longest. Most of the time there he was in isolation on the fourth floor. The time he spent with his convict friends while on the run was never very long. The longest liberty was eleven months, but most were just a few days or weeks.

Forrest commented, "I and my convict inmates had accumulated an unreasonable number of years in prison. So many years that we couldn't live long enough to serve out our sentences. Thus, escape was the only means we could gain our freedom, even if it was only for a brief time."

Forrest Turner was now seventy-five years old. "There is a lot I regret," he once said. "The grief and heartaches that I brought upon my family, especially during those war-torn years. I was raising hell with my prison buddies while others were giving their lives for their country."

Even after forty years since his parole, he couldn't forget the fellow convicts he left behind. Yes, he was proud of his accomplishments since his parole and was pleased with how his life turned out. At the same time, he was extremely disappointed in his fellow inmates. Many of whom were given the same opportunity to reform as he did but didn't. He felt sorry for those he left behind. He recalled their exploits as criminals during those forgettable years, the good and bad…mostly bad. They all have passed away and left behind their legacy of crime. He never saw or heard from them again after his parole. He wondered what became of James Lawrence, Tom Burroughs, Terrell Loughridge, Bryan Schwab, Jack Devine, Charles Bryant, Guy Ezell, Allen Billingsley, and a host of others who went with him in his escapes from Reidsville prison. All were eventually recaptured and were still in prison as of 1949.

Etched in his memory were the most notable inmates with whom he shared prison time and together managed many escapes. They included Robert Colton, Slim Scarborough, and Leland Harvey. He never forgot his brothers, Chester and Henry Turner, and school friend, Bill Baker. He considered these men as legendary criminals of their time. Each of them had an interesting past.

***

CHESTER TURNER

He reminisced about his brothers Chester, Henry, and Lee. Having grown up with them, Forrest regretted that he may have been partly responsible for their introduction to crime and Henry's untimely, tragic death. Henry was seven years older and Chester four years younger than Forrest. After the arrest of his older brothers, the youngest brother, Lee, learned his lesson and chose to avoid further encounters with the law.

Forrest remembered the events as if they had occurred yesterday, "They followed my footsteps down the path of crime as members of the 'Green Car Gang,' a name dubbed by a newspaper reporter. Originally, we were just the 'Turner Gang,' which included my brothers and me. We engaged in a few car thefts and holdups. When Bill and Robert joined the group, our gang proceeded to commit many more thefts. When we were eventually caught, charged, and sentenced, we all had different destinations. Chester was sent to the Cherokee County Work Camp.

"Like me, confinement did not agree with Chester. He successfully escaped in 1937 from Cherokee. While I was assigned to the Troup County Work Camp, Chester was on the run. He formed his own gang who took part in many robberies and holdups. He was subsequently arrested and sent to the state prison at Reidsville. At that time, I thought that he had learned his lesson and was headed in the right direction. But that was not to be.

"What became of Chester has always troubled me. While I was at the Dallas Work Camp in early 1941, my foolish brother, Chester, now twenty-three years old and serving a four-year term at Reidsville, escaped. He had less than two years to serve. He was recaptured and returned to Reidsville where he remained until August 1942, only to escape again.

"I was amazed as to how he and Wheat managed to escape. As were all of Reidsville's recaptured fugitives, they were first assigned to the fourth floor and isolation. When the warden decided Chester no longer was an immediate flight risk, he joined the other inmates who were assigned to one of the workshops to learn a skill. From there he was able to plan and execute his daring escape.

"I have often wondered how he managed to pull it off. The route he took to leave never occurred to me while I was there. Where did Chester find a ladder to climb up on the roof? Where did he get the courage to climb down five stories in total darkness? He should have been an easy target for the trigger-prone guards. He could have been shot or broken his neck, but instead he just broke his foot while on the run.

"He was recaptured, served out his sentence and was probated in May of 1943. When I decided to go straight, Chester was enjoying his short stint of freedom. But soon he was in trouble again," he remembered. "I never forgot Chester's continual disrespect of the law. In February 1945 he was a passenger involved in a collision with a cattle truck east of Dudley, Georgia. The 1941 Ford he and three others were in was stolen. He was arrested again. His un-lawful activities continued as he was arrested in September 1947 for burglary of a laundry business and the forgery of company checks. He received a conditional release in July 1948. The soap opera went on, however, as he was indicted in April 1951 for the robbery of Republic Engine Company in Hapeville near his for-mer home. While awaiting trial he was arrested in a hotel during a federal drug bust in February 1952. In April he was found guilty of armed robbery and sent back to Reidsville.

"Many thought that since Chester followed me into crime, that he would likewise follow me out of crime through rehabilitation. But he didn't. Chester was addicted to crime. He could not stop. Chester built a lengthy resume of crimes and spent approximate-ly twenty-five years in prison or as a fugitive before being pa-roled on November 3, 1961. He moved to Cayce, South Carolina where he lived his life in anonymity. After living a hard life,

Chester died in January 1972 at the age of fifty-three."

***

S.J. "SLIM" SCARBOROUGH

"I took a liking to Slim Scarborough when we met at Thomas County Work Camp. His real name was Simeon Joseph Scarborough, but everyone called him Slim. He was born in Florida in 1908. Wardens didn't want 'Slippery Slim' at their work camps because he was a 'runner.' He would escape at the drop of a hat. Since he was a 'life-termer' and saw no hope for freedom, he was always looking for a way out. During his prison career he had as many escapes as I did.

"After Slim Scarborough divulged the reason, he was in prison, I felt a bit of compassion for him. Neither of us had committed the crimes for which we were sentenced. Slim's mistake was being a passenger in a car where two other riders fatally beat the driver. His reward for turning state's evidence was a life term. My mistake was being a passenger in a stolen car for which I was sent to the Thomas County chain gang.

"After I escaped from the Thomas County Work Camp in 1937, I was determined to free Slim. I drove to Canton where he was working on a road gang. James Lawrence agreed to help me. The guards were not prepared to challenge the loaded machine gun I was aiming at them and allowed Slim to hop into my Ford. Thirty days later I was recaptured in a cabin and sent to Reidsville where I spent most of my time in solitary confinement. I was miserable and told the warden that I was going insane unless I could get some fresh air. I was sent to 'Little Alcatraz' in Paulding County where I was joined by Slim that summer. Shortly thereafter we made our daring escape.

"Slim enjoyed his newfound freedom with me. We were determined to live a lifestyle we had only dreamed about as boys. We had a fast car, wore fancy clothes, and had a pocket full of money, albeit all stolen. Back then the phrase 'If it's Illegal, It's Wrong' didn't apply to us.

"As I think back to the bank robbery, I often tell myself how foolish we were to have tried such a stunt. Who in their right mind wakes up the head of the bank before sunup and forces him to drive to the bank to unlock the safe inside the vault? Then when learning that the vault has a time delay combination lock, drive around for two hours until the time elapses allowing the vault to open? All the while, the bank manager's wife is at home sitting by the phone. Not knowing her husband's fate for nearly four hectic hours, she could have called the police at any time. It is one of the stupidest robberies I have ever committed. But as a result, we each pocketed twenty-five hundred dollars."

The fifty-one days that Slim Scarborough and Forrest Turner enjoyed time together as fugitives were the most rememberable. Not only did they rob a bank they also freed a truckload of convicts from a road gang in Harris County. Unfortunately, it ended when they were caught in South Georgia and sent to Reidsville. Although they worked together on the same road gangs, they did not attempt any further escapes together.

"I learned that 'Slippery Slim' managed to escape from Reidsville in September 1942 and fled to Florida. There he was busy committing robberies until he was recaptured and imprisoned there. Upon release he was sent back to Reidsville. As part of Wiley Moore's prison reform program, he was paroled to join the military. Since he didn't enlist, his parole was revoked and he later reentered prison. He escaped again. And while fleeing from the state patrol in Perry, Georgia he was shot in the leg, but recovered. After spending most of his life as a prisoner or as a fugitive, he was eventually paroled. He later married and moved to Florida. I was saddened when I heard that he had died in 1981.

***

ROBERT COLTON

"Robert Lewis Colton was somewhat of a 'loner' from Mississippi and two years older than me. He was in trouble from the day he was born. His career of crime began when he was arrested in Columbia, Mississippi for delinquency and truancy. Later he committed a string of crimes including burglary, grand larceny, and auto theft in Birmingham, Alabama, Parchman, Mississippi and Bogalusa, Louisiana. For his theft in Louisiana, he served time in the Atlanta Penitentiary and Alcatraz in San Francisco. For crimes he committed in Augusta and Atlanta he was sent to Thomas County Work Camp where our relationship began.

"When I met Robert at the Thomas County Work Camp, he already had an arrest record unequalled to the other convicts in the work camp. He was a thief. He had stolen everything from everywhere throughout the south. I felt sorry for him. God made him a little different from the rest of us. He was not all there at times.

"After my escape from the Thomas County Work Camp, I arranged to have him freed. Afraid of being recognized, I had a friend drive down to Thomasville and 'spring' Robert while he was working on a remote dirt road. I admit that while we were fugitives, we had our fun as members of the 'Green Car Gang' in 1937. It took a long time for Warden McMillan to get over our escape while in route to Thomasville. We were later cornered by a policeman in Augusta. I managed to get away, but Robert was caught. Two months later I was also recaptured.

"Our paths went in different directions. He was sent to the DeKalb County Camp, and I was sent to one of the Fulton County work camps. I knew that he was transferred to Hortense Work Camp in Brunswick where he made several escapes and was always recaptured. He was finally paroled in March 1949, about the same time as I was. He moved out of state, and I lost contact with him."

***

LELAND HARVEY

"I befriended Leland Harvey while we were at Reidsville. It was the shortest relationship I had with my five most memorable convicts. To cover the details of his life story would fill a novel. The first time I heard about him was his escape from the Henry County Work Camp in McDonough. I was nine years old and didn't live too far from the camp. During his lifetime as a criminal, he had amassed far more arrests and prison escapes than I had. He was intelligent, cunning, and clever, but incorrigible. He was charismatic in nature and used his charm to his advantage. We spent a great deal of time on the fourth floor at Reidsville, mostly in solitary confinement. I recall the private lunch I had with Leland in 1955 shortly after one of his paroles. The visit vividly brought back to memory some of the prison adventures we shared and some of his escapades of which I wasn't aware. The conversation started with his night club story back in 1929.

Leland began, "Two months after Aubrey Smith and I escaped from the Henry County Work Camp, we decided to check out a nightclub in Miami. We had pockets full of money which we had stolen and wanted to spend the evening celebrating our freedom. Around midnight after partying up a storm, buying drinks for every friendly couple, the waiter presented us with a bill. After complaining, I paid the bill and left. In a drunken state and enraged, I foolishly returned and robbed the employees and their guests."

"I chuckle when I think back to Leland's description of how well those couples danced with a pistol pointing at them. When the jazz band began playing, they started to do the Charleston. He didn't remember much after that. Just that he woke up in a jail cell with a splitting headache," Forrest recalls.

"Leland couldn't stop bragging about his escapes. He told me about the one of which he was the proudest. No one has ever managed to repeat his breakout since. I began to laugh as he continued to describe his arrest in Macon. Because he had a reputation for escaping, the local sheriff was afraid to keep him in his Macon jail. Instead, he transferred him to the escape-proof Georgia State Prison. While in the Milledgeville prison, they locked him in the most secure unoccupied cell on "Death Row." Not for electrocution but for safekeeping until his trial in Bibb County. Since he was from Macon, he knew a guard who he paid to smuggle in a file. Over several nights he filed and eventually kicked out one of the cell's iron bars. At one hundred and forty pounds, he soaped down his skinny body and managed to squeeze through the opening. When the guard did his nightly check, he overpowered him and took away his gun and keys. He had a friend waiting for him out front," Forrest remembered.

"The last time Leland and I were together was in Savannah in April 1943. A patrolman stopped the car in which we were riding. We were on the run after our incredible escape from Reidsville. Unfortunately, I was arrested while Leland and Allen Billingsly managed to flee. Three days later the police recaptured them near Macon."

Leland continued with his story telling, "I was not very smart by going back to Macon. Our great escape from Reidsville was big news and everyone in law enforcement was on the lookout for me. Believe it or not, it took me just twelve hours before I outsmarted the deputies at the Macon jail and escaped again. The next day the local newspaper mentioned that it was only the second such escape from the Macon jail in its seventeen-year history.

"Forrest, here's how I did it. First, I bribed a trusty to bring me wooden matches, a pistol, and ammunition. When the cell doors were opened for the usual inspection, unbeknownst to the guard, I stuck a match stem into the lock. By jamming the lock, the door did not seal properly. Later when only one guard was on duty on the floor, I pushed open the door, overpowered the guard, and forced him to clear my path out. A friend, who was told of my escape plan was waiting with a getaway car outside of the front gate.

"I enjoyed my meeting with Leland. I thoroughly enjoyed reminiscing about the prison days. I told him that I thought of myself as a clever escape artist. But I confessed that he was the best. 'No prison in the world could hold either one of us very long.'

"I knew that Leland had robbed a bank in Rome before I met him. It was 1936 when he was caught, sentenced, and sent to Alcatraz in California. After his release from Alcatraz, he returned to Reidsville to finish serving his sentence for his state crimes. He was credited with at least sixteen escapes by 1949. After he witnessed my parole, he made no more attempts. He had also made good as Trusty at the Jessup State Work Camp. As a result, the board paroled him when he was forty-eight years old.

"He went to work in Atlanta, married and had a child. His future was on the rise, but not for long. The pattern of wrongdoing resurfaced. In 1956 he was arrested on charges of kidnaping and attempted robbery. He was sent to Cobb County Work Camp, escaping again from a work detail. He was paroled again. In February in 1961, however, Leland Harvey did not go straight and again was arrested for robbery and jailed. After several more escapes, holdups, and re-arrests he was sent back to Reidsville. Following a period of good behavior, he was sent to the Colony Farm Correctional facility in Hartwick.

"That's the last time I heard of Leland's whereabouts. Based on his lengthy sentences, I suspect he most likely died in prison somewhere. Of all the convicts I had befriended, Leland was the most incorrigible. He received a full pardon in 1927 and was paroled in 1954 and again in 1960 only to get rearrested and returned to prison. He celebrated his seventieth birthday by escaping for the thirtieth time in May 1975. Leland may have been short in stature, but at five foot seven, few prisoners in penal history had accumulated such a long list of offenses as had Leland. When Leland died and went to hell, it wouldn't be a surprise if he hadn't escaped from there too."

***

VINCENT BILL BAKER

"Other than my brothers, I knew Bill Baker the best. We were neighbors in Hapeville and attended Russell High School together, albeit he was younger than me. I had mixed feelings about Bill. To describe my early friendship with him I recall an old wise tale. 'When you run with someone from the wrong crowd, you will soon find yourself in trouble with the law.' That's exactly what happened to me. Of all the convicts that I got to know personally, Bill Baker was the most prone to violence. He had a touch of meanness. In July 1937 he shot an unarmed guard while fleeing from the Troup County chain gang in LaGrange. He and two companions stole the prison pickup truck and fled. He was responsible for the kidnaping of a young girl in Gainesville which led to the shootout with police in College Park. It was there where brother Henry was killed," Forrest recollected.

Bill Baker
Exhibiting His Litberty
Tattoo

"I give Bill all the credit for me entering the Georgia prison system. I blame him for my first arrest and conviction of auto theft. As a result, I went to Thomas County camp, and he went to the Floyd County camp. After his escape Bill helped me flee from the chain gang in Thomasville. I will always be thankful to him for getting me out of that God forsaken place. After the breakup of the 'Green Car Gang,' I had little contact with Bill. What happened to him, I learned from one of my my brothers, who stayed in touch with him.

"When I think about Bill Baker, I admit that he was a little crazy when he entered prison. His propensity to commit crimes was influenced in part by his mental illness. Once in prison, the harsh conditions and isolation he experienced only worsened his condition."

When the subject of Bill Baker came up at a family gathering, he gave me an update. "Forrest, as you know, Bill, committed many crimes. The crazy fool escaped from the Troup County Work Camp twice. His freedom was short-lived as he was arrested in Birmingham after he and an accomplice robbed a bank. Since it was a federal crime, he was first sent to the Atlanta Penitentiary and later was transferred to the real Alcatraz in San Francisco. After serving out his sentence at Alcatraz, he was returned to Georgia to complete his pending twenty-three-year larceny and robbery sentence. In August 1949, the prison doctors recognized Bill's unusual behavior. They diagnosed him as being criminally insane. He was sent to the state mental hospital in Milledgeville for treatment," the brother said.

He continued, "In July 1953 he escaped from the Milledgeville State Hospital and fled to Michigan. For the first time in his adult life, while in Michigan, he managed to stay out of trouble. He remained a fugitive for three years until the F.B.I. in Detroit learned of his whereabouts. He was arrested and extradited back to Georgia to complete his prison sentence. He would be under psychiatric care for the rest of his life."

***

Forrest Turner had outlived all five as they died as broken men. They were penniless and soon forgotten by everyone except him. They were beyond correction. He considered them to be a habitual band of crooks. No jail or prison was able to hold them as they always managed to escape. "They wasted their lives," he said to those who were interested in listening. "We had some good times, but that was long ago." He wished they had taken his advice and left their evil ways behind.

39 THE GREAT ESCAPE

Forrest Turner's prison days were far behind him. It had been thirty-four years since he walked out of Bellwood as a free man. Approaching sixty years of age he continued staying active in his business and achieving his personal goals. His dental labs were doing well fulfilling dentists' prescriptions for dentures. He was often called upon by various public officials to render advice on prison security, most notably the DeKalb County Jail. He was still a popular guest speaker. During a speaking engagement he revealed unknown details of the infamous Reidsville breakout to a reporter.

***

Forrest Turner was politically connected. His lobbying for penal reform opened doors at the State Capitol. He had personal relationships with governors and members of the Georgia House and Senate. He became a friend and ally to all the commissioners on the State Board of Corrections. As a former escape artist, he had become an authority on prison security. He was often called on to review architectural plans for new prisons. They valued his opinion on whether the proposed construction was escape-proof. After a successful escape from one of the newly constructed prisons, he was asked to inspect the facility and recommend what changes were needed to prevent future escapes. "I hate to give away my trade secrets," he said. "But if I was locked in here and planned to escape, this is what I would do." He proceeded by pointing out the facility's vulnerable areas.

Forrest Turner was asked to inspect the DeKalb County Jail after three prisoners escaped. Located on Memorial Drive, the jail was near his home in DeKalb County. The dangerous prisoners were eventually recaptured, but not before creating concern among the prison officials. The new jail had cost the taxpayers two and a half million dollars.

After a quick tour Forrest Turner remarked to Sheriff Ray Bonner, "The facility would make a good old ladies' home, but as a jail it just doesn't make it. You can expect more breakouts unless some changes are made."

"The DeKalb County Jail is the least secure jail in the state," he reported. "I can assure you that I am right. I have seen or been locked up in most of them. From a security standpoint the jail is inadequately constructed. Concrete blocks may look strong, but a prisoner can kick a hole in them in no time. The prison bars are not case-hardened. With a piece of wire from a broom handle, I can cut the bars very easily. I like the TV surveillance cameras you installed, but you have too many blind spots. The bullet-proof Plexiglas that protects the guards is not fireproof."

Sheriff Bonner agreed whole-heartedly with Forrest Turner's assessment. "To make these changes I bet it would cost a half a million dollars," the Sheriff surmised.

***

In 1974 Forrest Turner was invited to address the inmates at Reidsville prison. At that time, the prison was receiving a great deal of attention. Not for Forrest Turner's arrival or a prison escape, but because of the filming of a movie. "The Longest Yard" featured lead actors; Burt Reynolds, as an ex-football player and convict with Eddie Arnall portraying the emotional warden. The highlight of the movie was the fictional football game between the convicts and the guards.

It was one of the few times he was able to walk into the prison without being handcuffed or shackled. It was quite an emotional experience. He was in the same dining room where he ate his daily meals. He was standing in the exact spot where Wiley Moore made his "Do Right, Get Out" promise to the "Eight-Ball Squad." He hadn't come to Reidsville to make the same promises, but to give advice. He brought a message of hope. "If you will let me show you the way, I know the path to freedom," Forrest told them. "The Bible is your survival not the nonsense your fella cons are preaching." When he finished, the inmates gave him a rousing ovation.

A local reporter who was at Reidsville to interview Burt Reynolds learned of Mr. Turner's visit. He could not resist a separate interview with him. Forrest Turner never turned down the opportunity to speak to the press.

"So how was your meeting with Mr. Reynolds?"

"It was a thrill to meet him. I have been a fan of his since he appeared on 'Gunsmoke,'" Forrest enthusiastically replied.

The reporter continued, "What do you think of a football game matching the guards against the inmates?"

"If they had had a real game while I was here, there would have been several serious injuries, if not deaths," Forrest answered with a grin from ear to ear.

On a more serious note, tell me Mr. Turner, "How did you manage to cut your way out of the cell back in 1943 when you helped two dozen inmates escape?"

"I have never told a soul outside of the prison," he replied with a grin and a gleam in his eye. "I didn't want to get anyone in trouble. Plus, I wasn't sure if I would ever need to use that trick again. To this day the warden never figured out how anyone could escape from an isolation cell on the fourth floor at Reidsville."

Forrest continued, "You know I was confined to my cell for twenty-three hours a day. I had one hour of exercise which was limited to walking back and forth in the hallway. I was under constant surveillance by two guards who were on watch. During that period, my meals were limited to one stick of cornbread and a meager bowl of stew. I believe the warden was trying to starve me to death. I was not allowed to send or receive mail. There were no reading materials available, not even a Bible. All I could do was lay on my bed and daydream. How am I going to get out of here dominated my thoughts?

"The cell bars in the newer prisons such as Reidsville were made of case-hardened steel. A regular file would not penetrate the super tough metal. The only tool that worked was some type of instrument with a diamond tip. Such a tool would have to come from outside of the prison. But how do you smuggle items in when only the guards were allowed on the fourth floor?"

I could tell the reporter was getting anxious for me to get to the answer. "I discovered that the third and fourth floor plumbing were connected. When I and the fella below me flushed our toilets, the waste fed into the same pipe. I began 'de-threading' my prison clothes, tying the threads together, and making a thin string. I made a ball out of the threads and tied it to the end of the string. I held on to one end of the string and threw the ball of string attached to the other end into the toilet. After several tries, I was able to flush the ball down the toilet to where the fella on the third floor could fish it out with a piece of wire. Over time he was able to attach the items I needed, which I pulled up. It was a nasty way to send messages, but it worked. I can tell you that there is nothing sanitary about a prison toilet.

"The third-floor inmates worked in the yard or on the road gangs. They had access to the metal shop. They were not considered flight risks, so they were not heavily guarded. It was easy for them to smuggle stuff into the prison. Since the guards assumed it was impossible for inmates on the fourth floor to have contraband they seldom checked. When they did, they had no interest in sticking their faces in the toilet for a closer look.

"I spent seven months grinding on the cell bars and planning the escape. I knew I needed help, so I shared my plans with Leland Harvey and Allen Billingsley who were in adjoining cells. Both had already made many successful escapes from other prisons. Harvey bribed a guard who managed to smuggle in a pistol. Once outside the cell it was easy to overpower the unarmed guard, unlock prison cells with the guard's keys, and take over the prison. The rest of the story you know."

In awe over the incredible secret Forrest Turner had divulged, the reporter was speechless. Finally, the amazed reporter responded, "You say you used the toilet, that's unbelievable."

Forrest continued, "After I was recaptured, one of the prison investigators agreed to pay me if I would tell him how I was able to cut those bars. I confessed to him with a straight face that I had help from the damn termites that had been highly active that year."

"Forrest, your 1943 escape is a record that was never broken," the reporter commented.

Forrest paused, then continued, "Let me be serious for a moment. I suspect the massive prisoner breakout from Reidsville was a tremendous achievement. However, the escape of which I am the proudest, is my escape from my criminal way of life. It was a struggle, but I finally saw the error in my ways."

40 FINAL TRIBUTE TO A LEGEND

Forrest Turner's life can be divided into three stages: growing up as a member of a large family in a small southern rural setting until the age of nineteen, spending the next fifteen years as a convict, prisoner or fugitive convicted of numerous hold ups and thefts, and then dedicating the remainder of his adult life repaying society for his wrongdoings by his being a "Good Samaritan."

***

Forrest Turner was born and raised in the McDonough, Georgia area. He moved to Hapeville as a teenager and attended high school there. His desire to go to college was not fulfilled, since the family did not have the means to send him. The Great Depression and the premature death of his father kept his mother, and her children financially challenged. His life took a turn for the worse when he was arrested. His punishment changed his life forever. From his terrible experience while on the chain gang, he felt that society owed him retribution. His revenge was felt by robbery victims and a host of policemen and detectives who could not keep him under lock and key.

The folk hero of the 1930s and 1940s was labeled, "Georgia's Number One Bad Boy" and "Public Enemy Number One." His eleven official escapes earned him more titles, "Jail Breaker," "Escape Artist," and "Georgia's Houdini." His fame continually made headlines throughout the state. Many said he was the most famous prison escape artist of the twentieth century and that only Houdini got more publicity than him. It was not just his many escapes from prisons, but the remarkable breaks into work camps and prisons that made him famous.

Unlike other criminals and gangsters of the era such as Bonnie Parker, Clyde Barrow, and Al Capone; Forrest Turner was non-violent. Armed with an arsenal of weapons he never used them against those who pursued him. He committed many robberies of individuals, filling stations and stores. Taking their money, goods and vehicles to further his lifestyle. His escapes were short-lived as Detectives Nahlik, Coppenger, and others apprehended him and returned him to prison. Each escape increased his sentence to a term that reached several decades.

In 1945 while confined to a solitary cell, Forrest Turner was in a state of depression. After the governor refused to grant him a pardon, he was destined to remain in prison forever. He became a member of the infamous "Eight Ball Squad." Weighed down by a heavy metal cannonball attached to his leg irons and under constant watch, the opportunity to escape and flee to Canada became impossible. He began to realize that the fame and newspaper hype bestowed on criminals were not worth the resulting imprisonment. He was just thirty years old and thus far had nothing to show for his pitiful existence. It was his darkest hour. He prayed for a second chance. An unexpected but timely ray of hope came from the new director of corrections. His penal reform plan promised parole to convicts, who became model prisoners and learned trades.

Forrest Turner took the challenge. He seized the opportunity to gain experience in the art of making dentures and took the position of dental assistant. He was transferred to Bellwood, where in the absence of a prison dentist, he was required to perform the dental services needed. After his release he became the dental assistant for a prominent Atlanta dentist. When the dentist closed his office, he eventually found a similar position at the Milledgeville State Hospital. Recognizing the need to make dentures affordable for the poor and elderly, Forrest Turner opened clinics in Jonesboro and Lilburn. He personally examined patients, made impressions, and created and inserted dentures until he was enjoined by the court.

The friendship with Pastor Bill at Bellwood totally changed his life. He became a Christian and volunteered to function as the assistant pastor. He chose not to become a minister but devoted much of his adult life to ministerial activities. He earned Trusty status and was eventually awarded parole in 1949. Not to forget the harsh treatment he received and the brutality he witnessed, he aggressively promoted further penal reform. To the youth he preached the consequences of breaking the law. To promote his cause, it was reported that he made over ten thousand speeches to youth groups, churches and civic organizations. He was a mentor to hundreds of prison parolees and was successful in keeping most of them from re-entering prison.

Of the sixty-three members of the "Eight Ball Squad," Forrest Turner was the only one to receive a full pardon and the return of his civil rights. Other than a traffic ticket and the violation of an injunction preventing him from providing dentures to the needy, he never had any further encounters with the law. His only visits to prisons were speaking engagements.

To promote his crusade against the high markup of dentures and penal reform, he ran for public office. He was narrowly defeated for the District 75 DeKalb County House of Representative seat. His foray into politics brought him to the forefront of the political leaders of Georgia. He served on the campaign committees of Herman Talmadge, Lester Maddox and Jimmy Carter. Forrest Turner was considered a spokesman for the humane treatment of prisoners. Through his testimonials and lobby of legislators he influenced the closing of work camps and the treatment of prisoners. He was named honorary member of the Georgia Penal Board.

Governor Vandiver commissioned him as Lieutenant Colonel, Aide de Camp for his past service as an advisor on his staff.

He became the most sought-after speaker in the State of Georgia. His fame earned him an invitation as a challenger on "What's My Line?." During his adult life and after his release from prison, Forrest Turner repaid more to society than he had taken earlier as a thief. He married June Young, a volunteer with the Baptist Training Union, whom he met during her visits to prison. He once said that without her support, he could never have achieved his lofty goals which he had set for himself.

He never lost his love for fast cars and was a fan of stock car racing. He only wished that he had been a free man so that he could have raced against his former bootlegging friends. He was certain that he, in his roadster, could have beaten them at Lakewood Speedway.

Forrest Turner was indeed one of the more interesting individuals in Georgia's recent history.

EPILOGUE

The concept that "bad boys build good roads" led to the creation of state-controlled work camps throughout Georgia. Once an accused was found guilty, he was summarily sent to one of the work camps to serve out his sentence. Robert Burns was given a six to ten-year sentence for stealing five dollars and change. First-offender Forrest Turner received an unfair sentence for riding in a stolen car with his friend. The petty crimes in many cases did not justify the stiff sentences imposed by the judges. Inhumane and harsh treatment of convicts became a focal point of newly elected Governor Ellis Arnall. During his administration he introduced sweeping prison reform. One of the prisoners to benefit from the new policies was Forrest Turner.

Detectives Nahlik and Coppenger were constantly on the trail of Forrest Turner. That ended when like many able-bodied Americans, his two adversarial detectives enlisted in the military. During the war Leo Nahlik served as a staff sergeant in the Marine Corps and Melvin Coppenger enlisted in the U.S. Navy.

Sargent Nahlik spent most of his time in the induction center at Fort McPherson. He never made it to Europe and was unable to liberate his countrymen in France. After the war Leo Nahlik returned to the Atlanta Police Department and solved many publicized cases. He retired in 1948 and became Chief of the DeKalb County Police Department. Lieutenant Coppenger did not return to the police department. Instead, he became the head of Georgia Tech University's security division until his retirement.

Many persons can be credited with bringing prison reform to Georgia. The four who made the most significant contributions in the twentieth century were Robert Burns, Wiley Moore, Pastor Allison, and Forrest Turner. Each affected the movement in different ways. Robert Burn's news editorials, books and movie introduced to the public the unknown cruelty and atrocities which were inflicted on chain gang convicts. Wiley Moore was the most influential public official to institute meaningful changes in the treatment of prisoners. Pastor Allison showed how kindness and compassion were a better method of reforming convicts in the state's institutions. And Forrest Turner lobbied for reform through his testimonials and speeches. He was a shining example of how humane, rather than harsh treatment reformed a convict; one of whom the prison system at one time labeled as incorrigible.

Reidsville Prison opened in 1937. In its history two hundred fifty-three inmates were executed before "Old Smokey" was moved in June 1980 to the Georgia Diagnostic and Classification State Prison in Butts County. The unclaimed remains of those who were executed or died in prison were buried in Reidsville Cemetery.

The number of escapes from Reidsville was astonishing. Most of those, however, occurred while convicts were working on road gangs or in the yard. The most remarkable escapes were achieved by Forrest Turner and others who managed to break out from the maximum-security cells. The Georgia Board of Corrections closed Reidsville's escape proof prison in 2022. The prisoners were moved to Rogers State Prison in Reidsville and Smith State Prison in Glennville. As of 2024 Georgia had thirty-four state prisons housing approximately forty-seven thousand inmates.

Forrest Turner could escape from every prison, but he could not escape from God. He and his wife, June, spent entire Sundays attending church services and speaking to congregations. *"From*

Crime to Christ" was his theme in addressing youth groups, civic clubs and church gatherings. His message was from the heart, sobering in nature and very convincing.

Herbert Brannan, the traveling salesman abducted between Hinesville and Ludowici by Forrest Turner and four convicts and accidently shot by a pursuing policeman, was reimbursed for his medical expenses. The House of Representatives passed a resolution requiring the state to pay him seven hundred fifty dollars.

Ed Long was shot by a policeman while resisting arrest, when he mistook him for Forrest Turner. In retribution the Fulton County Commission paid Mr. Long five hundred dollars.

After Forrest Turner and Slim Scarborough robbed the bank in Royston, its current management renamed the financial institution the Pinnacle Bank.

In 1955 Forrest Turner felt the compassion to brighten Christmas for the state's prison inmates. He recalled the loneliness he experienced while incarcerated during the holiday season. He gave each of the more than six thousand prisoners a Christmas gift. Many of which he personally delivered.

In May 1949 Georgia became the first state to ban the use of straps, shackles, and whips in its prisons. The forced work camps where Forrest Turner labored were all closed by 1973 after the Georgia Department of Transportation stopped its use of road gangs. The Henry County Work Camp closed in 1971. The main building became the future office of Henry County Family and Children Services. Bellwood, which housed Atlanta's largest chain gang, was converted to a public recreational area named Westview Park. The buildings are long gone, but the memories of what occurred there to the former convicts will be memorialized forever.

Nominated for ten Oscars, the original "Bonnie and Clyde" movie starring Warren Beatty and Faye Dunaway released in 1967 grossed seventy million dollars worldwide. The original "Longest Yard" movie released in 1974 starring Burt Reynolds grossed one hundred and ninety million dollars worldwide. The exploits of the legendary Forrest Turner caught the attention of Hollywood scriptwriters, who in 1978 wrote a screenplay "Turner's Gone Again." Forrest, however, objected to the contents of the script. Thus, to this day, his life's story has not been captured on the silver screen.

Forrest and June Turner continued to operate the dental labs. Since they were no longer seeing patients, only making dentures, the dentists resumed sending prescriptions. He no longer practiced dentistry without a license.

Forrest Turner outlived most of the people he encountered during his tumultuous life. In December 1956, Wiley Moore passed away in Washington, D.C. while attending a convention. In February 1969 former detective Leo Nahlik was laid to rest. Forrest Turner was honored to serve as a pallbearer at his funeral. Reverend Bill Allison died later that year in October. December 1997, former detective Melvin Coppenger met his Maker and was buried at Marietta National Cemetery. Robert Elliott Burns, who Forrest Turner had never met, passed away on June 5, 1955 and was buried in Beverly National Cemetery in New Jersey.

Forrest Turner, at the age of eighty-five died of lung cancer, even though he did not smoke. He was laid to rest at Lilburn First Baptist Church. Forty Georgia State Patrolmen in uniform were there to pay their respects for their honorary member of the Peace Officers Association. Former Governor Lester Maddox, many elected officials, friends, and family attended his funeral. Etched on his gravestone are the words, "Now at peace with his Savior." He was a legend in his time, leaving a legacy known to many; born February 8, 1915, died January 5, 2001.

On January 15, 2022, June Turner died at the age of ninety-two. She outlived her husband, Forrest, by eleven years. She joined him at a Lilburn cemetery, where they rest in peace. They left behind two daughters, Sherry, Maria, and three grandchildren.

ODE TO A LEGEND

The legendary tale of Forrest Turner was hard to believe.
What a young man from McDonough was able to achieve.
Moonshine runner, hold up man and thief he became.
Newspaper articles of his exploits enhanced his fame.
A long list of outraged and angry victims he did leave.

It began in the year 1934 when riding with a friend,
ending in an arrest for a crime he could not defend.
"This car has been stolen. To jail I am taking you!"
"But officer, of what you are accusing me; I did not do."
A sentence of 3 to 5 years on a chain gang to spend.

There, cruel treatment by the guards was a daily event.
Relief from the misery required a daring escape attempt.
But recaptured, resentenced, in prison he must remain.
Jailbreaker, Houdini, Escape Artist were now his new name.
Escaping eleven times was his incredible achievement.

He terrorized and threatened his victims with a loaded gun,
defying the law and satisfying his lifestyle while on the run.
The frequency of his robberies became a major concern,
as he confounded the police and detectives at every turn.
Soon he became "Georgia's Public Enemy Number One."

When recaptured his destination was solitary confinement.
Isolation caused depression, sadness and endless torment.
In a desperate promise to the warden and the governor too,

"If given a chance and paroled, I will do right by you.
For all my past wrongdoings I promise to repent."

With divine intervention a new Forrest Turner was born.
The once incorrigible prisoner was about to reform.
Dentistry and making dentures were the trade he learned.
As a model prisoner, the new role of Trusty he earned,
and to the position of assistant chaplain, he was sworn.

Parole after fifteen years of prison was granted at last.
Criminal acts and disrespect for the law were now in the past.
Counseling parolees and juveniles would be his penance,
as was making dentures for poor and elderly at no expense.
"I want to repay my debt to society; I promise to do my best."

Thousands of testimonials and speeches where he would say,
to churches, civic clubs and youth that "Crime does not Pay."
To promote his worthwhile causes for public office he ran.
Improvements to the prisons and camps were his demand.
Respect for the law, fellow man, and God were now his way.

The life and times of Forrest Turner had come and gone.
But the memories of his exploits and good deeds live on.
He returned more to the people of Georgia than he took.
The list of those he touched with his kindness fills a book.
An incredible turnaround for a man who started so wrong.

***

Dedicated to the friends and families of Forrest Turner, Legendary Escape Artist

February 8, 1914: Forrest Turner was born in Henry County, Georgia.

March 15, 1930: Forrest Turner's father, Justus Turner, died.

August 26, 1934: Forrest Turner tried to escape from courthouse after he and Bill Baker were sentenced.

October 25, 1934: Forrest Turner arrived at Thomas County Work Camp.

August 28, 1936: Forrest Turner escaped from Thomas County Work Camp.

December 12, 1936: Forrest Turner and his "Green Car Gang" were arrested on Boulevard Avenue in Atlanta by Detectives Nahlik and Coppenger.

January 26, 1937: Forrest Turner and Robert Colton escaped near Smithville, Georgia while being transported from Fulton Tower to Thomas County Work Camp.

February 8, 1937: Forrest Turner freed Slim Scarborough from Cherokee County Work Camp.

March 8, 1937: Forrest Turner was recaptured at tourist camp on Macon Highway south of Atlanta by posse led by Detective Nahlik.

April 1, 1937: Forrest Turner was transferred to Troup County Work Camp.

April 21, 1937: Forrest Turner arrived at Sandy Springs Work Camp.

June 12, 1937: Forrest Turner attended Henry Turner's funeral after he was killed in a shootout with police in College Park.

July 11, 1938: Forrest Turner led escape of Terrell Loughridge, Tom Burroughs, and three others from Georgia State Prison at Reidsville.

July 12, 1938: Forrest Turner and the other fugitives were recaptured in Riceboro, Georgia.

November 28, 1938: Forrest Turner hiding in a truck escaped Reidsville Prison.

January 3, 1939: Forrest Turner disguised as an attorney broke out five convicts from Cherokee County Work Camp.

January 30, 1939: Forrest Turner and Bryan Schwab were recaptured in Augusta, Georgia.

February 2, 1939: Forrest Turner was indicted for armed robbery by Richmond Grand Jury who recommended the death penalty.

July 19, 1939: Forrest Turner was transferred from Reidsville to "Little Alcatraz" in Dallas, Georgia.

August 14, 1941: Forrest Turner and Slim Scarborough escaped from "Little Alcatraz."

August 18, 1941: Forrest Turner and Slim Scarborough kidnapped manager and robbed Commercial Exchange Bank in Royston.

October 3, 1941: Forrest Turner and Slim Scarborough freed forty-one chain gang convicts working on roadway in Harris County.

October 4, 1941: Forrest Turner, Slim Scarborough, and Betty Ann West were captured in Ellenton, Georgia.

April 19, 1942: Forrest Turner was wounded in an escape from a Reidsville Prison's road gang accompanied by Guy Ezell.

April 20, 1942: Forrest Turner and Guy Ezell recaptured in Collins, Georgia.

October 31, 1942: Forrest Turner met with Governor Eugene Talmadge seeking parole to enlist in the military.

February 1, 1943: Forrest Turner escaped from Reidsville Prison and was recaptured the same day.

April 16, 1943: Forrest Turner, Leland Harvey, and Allen Billingsley led the escape of twenty-four prisoners from the fourth floor of Reidsville Prison.

April 24, 1943: Forrest Turner's final escape resulted in his recapture in Savannah.

October 19, 1943: Forrest Turner and the "Eight Ball Squad" were offered new path to freedom by Director, Wiley Moore.

November 1, 1945: Forrest Turner's chain gang predecessor, Robert Elliott Burns' sentence commuted by Georgia Board of Pardons and Paroles.

December 20, 1946: Forrest Turner was transferred to Bellwood Work Camp and became a Trusty.

December 21, 1946: Forrest Turner appointed Assistant Chaplain at Bellwood.

March 6, 1949: Forrest Turner was paroled by Georgia Board of Pardons and Paroles.

May 1, 1950: Forrest and June Turner had their first child, a daughter named Sherry.

August 13, 1954: Forrest Turner's political and civil rights were restored by Georgia Board of Pardons and Paroles.

January 2, 1957: Forrest Turner attended funeral of friend, Wiley Moore.

January 19, 1959: Forrest and June Turner had a second child, a daughter named Maria.

August 14, 1967: Forrest Turner ran for the House of Representative District 75 Post 3 seat.

August 28, 1968: Forrest Turner appeared on the television show, "What's My Line."

December 2 ,1968: Forrest Turner was enjoined from the practice of dentistry without a license.

October 20, 1969: Forrest Turner attended the funeral of Pastor Allison.

September 12, 1970: Forrest Turner ran for House seat District 75 Post 2.

January 21, 1971: Forrest Turner was found guilty of practicing dentistry without a license.

October 8, 1971: Forrest Turner ran for House seat District 75 Post 3.

July 15, 1974: Forrest Turner spoke to inmates at Reidsville Prison and met with Burt Reynolds.

June 26, 1975: Forrest Turner ran for House seat District 75 Post 3.

January 7, 2001: Forrest Turner was buried at Lilburn First Baptist Church Cemetery.

January 15, 2022: June Turner was buried at Lilburn First Baptist Church Cemetery.

February 19, 2022: Georgia State Prison in Reidsville was closed.

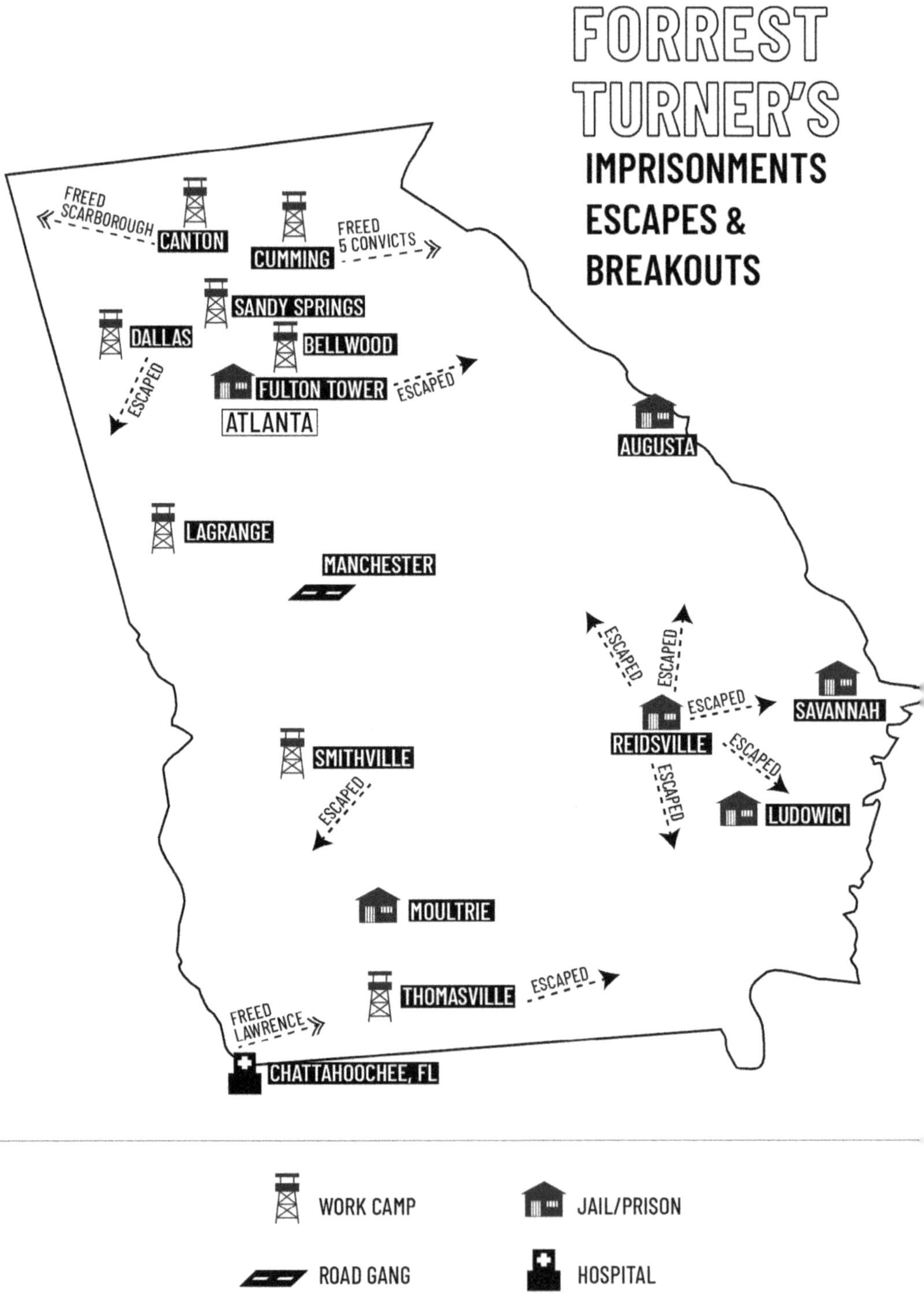

FORREST TURNER'S
IMPRISONMENTS ESCAPES & BREAKOUTS
FREED SCARBOROUGH
CANTON
CUMMING
FREED 5 CONVICTS
SANDY SPRINGS
DALLAS
BELLWOOD
ESCAPED
FULTON TOWER
ESCAPED
ATLANTA
AUGUSTA
LAGRANGE
MANCHESTER
ESCAPED
ESCAPED
ESCAPED
SAVANNAH
REIDSVILLE
ESCAPED
SMITHVILLE
ESCAPED
ESCAPED
LUDOWICI
MOULTRIE
THOMASVILLE
ESCAPED
FREED LAWRENCE
CHATTAHOOCHEE, FL
WORK CAMP
JAIL/PRISON
ROAD GANG
HOSPITAL

ABOUT THE AUTHOR

Hans Melchior Broder, Jr. was born July 6, 1947, in Bern, Switzerland and immigrated with his parents to Stockbridge in 1951 where he currently lives. Raised on the family's dairy farm, he is the oldest of eight siblings. He is married and has four children and ten grandchildren. He received a bachelor's degree in business administration from the University of Georgia. He began his working career as a Business Education teacher at Stockbridge High School in 1969. In 1971 he accepted a lending position with The First State Bank and became its CEO in 1975. He is a past Chairman of the Henry County Chamber of Commerce and served on several bank, civic organization, and church boards.

He is the author of *This Too Shall Pass*, a book about the failure of community banks during the Great Recession, the causes, and consequences. Motivated by the closing of Enterprise Banking Company in 2011, which he organized and managed; he takes his bank from its creation to its takeover by the F.D.I.C. The book provides insights and details of the challenges faced by the community bankers during that period.

In his second novel he writes about a tragedy that occurred in his hometown of Stockbridge. Many of his neighbors, classmates, and bank customers contributed to the events that occurred during a twelve-year period from the 1970s to 1980s in Henry County's past. It is these relationships that inspired him to author his book, *May All of You and God Forgive Me.*

As an inspiration for his next writing were his grandfathers. Both made their livelihood by working for the railroad in Switzerland. His book retells the diastrous train accident in McDonough, Georgia in 1900. To date it remains as the most tragic train wreck in Georgia history as thirty-nine on board died. *The Mystery Passenger* mixes real life facts with a touch of fiction. A mystery passenger who slipped on board miraculously survived the crash tells the story. The book covers railroads and the railroad men who are a part of its history.

Where is Forrest? Tales of an Escape Artist tells the life story of Forrest Turner, Henry County born young man, who along with a friend, were charged with auto theft. Only nineteen years old in 1934, he spent the next fifteen years in and out of work camps and prisons. During his escapes he committed many thefts of money and fast cars. He was dubbed as "Georgia's Number One Bad Boy" His escapades while a fugitive made him a folk hero. The uniqueness of his life occurred after his parole. Trained in making dentures while in prison, he used his skill to provide dentures at little or no cost to the needy. He found God and repaid society through his speeches, counseling of the youth, and benevolent works.

ABOUT THE ILLUSTRATOR

Michael Felix Broder is the brother of author, Hans Broder. He was born on December 18, 1952, and currently lives in Florence Alabama. Raised on the family's dairy farm in Stockbridge, he is one of eight children of Hans and Margrit Broder. He is married to the former Jacqueline Dale from West Lafayette, Indiana, and has four children and four grandchildren. He received an undergraduate degree in ag engineering from the University of Georgia and a master's degree from Purdue University. He retired from the Tennessee Valley Authority (TVA) after a lifelong career as an environmental engineer.

He realized he had a talent for art at an early age, impressing his teachers with his sketches and paintings in grammar school. Devoting his free time to the arts became an adult hobby. His mosaic depiction of an Indian chief, crafted from arrowheads he had found, won acclaim from Art Prize, an international art competition.